El Dorado County Library

In Memory of

Willette N. Strong

Dear Friends,

Was there a doubt in your mind after reading *Flirting with Disaster* that Amanda and Caleb would have their own story? Certainly not in mine.

Amanda O'Leary is exactly the sort of woman about whom I love to write. She's suffered through tremendous adversity and triumphed. On every page of *Flirting with Disaster,* she gets stronger. By the time she's ready for her own story, she's a more than even match for the wonderfully kind and protective Caleb Webb.

But naturally Amanda's struggles aren't over. All of her old issues with Big Max, her stubborn, difficult father, are about to surface in an unexpected way, and Caleb is right in the thick of it. When Amanda wakes up to discover the secrets he's been keeping, will she ever be able to forgive him? And will she be able to make peace with her father before it's too late? Just turn the page to find out.

In the meantime, welcome back to South Carolina's Low Country, one of my favorite places in the world. I've loved sharing it with you.

All best,
Sherryl

1

Sunday services were over and most of the congregation had gone home for the traditional midday dinner. Caleb, however, was still in the church office trying to feel his way through an unexpected and troubling counseling session. He studied the couple sitting across from him and wondered if he dared tell them what he really thought, that they were way too young even to be thinking about marriage. Mary Louise Carter was just a few months out of high school. In fact, with her stylishly short, sun-streaked hair, she looked even younger. Danny Marshall, every bit the preppy overachiever, was barely into his sophomore year at Clemson. In Caleb's opinion, they were years away from knowing what they really wanted out of life.

Unfortunately, he could predict exactly how they'd reply. They'd remind him that they'd known each other since grade school, been sweethearts since Danny's freshman year in high school. They both thought their marriage was inevitable. So what if having a baby on the way had kicked up the timetable by several years?

"It's not the end of the world," Mary Louise said, her adoring gaze on Danny.

Though she rarely looked away from her fiancé, she evidently didn't see the barely concealed panic that Caleb spotted. He'd counseled enough couples during his ten years as a minister to recognize the signs of a man being pushed toward a commitment he wasn't ready to make.

"Danny, is this wedding really what you want?" Caleb asked directly. Aware that Mary Louise's eyes had widened with dismay, he quickly added, "I know you love Mary Louise and I think it's wonderful that you want to take responsibility for the baby and do the right thing by Mary Louise, but there are other options."

Danny squirmed uncomfortably and avoided Mary Louise's hurt expression. "What kind of options?"

"You could acknowledge paternity and pay child support. Or you both could agree to give the baby up for adoption to a family more prepared to give a child the life he or she deserves," Caleb suggested, careful to keep his tone neutral.

Even so, Mary Louise leapt up. "No way," she said, quivering with outrage. She scowled at Caleb, then whirled on Danny. "This is our baby. How could you even think about giving away our baby, Danny Marshall?"

Danny gave her a sullen look. "I didn't say I'd do it. I asked Reverend Webb what the options are. Jeez, Mary Louise, settle down."

"I'm keeping the baby and that's that," she said fiercely. "If you don't want to marry me, then don't. I don't want you if you can't love both of us. And you can keep your stupid money, too!"

"I never said I didn't want to marry you," Danny said placatingly. "You know I love you, baby. It's just . . ."

"Just what?" she asked.

"How are we going to make it?" Danny asked reasonably. "I can't quit school. I worked too hard to get accepted and win a scholarship to throw it all away now. I don't want to wind up in some dead-end job for the rest of my life, like my dad."

"You won't have to. I can stay with my folks for now and keep working. It's only minimum wage, but I'll get another job. I can handle two," Mary Louise promised staunchly. "We can put all that money into savings so we'll have it when I have to go on maternity leave. I won't have to take off long. Once the baby comes, I'll move to be with you. We can figure out a schedule so you can take classes when I'm home. Then you can watch the baby while I work."

It was evident she'd already given this a lot of thought. Caleb admired her earnest conviction that she could handle a pregnancy and two jobs and that Danny could keep up with his classes and take care of the baby. But Caleb was more realistic. He knew the toll that would eventually take on the marriage and on Mary Louise and Danny individually. He also knew she'd never listen to him if he tried to tell her any of that.

However, he did know someone who might be able to get through to her in a way he couldn't.

"Okay, you two, I think that's enough for today," Caleb said. The pair needed a cooling-down period. "I'm sure this has caught both of you by surprise. You need to spend some time thinking about what you really want and what will be best for the baby. Danny, can you get home from college again next weekend, so we can talk some more?"

"I guess," Danny said, his reluctance plain, but the stoic lift of his chin told Caleb he would do it. He'd always been a good kid, one who took his responsibilities seriously. He'd worked hard to get a college scholarship, even harder to earn money to help with bills for meals and books.

"Great, then we'll talk again next week right after church," Caleb told them. "In the meantime, Mary Louise, there's someone I'd like you to meet."

She regarded him with evident suspicion, clearly not happy about the monkey wrench he'd thrown into her plans for a hasty wedding. "Who?"

"Let me speak to her first and get back to you," he said.

"I don't know why you're so opposed to this wedding," Mary Louise said to him plaintively. "You've known us forever. You know we're in love."

"I do," Caleb agreed. "But I want your marriage to have the best possible chance to succeed, and the way to accomplish that is to make sure you've given this serious consideration from every angle before you rush into something. I've seen too many young people who start out crazy about each other wind up bitter and divorced because they did the right thing and then resented each other afterward. I really don't want that to happen to you."

Danny gave him a grateful look. "Thanks,

Reverend Webb. I'll see you after church next week. Mary Louise, you ready to go?"

For a moment, based on her pouty expression, Caleb thought she might insist on having this out right here and now, but apparently she caught something in Danny's steady, unrelenting gaze that told her to wait till next time.

"Remember, I want both of you to do some soul-searching this week. See if there are some other solutions that might make sense. If marriage is what you both want, then think about the best way to make sure you have plenty of support," Caleb suggested. "And I'll be in touch with you, Mary Louise, probably tomorrow."

"Okay," she said, and followed Danny from the room.

Just outside the door, Caleb saw Danny reach for her hand and whisper something in her ear that put a smile back on her face. Caleb sighed and reached for his phone to follow up on his brainstorm.

Okay, he'd been looking for an excuse to call Amanda all day. Ever since he and the other church volunteers had finished building her house two weeks ago and had held a housewarming party just yesterday, he'd been suffering some weird withdrawal symptoms.

He'd fought his feelings for Amanda O'Leary, struggled to pretend that she was just another member of his congregation in need of help, but the time he'd spent with her and her kids had fulfilled him in unexpected ways. He'd come to admire her strength, to enjoy her sense of humor.

Before he actually dialed her number, he gave himself a stern lecture on remembering that he was her pastor, not a would-be lover, much as he might wish otherwise. It wasn't the first time he'd struggled to place duty above his needs as a man, but it was the first time he was right on the edge of losing the battle.

But the lecture didn't seem to stop the jolt to his heart when she answered the phone, her voice soft and a little breathless.

"Amanda, you weren't taking a nap, were you?"

"In the middle of the afternoon with three kids loose in the house?" she replied, laughter threading through her voice. "You must be kidding. No, if I sound out of breath, it's because Susie, Larry and Jimmy insisted I play tag with them in the backyard. They can't get over having so much room to run around in. I can't get over it myself. Thank you again, Caleb."

"Would you stop thanking me?" he

pleaded. "Getting that house built for you was something the whole congregation wanted to do." Well, except for a couple of obstinate holdouts, and eventually even they had come around.

"I just want you to know how much I appreciate it," she said. "If there's ever anything I can do to pay you back, let me know."

It was exactly the opening Caleb needed. "Actually, there is something you could do." He explained about Mary Louise and Danny. "I think Mary Louise needs to understand the realities of trying to work two jobs and care for a baby. Would you consider talking to her?"

"Of course I will," Amanda said at once. "But maybe I should clarify something. Are you asking me to help you talk her out of getting married?"

He considered the question, then answered honestly. "I just want her to know what's ahead. Right now she's all caught up in this romantic notion of living with Danny and having his baby and being happy forever. She needs to know how exhausting it can be and what a toll it might take on their marriage. These two kids have been in love practically as long as I've known them. I don't want them to lose that because this pregnancy has backed them into a corner."

14

"Will their parents help them?" she asked, an unmistakably wistful note in her voice.

Caleb knew what it would have meant to Amanda if her father, Big Max, had stepped up when her life fell apart, but the divide between them had been too great. Amanda had made a tentative overture, but as usual Big Max had blown the opportunity. Sometimes Caleb wanted to shake the stubborn old man, but instead, he'd settled for trying to gently nudge them back together. So far, he'd made precious little progress. And if Amanda ever found out what he'd been up to, she might very well hate him for his interference.

"Actually, even though I haven't spoken to them yet," he said, "I think their parents would help as much as they can. They're all good, decent people who want what's best for their kids. Even so, it's still going to be tough. Danny would probably have to give up his scholarship, quit college and come home."

"He could go to college here," Amanda reminded him. "It might take him longer, but he could do it."

"I suppose," he conceded, though he knew how much going to Clemson had meant to Danny. Caleb had made quite a few calls himself to assure Danny's acceptance there.

He'd even spoken to the scholarship committee on Danny's behalf.

"And both sets of grandparents could help out with babysitting if they're here," Amanda continued. "Maybe Mary Louise and Danny could even live with his folks or hers for a while. It wouldn't be ideal, but it might work. Have any of you considered that?"

"What are you saying?" Caleb asked, startled by the turn the conversation had taken. "Do you think I'm wrong for urging caution?"

"No, I think you're being a responsible, compassionate minister who's trying to make sure two kids get off to a good start, but sometimes things happen even when the timing sucks. Not every marriage is ideal at the beginning, but if the love is strong, a couple can weather almost anything."

"The way you and Bobby did," Caleb concluded.

"The way I *thought* we had," Amanda corrected. "I lived the illusion right up until the day he died. Then reality set in."

"I'm sorry."

"Hey, I'll make you a deal," she said, a teasing note in her voice. "I'll stop saying thank you if you'll stop saying you're sorry."

Caleb chuckled. "I can do that."

"So, knowing where I'm coming from, do

you still want me to speak to Mary Louise?"

"Absolutely," he said at once. "I think you'd be an incredible role model for any young woman. Will tomorrow afternoon work for you?"

"I'll need to come straight home from work because of the kids," she said. "Can you bring her by here, say, around six?"

"Will do," he said at once, trying to keep the pathetically eager note out of his voice. "Goodbye, Amanda."

" 'Bye, Caleb. See you tomorrow."

He hung up, a smile on his lips, then realized he was running very late for his standing Sunday get-together with Amanda's father. Big Max hated to be kept waiting. On the rare occasions it happened, he blustered and carried on about Caleb's impertinence and lack of respect.

Caleb had come to realize, though, that Big Max's temper didn't have anything at all to do with feeling disrespected. Big Max was simply impatient for every little tidbit of information he could get about the daughter he'd cut out of his life and was too proud to let back in. Caleb was simply the chosen messenger.

Still troubled by her conversation with Caleb and imagining the difficulties faced by the

17

young couple, Amanda settled at her kitchen table with a cup of tea. It was the first time all day she'd been able to stop touching things — the shiny new appliances in the kitchen, the glowing oak cabinets, the sheer curtains that billowed at the windows, letting in the pleasant early November breeze and filtering the pale, shimmering late-fall sunlight.

Now she reached yet again for the cool metal key that proved this brand-new house was all hers. The overwhelming feelings that swept through her temporarily pushed aside her concern for the young woman Caleb was bringing by tomorrow afternoon.

She and the kids had moved in barely twenty-four hours ago and it still felt like a dream. The boys had spent the day going from room to room, touching things as she had done, rearranging the toys and furniture that had been given as housewarming gifts in one final burst of generosity that had filled Amanda's heart with gratitude. The screen door to the new backyard with its brightly painted swing set had slammed a hundred times as the boys, trailed by their five-year-old sister, had gone out to explore this vast new space they had to play in, then rushed back in to tell her about everything they'd discovered.

Compared to the luxurious brick home they'd once had in an upscale Charleston suburb, or to Willow Bend, the gracious old plantation-style home in which she'd grown up, this three-bedroom frame house with its bright yellow siding could only be called cozy, and that was being generous. Even so, she loved every square foot of it with a passion she'd never felt for either of those other places, one that had been built on lies and deception and the other the home from which she'd been banished on her wedding day.

For one thing, she and the kids — even Susie — had poured their sweat and tears into building this home, along with the help of dozens of volunteers from their church and community. She'd made friends here, shared laughter. That counted for a lot. She viewed those exhausting but exhilarating days as a blessing, a promise that these rooms would always be filled with joy. She vowed she would never again take anything for granted as long as she lived in this house.

For another thing, she promised herself she would make this house into a real home, instead of the sham she'd unwittingly lived for years with Bobby O'Leary. Only when he'd died in a car accident had she learned the full extent of her husband's betrayal.

He'd pawned the few pieces of heirloom jewelry she'd owned and mortgaged their house and his business to the limit. Their credit card debt had been staggering. He'd cashed in insurance policies, too, so his death had left her no choice but to close the business and find work that could help her pay off the mountain of debt.

When she'd just about worked herself into exhaustion at two jobs to try to satisfy the creditors, and she and the kids were about to be evicted from their too-small apartment, she'd finally accepted that she had no choice but to declare bankruptcy if she was ever to regain some control over their financial future. A recent change in the law had made the process more complicated and dehumanizing than ever before, but Caleb had stood by her side every step of the way.

That humiliating day at the courthouse had sickened her, especially when she finally understood that Bobby had spent all that money in a wasted attempt to prove to her father that he was good enough for Amanda. He'd given her a lifestyle they couldn't afford and left her with debt she couldn't manage.

Oddly enough, even now when she was still working the same two dead-end jobs — one at a lovely boutique, the other at a superstore, when she had to deny the children anything more than the basic necessities, she couldn't hate Bobby. He'd made those misguided choices out of love for her and to counteract the sense of inadequacy her own father had instilled in him. No, she didn't hate Bobby. It was her father she despised.

William Maxwell, known far and wide in South Carolina Low Country as the benevolent Big Max, had been anything but benevolent when it came to Bobby O'Leary. He'd seen him as a no-account loser from the day they'd met and made no pretenses about it. He'd had big plans for his only child and they didn't include a blue-collar husband he believed would only hold her back. He'd done everything in his power to keep Bobby and Amanda apart, and when love had triumphed over his objections, he'd accused Amanda of squandering all the advantages he'd given her. He'd sent her packing with a warning never to look to him to save her from the mess she was making of her life.

Her father's unstinting disapproval had been one of the hardest things Amanda had ever had to endure until she'd lost Bobby. She'd never known her mother, who'd died giving birth to her, so from the time she was a baby, she and her father had been inseparable. He'd doted on her, taken her everywhere. She'd grown up sitting quietly in the

21

boardrooms of some of Charleston's biggest companies, not coloring or reading as some children might have, but absorbing the atmosphere of power around her.

Given that, she supposed it wasn't surprising that her father had held such high expectations for her. He'd anticipated her getting a business degree, then putting it to use and replacing him in many of those same boardrooms, maybe even getting into politics one day. He had the contacts, the will and the raw ambition to make it happen. There was no limit to what he thought she could accomplish. It didn't seem to matter to him that she'd never shared that vision.

He certainly hadn't expected her to throw his legacy back in his face by marrying a garage mechanic. It didn't matter to him that Bobby thought big and already had the beginnings of a small chain of well-run auto shops in half-a-dozen communities too small to attract the national companies. What mattered to Big Max was the loss of Amanda's potential to follow in his footsteps. He couldn't conceive of her achieving anything by the side of a man with grease under his fingernails. Her lack of ambition had appalled him.

Remembering the fight they'd had on the morning of her wedding still brought tears to

Amanda's eyes. Her father had tried one last time to make her see reason and she'd tried harder to make him see Bobby in another light. In the end, it had all dissolved into bitter accusations and her father's vow never to see her again. Amanda knew him well enough to take him at his word. Big Max was known throughout Charleston for his stubbornness and pride, a bad combination for any man, but especially for one who possessed a share of power to go with it.

If it hadn't already been too late, she would have grabbed Bobby and eloped, but Bobby had spent a small fortune to make sure she had the wedding of her dreams, even if it was over her father's vehement objections. Friends she'd grown up with had accepted the invitations. Most of her father's friends had not.

Filled with her own stubborn Maxwell pride, even though her heart was aching, Amanda had gone to the church alone, walked down the aisle alone with her chin held high and her eyes glistening with tears. In front of the minister, she had clung to Bobby's hand as if it were a lifeline.

Bobby knew her heart was broken, not just on her wedding day, but every day thereafter, and he'd done everything he could to mend it. He'd even gone to her father after their first child was born, taken pictures of Max's new grandson, but her father's heart hadn't softened. He tore the pictures up in front of Bobby's eyes and uttered words no grandfather should ever say about his own kin.

Looking back, Amanda realized that was when Bobby had started going overboard. He'd begun buying her things to make up for Big Max's intractable attitude. It had become his obsession to see that she and the children wanted for nothing.

Since Bobby took care of their finances, Amanda hadn't had any idea of the amount of debt they were accumulating. She should have paid attention to the mounting bills, questioned him more about their finances, but she hadn't wanted to indicate in any way that she didn't have total confidence in him. Maybe she should have reassured him more often that he and the kids were enough for her, that she didn't need more things as proof of his ability as a provider, but she'd assumed he knew that. She took for granted that he knew how to manage money. He'd been smart enough to expand his business; surely he could balance their personal checkbook. And basically he had, but only by mortgaging their lives to the hilt.

If only Bobby had known what fate had in

store, he might have made better choices. Instead, they'd lost it all. Worst of all, she'd lost Bobby.

Now, though, she and the children had a second chance, Amanda thought, feeling at peace for the first time since Bobby's death. With the soft afternoon sunlight spilling over her, she smiled. This room would fit into the pantry at Big Max's house. She had little doubt what he would think of it. He would treat it with the same disdain he had shown when she'd made a desperate attempt to reach out to him after Bobby's death had left her virtually penniless. She'd made that attempt only for the sake of her children, but being rebuffed once more had convinced her that the father she'd once adored was now only a bitter old man incapable of compassion.

"Doesn't matter what he thinks or what he does," she told herself fiercely. "My kids are healthy and this house is mine. We're getting back on our feet and that's what counts."

And if Big Max couldn't see that all his wealth, all his power didn't amount to a hill of beans without love, so what? Amanda had long since stopped caring what her father thought or how empty his life had become. She'd stopped because he'd given her no choice. If she hadn't, she might never have stopped crying.

"They've moved in?" Big Max asked Caleb when the minister finally turned up for their regular game of cards. For once Max didn't waste his breath complaining. He was too anxious to hear how things had gone with Amanda and the kids when she'd moved into her new house the day before.

Max and Caleb were an odd pair — the heathen and the man of the Lord, as Max liked to say. Maybe he was more worried about his immortal soul than he'd ever realized. He couldn't see any other reason for having gravitated to this man whose unwavering faith Max couldn't share. He'd lost his belief in God when he'd lost his wife, leaving him all alone to raise Amanda. For a man who'd never understood a thing about women, it had been a terrifying burden.

Yet, from the moment he'd gazed down into Amanda's trusting blue eyes, felt her tiny fist close around his finger, he'd been totally smitten. That girl of his had filled his heart with so much joy, it had dulled the pain of losing his beloved wife.

Severing all ties with Amanda when she'd chosen to defy him and marry that no-account Bobby O'Leary had just about ripped his heart out. He'd taken what he'd considered to be a calculated risk that day and he'd lost. The memory of it haunted him.

Stubborn pride had kept him from reaching out to mend fences. When Bobby had tried, Max had turned him away, embarrassed and shamed to have the boy attempt what he should have been man enough to do himself. When Amanda herself had come to him after Bobby's death, he'd been too quick to say hurtful, judgmental things guaranteed to turn her away. He'd lost a lot of sleep over the years knowing he was a damn fool and the price he'd paid for it.

"If you're this curious about Amanda, why don't you go and see for yourself?" Caleb asked. "Don't you think this feud has gone on long enough? You love your daughter, Max. You need to get to know your grandchildren. You've lost too many years already. Don't lose any more. Don't wait until it's too late."

"You don't know what you're talking about," Max snapped. "I've had more than one chance and I blew it. The girl hates me, and who can blame her?" He looked away. "Besides, if she ever found out . . ."

"Found out what?" Caleb prodded.

"Nothing. I don't want to get into it."

"Get into what? Don't you know by now you can tell me anything and I won't judge you?"

27

"You're a real saint, all right," Max said snidely, hoping to tick him off.

Caleb didn't react. He just sat there with the patient expression that made Max nuts.

"Oh, for goodness' sake, it was a slip of the tongue, that's all," Max grumbled.

"I doubt that," Caleb said.

"Look, all I'm saying is it's too late for Amanda and me."

"It's not too late until you're in your grave," Caleb retorted.

Maybe that was what Max liked about this young man. He didn't wilt under Max's scorn, didn't turn away when pushed to do just that. Caleb was a man with staying power. Max admired that, even if he didn't know how any man could devote himself to God's work when there was evidence all around that God wasn't paying a damn bit of attention to what was happening down here on earth.

"You gonna pray over me when I'm gone?" Max asked, taunting him.

Caleb grinned. "I pray for you every night as it is. If you weren't so ornery, I think maybe my prayers would have a better outcome."

Max regarded him with surprise. "I never asked you to pray for me."

"You didn't need to. It's what I do. I see a

need and I jump in."

"Well, you're wasting your breath," Max replied irritably.

"It's mine to waste," Caleb responded. "Besides, I think one of these days even someone as cantankerous as you will wake up and admit he's made a dreadful mistake and reach out to the one person on earth he cares about. In fact, you and I know you've already done that in a way. The only one who doesn't know and should is Amanda."

Max scowled at him. "You tell her I bought that land her new house is sitting on and she'll move out by morning," he said with absolute conviction. "That girl got my stubbornness and doubled it."

"Maybe," Caleb said. "But maybe she'd see it as a gesture that's been too long coming."

"Stay out of it, Caleb. You don't know what the hell you're talking about." He frowned at the pastor. "And don't go dropping any hints to her, either. You and I made a deal. She's never to know about me buying that land. You spill the beans to her and I will see your sorry butt in hell."

Caleb's steady gaze never wavered. "You don't scare me, Max. Don't you know that by now?"

Max was flustered by the amusement in

Caleb's voice. Most men in Charleston would have been quaking in their boots. Most men understood that he never made idle threats.

"Well, I *should* terrify you," he said testily. "Now, are we going to play cards or are we going to sit around here all night gabbing like a couple of old women?"

"Bring it on, old man." After he'd dealt the cards, Caleb pulled a piece of paper from his pocket and smoothed it out. "Let's see here. You already owe me $7,403.62."

Max chuckled at the precise accounting. "Just think what kind of stained-glass window you could have bought for the church by now if we played for more than small change."

"And isn't it lucky for you that I don't approve of gambling except for a worthy cause?" Caleb retorted. "The stained-glass windows can wait. This money will come in handy at the church's food bank. I think when we get to a nice round ten thousand, I'll ask you to cut me a check."

Max looked at the hand he'd been dealt and muttered an oath. "Sure as hell looks like I'm about to make another contribution tonight."

Caleb laughed. "Who're you kidding, old man? It looks that way every time we play."

"True," Max conceded. It was a small-enough price to pay, though, for some decent company. Add that Caleb kept him abreast of what was going on with Amanda without gloating about it, and Max was perfectly content to lose a few dollars once a week. Hell, he'd give up his entire fortune for the chance to go back in time and do things differently. So many things. Some that only a small handful of people knew anything about.

Since going back wasn't possible, he'd have to make do with the way things were.

2

Amanda was rushing to get out the door at the boutique where she worked when Maggie Parker halted her exit.

"Hey, where's the fire?" Maggie asked. "I came to see if you and the kids would like to have dinner with me tonight. Josh had to run over to Atlanta to take a look at that historic renovation project he and Cord are starting next month."

Amanda regarded Maggie with surprise. Though she'd been a bridesmaid in Maggie's wedding to Josh, she'd always thought Maggie had made the gesture to appease Josh. While Maggie had never been outright rude to her, the wedding was just about the only occasion she had been openly friendly. Maybe now that she and Josh were married, she was putting aside the irrational jealousy she'd once felt toward Amanda and turning over a new leaf. Still, Amanda couldn't help being skeptical.

"You want to have dinner with us?" Amanda said. "Me and the kids?"

Maggie shrugged. "Sure. Why not?"

"Maybe because a part of you still wonders if there wasn't something going on between me and Josh," Amanda said candidly. "I know it bothered you that there was a bond between us when he was in charge of the crew building my house."

Maggie winced. "Okay, I acted like an idiot. I took my insecurities out on you."

Amanda grinned at the admission. "Yes, you did, especially since Josh could barely untangle his tongue whenever you were around."

"I guess I missed that, at least at first," Maggie conceded. "I swear to you I'm over it. Come on, Amanda. I know you're not the type to hold a grudge."

"Not usually," Amanda agreed. "Something tells me, though, that this was Josh's idea, not yours."

"It most certainly was not," Maggie declared with a pretty good show of indignation, then sighed. "Okay, maybe it was, but he's right. It's past time for me to get over that ridiculous jealousy, especially now that he and I are married. I really do want us to be friends, Amanda. You and the kids mean

33

a lot to Josh and to his mother. We're bound to be thrown together from time to time. Can't we get past my bad behavior?"

Amanda could see her obvious discomfort. Maggie Parker was the most self-confident woman Amanda had ever met, with the possible exception of Maggie's best friend, Dinah Beaufort. Amanda envied them, and she was still a little astounded that Maggie had thought even for a second that Josh was interested in her, not Maggie.

"I'd like that," Amanda told her sincerely. Real friends had been in short supply since her marriage to Bobby. And since his death, there hadn't been time to make new ones. "But I can't tonight. I have to get home."

"The kids are invited, too," Maggie reminded her.

"I know, but actually I already have plans. Caleb's coming by."

Maggie's expression immediately brightened with curiosity. "Really? Do tell," she said.

Amanda shook her head. "Stop that. It's not what you think."

At the quick denial, Maggie grinned. "Then, please, tell me what it is."

"He wants me to talk to someone. He thinks I might be able to offer a perspective that he can't. That's it."

34

Maggie regarded her with blatant skepticism. "So, this seasoned minister who's counseled who knows how many people about every problem under the sun is turning to you?"

Amanda frowned at the hint of amused disbelief in Maggie's voice. "In this particular situation, apparently I'm the one with firsthand experience," she said.

"Of course you are. And Caleb's sudden recognition of your expertise doesn't have anything at all to do with the fact that he has the hots for you?" Maggie inquired.

Immediately Amanda's cheeks flooded with color. "Maggie!" she protested weakly. "You can't say things like that. Caleb's a minister."

"I know. I worried about the same thing when Dinah pointed out that Caleb practically salivates when you're nearby, but then I caught on that he's a man, not a saint. It's not as if either one of you is off-limits in any way. The only shocker is that in his seven years here in Charleston some woman hasn't already snapped him up."

Amanda had had similar thoughts from time to time. Aside from being gorgeous, Caleb was the kindest, most decent man she'd ever known. It didn't make sense that he wasn't married. She, however, wasn't the woman to change that. She was just beginning to get back on her feet emotionally. She needed time to prove to herself that she was strong and capable. She was not about to let some man promise to bail her out, only to have him abandon her. She'd learned to prize her independence. If her life ever fell apart again, it would be her own doing, not someone else's.

"That woman won't be me," she told Maggie emphatically.

"Then you don't see what a catch he is?" Maggie asked skeptically.

"Of course I do."

"Well, then?"

"I'm not looking for a catch, even one as terrific as Caleb," Amanda insisted. "Now, I really do have to go."

Maggie stepped aside. "We'll do the dinner thing another time, okay? Maybe later in the week when Josh gets back. I'll ask Nadine, too, though these days Josh's mother rarely goes anywhere without George Winslow in tow. Would that be okay with you?"

Amanda considered the question seriously. George was one of her father's best friends, and initially he'd been one of the most outspoken critics of the church's plan to build her house. That was the downside. On the upside, since he'd gotten involved

36

with Nadine, he'd mellowed.

"I can tolerate George," Amanda said eventually. "Nadine's pretty good at keeping him in check."

"Okay, then, I'll be in touch with the details," Maggie said, a faint hint of relief in her voice.

Once again Amanda was astounded by the trace of vulnerability in a woman whose strength and self-confidence she admired. Maggie had faced down a madman who'd trapped her in her art gallery not that long ago, but she seemed to be genuinely uneasy around Amanda.

"Maggie, can I ask you a question? Why is this so important to you?"

Maggie looked disconcerted by the direct question. "I told you. I know I misjudged you and I want to make amends. You're important to Josh and to Nadine and other people I admire and respect, so I'd like us to be friends, too."

"Then we will be," Amanda said. "If I've learned nothing else since my husband died, it's that friendship is important." Impulsively, she reached out and gave Maggie a hug. "Besides, as far as I'm concerned we've been friends since the minute you showed up to help build my house. That was an act of kindness I'm never likely to forget."

Maggie regarded her with surprise. "You really mean that, don't you? Even after everything I did to keep you at arm's length?"

"Believe me, I understood what that was all about. You were protecting your turf, even though you had nothing to fear from me. I knew in time you'd figure out that I wasn't a threat to your relationship with Josh."

"Well, I'm sorry just the same. We're starting over right now, okay?"

"Okay," Amanda agreed at once.

Maggie gave her a conspiratorial grin. "You know what that means, don't you?"

"What?"

"I get to have free rein to meddle in your relationship with Caleb."

Amanda gave her a horrified look. "I don't have a relationship with Caleb."

"You will when I'm through," Maggie said cheerfully. "Enjoy your evening."

She was gone before Amanda could formulate a reply. This wasn't good. Not good at all. Maggie meddling all on her own would be bad enough, but if she brought the romantically irrepressible Nadine into it — and she very well might — who knew what mischief they could stir up for Amanda and Caleb?

Caleb took in Amanda's flushed cheeks and

too-bright eyes and tried to figure out what had brought on this sudden attack of nerves. It couldn't be because he and Mary Louise were the first official guests at her new home. Amanda had grown up entertaining for Big Max. She'd been hosting dinner parties for Charleston's power brokers by the time she was thirteen. So why was she fluttering around the living room, fussing over a plate of cheese and crackers and a couple of soft drinks?

He captured her hand as she was about to take off for the kitchen once again. "You okay?" he asked.

"Fine, just fine," she said too cheerfully. She turned to beam at Mary Louise. "Just let me get some napkins and we can talk."

"There are napkins on the table," Caleb pointed out.

Her good cheer evaporated. "Oh, of course there are. What was I thinking?" She sat down on the edge of a chair. "Mary Louise, why don't you tell me a little bit about you and Danny?"

Mary Louise, who'd been tense ever since Caleb had picked her up and hadn't said a word on the ride over, launched into a dreamy description of their relationship. If it had been written down, it would have been punctuated by hearts and flowers.

Amanda grinned at the romantic picture the girl was painting. "Then you've been in love with him practically forever?" she summarized.

Mary Louise nodded. "That's why I don't understand what all the fuss is about us getting married a little sooner than we planned."

Caleb was about to explain when Amanda asked, "What's Danny studying at Clemson?"

"Architecture," Mary Louise said.

"Is he excited about it?" Amanda asked.

"He loves it. Who could live around here and not care about all these historic old buildings? He really wants to find ways to preserve them."

"I have a couple of friends who do historic preservation work," Amanda told her. "It requires a real passion and understanding to do it right. How are you going to feel if Danny has to give that up?"

Mary Louise looked startled. "Why would he have to give it up?"

"Supporting a family means bringing in a paycheck and putting food on the table," Amanda explained. "It means doctors for you and the baby. It means paying rent for someplace to live."

"I can work," Mary Louise said staunchly.

"For a while," Amanda agreed. "What about once the baby comes?"

"We can manage," Mary Louise insisted.

Just then Larry, Jimmy and Susie raced in from the backyard demanding Amanda's immediate attention. In Caleb's opinion, their timing couldn't have been better.

"Mommy, they wouldn't let me swing on the swing," Susie said, tears rolling down her cheeks. She cast an accusing look at her big brothers. "They're mean and I hate them!"

"Susie!" Amanda said. "You do not hate your brothers."

"Do, too," she said with a sniff.

"She's just a big ole baby," Jimmy countered.

"Am not," Susie retorted.

Before the battle could escalate, Amanda scooped up Susie, then directed a forbidding look at the boys. "Come with me," she said.

"I can take them," Caleb offered.

"Not this time," Amanda said tersely, heading to the back of the house.

"But it's not fair," Jimmy wailed just before one bedroom door slammed shut.

"They were being mean," Susie repeated, her voice thick with tears. "How come I have to go to my room?"

Caleb couldn't hear Amanda's murmured reply, but then a second door closed. She came back, looking faintly harried.

"Sorry. Where were we?" she asked Mary Louise.

"I was telling you that Danny and I can figure all that out," Mary Louise said, though her gaze seemed to be drawn in the direction of the unmistakable sobs coming from down the hall. She looked shaken.

"You'll need to get used to that," Amanda told her mildly. "Kids cry, especially babies. It'll make it tough for Danny to study, at least at home. Next thing you know he'll either have to drop out of school or spend all his free time in the library so he can keep up with his classes."

Mary Louise reacted with dismay. "It's one little baby," she protested.

Amanda smiled. "You have no idea what a ruckus one little baby can create, especially if he or she happens to be colicky. Jimmy didn't let me get a decent night's sleep for months."

"Didn't your husband help?"

"Some, but he was working. He needed his sleep, just the way Danny will need his if he's going to keep up with his studies." Amanda's expression turned sad. "Bobby and I fought all the time during those months."

"How come?" Mary Louise asked.

42

"He thought I ought to be able to do something to stop the crying. It was like he was accusing me of being a bad mother. It tapped into every one of my insecurities, so I lashed back."

The memory still seemed to touch a raw nerve and Mary Louise seemed to get that. "How old were you when you got married?" she asked.

"I was nineteen, just a year older than you," Amanda told her.

"But your husband wasn't in college, right?" Mary Louise said, seizing on some slim difference between him and Danny. "He was working."

"Right. He was getting his business off the ground. He was gone all the time, so everything at home was up to me."

"If you were in love, though, I'll bet it was worth it," Mary Louise said, her expression hopeful.

"In many ways, yes," Amanda agreed. She exchanged a look with Caleb. "But I won't lie to you, Mary Louise, the exhaustion and stress pretty much sucked the romance right out of it. Bobby and I were lucky, though. No matter how tough things got, no matter how many fights we had, we stuck together. We both knew we didn't have anybody else to fall back on. We had to make it work. It might

43

have been easier, though, if we'd waited."

"But Reverend Webb told me your husband died," Mary Louise said. "What if you hadn't had that time together? Aren't you glad you had that?"

Caleb saw the unmistakable sadness in Amanda's eyes. It was always there when Bobby's death was mentioned. It was always there, as well, when anyone mentioned her father. That loss ran just as deep.

"Yes," Amanda whispered. "I'm glad for every minute we had. No one can live their life, though, based on what-ifs. You have to be smart and base your decisions on what *is*."

"Danny and I are having a baby," Mary Louise said. "That's what is." She aimed a fiercely determined look at Caleb. "And I'm not giving the baby away. It might be hard and scary, but this is what I'm doing and nothing you say will talk me out of it."

Caleb recognized that level of determination and knew that Amanda had hit the nail on the head. He, too, had to deal with things the way they were.

"Okay, then," he said. "I'm going to see you and Danny again on Sunday and then afterward I'm going to ask your folks to join us. Let's see where we stand and what we can do to make sure this baby has not just two parents who will love it, but a whole support system."

"Really?" Mary Louise said, her eyes wide. "You're going to marry us?"

"One step at a time," Caleb warned. "Let's get Danny and your folks on board first. You don't want Danny to feel like he's been backed into a corner, do you?"

"No, of course not. He wants this as much as I do. You'll see," she insisted.

Caleb had his doubts about that, but maybe there was a way to bring him around, especially if he could come up with some way to ensure Danny didn't lose his career dream in the process.

Once Amanda had gotten over her case of the jitters, thanks to that untimely and provocative conversation with Maggie, she'd been able to focus on the young woman Caleb had brought over. She'd totally empathized with Mary Louise's unshakable optimism in the face of an unexpected pregnancy that threatened to change her life forever. She'd done what she could to explain the harsh realities of marrying and having a family too young, but a part of her had been rooting for Mary Louise to stick to her guns and fight for what she wanted. It was that sort of spunk that would be needed if she and Danny were to have even half a chance of making it.

As soon as Mary Louise and Caleb had left, she'd wilted as she considered the confrontation that awaited with her own squabbling children. With no siblings of her own, she was always taken aback by the battles among her three children. She'd always had this rosy picture of them loving one another through thick and thin. The reality was that there were plenty of times when they barely tolerated one another.

Before she gave them permission to leave their rooms, she fixed a quick dinner of spaghetti and meatballs, one of the few meals they all loved. Maybe that would facilitate peace.

When the food was on the table, she went to the boys' room first. "Okay, you two, dinner's ready, but I want you at the table only if you can promise me that there will be no fighting with your sister. You know how I hate it when you gang up on her."

Larry and Jimmy regarded her with tear-reddened eyes.

"I'm sorry, Mom," Jimmy said first.

"Me, too," Larry added. "We really weren't being mean. We were scared she'd fall out of the swing like she did yesterday."

Amanda's mouth gaped. "Susie fell out of

the swing yesterday?"

Jimmy nodded. "Twice. She made us promise not to tell, 'cause she was afraid you wouldn't let her get on the swing anymore."

Amanda sighed. "Then you were trying to protect her?"

Both boys nodded solemnly.

"Then I'm the one who's sorry," she told them. "I should have given you a chance to explain."

They wrapped their arms around her waist and leaned into her.

"It's okay, Mom. You were kinda busy with Caleb and that lady," Larry said.

She looked down into their upturned faces. "How about I make it up to you with ice cream after dinner?"

"We have ice cream?"

"No, but we'll take a walk and get cones," she said.

"Susie, too?" Larry asked indignantly.

"Something tells me she's learned her lesson," Amanda said. "She was sent to her room, too."

Both boys seemed to consider that for a moment.

"Okay," Larry said eventually. "But we get double dips and she only gets one, 'cause we're bigger."

Amanda laughed at the twisted logic that

gave them a triumph over their little sister. "That sounds fair."

Caleb returned to Amanda's just in time to meet her and the kids on the sidewalk.

"We're going for ice-cream cones, Mr. Caleb," Susie announced, holding out her arms to be picked up. The red band holding her hair in a ponytail had slipped and curls were poking out in every direction. There was a streak of spaghetti sauce on her cheek and another on her purple T-shirt.

He scooped her up just as Larry tugged on his shirtsleeve.

"We get two scoops, but she only gets one," he told Caleb.

"Because you're older," Caleb guessed.

"And because Mom's 'pologizing to us," Jimmy added.

Caleb glanced at Amanda. "Oh?"

"Long story," she said. "What brings you back?"

"I was hoping we could talk some more about the Mary Louise and Danny situation."

Amanda looked vaguely uneasy. "Sorry I wasn't more help."

"Actually you were a huge help."

She seemed startled by that. "Really?"

"Seems I'm the one who came away from

48

the talk with a whole new perspective," he admitted. "Have you ever considered going back to school and getting a degree in psychology, so you could counsel young people?"

She stared at him as if he'd grown two heads. "Me? No way. I barely have my own life together. I certainly don't want to tell anyone else what they ought to be doing."

"That's just it, you weren't telling Mary Louise what to do at all. You were showing her what lies ahead and letting her draw her own conclusions."

"She came to the wrong one, according to you," Amanda reminded him.

"No, I suspect she came to the right one for her. Or, if she didn't, at least she's moving ahead with her eyes wide open. That's the best we can hope for." He met her gaze. "I'm serious, Amanda. I think you could do this. I could certainly use someone like you to work with the kids at church. Maybe you could do that on an informal basis."

"How?"

"Just be one of the sponsors of the youth group, sort of a mentor. You wouldn't need formal training for that." And, he thought, it would mean they'd be working together on a regular basis. He recognized that God would probably find some way to slap him silly for the ulterior motives behind his pitch.

"I don't know," she said doubtfully. "I really don't have that much time."

"You've been looking for a way to give back to the church for helping you get a house," he said, forcing aside the instant twinge of guilt that assailed him for playing that particular card.

"I'll think about it," she promised.

"Seriously," he pressed.

She regarded him with amusement. "Yes, Caleb, I promise I will think about it seriously. I will not crack up laughing at the mere idea of turning myself into anyone's mentor."

Before he could respond to that, Susie patted his cheek to get attention.

"Mr. Caleb, what kind of ice cream are you gonna have?"

"Strawberry fudge," he said at once, knowing it was her favorite.

She grinned. "Me, too!"

He feigned shock. "Really?"

"I'm gonna have one scoop of chocolate and one of cherry vanilla," Larry said enthusiastically.

"I want two scoops of chocolate," Jimmy said.

Caleb turned to Amanda. "What about you? Is this a plain old vanilla night or are you going to live dangerously?"

He saw the precise instant when she rose to the dare in his voice. Her eyes began to shine with a rare sparkle.

"I am having," she began, pausing for drama, "a banana split." She looked each one of them in the eye, saving Caleb for last. "And I am not sharing."

He laughed. "Not even one little bite?"

"Not even if you beg," she declared.

Caught up in the moment, he locked his gaze with hers. "Bet I can make you change your mind."

Bright patches of color rose in her cheeks, but she didn't blink or look away. "Bet you can't," she said in a voice barely above a whisper.

Caleb once again admired her willingness not to turn away from something that so clearly scared her. He could have let the whole thing die right there, satisfied with the response he'd managed to stir in her, but he, too, was feeling just a little bit reckless and daring tonight.

With her steady gaze still even with his, he leaned slowly down and brushed a daring first kiss across her lips. When he pulled away, she looked shaken, but undaunted.

"You think that will change my mind?" she scoffed. "We're talking a banana split here."

He grinned. "*That* might not change your mind," he agreed. "But how about if I tell you that if you *don't* share, there's a whole lot more where that kiss came from."

She faltered for just a second, then chuckled. "You know, for a minister, you certainly know how to play dirty."

"It would be wise, Amanda, if you'd remember that when it gets right down to it, I'm a minister, not a saint. Trust me, there's a difference."

"Yes, I'm beginning to get that."

Oddly enough, it didn't seem to scare her half as much as he'd expected it to.

And that gave him unexpected hope for the future.

3

Mary Louise had worked a double shift at the Stop and Shop and her feet were killing her. She was determined, though, to show Danny that she was willing to make good on her word to earn all the money they would need to get by once they were married.

"Is Danny coming home again this weekend?" Willie Ron asked as she closed out for the evening and he prepared to take over.

Willie Ron Dupree was only twenty-six, but he had been working the graveyard shift for ten years to help support his disabled mother. He never talked about whatever hopes and dreams he'd had before his mother's illness had made her unable to work. If he'd had to give up college or anything, Mary Louise had never heard him complain about it.

Willie Ron was one of the nicest guys she'd ever known, always willing to come in early if she needed to take off, always ready to listen when she had a problem. And he always asked about Danny. She wondered what he'd have to say if he knew about her pregnancy, if it would make him think less of her, or of Danny, for that matter.

"Hey," Willie Ron said, concern in his voice. "You okay? I asked about Danny and for once you didn't launch into a full-scale recitation of all the guy's good points."

Mary Louise shrugged. "Guess my mind wandered," she said. "He should be here any minute. He was driving over from Clemson after his last class today. He promised he'd be here in time to pick me up after my shift."

"Girl, you got that boy wrapped around your finger," Willie Ron teased, his smile showing off a row of glistening white teeth. "No woman's ever going to tie me up in knots like that."

"Just wait till the right one comes along," she goaded him. "You'll treat her like a queen, the same way you do your mama."

"My mama's raised eight of us, and done a good job of it," Willie Ron said, his expression turning serious. "She deserves being spoiled. Haven't met anyone yet who's her equal. Even when she was laid low by a bad heart, my mama kept her spirits up. She raised all of us to count our blessings and not be crying over things we can't fix."

"You'll find someone just like her someday," Mary Louise told him. "I know for a fact that Li'l Bit Gaines comes in here just to see you."

If it was possible for a black man to blush, Willie Ron's cheeks would have been flaming. "Li'l Bit just likes her nightly candy fix. She comes in here for a Snickers bar. Got nothin' to do with me."

"Yeah, right," Mary Louise responded. "I know better. How many people rush out to indulge a chocolate craving after eleven o'clock at night?"

Willie Ron frowned. "Maybe instead of messin' in my love life, you ought to be checking your lipstick before that boyfriend of yours gets here," he said. "Though I don't know why you'd bother since he's likely to kiss it right off. I haven't seen you two make it to the car yet before that man's sneakin' himself some sugar."

Ignoring the taunt, Mary Louise hurried to the back of the convenience store to put on another coat of Sugarplum lip gloss. But even as she locked the door to the restroom she kept spotless, she wondered just how much kissing she and Danny were likely to do. He'd gone into a hands-off mode the minute he'd heard about the baby. Kinda like shutting the barn door after the horse has gone, in her opinion. Seemed like they ought to be taking advantage of this time, since any fooling around they did couldn't lead to another pregnancy. They were already in as much trouble as it was possible to get.

When she emerged from the back, Danny was standing at the counter talking to Willie Ron. She took a moment to admire the way Danny looked in his carefully pressed chinos and dark green polo shirt. It was her favorite because it made his eyes look even greener than usual. He looked like the fancy college boy he was, and she was amazed that she'd been lucky enough to be the girl he'd fallen for.

"Hey, handsome," she called out. "Did you come straight from the fraternity house?"

"You know I'm no frat boy," he chided, then gave her an appreciative once-over. "But you could put most of those sorority girls to shame, Mary Louise."

It was a sweet thing to say, especially since he knew she sometimes felt inadequate because college had been beyond her family's reach. Until she'd gotten pregnant, she'd been hoping to put enough money aside to take some classes here in town so Danny wouldn't be ashamed of her lack of education.

"You two have big plans for tonight?" Willie Ron asked, regarding them like an indulgent big brother.

"Actually we have some talking to do," Danny said, his gaze locked with Mary Louise's. "I thought we could take a drive or something."

Willie Ron didn't look as if he believed for a second that they'd be driving around all evening, but he kept his comments to himself for once as he shooed them out the door. "I'll see you on Monday, Mary Louise. You say a prayer for Mama in church on Sunday, you hear."

"I always do," she said, then grinned. "And I ask God to find you a girl worthy of you."

"You go on now," he said with a roll of his eyes.

Mary Louise turned to find Danny grinning at her. "You like embarrassing that man, don't you?" he asked as she slipped her hand into his and headed for the car.

"Embarrassing him how?" she asked. "He needs a girlfriend and a life. All he does is work and look out for his mama."

"I think he's old enough to find his own woman."

"But Willie Ron's shy. He needs a nudge," she protested as Danny held the car door for her the way he always did. His folks had taught him manners, that's for sure. It was one of the first things she'd noticed about him.

"Don't you think your time might be better spent figuring out what we're going to do, instead of worrying about Willie Ron?" Danny asked, a sudden edge to his voice.

Fortunately before she could respond, he closed the car door, then went around to get behind the wheel. It was just enough time for her quick flash of temper to cool. There was no point getting into some silly argument right off the bat when they had more important things to talk about.

"I have been thinking about our future," she said calmly. "All week long, in fact. What about you?"

He sighed. "It was the only thing I could think about. Jeez, Mary Louise, this couldn't have happened at a worse time."

"Well, I'm sorry as hell about that, but it's not like I planned it, Danny." She scowled at him and noted the faint flicker of doubt in his eyes. "You don't believe me, do you?" she demanded in a shocked tone. "You think I planned this." Her temper shot right back into high gear. "Well, you can just think again, Danny Marshall. This messes up some things I'd been counting on, too."

"Such as?"

"Taking college classes right here in Charleston. I never intended to just drift along working at the Stop and Shop for the rest of my life. I might not have had the grades to win a scholarship to Clemson, but I'm smart. I have dreams, too. You should know that. We talked about them enough."

His hands tightened on the steering wheel. "I do know that," he said eventually. "I'm sorry. It's just that everything is such a mess. I flunked an important math test this week because I couldn't concentrate. I can't help thinking that's what it's going to be like from now on."

"It'll get better once we make some decisions," she consoled him. "It's the worry that's distracting you."

"And you think that's going to stop just because we get married?" he scoffed. "That'll just be the start."

His words echoed the warning Amanda O'Leary had given her and that scared Mary Louise. Desperate to reassure him — and herself — she reached for his arm, then massaged the tight muscle until it began to relax. "I swear I didn't mean for this to happen," she whispered. "I never wanted to ruin things for you."

He faced her, his expression earnest. "Then let's think about what Reverend Webb said. Let's at least consider the possibility of having the baby adopted," he pleaded. "It's the only thing that makes sense. Let somebody who desperately wants a baby give ours a good home. We're not ready to do that, Mary Louise. At least, I'm not."

Tears welled up in Mary Louise's eyes. A part of her wanted to go along with him, if only to make his life easier. Heck, it would make her life easier, too. She wasn't holding out because of stubbornness, either, though she knew that's what Danny thought. How could they give up their baby and ever have any chance at a future? Every baby that might come later would be a bittersweet reminder of the one they'd given up. Sooner or later that loss would eat away at them. The way she saw it, giving up this baby would be a sure way to end things between them forever.

"Do you love me, Danny?" she asked, her heart in her throat.

He took his eyes off the road and glanced at her. "You know I do," he said with unmistakable sincerity.

"Then how can you not love our baby?"

He didn't answer for the longest time, but when he did, he said, "Because it's not real to me, I guess. And I'm scared, Mary Louise. Really scared."

"Of the baby ruining your life?"

"There's some of that," he admitted. "And I know it's selfish, but there's more, too. I'm afraid it will come between us, that I'll resent you, just the way Reverend Webb said, and even worse that I'll resent the baby and won't be able to love it the way a baby deserves to be loved."

He gave her a sad smile. "I used to think about what it would be like when we finally had our first baby. I could imagine holding that little guy or girl in my arms, teaching it stuff, reading stories. Now all I can think about is how exhausting it would be to cope with middle-of-the-night feedings and all the crying and stuff when I've got exams coming up and studying to do."

Maybe because Amanda had helped open her heart to it, Mary Louise heard the depth of his emotional struggle in his voice. In that instant she knew that she really did have to consider Danny's point of view and not just her own blind optimism that everything would be fine.

"Will you take me home?" she said, her voice tight.

61

"Don't be mad at me, Mary Louise," he begged. "I'm just trying to be honest."

"I know, and I'm not mad, really I'm not," she said sadly. "That's why I want to go home. I need to think about what you said before we meet with Reverend Webb again on Sunday."

"Do you want to get together tomorrow and talk some more?" Danny asked.

She shook her head. "No, you've given me some more to think about and I need to wrestle with it on my own. I'll call you if I change my mind. Otherwise I'll see you when you pick me up for church on Sunday." She lifted her gaze to his. "Have you talked to your folks at all?"

He shook his head. "Not yet. You?"

"No."

"Do you think we should tell them before Sunday?" he asked. "If Reverend Webb wants to see them, too, we should probably give them time to absorb all this."

"I want this to be *our* decision," Mary Louise argued. "You know they'll get all weird, and the next thing we know, they'll be making all the decisions."

"I suppose you're right," he admitted. "But it's not really fair for them to be blind-sided."

"Maybe we can just meet with Reverend

Webb and decide what we're going to do, then go tell them together," she suggested. "First yours, then mine."

"Why mine first?" he asked.

"Because mine might kill us," she said, only partially in jest. "Or you, anyway."

Danny pulled the car to a stop in front of her house and cut the engine, then rested his head on the steering wheel. Mary Louise sat beside him, fighting tears. When Danny finally turned toward her, his eyes were damp, as well.

"I'm sorry," he whispered. "I wish I were as excited about this as you are."

"I wish you were, too," she said, reaching for him. "But we're going to figure this out, Danny. I know we will. And when we do, it will be what's best for all of us."

Amanda was pretty sure a person could go straight to hell for having the kind of thoughts she was having on Saturday afternoon as she watched Caleb struggle to wrestle the armoire she'd bought at a flea market into her new bedroom. What kind of joke had God been playing when he'd created a minister with broad shoulders and rock-solid abs that belonged on the cover of a fitness magazine?

She'd noticed the man's muscles far more

than she should have during the months they'd worked side by side to build her new home. He had a very dangerous habit of stripping off his shirt when the sultry Charleston temperatures climbed. She wasn't the only woman working on the house whose mouth had gaped at the vision of male perfection he'd presented. Add in Maggie's taunting remarks just the other day, and Amanda's imagination had traveled in a very steamy and unsuitable direction. Just last night she'd had a dream about him — about the two of them — that had left her lying awake, restless and hot.

Amanda figured it was ironic that she felt such stirrings of desire only when she was around the most inappropriate man in all of Charleston. Then, again, maybe this was God's way of showing her she wasn't dead, after all, without putting her heart at risk in the process. Being attracted to Caleb was safe, thanks to his profession. He certainly wouldn't be trying to tempt her into some casual liaison, that was for sure, and a fling was all she could imagine for herself for the foreseeable future.

And when it came down to it, she was the last woman on earth any minister would want. She didn't really believe in God, at least not a benevolent one, mostly because of the way she'd been brought up. Her father's bitterness over her mother's death had instilled the impression that only an uncaring God could have allowed such a thing to happen. Even as she'd grown up and started thinking for herself, Amanda couldn't disagree. As much as she'd loved her father, she'd missed having a mother. She'd felt cheated out of something important. With no one else she could think of to blame, she'd pointed her anger toward God and kept her distance.

Despite her apathy, Bobby had insisted they make at least perfunctory appearances at church for the sake of the children. She'd gone along with it, using the quiet time to reflect on things. The hymns had been lovely, a few of the prayers meaningful, but she'd made little attempt to absorb the messages in the sermons.

Ministers had come and gone, and she'd paid scant attention — until she'd had to make arrangements for Bobby's funeral. That was when she'd seen the compassion in Caleb's eyes and felt a much-needed steadiness in him that had gotten her through those first awful months when everything in her life had unraveled.

It had been his idea that the church come together to build this house for her. And, remarkably, as the weeks had passed and she'd seen her home taking shape, her life had come together, as well. She'd felt stronger, more capable of facing an uncertain future.

And when they'd handed her the keys on that last day, she'd looked around into the faces of her new friends and felt whole again. Despite all the adversities she'd faced, her life truly was blessed. She'd looked across the room and met Caleb's gaze and knew that he'd understood all along how desperately she needed what she'd found in this house and the building of it. She'd reclaimed her self-respect.

"Thank you," she'd mouthed.

To her utter shock, he'd winked. That tiny, flirtatious wink had rattled her so badly she'd turned and fled. For months she had tucked Caleb into a nice, safe niche in her life. After the turmoil of living with Bobby and the chaos after his death, Caleb epitomized a quiet serenity she craved. That wink, however, had suggested there was another side to him, a human and very male side she wasn't ready for.

But even though he continued to disconcert her, for some reason she hadn't been able to insist he stay away. The stakes escalated more every time they saw each other.

She knew it and she was pretty sure he did, too. That kiss the other night had been as innocent as a peck on the cheek between friends, but way too much passion had simmered just below the surface. The depth of it had shaken her. Yet when she'd needed help transporting the armoire today, Caleb was the first person she'd thought of. And he'd agreed readily in fact, with an eagerness that told her he'd missed her during the week as much as she'd missed him.

Amanda felt a tug on her sleeve and looked down into the too-serious face of her five-year-old daughter.

"Hey, baby, what's up?" she asked Susie, relieved by the distraction.

Susie frowned. "I'm not a baby."

Amanda scooped her up and tickled her. "You're my baby. You always will be."

"Even when I'm ten?" Susie asked in a dismayed voice.

"Even when you're thirty," Amanda replied.

"How old is thirty?"

"Almost as old as me," Amanda said.

"But you're not a baby," Susie protested.

Amanda knew she was in one man's eyes, or had been, anyway. Sometimes knowing she'd lost that relationship hurt more than she could bear. Knowing that her once-beloved father had willingly tossed it aside hurt even more.

"No, I suppose not," she said, biting back a sigh. In fact, she was the only grown-up these children had. Sometimes the pressure of that was overwhelming. It would have meant the world to be able to lean on her father from time to time, to share the joy of her three kids with him. But there was no point in wishing for things that simply couldn't be.

"So can he?" Susie asked, apparently completing an entire line of conversation Amanda had missed.

"Can who do what?"

"Can Mr. Caleb stay for dinner?" Susie asked impatiently. "We could have pizza, like last time."

"You have to stop thinking that we're going to have pizza every time Caleb comes over," Amanda told her daughter.

"Why is that?" Caleb asked, coming back into the living room, wiping away his sweat with a towel, which only drew attention to those fabulous abs again. It was all Amanda could do not to sigh.

"I love pizza," he declared. "And who wants to order a large pizza just for one person? You guys give me the perfect excuse."

Susie's eyes glowed with excitement. "See, Mommy. Mr. Caleb likes pizza as much as I do. So can he stay?"

Amanda gave Caleb a look of mock severity. "Did you put her up to this?"

He winked at Susie. "Absolutely not," he swore solemnly. "I just figure that a man who's risked his back to haul furniture for you ought to get something out of the deal."

"And you want to be paid in pizza?" Amanda asked doubtfully.

"Actually, I'm buying the pizza. Your company is enough payment."

Amanda regarded him warily. "You can't keep doing this," she said.

"Doing what?" he asked, his expression all innocence.

"Dreaming up excuses to feed us." She set Susie down. "Go get your brothers and tell them to wash up for dinner."

As soon as her daughter was gone, she faced Caleb, determined to set some long-needed parameters. "You've done enough, Caleb. I won't let you go on treating us like your pet charity. My budget's not that tight. I can afford to pay for pizza once in a while. And now that we have this brand-new kitchen, I can even cook a meal for all of us."

"But why should you cook after working hard all day or pay for pizza when I can?" he asked reasonably.

"Because getting back on my feet means

being on equal footing with my friends. I need to do things for you once in a while. Otherwise, I'll start feeling indebted to you. I don't think that sort of thing is good for a friendship, do you?"

He nodded slowly at that. "Point taken. You can buy the pizza tonight."

"And next time," she said firmly, knowing there would be a next time, no matter what excuse he — or she — had to dream up to make it happen.

"We'll table that discussion till the next time," he said just as firmly. "We men have our pride, too, you know."

Amanda had lived with two males who'd had it in spades. She gave Caleb a wry look. "Believe me, I know. It's not something I'd brag about, if I were you."

He regarded her with understanding. "Lumping me in with Bobby or your father, Amanda? Do you really think there's any comparison?"

"Not yet," she replied. "But you could be standing on the edge of a slippery slope. Now seems like the time to drag you back."

He laughed at that. "You go set the table. I'll call for the pizza," he said, then added, "Paper plates will do."

"Not in my house," she called back. "Not for guests."

She was in the kitchen distributing plates and silverware when Caleb joined her, his expression oddly troubled.

"Don't tell me the pizza place is closed," she joked lightly.

"No, the pizza's on the way. I got a salad, too."

"Then what's with the somber look? Bad news?"

"No, it was something you said."

She tried to recall what might have put that look on his face. She couldn't come up with anything. "What?"

"You still think of me as a guest," he said.

Amanda didn't see the problem. "Isn't that what you are?"

He shrugged. "I guess I was sort of hoping by now you'd start thinking of me as part of the family, or at least as the kind of friend who doesn't require going to any trouble."

There was no mistaking the genuine dismay in his voice, so she guided him toward a chair. "Sit."

A grin tugged at his lips. "Bossy, aren't you?"

"You have no idea," she said dryly. She might be out of practice, but she'd once excelled at getting things done to her satisfaction. It was a trait she'd learned at her daddy's knee.

"Now, you listen to me, Caleb Webb," she lectured sternly. "You've been the best friend this family has ever had, which is exactly why I want to show you some respect when you come here. Maybe in your world that means eating off paper plates and not going to any trouble, but in mine it means observing some of the niceties."

"Yes, ma'am," he said, his eyes twinkling despite the meek tone.

She frowned at the interruption. "I might not be able to pour fine wine into crystal goblets in my house," she continued. "I can't serve you on bone china that came over from England a couple of centuries ago for my great-great-grandmother's wedding, but I can at least treat mealtime as an occasion."

His grin spread as she spoke. "Okay, then. Guess that means I ought to at least put my shirt back on."

"You should," she said, though not without regret. "And wash your hands."

He snapped a salute and started toward the bathroom, then came back and dropped another one of those sneaky, sizzling little kisses on her mouth.

"Have I mentioned how adorable you are when you get up on your high horse?" he asked.

Her gaze narrowed. "That sounds suspiciously close to telling me I'm cute when I'm angry."

He held up his hands. "Not a chance, darlin'. I know better than that. The last thing I want to do is set off World War III around here right before dinner. It's bad for the digestion."

She gave him a wry look. "I think the pizza will take care of that, especially if you ordered pepperoni, jalapeños and onions again."

"Only on my half," he reassured her.

Amanda shuddered. "Who would have thought a preacher would have a cast-iron stomach?"

He gave her an amused look. "Did you think we lived on oatmeal or something?"

"I think I always imagined you lived on Sunday dinners of fried chicken, peas, mashed potatoes and apple pie at some parishioner's home. Beyond that, I guess I never gave it much thought. The burgers we consumed while we were building the house should have been a clue. You put jalapeños on those, too, didn't you?"

"Every chance I got," he told her. His gaze met hers, then held it. "What can I say? I like a little spice in my life."

He's talking about food, Amanda reminded herself sternly when he walked away, his lips twitching. He had to be. Preachers surely didn't flirt so outrageously.

Or did they? How on earth was she supposed to know what preachers did? Caleb was the only one she'd ever known beyond the most casual greeting at some function or another. Amazingly, he suddenly struck her as someone who was all too eager to break a few rules, or at least to bend them.

Was she ready to do the same? She tried to imagine opening up her heart again and she couldn't. Not even to a man as rock-solid and dependable as Caleb.

For one thing, it was becoming clear that under that steady, staid exterior beat the heart of a man capable of a few surprises, and Amanda had had all the surprises in life she could handle. She'd vowed on the day they'd put Bobby in his grave that she'd never risk another one, not for herself, not for her children.

For another, there was the whole independence thing. She still needed to prove to herself that she had what it took to make a success of her life, to give her children what they needed to become good people. Her father had been so sure she couldn't do that, not with Bobby by her side and certainly not on her own.

She sighed at the thought. And wasn't it

ironic that even after all this time and all her disclaimers to the contrary, her father's opinion still drove some of her decisions? Obviously she still had some work to do to claim that independence she prized so much.

4

As he dutifully washed his hands as ordered, Caleb thought about the twists and turns his life had taken. He wasn't entirely sure when he'd fallen for Amanda with her chin-up pride and stubbornness and her sad, vulnerable eyes, but the knowledge of the attraction had been eating at him for a long time now. There were so many things wrong with it, he couldn't begin to count them all.

She was a member of his church for one thing. For another, after her husband's death, she'd needed his counseling and his comfort. He couldn't do that objectively if his own emotions kept getting in the way.

And then there was Max. There were times when Caleb thought he'd made a deal with the devil when he'd agreed to Max's scheme to help his daughter get out from under the mountain of debt she'd been left in after Bobby's death. He'd known buying the land for her house anonymously was the only way Max could make himself reach out, but Caleb had done everything he knew how to do to convince the stubborn old coot to go about helping in a more straightforward way.

His entreaties had fallen on deaf ears, and now Caleb was burdened with this secret that stood squarely between him and Amanda. If she ever discovered what he'd been keeping from her, he doubted she'd forgive him. The animosity between her and Max ran too deep. She wouldn't take kindly to the fact that Caleb had been in cahoots with him behind her back, even with the best intentions.

But despite the potential for heartache, Caleb couldn't seem to stay away from this woman whose strength he'd come to admire. Nor could he seem to keep himself from stealing an occasional kiss, just as he had earlier. He knew it disconcerted Amanda. Heck, it disconcerted him. He wasn't in the habit of tossing out innuendoes and hoping for a quick rise of color in a woman's cheeks. In his own way, he was every bit as skittish about love and commitment as Amanda. He believed in it in the abstract. He preached about its importance in church and coun-seled couples on ways to make the love stronger in their marriages. But he doubted he'd ever take another chance on it himself.

All that sage advice and supposed wisdom hadn't done a thing to keep his *own* marriage from crumbling. Feeling like a fraud after the divorce, he'd kept to himself, deftly avoiding all the attempts by friends and parishioners to do any matchmaking on his behalf. He'd cut back on premarital counseling, then seven years ago he'd changed churches to get away from all the reminders of his failed marriage and especially anything that reminded him of why it had fallen apart. He wasn't sure he would ever come to terms with that.

Nor would he ever do anything that might lead to another devastating rejection. Watching his wife walk out on him over something that was beyond his control, losing her and, maybe worst of all, not really blaming her for her choice had nearly destroyed him. He'd been devastated, but so had his wife. He couldn't bear hurting Amanda in the same way.

For a time he'd lived by one principle, guiding his congregation, offering solace when needed, but pretty much keeping everyone at arm's length. When he'd gotten to know Amanda after Bobby's death, he'd recognized a kindred spirit, a lost and wounded soul. And somehow his own resolve to remain uninvolved had melted. During the building of her house, he'd forged real friendships, just as she had.

Maybe it was because of Amanda herself or maybe it was because she had the family he'd always wanted for himself, but he'd gravitated to all of them and now couldn't seem to make himself pull back. They represented his dream, the one he'd thought gone forever. In them he saw that hope for a warm and loving family in all its tempting glory. In many ways, though, it was still oh-so-sadly out of reach.

Aside from his own fears and reservations, the biggest obstacle to making this family a real part of his life was the way Amanda danced so skittishly away from him. As she had yet again tonight, she repeatedly told him what a wonderful *friend* he was, how lucky she was to have such a good *friend* come into her life when she needed one so desperately. He was growing weary of the word.

One of these days, she was going to start to utter it and he was going to cover her mouth with his just to silence her. This time it wouldn't be one of these quick little pecks he was stealing, but a full-fledged, no-holds-barred kiss that he figured would pretty much destroy the whole friendship masquerade she was so determined to cling to. It would also end the illusion that he had tight control of his own emotions.

Of course, she might very well kick him to the curb in the process. That was the one thing that had made him keep his distance.

For now. And, if wisdom overcame need, forever.

Caleb walked back into the living room just as the pizza arrived. He had his wallet halfway out of his pocket when Amanda shot a warning look in his direction and grabbed her purse.

"Sorry," he murmured. "I lost my head there for a minute."

"Don't let it happen again," she said, handing him the boxes of pizza, then turning to pay the delivery boy.

"Are the kids at the table?" he asked. "Or do I need to chase them down?"

"They have sensors when it comes to pizza delivery," she assured him. "I'm sure they're already on their way."

Sure enough, all three of the children were seated at the kitchen table when Caleb arrived with the two pizza boxes. He'd wound up ordering two mediums, rather than a large, so there would be leftovers for the kids and Amanda tomorrow.

"I want pepperoni, jalapeños and onions, like Mr. Caleb," Jimmy announced.

Amanda frowned at her towheaded son. "I don't think so."

"How come?"

"Remember last time?" she asked.

Jimmy's eyes widened. "Oh, yeah. I hurled."

"Exactly," Amanda said. "You stick with the plain pizza. One slice."

"But I can eat at least two," Jimmy argued. "Maybe even three."

Amanda shook her head at the boast. "We'll see."

"What about me?" Larry asked. "I didn't get sick."

"Then you may have one piece of Caleb's pizza," Amanda conceded. "If he says it's okay."

Caleb grinned. "Hey, I'm all about sharing." He handed a piece to Larry, then looked at Susie. "You having plain, young lady?"

She nodded. "That other stuff's yucky. Only boys would eat that."

"You're just a baby," Jimmy taunted.

Amanda scowled at him.

"Sorry, Susie," Jimmy said meekly.

Caleb bit back a grin. Despite all they'd

gone through, all the things they'd lost and continued to be deprived of, these three kids were as normal as any he'd ever met. They squabbled among themselves, but if any outsider threatened any one of them, they united. Amanda had done a fantastic job with them. Caleb admired the strength it must have required for her to do that, especially on days when a lesser woman would have caved in under all the pressure.

"Hey, Mom," Larry said. "Me and Jimmy have this really cool idea."

"Jimmy and I," Amanda corrected.

Larry stared at her blankly.

She sighed. "Never mind."

"Anyway, that tree out back is really, really big, so we were thinking it would be just right for a tree house," he said enthusiastically, his pizza momentarily forgotten. "So, can we build one?"

"I don't know," Amanda began, casting a worried look in Caleb's direction.

"Maybe we could take a look after dinner," he said, treading cautiously. He knew the kids turned to him when they sensed their mother's disapproval. They hoped that as a guy he'd be an ally. His gaze on Amanda, he said, "There might be some sturdy branches not too high off the ground that would hold one. I think that would put your mom's anxiety to rest."

Larry regarded him gratefully. "Then would you help us build it? Not just some platform, but a real house with walls and everything," he said excitedly. "Maybe Mr. Josh would help, too. He did a great job on our house. And I'll bet he has some extra wood and stuff he could give us."

Caleb caught Amanda's frown, so he took a step back. "Let's see what the tree looks like before we get too carried away. Remember, when it comes down to it, it's your mom's call."

"She'll say yes," Larry said confidently, giving her a huge smile. "I know she will." He put down his barely touched slice of pizza. "I'm done. Can we go look now?"

"Other people haven't finished eating," Amanda said at once. "And neither have you from the looks of that pizza slice."

"I've finished mine," Jimmy said loyally, stuffing the last bite in his mouth.

"I'm not finished, but I'm all filled up," Susie added, clearly determined not to be left behind.

Amanda sighed. "Then you three can go outside. Caleb and I will be out later," she told them. "And do not, under any circumstances, climb that tree. Understood?"

"Yes, ma'am," Jimmy said dutifully. Larry

reluctantly echoed the promise.

As soon as they'd raced outside with a slam of the screen door, Amanda turned to Caleb. "What are the odds we'll find them up in the tree?"

He grinned. "If I know those two, it depends on how long it takes us to get out there. Maybe we ought to go now. We can warm up the pizza later."

She looked relieved. "Do you mind?"

"Not if it's in the interest of preventing broken bones," he said.

Sure enough, they found Jimmy and Larry at the foot of the tree studying it in a way that suggested they were plotting which way would give them the best access to the lower branches. At their first glimpse of Amanda and Caleb, they stepped back guiltily.

"What do you think, Mr. Caleb? Can we build one?" Larry asked.

Caleb glanced at Amanda, then turned his attention to the old pin oak. There were some branches that appeared solid enough to hold a tree house big enough to accommodate these two without putting them at too much risk.

"It could be done," he said carefully, his gaze on Amanda. "What do you think? A tree house would be pretty cool. I had one when I was their age. There was nothing better than going up there to read a book or hang out with my friends. I thought I could see the whole world from up there."

Amanda winced, probably at the reminder of the tree house's height off the ground.

"It wasn't *that* high," he told her. "I had a vivid imagination." He grinned. "And I never fell out."

"Never?" she asked.

"Not even once. Not even a scratch on me from climbing up there."

"And you'd help them build it?" she said.

He knew what lay at the heart of her concern — not just the prospect of the little daredevils tumbling out of the tree, but helping themselves to dangerous tools in their eagerness to get the tree house constructed. "Absolutely," he assured her. "They'd never touch a tool without me around, right, boys?"

Both of them nodded solemnly.

"And you wouldn't go up in it without an adult around?" she asked.

They looked a little more hesitant over that one, but Caleb gave them a surreptitious nod.

"Sure, Mom," Jimmy said.

Amanda clearly caught the lack of enthusiasm for that particular rule. "That one's a deal breaker," she said adamantly.

"Okay, okay," Larry grumbled. "We'd never go up there without a grown-up around, right, Jimmy?"

"Right," he said.

Susie had listened intently to the whole exchange. "What about me?" she asked. "I wanna go up, too."

"No girls," Jimmy said fiercely. "It's only for boys."

"That's not fair," Susie protested, near tears.

Amanda picked her up. "Trust me on this one, you don't want to go up there, anyway. Trees are all full of bugs and stuff."

Susie didn't look convinced. "I'm not scared of bugs."

"Snakes can climb up there, too," Jimmy exaggerated. "And big ole birds can swoop in and carry little kids away."

Susie's eyes widened. "You're not that much bigger than me. How come they won't get you?"

" 'Cause we're tough," Larry said.

"And we're boys," Jimmy added. "They only come after girls."

Caleb listened to the exchange with amusement, then waited to see what Susie's response would be.

She hugged Amanda a little tighter, then announced imperiously, "I don't want to be in your ole tree house. Mr. Caleb and me are gonna build a playhouse down here and I'm gonna have tea parties and cookies and you can't come in, so there." She gazed into Caleb's eyes. "Is that okay?"

"Absolutely, short stuff. It'll be the best playhouse in all of Charleston," he promised.

"And only me and you and Mommy can come inside," she added emphatically.

"Seems fair to me," Caleb said.

"Okay, now that we've agreed to all these building plans, I think it's time for you guys to take your baths and get to bed. Scoot," Amanda said, setting Susie back on her feet.

All three kids headed for the house, but Susie ran back and held her arms out to Caleb. When he'd picked her up, she kissed him. "I love you, Mr. Caleb," she said.

"Love you, too, little one."

He put her down reluctantly and watched her run off.

"I'm sorry you've gotten dragged into yet another housing project for this family," Amanda told him. "You don't have to do it, if you don't have time."

"Nothing would give me greater pleasure," he assured her. "I like your kids." He hesitated, then added, "I can think of someone else who might want to help."

She studied him with a narrowed gaze. "Oh?"

"Why don't you give your father a call? I'll bet he'd enjoy giving the boys a hand."

"Are you crazy?" she retorted bluntly. "Why on earth would I call my father under any condition? And what makes you think he'd even take the call, much less come over here?"

"A lot of time has passed, Amanda."

"Not since the last time I reached out to him. He all but laughed in my face when I tried to turn to him for help after Bobby died. I swallowed my pride then, Caleb. I won't do it again." She studied him with undisguised dismay. "Why would you even suggest such a thing?"

He regarded her somberly. "Because I know a day will come when it's too late and you'll regret it with all your heart that you didn't try harder."

Her expression remained stoic and determined. "I've long since learned to live with regrets. My relationship with my father is what it is. There's nothing I can do to change it."

"Amanda, surely you know better than that," he chided. "Aren't you even willing to try?"

"Stop pushing me on this, Caleb," she responded heatedly. "Stop trying to make it sound as if I'm throwing some stubborn little snit. It was my father's decision to cut me out of his life. He's going to have to be the one to reach out. I'm done."

Caleb heard the unyielding tone in her voice and decided it would be prudent to back down. Otherwise she might start asking a whole lot of questions he didn't want to answer, such as when he'd become such an advocate for Big Max.

"Okay, you've made your point," he said quietly, trying to hide his disappointment.

She frowned at him. "Don't you dare look at me like that," she snapped.

"Like what?" he asked, genuinely puzzled.

"As if I'm disappointing you."

"Sorry. It's the circumstances that disappoint me, not you specifically. Nothing is more important than family, and I hate seeing people turning their backs on the ones they have."

"Then go have this chat with Big Max. He's the one who's raised rejection to a whole new level."

"Maybe I will," he said mildly, wondering if she hadn't inadvertently given him the perfect excuse to do what he'd already been attempting to do — build a bridge between these two.

She seemed startled by his response, but then her shoulders squared stiffly. "Just don't bother reporting back to me. I don't want to hear anything you might have to say about my father."

Caleb sighed. "Look, I'm sorry I brought it up, okay? Let's get back to the tree house for a minute. Maybe the boys are right and Josh will help. I can probably put it together, but it's bound to be sturdier with an expert on the premises. He'd be a help with Susie's playhouse, too. And he may well have left-over supplies, so there won't be many expenses. I'll give him a call." He forced a smile and moved on. "Did you see the look in your sons' eyes when you agreed to let them do this? They're over the moon."

Amanda's anger visibly faded and she smiled slowly. "They were, weren't they? For the first time in I can't remember how long, it feels good not to have to deny them something they want."

"A little denial isn't bad for a child," he reminded her. "It helps them learn that sometimes you have to work hard to earn the things you want."

"I know, but I would give them everything if I could," she said.

He understood the sentiment, but he couldn't help reminding her, "That's how

Bobby felt, and look where it led."

"Believe me, no one is more aware of that than I am," she said soberly. "And if I forget it from time to time in my desire to make up to them for the bad times, I hope you'll bring me back in line."

"You're a good mother, Amanda. I don't think you need me to tell you what's right."

A part of him wanted to tell her, though, that he'd always be around if she needed him to fall back on, but it was the wrong thing to say, the wrong time to say it.

"I should go," he said instead. He needed to remind himself that this wasn't his home, wasn't his family and that he'd already over-stepped the boundaries tonight.

"But you barely ate any of your pizza," she protested.

"I'll take a couple of slices home with me. I can eat while I'm going over my sermon for tomorrow."

He thought he detected disappointment in her expression, but she was quick to recover and offer a bright smile.

"I'll wrap it up for you," she said. "I wouldn't want you to stand up there in front of the entire congregation and have to wing your way through a sermon, though some-thing tells me you could do it. You have quite a way with words."

"It's probably best if we don't put that theory to the test," he said.

Inside, he accepted the pizza from her, then headed for the door. "Good night, Amanda. Thanks."

She regarded him with surprise. "For what?"

For sharing your family, he wanted to say, but he doubted she'd understand how much it meant to him. It was probably best if she didn't even try.

"The pizza, of course."

"Thank you for hauling that armoire in for me."

Caleb looked into her eyes and couldn't seem to tear his gaze away. There was a time in his life when he would have responded to the need that was so plain in her eyes, when he might have reached for her, kissed her thoroughly and left wanting more. Now he simply left.

No, he thought as he got into his car. It hadn't been that simple. Even without the kiss, he still wanted more.

Mary Louise hadn't heard a single word of Reverend Webb's sermon. Instead, she'd been clutching the prayer book in her hands so tightly it had carved lines in the palms of her hands.

Beside her, Danny was staring straight ahead, his shoulders slumped, looking miserable. It made her heart ache, seeing him like that.

She knew what she had to do this afternoon after church. As much as it was going to hurt, as furious as her parents were going to be, she had to let Danny go. She loved him enough to do that. She wanted him to be everything he'd dreamed of becoming, a brilliant architect and historical preservationist. She couldn't stand in the way of that. She couldn't let one mistake change the course of both their lives.

She reached over and gave his hand a reassuring squeeze. In less than an hour, they would be in Reverend Webb's office and she would be giving Danny his freedom. She didn't know what would happen to her after that, but she knew it was the right thing to do. If Danny wanted to be a part of his baby's life, well, they'd find a way to make that work, even if it just about killed her to see him and know it was over between them.

The sermon ended, the collection plate was passed and then there was one last hymn and the recessional. It all went by in a blur. It all happened too fast.

Danny looked over at her. "You ready?"

Mary Louise nodded.

Instead of going out the front door where they'd have to speak to everyone, they slipped out a side door and went straight to Reverend Webb's office. He came in right behind them and closed the door.

"Will your folks be joining us later?" he asked.

"We decided against asking them to come," Mary Louise said. "We needed to make this decision on our own. Once we've talked it over with you, we'll tell them what's going on."

"Don't you think they might have been able to offer some sound advice?" Reverend Webb asked.

Mary Louise gave him a wry look. "You mean after they stopped yelling at us and calmed down?"

He laughed at that. "You might have a point, though I'm not sure you're giving me much credit. I might have been able to keep the yelling to a minimum."

"Not with my folks," Mary Louise said, resigned to the explosion that lay ahead. "They're going to have a hissy fit."

"Mine, too," Danny said bleakly. "Especially when they find out I'm going to be blowing off a college scholarship."

"Then you've decided to move back here and get married?" the minister asked, his tone pretty even for a guy who'd been advocating against that.

Mary Louise shook her head. "Actually, that's not what we've decided," she said, proud that her voice hardly wavered at all. She met Danny's startled gaze and held it. "I think getting married is a bad idea. It's not what Danny wants, not now, anyway, and I don't want to live with knowing that I ruined his chance to go for his dream."

There was no mistaking the relief in Danny's eyes, but he asked quietly, "Are you sure about this, Mary Louise? I've given it a lot of thought, too. We could make it work if we had to."

If we had to. That grudging phrase told the whole story. "No, we couldn't." She avoided Danny's gaze and faced Reverend Webb. "You see, I really did listen to what Mrs. O'Leary said the other day, and I saw how frazzled she was when the kids started acting up. I know we'd only have one baby, but even one would probably make a lot of noise. Danny would wind up being tired all the time and missing classes and stuff or failing tests. It's not fair. Sooner or later, he would resent me and the baby. I get that now."

"It's not fair that you'll have to cope with all that alone, either," Reverend Webb said gently. "Is that what you're suggesting? Do

95

you still plan to keep the baby?"

Mary Louise nodded emphatically. "I want this baby. I won't give it up, but this is my choice, not Danny's."

Reverend Webb turned to Danny. "This girl of yours is pretty amazing."

Danny's eyes glistened with tears. "I know that. And she shouldn't be the only one making a sacrifice. We made this baby together."

Mary Louise saw that a part of him wanted still to do the right thing and she loved him for it, but she couldn't do this by half measures. "Danny, this is what I want. That's the difference between you and me. You see what you'd be giving up and I see what I'm getting. It's my decision to keep the baby and it's my decision to let you go. We can decide later about custody and stuff. I'll never keep you from the baby, but I won't expect you to be a part of its life, either. That's up to you." She managed to get the words out without a single tear leaking out. She was proud of herself.

"I'll make support payments," Danny said, sitting taller. "That's only right. It might not be much at first, but we can set it up so it's more later, once I graduate and get a halfway decent job." He looked toward Reverend Webb for support. "Is that fair?"

"I think so," the minister said.

96

"And the baby?" Mary Louise asked, her heart thumping unsteadily. "Will you want to see the baby?"

Danny hesitated, his eyes filled with uncertainty. "I . . . I don't know," he whispered. "Can we decide that later?"

The last shred of hope inside Mary Louise died. Their baby still didn't matter to him, not the way it did to her. "Sure," she said stoically. "Later's good."

Maybe later her heart wouldn't ache as if Danny had just stuck a knife into it.

5

Amanda's backyard was crawling with people. Okay, there were only six adults besides herself, but the way the kids were scurrying around and getting in everyone's way, it felt like more. Maggie had called Saturday morning and announced that she and Josh were coming by to help with the tree house construction and they were bringing Dinah and Cord, along with Josh's mother, Nadine, and George Winslow.

"I take it Caleb recruited you all," Amanda said.

"He mentioned it to Josh, who called Cord," Maggie said. "I'm the one who decided the guys shouldn't have all the fun. You, Dinah, Nadine and I can make curtains and stuff for Susie's playhouse, which I gather is the next construction project. Something tells me these kids are going to be the envy of the whole neighborhood, if not most of Charleston. Our men must have had very deprived childhoods. They're really getting into this. I haven't seen Josh this excited about building something in ages."

"And you're not as into it as he is?" Amanda teased. "It sounds as if you're already working on an interior-design plan for the playhouse."

"It's curtains," Maggie protested. "I can whip those up with my eyes blindfolded."

"I can't get over the fact that you sew, too," Amanda said, feeling instantly inadequate. Maggie seemed to possess all sorts of skills Amanda didn't have. She'd even worked right alongside the men on the construction of Amanda's house.

"In my world, little girls learned to paint and sew," Maggie admitted. "Some of it took before I rebelled and learned how to use a hammer and saw. I much preferred playing with boys to doing sissy stuff with girls."

"I'm in awe." Amanda's father hadn't pushed her to learn any of the so-called feminine pursuits. He'd steered her toward his own interests. Instead of a little patent-leather purse, he'd given her a custom-made miniature briefcase. She'd had to beg for a doll, and then he'd managed to custom order one dressed in a designer business suit.

"I can barely hem the kids' clothes, much

less make something from scratch," she told Maggie.

Maggie laughed. "Hey, don't get the idea I'm on a par with a professional seamstress. The curtains will be frilly and they'll do the job. They won't be perfect."

"Susie will love them no matter what," Amanda said. "Now, what can I do for this gathering? It's short notice, but I can whip up some hamburgers and potato salad for lunch."

"Not necessary," Maggie said. "Caleb said he'd have that covered. He's going to be running late, so he'll bring lunch for the whole crew with him. And Nadine said she'd make some lemonade and pick up sodas."

A part of Amanda chafed at the generosity. It smacked of more charity. "I should be doing something," she protested.

"Paper plates and napkins," Maggie suggested. "Or maybe once the guys get there, you and Susie would like to meet Dinah and me at the fabric store. Susie might like to choose the material."

Amanda declined. She'd wanted to make sure the house was spotless before her first impromptu party. She didn't want any of these people to think she didn't prize the home they'd built for her and couldn't care for it properly.

Of course, the men had barely spared the inside of the house a glance as they'd headed straight for the backyard. And the women had immediately congregated in the kitchen, which had been turned into a sewing room and was now covered with yards and yards of pink eyelet fabric.

"I had curtains made out of material just like this when I was six," Dinah said, her expression nostalgic. "It was the prettiest room I ever had. When I have a little girl, I'm going to do her room exactly the same way." She scowled as the needle she was using to sew a hem pricked her finger. "Of course, someone else is going to make the damn curtains."

Maggie regarded her with interest. "Any timetable for the arrival of this girl?" she inquired.

To everyone's surprise, Dinah blushed. "Could be sooner rather than later."

"You're pregnant?" Maggie asked delightedly. "Does Cord know?" She shook her head. "Of course he does. You'd tell him first, wouldn't you? When's the baby due? How soon will you know if it's a boy or a girl? Oh, Lord, this is going to give Josh ideas." She sat back, looking stunned.

Amanda laughed. "I have never heard one woman's good news cause such commotion for someone else before."

"Then you haven't spent nearly enough time around Maggie," Dinah said dryly. "Trust me, she is not worried about this giving Josh ideas. She's the one who's always had to do everything I do and twice as fast." She grinned at Maggie. "Sorry, sweetie. Not this time. I've got an insurmountable head start."

Maggie's gaze instantly narrowed. "How much of a head start?"

Nadine draped an arm around her daughter-in-law's shoulders. "Maggie, honey, when it comes to babies, it's all but impossible to make up any kind of a head start. Nine months is pretty much the rule. You can't set out to have your baby in eight, though I for one would certainly like to see you try. I'm ready to be a grandmama."

"But with those early pregnancy tests, Dinah could be only a few days pregnant," Maggie argued. "If I take Josh home right this minute —"

"Give it up, Magnolia," Dinah said. "This is one contest I'm going to win. Do you think I'm stupid enough to tell you news like this when you might have time to catch up?"

"So when is the baby due?" Maggie asked. "It's November now."

"I'm not telling," Dinah said, her lips twitching with amusement.

Maggie headed for the door. "Cord will tell me. I always could wrap that man around my finger."

"Not this time," Dinah retorted. "I've put him on notice that he is not to tell you a blessed thing about this baby's due date."

Amanda listened to the two of them sparring as only best friends could and regretted that she'd never had a friendship that ran that deep. Her father had been her best friend, and then Bobby had taken his place. Now with both of them out of her life, she recognized the foolhardiness of not making more of an effort to surround herself with women like these.

"Hey, you okay?" Nadine asked, studying her worriedly.

Amanda nodded. "Just feeling a little envious, I guess."

"Because of the baby?" Dinah asked. "Would you like to have another one someday?"

"Sure," Amanda said without hesitation. "I loved every second of being pregnant, even the morning sickness. I loved it when the baby started to move inside me. I can't say I was crazy about the pain of getting those little monsters into this world, but holding them in my arms for the first time was amazing. When they call it one of God's

103

greatest miracles, they get it exactly right."

No sooner had she spoken than she looked up and spotted Caleb standing on the other side of the screen door. He looked as if someone had just delivered devastating news.

"Caleb?" Amanda asked, regarding him with concern. "Are you okay?"

He smiled, but she knew him well enough now to recognize that it was forced.

"I'm great. Just loaded down with all this food," he said, juggling several bags. "Can somebody get the door for me?"

Nadine sprang up to do it. Maggie and Dinah immediately began poking in the bags to see what he'd brought for lunch, pulling out huge containers of coleslaw and barbecue and potato salad.

"Pickles?" Dinah queried. "Where are the pickles?"

"Right here, little mother-to-be," Maggie responded, retrieving a plastic container of dill pickles. "I imagine you think they're all for you."

"Of course," Dinah said, reaching for them.

During the exchange Amanda kept her gaze on Caleb. She'd never seen him looking quite so out of his depth before. She crossed the room. "Can I get you something to

104

drink? A soda, maybe? Or the guys have beer in a cooler outside."

"No, I'm fine," he said with another of those halfhearted smiles.

"Do you want to tell me what's going on?" she pressed, keeping her voice low while Maggie, Nadine and Dinah chattered on.

"Nothing's going on," he said more tersely than he'd ever spoken to her before. He immediately winced. "Sorry. Bad morning, I guess. I'll go outside and take out my foul mood on some wood. Hammering a few nails should make me feel better."

Amanda reluctantly let him go. How could he claim that the two of them were friends when it was apparently so one-sided? He was always there for her, but the one time he looked as if he needed a friend, he shut her out.

She might not have a lot of experience with friendship, but she knew that wasn't the way it was supposed to work, which meant that the minute this crowd dispersed, she and Caleb were going to have a chat. She was going to get to the bottom of whatever had put that lost and devastated look on his face.

Caleb wanted to kick himself for betraying even a hint of his reaction to Amanda's comments about having another baby. Thankfully she'd only picked up on the fact that there was something wrong, not what had triggered his mood. He had a hunch, though, that he hadn't heard the last of it. She was going to get in his face the very first chance she had.

Which meant, of course, that he needed to be away from her house one step ahead of everyone else. The minute the food had been served and the kids had gone inside for their naps, he made his excuses and started around the side of the house. Even though it made him feel like the worst sort of coward, he did it while Amanda was inside.

Unfortunately, the woman apparently had radar. She met him the second he turned the corner into the front yard.

"Going somewhere?" she inquired sweetly, her expression knowing.

"I have an appointment," he said. It was only a slight stretch of the truth. He was going over to Mary Louise's later to talk to her parents about the baby. She'd called that morning and asked him to be there when she broke the news. She'd sounded so nervous and uncertain, he'd agreed immediately.

There it was again. The whole baby thing. It seemed like everywhere he turned these days people were talking about babies. It was beginning to take a toll.

"Oh?" Amanda said, her expression skeptical. "Anything you'd care to talk about?"

"Sorry, it's confidential," he said evasively. "And I really do need to get going."

She studied him with apparent disappointment. "I thought you trusted me more than this."

"I told you, this appointment is confidential."

"I'm not talking about that," she said impatiently. "I'm talking about the fact that you're obviously upset and you're trying to hide the reason from me."

"I can't talk about it, Amanda. I really can't." He'd never discussed it with anyone, and Amanda was the last person with whom he'd share it. He hated the idea that it might change the way she looked at him.

"Then it's all part of this confidential meeting you're going to?" she asked.

For the first time since he'd known her, Caleb lied. "Yes," he said. He could live with the lie far more easily than he could live with Amanda ever knowing the truth.

She regarded him sadly. "I wish I believed you."

She turned and walked away, leaving him standing there knowing that he'd just lost something that really mattered. He'd lost her trust, something he'd spent months and months trying to earn. He couldn't help wondering if, once all the truths started coming out, he would ever get it back again.

Mary Louise wished her mom and dad weren't looking at her like that, as if she were such a terrible disappointment to them. The minute she'd told them about the baby, her mom's eyes had filled with tears and her dad had looked as if someone had punched him in the stomach.

"Where the hell's Danny?" her father asked furiously. "Why isn't he sitting here beside you? What kind of coward leaves his girl to break this kind of news alone?"

"I didn't want him here," Mary Louise said, looking to Reverend Webb for support. He gave her an encouraging smile. "Danny and I talked about this and we've met twice with Reverend Webb. We know what we're going to do, or I guess I should say what we're not going to do."

Her mother's hand covered a gasp. "Please don't say he's not going to marry you, Mary Louise."

"Mom, it's for the best," she said urgently. "Getting married now would ruin all of Danny's plans for the future, and sooner or later he'd come to hate me and the baby.

That's the last thing I want."

Her father rose to his feet, his face red. "You're going to sit here and tell me that boy is not willing to make an honest woman of you? We'll see about that. I have a shotgun in the other room that says otherwise."

"That's not an answer, Chet," Reverend Webb said mildly. "Forcing two kids to get married when they recognize all the pitfalls won't help anyone, least of all your grand-child."

Her dad scowled at Reverend Webb. "At least my grandchild would have its daddy's name."

"And now it will have mine . . . and *yours*," Mary Louise stressed with a touch of defiance. "And that's okay. I've made my peace with raising this baby on my own." She gave her father a hard, unyielding look. "And I can do it completely on my own, if that's the way it has to be."

"Oh, Mary Louise," her mother whispered, her voice thick with tears. "Are you sure you want to do this? You could . . ." Her voice faltered.

"What? Have an abortion? Give the baby away?" Mary Louise said. "No way. Neither of those is an option. This is Danny's baby and I want to keep it."

Her mother turned to Reverend Webb.

"Talk to her. Tell her how difficult this is going to be."

"I think she knows," he said gently. "Your daughter is very mature. You should be proud of her. She hasn't come to this decision lightly. Neither has Danny. I can vouch for that. In the end, they made the decision together. He'll acknowledge the baby and pay what he can in support."

"Well, that's mighty damn big of him," her father blustered. "Seeing as how he's the one who got her into this fix."

"We made this baby together," Mary Louise corrected him staunchly. "Don't blame it all on Danny. He's a good guy. He's just not ready to be married or to be a father."

"Well, ready or not, it looks as if he's about to be a daddy. He ought to be man enough to be a husband, too," her father insisted. "I don't care what the rest of you say, I'm going over there to talk some sense into him. I imagine his folks will see my side of it, especially when I ask 'em how they'd feel if it was that little princess of theirs. I imagine if Cindy came to them with this news, they'd want the boy to do the right thing."

He stomped out of the room. Mary Louise sent a pleading look toward Reverend Webb. "Please, talk him out of this. I don't want it to get ugly."

He gave her hand a squeeze. "I'll do my best," he promised, heading after her father.

Mary Louise turned to her mother. "Please don't hate me, Mom."

"Oh, sweetie, we could never hate you. It just makes me sad to think of all the difficulties you're bound to face. There will be talk, you know. That'll be hard on you and on the baby. And being a single mom might be common these days, but it's not easy."

Mary Louise crossed her arms protectively over her still-flat stomach. "I don't care about 'easy.' I already love this baby. I can't wait for him or her to get here. It's seven more months, but I already wish it were tomorrow."

Her mother gave her a watery smile. "My first grandbaby," she said. "You know once your father gets over the shock, he and I will do anything we can to help you."

"Do you think Daddy will calm down and leave Danny alone?" Mary Louise asked, worriedly glancing toward the door. She could still hear her father's raised voice and Reverend Webb's quieter responses outside.

"You're his little girl. He only wants what's best for you," her mother said. "He'll settle down once he accepts that this is the way you want it." She studied Mary Louise's face intently. "It is the way you want it, right? Because your daddy will change Danny's mind if you still want a wedding."

Mary Louise regarded her mother sadly. "I do, but not if it means being divorced a year from now. I think this is the only way Danny and I might eventually have a real chance."

Her mother crossed the room and sat next to her, then drew her into a fierce hug. "Reverend Webb's right. You're wise beyond your years, Mary Louise, and I am very proud of you."

Tears, never far from the surface these days, spilled down Mary Louise's cheeks and mingled with her mother's. Being wise pretty much sucked.

"What put you in such a sour mood?" Big Max asked Caleb when he showed up on Sunday evening. "If you're going to sit there looking as if you just lost your best friend, you might's well go on home. Things get gloomy enough around here without you adding to the misery."

"And who's fault is that?" Caleb retorted heatedly, his patience worn thin by too many people poking into his business the past couple of days. "You could change the way things are around here with one phone call."

"We were talking about you, not me," Big Max responded. "Don't try to twist it into another one of your pitches for me to crawl back to my daughter."

"It wouldn't hurt you to grovel, Max. You could use a healthy dose of humility in your life."

"I've got plenty to keep me humble," the old man said. "And I'm sure you'll see to it that I'm brought down a peg or two when I need it. Now, what got your knickers in a knot? There's no point playing poker if your mind's not going to be on the cards. What happened in church today? Did somebody tell you your sermon stank like day-old fish?"

Caleb bit back a laugh. "My sermon was just fine. Several people said so."

"Did somebody dump a problem in your lap that you can't solve?" Big Max pressed. "You're not the Lord Almighty. You can't fix everything. To tell you the truth, it seems to me *He's* at a loss from time to time, too."

Caleb thought of how ineffective he'd been yesterday when he'd been trying to help Mary Louise's parents cope with the news of her pregnancy and guide them toward a workable solution they could all live with. Chet Carter had been all for taking his shotgun over to the Marshalls' and using it to nudge Danny down the aisle. Eventually, Caleb had been able to make him see that a

113

forced marriage wasn't a good solution to anything, but Caleb wasn't convinced Chet wouldn't go back to his plan before all was said and done. He was still mad as hell that his daughter was facing this pregnancy alone.

"I do have a parishioner in need of some help," he told Big Max, hoping to throw him off the scent. "I suppose that's why I'm so distracted tonight."

Big Max studied him skeptically. "That's it? That's all you're going to tell me?"

"That's all I *can* tell you," Caleb said.

"Well, hell's bells, if you can't do better than that and you can't concentrate on poker, get on out of here. You're wasting my time."

Relieved by the prospect of an early end to the uncomfortable evening, Caleb was about to take him up on it when Big Max suddenly looked a whole lot less feisty. "Is everything okay?" Caleb asked him, worried by the sudden uncertainty he saw in the older man's eyes.

"Sure. Why wouldn't it be? You're the one acting crazy tonight," Big Max grumbled. "Don't know why you showed up here in the middle of the week, anyway."

Caleb regarded him with real concern now. "Max, it's Sunday night, same as always," he said gently. "You asked me about church not two minutes ago."

Big Max looked flustered, but he covered it with anger. "Of course it is. Stop trying to confuse me. Go on, now. I'm going to bed."

Caleb wasn't about to leave, not unless there was someone else around. "Is your housekeeper here?"

Max glowered at him. "Why do you care about that? You hoping Jessie will send you home with another piece of pie?"

"Exactly," Caleb said, unwilling to admit that he wanted to be sure that there would be someone nearby in case something really was wrong.

"Well, I sent her home, so you're out of luck," Max said ungraciously. "Now, stop dillydallying and go."

"I wouldn't mind staying for a while," Caleb offered. "That drink you made went to my head. I'd like to make myself a cup of coffee."

Though the old man would never admit it, Caleb thought he detected relief in Max's expression.

"Knew you couldn't take a real drink," Max gloated. "Stay here. I'll make the coffee. I know my way around the kitchen."

He left Caleb sitting alone, staring after him, concern suddenly eating away at him. Tonight wasn't the first time Max had seemed a little . . . off-kilter. Caleb had chalked up all the other incidents to mere forgetfulness, but tonight he had to wonder if it might not be something more.

Then again, Max insisted on living out here all alone. He rarely ventured into town anymore, not even for the board meetings he was expected to attend. He'd turned into a recluse, but most people in town talked about his behavior as nothing more than the eccentricity of a wealthy man.

George Winslow ignored Max's bad temper and lack of welcome and continued to visit from time to time. Caleb came by regularly, but if others dropped in, Caleb didn't know about them. It was little wonder Big Max occasionally lost track of what day of the week it was. He supposed that the real surprise was that it didn't happen more often.

When Max came back, he brought a Coca-Cola loaded with ice. "Here you go," he said. "That ought to fix you up."

Caleb accepted the cold drink and dutifully took a sip, trying his best to hide his shaken reaction. Had Big Max concluded that coffee was too much trouble? Or had he simply forgotten why he'd gone into the kitchen in the first place?

6

Amanda rarely set foot in Caleb's office, mostly because there were so many other opportunities to see him. Unfortunately, ever since that Saturday when he'd been so obviously upset, he'd been avoiding her and the kids. Afraid that she'd inadvertently said or done something to offend him or that he was going through some sort of personal crisis and needed help he'd never ask for, she concluded it was time to take action.

As soon as she left her job at the boutique, she set off for the church. Nadine and George, who'd unexpectedly turned themselves into surrogate grandparents for Susie, Larry and Jimmy, were taking the kids to a movie, so Amanda had the entire evening to wrangle the truth out of Caleb.

On her arrival and drawn by some emotion she couldn't quite explain, she wandered into the church, rather than going in

117

search of Caleb. Only dim lights near the altar lit the way. She liked it in shadows like this. It felt peaceful and oddly welcoming to someone like her, someone not sure she had any right to be there, given her history and lack of faith.

She slipped into a pew toward the front and let the serenity steal over her. After the past couple of weeks, she needed a few minutes of solitude to gather her thoughts before facing Caleb and whatever secrets he was hiding from her. The kids had been a handful for days now. Even their teachers had called to complain, wondering if there might not be something wrong at home.

The only thing unusual that Amanda could point to was Caleb's absence. Maybe this was a warning that her children were growing too dependent on him, expecting him to fulfill their need for a father. That was a burden he shouldn't have to shoulder. Perhaps he'd sensed that himself and that was why he'd pulled back. It was something they needed to discuss.

As she wrestled with that, a side door opened softly, letting in a shaft of brighter light.

"Amanda!" Caleb said, obviously startled to find her there.

She jumped up guiltily. "I'm sorry. I probably shouldn't be in here."

He frowned at her reaction. "Why on earth shouldn't you be here? The church is open to everyone. Sit back down. I can leave you alone, if you'd prefer."

There it was, she thought, that compassionate tone that made her long for things she hadn't had in a long time. She'd missed having someone to share her day with. She and Bobby had talked about everything after the kids were in bed, or at least she had assumed they had. It turned out she'd been wrong, but at the time, those talks had been the best part of her day.

More and more lately she'd looked to Caleb for that kind of sharing. Maybe she'd been leaning on him too much. That was something else they should discuss.

She looked into his worried eyes. "No, stay, please," she said. "Actually I came to see you. I walked in here on impulse and it was so peaceful, I stayed."

Caleb crossed to sit beside her. "What brought you here to see me? You don't usually stop by the church."

She gave him a wry smile. "Because you're usually underfoot at the house. You haven't been by for a while now."

"I should be flattered that you've noticed," he said, though he sounded anything but pleased. In fact, he looked uneasy. "I've been busy."

"You're always busy," she noted. "That's never kept you away before."

He sighed, then looked directly into her eyes. "It's not my absence that's on your mind, is it? It's something more specific."

She thought about the question before answering. "The kids do miss you," she said honestly. "They've been acting up in school this week. I think it's because they're feeling abandoned. Frankly, so am I."

His expression troubled, he murmured, "I'm sorry. I should have thought of that and explained to them."

Amanda regarded him with frustration. "Don't you dare apologize, Caleb. You don't owe us anything. You've already been more than generous with your time and everything else." She studied him intently, then forced herself to ask him directly, "Are you afraid we're all getting too attached to you, Caleb? Is that it? Because if it is, I understand. I'll make the kids understand, too. We can't rely on you to fill the void Bobby left in our lives. You've already done more than we have any right to expect."

He frowned at her. "You and the kids haven't expected anything from me that I haven't been more than willing to give," he said with unmistakable sincerity. "I'm not sure I can explain this so you'll understand, but there have been some things going on that I needed to deal with."

"Personal things?" she asked, watching him closely.

He never once met her eyes, but he nodded. "At least some of it. The rest has to do with other people."

"And you couldn't share with me whatever it is that relates just to you?" she asked. "I thought friends were supposed to be there for each other, the way you've been there for us. I told you that at my house before you ran off the other day. I guess you still don't get it."

"If this were just about me, you'd have a point," he said. "But it's not. Can you try to accept that? There are going to be times when I simply can't talk to you about what's on my mind."

She studied him closely, saw the conflict in his eyes. "If these are things you're supposed to keep confidential, then of course I can accept that," she told him. "But you've just admitted that you're hiding something else from me, something that's more personal. I have to tell you that hurts, especially after all the things Bobby kept from me."

He winced. "I'm sorry."

"Stop saying that," she chided. "You're missing my point. Don't you know there's nothing you can't discuss with me? You certainly know all the secrets in my life."

He hesitated for a very long time before drawing a deep breath. "I know," he said at last. "And you already know that I value your opinion. I came to you about Mary Louise, didn't I? And I asked you to consider helping with our young people's group here at the church." He met her gaze with a challenging look. "You never did give me an answer to that, by the way. Have you thought about it?"

She grinned at him. "Very smooth, Reverend. Things get a little uncomfortable, and you turn the tables on me. Yes, I've thought about helping out, but we're talking one evening a week, right? What would I do about the kids?"

His lips twitched at the unmistakably flimsy excuse she hoped to latch on to. "Who has them now?"

"Nadine and George," she said, then chuckled at his stunned expression. "I know. It blows my mind, too, but they all get along and I think George is still feeling guilty that he tried to interfere in having the house built for us. Plus the man is so smitten with Nadine, he'd jump in front of a bus if she asked him to."

"Then I'm sure they'd be happy to help out if it meant you'd be freed up to do something worthwhile for the church and these kids."

She shook her head. "I can't ask them to babysit every week. That's too much."

"You're making excuses, Amanda. I don't imagine they'd mind," he countered. "And I think Dinah and Cord might be happy for the experience now that they have a baby on the way. I don't think finding a baby-sitter would be a problem. You could even bring the kids along, if you had to. It's mainly a chaperoning thing right here at the church. The young people get together, order in pizza, play a little music, plan some fund-raising activities. Sometimes we have speakers."

"And you'd be here?" she asked.

"I'd be here," he said, then grinned. "And on my very best behavior. I guarantee there would be no stolen kisses in the choir room. It would set a very bad example."

"No stolen kisses, huh?" she said, struggling not to show even a hint of disappointment.

His grin spread. "Unless, of course, you wanted them to be a part of the deal," he said. "Then I might find a way to make it work."

"Very funny," she said. "Let me talk to Nadine and Dinah and even Maggie. If they're willing to take a turn with the kids from time to time, then I'll consider helping."

"Fantastic!"

"Hold on," she cautioned. "What exactly do you want me to do?"

"Like I said, it's mostly chaperoning and offering some adult supervision when their ideas get a little too ambitious. Every now and again, you'd have to do some informal counseling. The kids may come to you with problems. All they really want is someone who'll listen."

"Shouldn't they be going to their parents?"

"Of course, that's exactly what I encourage them to do, but sometimes they need an outside perspective, or maybe their parents are the problem. And, let's face it, not all parents are around these days. A lot of teens have to make too many difficult decisions on their own, and they don't always make the best ones."

"And you really think I can help them?" she asked doubtfully.

"I think you have a huge heart and a good head on your shoulders. Of course you can help. And if you're at a loss, send them to me."

She nodded. "You're definitely the better bet."

"Not always," he said, that sad, distant expression back in his eyes.

"Caleb?"

"What?" he asked, avoiding her gaze, a sure sign that she was treading back into territory he didn't want to explore.

"There is something you're keeping from me. I can see it in your eyes. It's something that's really weighing on you."

"My problem, not yours," he insisted.

"I could have said the same thing when you pushed your way into my life," she reminded him.

He chuckled. "You did. Several times, as a matter of fact."

"And remember what you did?" she asked. "You kept right on pushing." She smiled at him cheerfully. "Consider this payback time."

Caleb looked a little shaken by her response. Good, she thought. Maybe he'd open up sooner if he figured out that there was no way around it.

Caleb had known Amanda wasn't going to let him get away with avoiding her questions forever. Her showing up at the church had proved just how well he understood her. He thought, though, he'd done a halfway-decent job of distracting her this time. He was going to have to get a whole lot better if he was to keep the situation with Max from her.

He had dropped in on Max several times since the night Max had mixed up the days and then brought him Coke instead of coffee. He still wasn't absolutely certain both things hadn't been innocent mistakes, but he was worried just the same.

So far, on most of his visits nothing had seemed amiss. In fact, Big Max seemed so perfectly normal that Caleb was beginning to think he'd made too much of the earlier incidents. There could be a dozen different reasons for the old man to be having an off night. None of them had to be dire.

Still, he kept going back.

Tonight he'd barely set foot in the door when Big Max pointed him toward a chair.

"Sit," he ordered. "Would you mind telling me what the hell you think you're up to?"

Caleb flinched. He thought he'd done a better job of dreaming up excuses to stop by. Apparently Big Max wasn't buying any of them. Still, he hedged. "I don't know what you're talking about."

"Sure you do. You've been sniffing around

out here like a dog on a scent. If you've got a genuine reason for being underfoot every time I turn around, it's time you told me."

Caleb debated how straightforward to be, especially in light of there having been no new incidents when Max seemed especially confused. He opted for being candid.

"You worried me a couple of weeks ago," he admitted. "You seemed a little confused."

Max regarded him blankly. "Confused how?"

"Not knowing what day of the week it was. Bringing me a soda when you left the room to get me coffee."

The air seemed to go out of Max. "I knew I'd gotten that wrong," he said, looking shaken. "But you didn't say anything, so I thought maybe it was okay."

"Then you've noticed things, too," Caleb said gently. "Have there been any other incidents of forgetfulness?"

"Nothing I couldn't explain away," Max said defensively. "You're making a mountain out of a molehill."

Caleb didn't intend to let him off the hook that easily. "Have you seen a doctor, Max?"

"No."

"Why not?"

"Same reason most people don't go, I imagine. I don't want to know the truth. If

I've got that old-timer's thing, what good's it going to do knowing? They can't cure it."

"There are things you could do, medicines that might help," Caleb corrected. "And maybe it's something else entirely, just a vitamin deficiency or something."

"You don't believe that any more than I do," Big Max scoffed. "Look, I've got money so somebody can take care of me, if it comes down to that. In the meantime, I'll just go along the way I have been."

"But Amanda —"

"Is not to know a damn thing about any of this," Max said heatedly. "I mean that, *Reverend.*" He said the last as if it were a curse, rather than a title of honor. "There's nothing to tell, anyway."

"At least see a doctor," Caleb pleaded. "I'll go with you. I'll help you deal with it, whatever the outcome. Don't just let this disease win, Max. Fight it. Get whatever help is out there."

"Will it get you out from underfoot if I say yes?" Max asked.

"For tonight," Caleb responded.

"That's not much incentive," Max said. "So I won't give you much of a promise. I'll think about what you said. That's the best I can do."

Caleb looked into his eyes, detected the

fear Max would never admit to having. "Make the appointment, Max. It's always better to know what you're dealing with."

Max gave him a wry look. "Is it really? I wonder if you'd be saying that if you were sitting here in my shoes."

Caleb gave his shoulder a squeeze. "You're tough enough to take the truth, Max." He leveled a look directly into his eyes. "So is Amanda."

"But she won't hear the truth, not from you," Max said to him urgently. "I have your word on that."

Caleb sighed. He knew that without his commitment, Max wouldn't see the doctor. He'd view that as the one sure way to make sure there was no truth to tell.

"If you're sick, she'll need to know, Max," he said firmly. "But for now I'll leave it to you to decide when it's time to tell her."

As he left the house, Caleb had the uneasy sense that he'd just made another pact with the devil and that it was one he was going to have plenty of time to regret.

Mary Louise couldn't seem to quit throwing up. She'd been munching on saltines and sipping ginger ale all day, but the stupid morning sickness was worse than the flu. It just wouldn't go away.

She knew she must look like a total wreck, because Willie Ron came into the Stop and Shop to get his check, took one look at her and ordered her to get out and go home to bed.

"Come back to work when you're over this flu bug," he said. "I can cover your shift and mine till then."

"I can't leave. I'm supposed to work a double shift," she told him.

"And I'm here," he pointed out. "I'll fill in."

"But you just stopped by," she protested. "It's not fair to ask you to cover for me on your day off. You've probably got plans."

"Nothing that can't wait, and you didn't ask. I offered," he said. "Besides, somebody's liable to come in and rob the place if they know you're locked in the bathroom every fifteen minutes."

That possibility had actually crossed her mind, too. She was always careful to lock the register before going into the bathroom, but if anyone hung around and noticed her repeated absence, who knew what they might decide to do? Even if they only stole some beer or candy, she didn't want it happening on her watch. The manager would eventually catch on that inventory was going missing on her shift and she'd be fired, no questions asked. Even though she wasn't on some career track here, she didn't want to lose this job, not now when every penny was going into savings for the baby.

"Okay," she said at last. "But why don't I at least stay and keep you company? That way if Mr. Garrison shows up, he won't think I'm blowing off work."

"And why don't I just tell him that we switched shifts?" Willie Ron suggested. "He doesn't care as long as the place is covered and he doesn't have to cut us a check for any more money. Besides, what makes you think I want that flu bug you've got?"

"I suppose you're right," she said at last. If he was going to cover for her, then he had a right to know the whole story. He'd be the first person outside the family and Reverend Webb she'd told. "Willie Ron, there's something you should know. I'm not going to get better, at least not anytime soon. I can't keep asking you to sub for me."

His dark brown eyes widened as understanding dawned. "You telling me this ain't the flu? You got a baby coming, Mary Louise?"

She gave him a weak smile. "Seems that way."

"Well, praise the Lord, if that ain't the best news I've heard in a long time." He shook

131

his head, looking dazed. "A baby. You and Danny, huh? He must be pretty excited." At her lack of a response, his gaze narrowed. "He is excited, isn't he?"

"Not exactly."

He regarded her with undisguised indignation. "That boy ain't going to marry you?"

She shook her head. "No, but I don't want to talk about it, okay? This is for the best."

Willie Ron looked as if he had a whole lot more he wanted to say, but he must have seen something in Mary Louise's expression that stopped him.

"Well, the man's a fool, that's all I've got to say," he huffed at last. "And no matter what you want, I intend to tell him that if he shows his face around here."

She smiled at his indignation. "Thanks for the support."

"You need anything, you come to Willie Ron, you hear? I'll fuss over you," he promised. "Your parents okay with all this?"

"They're getting there," she said. "Actually, they've been pretty great. I know they wish things were different, but they've stopped giving me those awful pitying looks and my dad's not talking about getting out his shotgun anymore."

Just then her stomach rolled. "Oh, hell, here we go again," she moaned.

"Go," Willie Ron said. "I'll have some nice cold ginger ale for you when you come back."

Mary Louise sprinted for the bathroom. Inside, once the heaving stopped, her eyes filled with tears. Why couldn't Danny have been the one waiting out there with ginger ale? Why did she have to go through this pregnancy with only her folks and Willie Ron in her corner? And Reverend Webb, she amended.

Then she thought about how generously her folks had rallied on her behalf, how solidly Reverend Webb had stood by her when she'd had to face her folks and how sweet Willie Ron had been just now. Maybe she should stop feeling sorry for herself and count herself lucky for having four decent, strong people on her side. There were lots of girls in her shoes who had no one. Whenever she got low, she needed to remind herself of that.

Caleb was pretty proud of himself for finessing that deal to get Amanda to help out with the church's youth group. It was going to be good for all of them, her included. She needed to prove to herself that she had something to offer the world. He was convinced that at some point in the future she could go back to school and get a degree in psychology, if she felt so inclined.

Then again, maybe she'd prefer to put to use those business courses she'd taken before dropping out of school. He had a hunch she'd downplayed those courses during her job hunt so folks wouldn't think she was overqualified to be a clerk in a boutique and working a register out at the new superstore. Maybe he'd take a look at the classifieds himself and see if there weren't a few jobs out there that would help her bring in more than minimum wage.

In the meantime, knowing that he'd be seeing her on a regular basis on his turf was a side benefit, as well, even if it was going to add to his frustration. He wanted so many things when he was with her, but some of them were simply out of reach. A few Saturdays ago at her house, he'd been forced to accept that when he'd heard her talking about her dreams for the future and how much she wanted to have another baby.

He told himself it was just as well to know right now that he couldn't fit in with those dreams, especially since she was going to flip out when she found out he'd been spending so much time with her father. At least now he'd more or less accepted that things were going to end between them. It was only a matter of time. The blowup over him hiding his relationship with Big Max would just finish things off.

And given what might be going on with Big Max's health and his own determination that Amanda needed to know, that blowup was going to happen much sooner than he might have preferred.

"Hey, Caleb, you look as if you're a million miles away," Cord observed when he walked into Caleb's office. "Troubles?"

"Anticipating trouble," Caleb responded grimly. "What brings you by? Did we have an appointment?"

"Nope. I just took a chance you might have some time."

"Of course." Caleb studied him intently. "You worried about becoming a dad?"

Cord's expression brightened. "No way. I can hardly wait. Of course, if I keep on fussing over Dinah, she's likely to leave me long before the baby comes. She's determined to work right up till the labor pains start," he said, a disgusted note in his voice. "Would you tell me why any woman would balk at a little pampering?"

Caleb chuckled. Dinah had been an internationally recognized foreign correspondent before coming home to Charleston and marrying Cord. She was used to her independence. "I don't imagine it's the pampering she's objecting to," he told Cord. "Something tells me you're trying to control how she spends her days."

Cord flushed guiltily. "I just want her to have a happy, healthy baby."

"Don't you think that's what she wants?"

"I suppose," Cord said grudgingly. "But she goes chasing all over town in that satellite truck the TV station has. I've seen the way those cameramen drive. They're maniacs when they're on the scent of a story."

"And your wife isn't?"

"Of course she is. I'd just like it better if one of the people in the truck remembered that there's a baby on board," he grumbled, then sighed heavily. "Nothing I can do about it, though."

"Not unless you want a full-scale war," Caleb agreed. "So, if it's not about impending fatherhood, why did you come by?"

"Actually it was something George Winslow said the other day when we were building that tree house for Amanda's kids."

"Oh?"

"He said it was a shame we couldn't build another house for another family in need of a decent place to live."

Caleb didn't even try to hide his surprise. "Really? George actually said that?"

136

"He even said he'd be willing to find some land, if Josh and I would consider building on it. He thought you'd probably know of another family who deserves to be helped out." He met Caleb's gaze. "So what do you think?"

"Do you and Josh have the time?" Caleb asked, trying to contain his enthusiasm. He had half-a-dozen families who'd approached him after hearing about what the church had done for Amanda. It had been disheartening to tell them all that her house had been a one-shot deal. "I know you have a big new historic renovation project over in Atlanta. Isn't that going to take all your time?"

"Not really. Since we managed to train so many volunteers who worked on Amanda's house, it wouldn't require much more than supervision from the two of us," Cord said. "I think we could do it mainly on the weekends. It wouldn't go fast, but we should be able to get another house up by spring, if we don't have a hard winter around here. I think we all came away from this last project feeling real good about what we accomplished. Why stop there?"

Caleb beamed at him. "I think it's a wonderful idea. And I certainly don't think we'll have any difficulty at all finding the right family for it. I have a list in my file right now."

137

"A list?" Cord repeated, looking startled. "How many families?"

"Six," Caleb said.

"Have you checked them out? Are they all legitimately in need of something like this?"

"I haven't done that yet, since I didn't think there was any way we could help them, but I'll do it first thing tomorrow."

Cord's expression turned thoughtful. "Let me know what you find out, okay? As soon as possible."

Caleb dared to get his hopes up. "What are you thinking?"

"That when I tell George to look around for some property, I'll tell him to make sure it has room for several houses," Cord said. "It'll do him good to spend some of that money's he's squirreled away on a worthy cause. Maybe I can set up a small division within Beaufort Construction to keep a supervisor on the payroll for these housing projects. It would be good PR for the company."

Caleb thought about an idea that had been simmering in the back of his mind for a while now. Since Cord was here and in a benevolent mood, he decided the timing was right.

"Mind if I ask another favor of you?" Caleb asked.

"Shoot."

"Do you know Danny Marshall?"

"Tall, good-looking kid who won a scholarship to Clemson?" Cord asked.

Caleb nodded.

"Sure. What about him?"

"He wants to study architecture. His real interest is in historic preservation."

Cord leaned forward. "Really? I didn't know that."

"What would you think about hiring him on during school breaks and next summer? Seems like it would be a perfect match. The kid's a hard worker and he's highly motivated to make some money these days."

"Oh?"

"He has a baby on the way."

Cord winced. "Married at his age? And in college? That's tough."

"He's not married, but he wants to do as much as he can for the baby and for its mother," Caleb said. "He's a responsible kid and Mary Louise is terrific. It took a lot of guts for both of them to come to this decision. I think, given the right chance, they could wind up together as long as they don't put too much pressure on themselves or expect too much too soon."

Cord studied him with a narrowed gaze. "This is about more than a job, isn't it?"

Caleb gave him an innocent look. "A job's

all I mentioned."

"But I know you, Reverend. You always have ulterior motives up the wazoo."

"I should probably be insulted that you'd say such a thing," Caleb said, but he could hardly deny the truth.

"Come on," Cord prodded. "Out with it. What do you really want?"

"It wouldn't hurt if you and Dinah took those two under your wings, so to speak."

"And do what? Push them down the aisle?"

"Absolutely not. Just mentor them. Amanda's already been a big help, but I think you and Dinah could take up where she left off. You show Danny how to get on the path you followed and Dinah can help Mary Louise find her way. Mary Louise needs someone — another woman — to confide in. If she and Danny happen to find their way back to each other in the process, well, that wouldn't be such a bad thing, would it?"

Cord regarded him with admiration. "You're a very sneaky man and a romantic to boot."

Caleb grinned. "And not the least bit ashamed of it," he countered. Not when it was for a worthy cause.

If ever two kids needed a strong support system, it was Danny and Mary Louise.

Caleb might agree with their decision not to rush into marriage, but that didn't mean he wanted to see their love wither and die. In some ways, the wise decision they'd made told him just how strong that love was, especially on Mary Louise's part. Who knew what the future might hold for those two?

7

On Friday night as she was fixing dinner, Amanda heard shouts in the backyard and went running out the door. "What on earth?" she muttered as she saw boards flying out of the tree house. "Larry O'Leary, Jimmy O'Leary, you come down from there right this instant."

The destruction continued.

"I mean it," she shouted. "I want you down from there right now!"

The two boys slowly climbed down. Larry's expression was mutinous.

"I'm not going to 'pologize," he said fiercely. "I'm not. I hate that tree house!"

"Me, too," Jimmy said, though far less forcefully. Tears were streaking down his cheeks.

Ignoring the destruction for the moment, Amanda hunkered down in front of them, hoping to make sense of their shattered expressions. "I thought you both loved the tree house. You begged Caleb to help you build it. What happened?"

They exchanged a look, but neither boy responded.

"If you don't give me an answer, then you're both going to be grounded for a very long time," she said quietly but emphatically. "Caleb, Josh and Cord worked very hard to build that for you and you were up there wrecking it. I don't understand how you could do such a thing or why you'd want to."

She focused her attention on Jimmy, who could usually be counted on to cave in first. "Why do you suddenly hate the tree house?"

"Because," he began, only to be cut off by a scowl from his brother. He scuffed the toe of his sneaker in the dirt and avoided her gaze.

"Because why?" she asked patiently.

Jimmy kept his lips clamped tightly together. Larry's expression remained equally unyielding. Amanda sighed. When they were like this — united as loyal brothers — she couldn't get anything from them. She could only dole out punishment, let tempers cool and hope for more forthcoming answers later.

"Okay, then. I want you both to go into

the house, get your schoolbooks, then have a seat at the kitchen table. You can spend the rest of the evening doing homework."

Jimmy's gaze shot up. "But we never have to do homework on Friday night."

"Tonight you do," she said firmly.

"What if we finish?" Jimmy asked.

"Then you'll read ahead on all your assignments until I say you can leave the table."

"But that's mean," Larry protested.

"So is destroying something that other people were kind enough to build for you," she said. "That's both mean and ungrateful. Think about that while you're in there."

"What about Susie? Are you gonna punish her, too?" Larry asked angrily.

Amanda's startled gaze flew back up to the tree house. "Is she up there?"

"No, she's in the playhouse," Larry said. "But she's gonna tear it down, too. We were gonna help when we got finished with the tree house."

"I see," Amanda said wearily. "Go inside now. And I expect to see you hard at work on your homework when I come in. Otherwise, you'll spend tomorrow in your room thinking about this some more."

"Can we . . . ?" Jimmy began.

She frowned before he could finish the request. "No snacks," she said, anticipating him.

"But you just baked cookies," he whined.

She leveled a look into his eyes. "I know, but they were for kids who'd been behaving themselves. Now I'm going to take them down to the church on Sunday for the coffee hour after the morning service."

Jimmy whirled on his brother. "I *told* you we were going to get into trouble."

"And I told you I didn't care," Larry retorted unrepentantly.

Amanda waited till they'd gone into the house before crossing the lawn to the playhouse. She opened the door and stepped inside the single room with its pretty pink eyelet curtains and child-size furniture. Susie was sitting in a rocking chair clutching her favorite doll, tears streaming down her face. Thankfully there was no indication she'd tried to destroy anything.

"Okay, Susie, what do you know about Jimmy and Larry wrecking the tree house?" Amanda asked, not the least bit ashamed of her divide-and-conquer technique. Sometimes it was the only way to stay one step ahead of her kids.

Susie's lower lip quivered. "Nothing," she said.

"Really? They told me the playhouse was

going to be next," Amanda said. "Is that true?"

Her daughter looked miserable, but she nodded.

"Why?" Amanda asked, then waited, her gaze steady.

"Because we're mad," Susie admitted eventually. "And they don't want the dumb old tree house anymore."

"And you don't want your playhouse?"

Susie looked less certain about that.

"Did you want to tear it down?" Amanda asked.

Suddenly Susie flew out of the rocker and threw her arms around Amanda's neck. "I love my playhouse," Susie whispered, her voice muffled against Amanda's neck, her tears dampening Amanda's T-shirt. "But I'm mad, too."

"Why, baby? Who are you mad at?" Amanda asked, though she was pretty sure she already knew.

"Mr. Caleb," Susie said, a hitch in her voice. "He left us, just like Daddy."

Amanda had seen this coming a mile away, but that didn't make it any easier to hear. "Oh, sweetie, it's not like Daddy at all. Your daddy didn't want to leave us. It was an accident. And he can't come back. Caleb just gets busy with other people sometimes and can't spend as much time with you as he wants to. He's our friend and we have to share him. It's not as if he's part of our family."

"But I want him to be," Susie said stubbornly. "If Daddy can't ever come back, then I want Mr. Caleb to be my new dad. That's what Jimmy and Larry want, too. Why can't he do that?" She regarded Amanda hopefully. "We'd promise not to be any trouble."

"Tearing down the tree house he built isn't a very good way to show him that, is it?" Amanda said wryly.

She gazed into Susie's misery-filled eyes and wondered how on earth she was supposed to make a five-year-old understand that life didn't work like that, that she and her brothers couldn't simply pick someone to be their new dad and make it happen. For that matter, how was she going to explain it to her sons, who were older, but obviously no less desperate to fill their father's shoes?

She clearly had to tell them something, though. She couldn't let them hate Caleb for something that was probably her fault, not his. She'd seen this moment coming, she'd even mentioned it to Caleb, and yet she'd done nothing to discourage their growing dependence on him. She hadn't even done a

147

very good job of keeping her own attachment in check.

Her heart aching for all of them, she said, "Come on, sweetie. Let's go inside. I think we all need to have a talk."

Susie regarded her hopefully. "Caleb, too?"

"No, this is just about the four of us — you, me, Jimmy and Larry," Amanda said.

"Oh," Susie said sadly.

Outside the playhouse, Amanda scooped up Susie, even though she was more than a handful to carry, and went inside. To her relief, both boys were doing exactly as she'd instructed them to do. Their schoolbooks were open on the kitchen table and they were doing their assignments. Apparently they'd concluded that they'd tested her patience enough for one night.

"Okay, time out," she said, settling herself and Susie into another chair. "Let's talk about what happened tonight and why."

Both boys stared at her resentfully, waiting.

"I understand that you're all upset because Caleb hasn't been around lately," she said quietly.

"You told!" Larry shouted, turning his angry gaze on Susie. "You're nothing but a little tattletale!"

148

Susie clung to Amanda more tightly.

"Yeah. And we're never telling you anything ever again," Jimmy added.

"Enough!" Amanda commanded. "The point is that I do get why you're feeling bad and why you were lashing out and trying to wreck your tree house. I really do."

"No, you don't," Larry muttered.

"You were feeling abandoned by someone you'd started to count on," Amanda said, her gaze locked with his. "Isn't that right?"

Both boys seemed surprised that she'd gotten that.

"I guess," Larry finally agreed.

"But who did you really hurt by tearing apart your tree house?" she asked. "Now you all don't have something you really wanted. Do you think that will get even with Caleb? Won't it hurt you more in the end?"

Their gazes faltered as they considered that.

"Well?" she prodded.

"I guess we really blew it, huh, Mom?" Jimmy murmured eventually, looking chagrined.

"I think you did," she said. "How about you, Larry?"

He gave her a grudging nod.

"So, what might have been a better way to handle your anger?" she asked.

They stared at her blankly.

"Maybe you could have talked to me about it," she prompted. "Or maybe you could have given Caleb a call and asked him where he's been. Maybe if he'd realized how much you miss him, he would have worked something out to spend time with you. I know he adores you guys. He would never intentionally hurt your feelings."

"Can we call him now?" Susie asked excitedly. "Maybe he'll come for pizza."

Amanda gave her daughter a quick hug. "Not today, sweet pea. The boys are still being punished for what they did. I'm not canceling that, but I will lift the restrictions after today now that I understand why you were so upset."

"Then we can call Caleb tomorrow?" Jimmy asked, his eyes brightening. "Can we invite him for dinner?"

"Yes," she agreed, then leveled a look at each of them in turn. "But listen to me, if he says he can't come, if he already has other plans, you need to accept that. It doesn't mean he doesn't care about you. I'm sure he'll make time for you as soon as he can."

And in the meantime, she would do everything in her power to figure out how to extricate them all from a relationship that had suddenly gotten way too complicated.

■ ■ ■ ■

Max's hands trembled so badly he had to clutch the arms of the chair to steady them. "Say that again," he commanded Doc Mullins, as if daring him to repeat the diagnosis.

"I don't know how many times you need to hear this, Max, but I'll keep repeating it as often as you need me to. You have the beginning stages of Alzheimer's. There's little question about it," the man who'd been Max's doctor for forty years repeated bluntly. "I'm sorry, Max."

Even though he'd been expecting it, the instinct to deny came on strong. "I forget a few things. What's the big deal? Everybody does. It doesn't mean I have Alzheimer's," Max insisted, wishing he hadn't pushed the doctor to open his office on a Saturday so he could get this visit over with.

Once Caleb had forced his hand, he'd seen not just Doc Mullins, but several specialists. They'd all come to the same conclusion. Hearing it over and over had become tiresome, but he'd kept holding out hope that someone would offer a different diagnosis. Now, with his old friend once again repeating it, he could no longer ignore the truth.

"You've forgotten enough things that it brought you here to see me," Doc Mullins

151

reminded him. "All those big shots you asked for second opinions agree. You can't hide from this, Max. It won't do you a bit of good."

"How long have I got?"

"Before you die? Years probably. The Alzheimer's won't kill you, not by itself. And overall you're in good health for a man of sixty-six."

"No, not till I die," Max said impatiently. "Before my mind goes completely?"

"There's no telling," Doc Mullins said. "There are a lot of new drugs on the market that are helping people retain their memory longer, and there's more research being done all the time."

"I imagine that's what they told people ten years ago, too," Max said. "How many of them are still alert enough to hold out hope for a cure?"

"Sarcasm's not going to help you."

"Doesn't seem to me like there's much that will," Max retorted.

"So . . . what? You going to lie down and wait to die?"

Max stared into his old friend's eyes. He wondered how long it would be before he didn't recognize him. "You know me better than that, Doc. I'd have gone on in blissful ignorance, if I could have, but certain people were against that. Now that I do know, I'll go down fighting. You write those prescriptions for me and I'll write you a check for the best, most promising research team out there. You tell me where to send it."

"That's more like it," Doc said approvingly. He took off his glasses and set them down carefully before meeting Max's gaze. "You going to tell Amanda?"

Max felt himself shrink at the question. "No," he said softly.

Doc regarded him with undisguised impatience. "Why the hell not, Max? She's your daughter. She has a right to know."

"Maybe so, but I lost the right to turn to her when I kicked her out of my life," he said sadly. "How can I ask her back into it now?"

"You just do," Doc said. "That girl idolized you. She'd want to know."

"Maybe once, not now," Max said with a finality that finally shut his friend up.

"I hope to hell you know what you're doing," Doc muttered as he wrote out his prescription.

"Some would say I'm living with the consequences of my actions," Max said wearily.

Doc scowled at him. "And some would say you're nothing but a damn fool."

Wouldn't be the first time someone had

called him that, Max admitted. Himself included.

Caleb was alarmed by what he found when he went to see Max on Sunday evening. The house was spotless, as usual, thanks to his diligent housekeeper, but Max looked as if he hadn't bathed or changed his clothes in days.

"What's going on?" Caleb demanded. "Are you sick?"

"That's what they tell me," Max said dully.

"So you finally went to see the doctor," Caleb concluded, knowing at once that the news hadn't been good.

"Saw a bunch of them," Max admitted. "They all said the same thing — just what you and I anticipated."

"Alzheimer's," Caleb said, his heart aching at the thought of what lay ahead for this man he'd come to admire, even when he disagreed with some of the choices he'd made. Soon enough the sharp wit would dull and he'd retreat into the past.

Max regarded him wearily. "I never thought I'd go this way. I always thought I'd drop dead of a heart attack or get cancer like my daddy did. That was bad enough, but this seems a thousand times worse."

"We don't get to choose the way we die,"

Caleb reminded him. "Only the way we cope with it. You might want to consider coming back to church, Max. You've spent a lot of years angry at God. He might be able to help you now."

"You know how I feel about all that. God didn't keep me from losing Margaret. Why should I believe He'd be there for me now?"

"Because He's always there, even if the answers He gives aren't the ones we were hoping to hear," Caleb said. He took a deep breath and leveled a look at Max. "Even if you won't consider coming back to church, it's time to call your daughter."

"Don't you start down that road again," Max said. "I've given it a lot of thought since I got the news, and I've already made my decision. Amanda's not to know. I don't want her back here out of pity."

Even though Max spoke with conviction, Caleb was certain he didn't mean what he was saying. He was protecting himself from the possibility that Amanda would turn her back on him, as he had on her.

"What are you really afraid of, Max? Are you afraid she won't come?" Caleb pressed.

Caleb knew from the way his friend avoided his gaze that he'd hit the nail on the head. "Amanda would never do that to you," Caleb said, praying he was right. The rift was

155

deep and she certainly had justification for staying away, but he knew she had a big heart, and despite everything, he believed there was room in it for the father she'd once adored.

"I'm telling you I don't want her here out of pity," Max insisted stubbornly.

"Then don't tell her you're ill," Caleb said. "Just mend fences. Tell her the rest in time."

For the first time since Caleb had known him, Max looked old and defeated, but he nodded slowly.

"I'll give it some more thought," Max promised.

That might have been good enough another time, but it wasn't nearly enough under these circumstances. Caleb resolved to get the wheels in motion. If nothing else, maybe he could ensure that Amanda was a little more prepared, a little more receptive when Max made an overture. Of course, there was always the chance that his meddling wouldn't fix anything between Max and Amanda and would wind up putting more distance between father and daughter. He had to risk it, though, for everyone's sake.

Fortunately he was planning to be at Amanda's tomorrow night. The kids had called on Saturday telling him they missed him and begging him to come for dinner. He hadn't been able to make plans for Saturday or for tonight, but he'd promised to be there on Monday. Amanda had reluctantly agreed, even though it was a school night, which told him there was more going on over there than he realized. Hopefully, no matter what it was, he could still find some time to be alone with Amanda so he could broach the subject of her relationship with Max.

Maybe he ought to consider borrowing a flak jacket from Dinah. After all her years in war zones, she probably had one stashed somewhere. Then again, he doubted even that would be enough protection once Amanda heard what he had to say.

The kids were as wound up as if they'd been consuming sugar by the spoonful all afternoon. Amanda was just about at her wit's end. "Guys, it's just Caleb. Settle down. He's coming for spaghetti, not to play catch in the backyard, Jimmy, or have a tea party with your dolls, Susie. It's a school night, so he's staying for a couple of hours, tops, because you have homework to do."

"I did mine," Larry said. "Can I play catch with him after dinner?"

Amanda sighed. "We'll see what time it is."

157

"I want to play catch, too," Susie insisted, scowling at her big brother. "I don't even have homework."

"No, but you have an earlier bedtime than the boys," Amanda reminded her, beginning to regret that she'd agreed to this visit. Then she saw their excitement and knew she could never have deprived them of a chance to see someone who'd become so important to them.

"Is the table set?" she asked Larry.

"I did it," Jimmy said.

"I helped," Susie added. "I put the napkins on the plates. Is that right?"

"Good enough," Amanda said just as the doorbell rang. All three kids took off running.

"I'll get it," Jimmy hollered.

"No, me," Larry said.

"I wanna," Susie screamed, on the verge of tears.

Amanda listened and sighed. She hoped Caleb was prepared for this. She was pretty sure he'd never had to deal with kids — at least her kids — when they were this wound up.

The squeals from the living room reached whole new decibel levels before finally settling down. Caleb appeared in the kitchen, Susie clinging to his neck and a boy clutching each hand. He looked a little dazed.

"I see you've met the welcoming committee," she said.

"They seem to have missed me," he said, looking vaguely surprised.

"You have no idea." She gave the kids a stern look. "Let the man breathe, okay?" She met his gaze. "Want a beer? Some water? Iced tea?"

"Tea would be good," he said. "Anything I can do to help?"

"Nope. Dinner will be ready in about fifteen minutes."

He sniffed the air. "Spaghetti?"

She nodded. "I made the sauce over the weekend. I usually freeze a couple of batches, so we have it on hand. It makes things quicker when I get home from work."

"I don't know how you do everything you do," he said, regarding her with admiration.

"Organization," she said. "And a healthy dose of patience. Some days are better than others. Maybe you should go outside with the kids while I get dinner on the table. The boys have something they need to show you."

Larry and Jimmy nodded, their expressions suddenly subdued. "We need to 'pologize," Larry said meekly.

"Oh?" Caleb said, turning a questioning

159

gaze in her direction.

"They'll explain," she said, watching as they trooped outside.

When they were gone, she bit back a sigh of relief. She realized that she'd been every bit as eager to see Caleb as the kids had been. She simply hadn't wanted to admit it. Feeling the hop, skip and jump of her pulse when he'd arrived had pretty much put the lie to the idea that his absence hadn't affected her. She wondered how much her own longing — to say nothing of the dreams in which he'd appeared stripped down to a pair of snug-fitting jeans — had influenced her decision to let the kids ask him over for dinner. The possibility that she'd used her kids to get something she wanted made her grimace. What kind of mother would do such a thing?

One who was lonely and who'd found someone who seemed to understand her, she confessed to herself. Pitiful.

She put the spaghetti on the table, then called everyone in. Caleb lingered at the back door as the kids raced into the dining room.

"I had no idea they'd miss me that much," he told her. "We need to talk about this."

"I know," she agreed. "But not now."

"After dinner, then," he said. "And there's

something else I want to talk to you about, as well."

She heard an unexpectedly somber note in his voice that set off alarms. "What?"

"After dinner," he said.

"Caleb, if whatever it is will upset me, just tell me now and get it over with," she said.

"It can wait till we've eaten," he insisted, slipping past her and going into the dining room.

Amanda stared after him. Something told her that whatever was on his mind didn't have anything to do with the kids. And she could think of only one thing that he might want to postpone discussing — her father.

But why on earth would Caleb have anything at all to say to her about Big Max? As far as she knew, they'd never even met. Was her assumption wrong? Had the two of them been conspiring behind her back?

"Okay, my imagination's running away from me," she muttered. She'd know whatever was on his mind soon enough. She just had to get through dinner and sending the kids off to bed. A couple of hours at most.

So why did it suddenly seem like an eternity? And why, when she'd been so happy only moments ago, was there now a sick feeling in the pit of her stomach?

8

To his chagrin Caleb let himself be swept along in the fantasy that this was his family and this was a perfectly normal night. It was exactly the way he'd always imagined marriage and family life to be. He'd envisioned coming in after a long day, dealing with whatever commotion the kids had caused, settling disputes, sharing an occasional simmering look with the woman he loved. It was a dream that had been tantalizingly out of reach for too long now.

It was nothing like his own marriage had been, at least not in those final months when tension had run high. Meals were eaten in icy silence, when they were shared at all. Accusing glances had become the norm. In the end, he'd all but forgotten a time when his relationship with his wife had been any other way, though it must have been once. There must have been love and passion in the early years before he'd failed her, before God had failed *him.*

If the kind of family he'd always wanted was so close at hand now, it was because of Amanda. He wondered if she knew how grateful he was to have this ordinary, normal family meal. He glanced across the dining room table and caught her studying him curiously. Because he knew it flustered her and because he couldn't resist, he winked. Just as he'd anticipated, she blushed.

"Did I mention I brought dessert?" he asked.

Three pairs of eyes turned toward him.

"Really?" Susie asked, bouncing in her chair. "Is it ice cream?"

"Nah," Jimmy scoffed. "Ice cream would be all melted by now if he left it in the car."

"Cookies," Larry said. "I bet it's cookies."

Caleb turned to Amanda. "Do you have a guess before I send these guys out to the car to get it?"

She tilted her head, her expression thoughtful. "Double fudge cake with buttercream frosting," she said slowly, then grinned at his astonishment. "Got it, didn't I?"

He stared at her incredulously. "How on earth did you know that?"

"I should probably let you think I'm omniscient, but the truth is, Betty Wickham came into the boutique today and told me she'd baked one for you," she admitted. "She says it's your favorite. Of course, Minnie Green thinks peach pie is your favorite dessert and Letitia Baker is sure it's lemon meringue. My money would have been on strawberry fudge ice cream."

He chuckled. "Do you honestly think I'm going to admit to favoring one thing over another? My dessert pipeline would dry up."

"So, whatever happened to honesty?" she inquired tartly.

"I totally advocate it," he replied. "Except in cases when diplomacy's called for."

"A pretty self-serving value system," she said.

Caleb laughed. "I can hardly deny it now, can I? Okay, kids, go get the cake and be very, very careful. It's a thing of beauty. There's shaved chocolate on top of the frosting."

"If it's that precious, shouldn't you get it yourself?" Amanda asked.

He shook his head. "I trust them to be careful."

All three kids raced eagerly from the room. Left alone with Amanda, Caleb was suddenly at a loss. There was too little time to discuss any of the topics that really mattered and too much to sit there silently. Yet he couldn't seem to make himself begin. Instead, he just looked at her, memorizing the way she looked with her cheeks flushed, her hair a bit mussed. It was the way he imagined she'd look after sex. He wondered if he'd ever have the chance to discover if he was right about that.

"I should clear the table," Amanda said, obviously feeling rattled under the intensity of his gaze.

"Let me," he said at once, realizing how just a little time and distance had changed things between them. There was an unfamiliar awkwardness that had never been there before.

They bumped into each other reaching for the serving bowls in the center of the table. Both of them promptly jumped back as if they'd been singed. Or maybe he'd gotten it wrong and it wasn't awkwardness on her part at all. Maybe her thoughts had been as steamy as his own.

"This is crazy," Caleb said, meeting her eyes. "We're acting as if we've never been alone together before."

"I know. It's ridiculous." Her gaze never left his.

"Amanda," he began, ready to reach for her and pull her into his arms.

Just then the kids burst through the back

door, letting the screen door slap shut behind them. The moment of intimacy was lost to the pounding of feet and shrill clatter of excited voices.

Amanda finally tore her gaze away. "Careful with the cake!" she called out to them. "Sit it on the counter. I'll be right there to cut it."

"It's totally awesome," Larry announced gleefully.

"And the icing is —" Jimmy began, only to be cut off, most likely by his brother.

Amanda exchanged an amused look with Caleb. "There'll be fingerprints in the frosting," she warned him. "I hope that won't ruin it for you."

"Not as long as they left some icing for me," he replied.

"You really are a go-with-the-flow man, aren't you?" she said with evident admiration.

"Considering the number of surprises life has in store, it seems like the sensible way to live," he said.

"You'd make a great father," she told him. "Nothing would rattle you."

"Not true," he said, only able to deal with one part of her comment. "Seeing the damage they did to the tree house certainly shook me up. There was a lot of anger behind that."

"I know."

"My fault, I assume."

"No, not entirely," she said. "We both share the blame. Obviously neither of us realized how much they'd come to count on you."

"Any idea how we're going to fix that?" he asked.

"No," she said, then regarded him earnestly. "But we do need to fix it, Caleb. I can't watch my kids get attached to someone who's going to disappear from their lives."

"I'm not going to disappear," he assured her.

"Then there have to be parameters they can understand," she insisted.

"Mom!" Larry shouted, interrupting. "We want cake."

"I suppose we're going to have to table this till they're in bed," Amanda said.

Caleb nodded. It was just as well. He had a hunch Amanda wasn't anywhere near ready to hear the solution he had in mind — making himself a permanent fixture in their lives.

Then, again, he acknowledged with regret, that was as much a fantasy as any of the other thoughts he'd had about her. For he knew he would never make that offer. While she could give him everything he'd ever dreamed of — a deep and abiding love and a family — he couldn't give her something he'd heard her tell Dinah and Maggie she truly wanted. More kids. And explaining that to her would destroy whatever was left of his pride. Pride might be a sin and honesty was certainly something he prized, but in his own case, he was weak and willing to admit it.

Amanda came down the stairs slowly, the sound of Caleb's voice drifting along behind her. He was reading a bedtime story to the boys after tucking Susie in. They'd clamored for him to read one more chapter of the latest Harry Potter book, so Amanda had made an excuse to leave them alone.

She needed to gather her composure. Sitting there while Caleb read had filled her with memories. Good ones, for a change. Bobby had loved reading aloud to the kids until they fell asleep. It didn't matter whether it was *Goodnight Moon* for the hundredth time or a chapter from *Huckleberry Finn*, he'd enjoyed bringing the stories to life and making the kids laugh sleepily before they drifted off. *Harry Potter and the Goblet of Fire* was one of the last books they'd read together.

Amanda had enjoyed those times as much

as Bobby had. She'd felt safest and most in tune with her husband. If only Bobby had understood that those moments of simple pleasure meant far more to her than all the material things.

Tonight, listening to Caleb, she'd felt those emotions stir again, felt that longing for a connection with another person, and that, she told herself, was dangerous.

She was no longer able to maintain the illusion that Caleb was safe, either because of his profession or his gentlemanly demeanor. Too many times now, she'd seen the desire in his eyes, felt the simmering passion sparking between them. And too many nights, she'd stirred restlessly in her bed, thoughts and dreams of Caleb turning wickedly hot. She'd imagined his hands on her, not in comfort, but exploring, stroking and caressing until she remembered what it felt like to be a woman.

Shaken yet again by those images, she retreated to the kitchen where she could no longer hear Caleb's voice. The familiar, uncomplicated task of washing and drying the dishes kept her from thinking too much, wanting too much.

Even so, she jumped when Caleb appeared suddenly and announced, "They're all asleep."

She turned and smiled. "Thanks for reading to them. They miss having Bobby around to do that. I'm afraid I don't have the same talent for drama when I'm reading."

"I think I enjoyed it as much as they did," Caleb admitted.

"Would you like another cup of coffee? More cake?"

"Sure," he said. "But I'll get it. You sit. How about you? Can I get you anything?"

"Nothing for me. The coffee and chocolate would keep me awake all night." And only add to the nerves she was feeling now that they were alone with too many hard decisions to make, too many yearnings to ignore.

Caleb poured himself a cup of coffee, cut another slice of cake, then joined her at the kitchen table.

"I'm truly sorry I upset the kids," he told her. "I had no idea my staying away would affect them like that."

"I didn't realize it, either, at least not right away. When I figured it out, I tried to explain that you were a busy man with obligations to a lot of people, that they couldn't expect you to be around all the time."

He looked oddly guilty. "But I had been making time with no problem at all," he said. "And the truth is, I wasn't that busy."

Amanda wasn't all that shocked by his revelation. "Just avoiding me," she guessed. "Are you ready to tell me why? What happened when you were here that Saturday to build the tree house? It goes back to that afternoon. I'm sure of it."

He regarded her with a troubled expression. "I know I owe you an explanation, especially now, but it's just not something I can talk about."

"Not even to me?" she asked, not trying to hide her hurt.

"It's too painful," he said. "It goes back to a time in my life I've worked very hard to forget."

"But you haven't forgotten it at all, have you?"

He shook his head.

"Then perhaps talking about it would help."

"Talking is a waste of time. It can't be changed," he said tersely.

She regarded him with surprise. She'd had no idea there was anything in his past that might have been devastating. She'd seen only his compassionate, caring side and taken for granted that was all there was to him. Because he was good and decent and cared for everyone else, she'd assumed he'd gotten only kindness and compassion in re-

171

turn. Now it was evident to her that some-one had hurt him deeply.

"Now I'm the one who feels like an idiot," she said. "I thought I knew all there was to know about you, and obviously I have no idea what went on in your life before you came to Charleston."

"Everyone has a history, Amanda," he said, smiling ruefully.

"And mine is pretty much out there for everyone to see," she said. "I guess I took for granted that yours was simply more of the same generous acts that have endeared you to everyone at the church."

He grinned. "Oh, there were a few kind acts before I turned up here," he conceded, "but believe me, there was more to my life. Not all the memories are good ones."

She studied him intently. It had been a long time since she'd pried into someone else's life, especially a man's. What sort of basic questions should she be asking?

"Have you ever been married?" she asked when she realized that a man as amazing as Caleb surely had to have had a woman in his life at one time or another.

Something that might have been pain flickered in his eyes, then was gone. "Yes," he said. "I was divorced six months before I moved here."

She hid her surprise well, she thought, and refrained from prying into the reasons for the divorce. It was obviously a touchy subject.

"Kids?" she asked instead.

"No." Again, that hint of pain, though this time he wasn't able to hide it as quickly.

"And you regret that," she guessed. A man as great with children as Caleb was surely had wanted some of his own.

"Amanda, let's not get into this, okay?"

There was enough misery in his expression to convince her to drop the subject for now, even though she had a hunch she was just scraping the surface of the real issue that stood between them. She moved on to more innocuous turf. "Did you always want to be a minister?"

He regarded her with undisguised relief. "Not always," he said. "There was a time when I wanted to be a firefighter and another summer when I was sure I was going to be a major league ballplayer."

"What happened?"

"I realized that firefighting was dangerous," he said, "and that there were other ways to save people."

"What about baseball?"

"I crashed straight into reality on that one," he said, another smile tugging at his lips. "Couldn't hit worth a darn and my fielding left a lot to be desired."

"That pretty much rules out baseball, all right."

He took a sip of his coffee, studying her over the rim of the cup, then set it aside. "Okay, my turn to ask the questions."

Amanda frowned at him. "You know everything there is to know about my life."

"Not everything," he said. "I don't know what you were like as a little girl. I'm picturing curly hair and pink bows and patent-leather shoes."

Amanda laughed. "Not even close, especially about the bows. My father was basically inept in the hair department. And I rarely held still long enough for Jessie to do anything special with my hair." It was the first time in ages she'd mentioned Big Max without rancor. "Besides, I was supposed to grow up and take over the world. Bows were too frilly. If they'd made power suits for six-year-old girls, I would have had an entire wardrobe of them. I did by the time I was seventeen."

"And then came Bobby," Caleb guessed.

She nodded, her lips curving at the memory of the way he'd blasted into her life on a motorcycle and captured her heart. "And then came Bobby," she confirmed.

"Did your father hate him from the beginning?"

Though the question threatened the tender skin covering an old wound, Amanda thought back, then shook her head. "No, at first I think he regarded him as nothing more than a nuisance. He was convinced I'd tire of him and move on to someone more appropriate. Things didn't get ugly till he realized that wasn't going to happen."

"You fought?"

"All the time." She remembered the confrontations as if they'd been yesterday. Each one had carved another piece out of her heart. She'd been torn between two men she loved more than life itself. "Ironically, now that I've had time to think about it, I'm not sure it was even Bobby he hated so much, but rather the destruction of all his dreams for me. He couldn't imagine me doing everything he'd planned for me with a man like Bobby by my side, rather than some doctor or lawyer he'd handpicked for his son-in-law."

"Yet you defied him and married Bobby, anyway," Caleb said.

"The power of love," she said glibly, as if that explained it all. It didn't even begin to describe the emotions that had driven her to choose Bobby over Big Max. It was a choice

175

she never should have had to make.

"Was it love?" Caleb asked. "Or rebellion?"

"I loved my husband," she said heatedly. "And I had no reason to rebel against my father. Until Bobby came into my life, he had been the most supportive father in the world. We weren't like other parents and teenagers. It had always been just the two of us, so we were a team. I guess that was why I was so shocked when he refused to accept how good Bobby and I were together. I'd thought I could make him understand. Before Bobby came along, he'd always given me the courtesy of listening when we had disagreements. I couldn't always change his mind, but at least he heard me out, and then we'd find a compromise."

"But this time nothing you said made any difference," Caleb said.

"Nothing. His mind was dead-set against the marriage, and that was that. Bobby and I went ahead and made our plans. Bobby paid for everything. All I asked of my father was that he give me away. Instead, he waited till the morning of the wedding to tell me he wouldn't walk me down the aisle to 'that man who's going to ruin your life.' "

"That must have hurt," Caleb said, his gaze filled with understanding.

"You have no idea," Amanda said. The memory ached as if it had happened yesterday. "Even so, I think I could have gotten past that if he'd bent even a little as time went on. Bobby tried so hard to prove what a good husband he was. But when my father stood right in front of him and ripped up the picture of Jimmy, his first grandchild, I knew that he would never accept my choice or let me back into his life."

"Surely he's mellowed by now," Caleb suggested.

"He hadn't when I asked him for help after Bobby died," she said, still bitter over the way he'd dismissed her then. It wasn't just that he'd turned her down; it was the callous way he'd done it. "I went to him and groveled, not for myself, but for his grandchildren, and he turned me away. He couldn't resist gloating, either. He told me I'd gotten what I deserved for not listening to him in the first place. My husband had died and my father thought I deserved it."

She shuddered at the memory. "Why are we talking about my father, anyway? He's part of my past. I simply have to accept that."

Caleb gave her a chiding look. "Remember the Ten Commandments?"

"Of course. I have picked up a few things

taking the kids to church on Sundays."

"What about honoring your father and mother, then?"

"I did," she countered. "I respected my father more than anyone on earth until the day he cut me out of his life."

"I don't think God put any qualifiers or time limits on those Commandments," Caleb said. "I'm pretty sure He meant them to last for the parent's lifetime, even when that parent is seriously flawed."

Amanda clenched her fists at the thought that Caleb was judging her for doing what anyone else with an ounce of pride would have done in the same circumstances. Suddenly all the joy of the tranquil evening fled.

"Why dredge this up now? Haven't I told you repeatedly that I don't want to talk about my father?" she said tightly. "Not now, not ever again."

Caleb's lips curved slightly. "Maybe that's exactly why you should, because it's still so painful."

Thoroughly agitated, Amanda shoved her chair back and began to pace. Eventually she stopped in front of Caleb and scowled at him. "I don't understand you. You refuse to discuss your past because it's painful. Why should I? You know how I feel. You've seen the damage he did to me and my family. Why are you pushing so hard to get me to open up about him? I hate him," she said fervently. "I think I have good reason. If you disagree, that's not my problem. I'm just not as good a person as you are."

"We both know that's not true. I certainly have my flaws, but you're not an unforgiving woman, Amanda," Caleb said mildly. "And hate requires an awful lot of energy. Something tells me there's a part of you that would like to see things made right with him again."

"I'd like a million dollars and a BMW convertible, too," she snapped. "It's all out of reach. I've come to accept that."

Caleb gave her a disbelieving look. "Have you really?"

"Yes, dammit! This subject is nonnegotiable, Caleb. I didn't cut my father out of my life. He kicked me out of his, because he didn't like my choice for a husband. It's up to him to fix this, not me. Personally, I don't see that ever happening. If you knew him, you'd get that. He's too stubborn to ever change his mind."

"Couldn't you be the bigger person and try one more time?"

"No," she said flatly. "It's too late."

"Only if you let it be."

She stared at Caleb. "I still don't get it.

Why is this so important to you all of a sudden? You've never given two hoots about my relationship with my father before."

He smiled at that. "Maybe I've been biding my time," he suggested. "Or maybe I've just realized how important a reconciliation would be for you, whether you're ready to admit it or not."

"Which is it?"

"Does it really matter?"

She sighed heavily as she dropped back into the chair next to him. "No, I suppose not, especially if you'll just shut up about it."

"I won't."

She gave him a plaintive look. "Please."

He shook his head. "I can't. It's too important."

Amanda thought back to a time when her father had meant the world to her. It seemed so long ago and there'd been so much water under the bridge since then. There'd been a thousand times she'd longed for things to be the way they once were, but she'd finally accepted they never would be. To try to fix things one more time, only to be rebuffed one more time, would kill her.

"Leave it alone, Caleb." She met his gaze evenly. "Don't let my father come between us, too."

She saw understanding dawn in his eyes

and knew she'd hit on the one warning he might take seriously, the one warning that might get him to back off.

Then he smiled. "Nice try, darlin', but I'm not the one who scares easily."

She frowned. "I'm not scared of my father."

Caleb's expression sobered at once. "What about me, Amanda? Aren't you just a little bit afraid of me?"

"What?" she scoffed. "Are you threatening to take away your company, your respect, if I don't mend fences with my father? I know you'd never do that. You'll keep at me till you get your way or hell freezes over, whichever happens first."

His lips twitched. "You're right about that."

She regarded him uneasily. "Then I don't know what you mean," she claimed, fairly certain she was compounding her sins with the blatant lie.

Caleb tucked a finger under her chin and kept his gaze steady on her face. Amanda could feel the heat climbing into her cheeks, feel the sudden dip and sway of her pulse even before he leaned forward and touched his mouth to hers.

And then her head went spinning, her heart thumping wildly and she was lost —

not *scared,* she told herself fiercely — just lost in a sea of sensation. Who would have thought quiet, steady-as-a-rock Caleb could take her on such a ride?

Especially when not five seconds ago she had wanted to wring his neck.

9

Caleb hadn't meant to kiss Amanda, but once he'd started, he couldn't seem to stop. Months of pent-up yearnings went into that kiss. His blood was stirred in ways he'd almost forgotten.

And then he remembered that this was Amanda, a woman whose dreams didn't mesh with his own, a woman whose children were already confused about how he fit into their lives. And here he was muddying the waters again. Clearly he needed to take a step back and reassess everything that was happening between them. That's what the noble man she thought him to be would do.

And he would do it, too — but not until he savored just one more kiss, not until he tasted the faint hint of chocolate still on her tongue, not until he learned the shape of her mouth and felt the satiny texture of her cheeks against his palms. If that made him weak, so be it. He'd never pretended to be a saint, despite what some thought.

Finally, reluctantly, he released her, then sat back. He reached for his now-cold cup of coffee and clutched it to keep from reaching for Amanda again. He wanted her with every fiber of his being, more than he'd even realized.

"We can't . . . Caleb, this is . . ." Her dazed eyes locked on to his. "What's going on here?"

He set the cup back on the table and raked a hand through his hair. "I wish I could explain it," he murmured, wrestling with the same conflicted emotions that were evidently torturing her.

"Try," she insisted.

He'd counseled honesty often enough that he couldn't ignore it now when it was so important. "There's an attraction here," he began.

"No kidding," she said, amusement lurking in her eyes.

"It's a bad idea," he said staunchly.

"No argument there," she agreed. "So why does it keep happening? It's not as if we're a couple of kids who can't control our hormones."

"Speak for yourself," he said ruefully. "Not about being kids, but the whole control thing. I seem to lose it when I'm with you, Amanda. All the sane, rational reasons why a relationship is impossible fly right out of my head."

She grinned then. "I've noticed," she said, then sobered. "I'm no better."

He let himself relax slightly at the admission that he hadn't been the only one losing control. "No kidding," he said, echoing her words.

"What are we going to do about it?" she asked. "You're a minister. You can't go around having flings with members of your congregation." She paused as if considering the possibilities, then looked into his eyes. "Can you?"

"Definitely a bad idea," he admitted with reluctance. And who'd said anything about a fling? he wanted to demand. The part of him that yearned for love and family and happily-ever-after wanted a hell of a lot more than that. He just knew it was impossible.

"Bad idea. Right," she said. "Okay, we're agreed on that." Her expression seemed a little sad, but she shook it off and added, "And then there are the kids to be considered. They're confused enough as it is."

He thought of the destruction of the tree house. "No question about that."

"But they need you in their lives, Caleb,"

she said urgently. "We have to figure out a way to make that happen without any more of this."

Pure devilment made him ask, "This?"

She frowned at him. "You know perfectly well what I mean. The whole kissing thing. Isn't that what we've been talking about?"

Caleb had never been more torn in his life. A part of him wanted to throw caution to the wind right now and tell Amanda that he was falling in love with her, that the kissing wasn't going to stop. Another part knew that such a declaration would eventually blow up in both their faces, especially when she found out everything he'd been hiding from her — his friendship with her father, his own dark secrets. Not just Amanda, but her children, needed to be protected from that kind of fallout.

"How about this?" he asked eventually. "Since I can't swear I won't be tempted to keep right on stealing kisses from time to time or even that I won't try to seduce you . . ."

Alarm, and perhaps just a hint of interest, flared in her eyes. He worked hard to ignore it.

"Let's make a pact," he continued.

"A pact?"

"Nothing complicated. We just agree that

we'll avoid being alone together. That way I can spend time with the kids, but there won't be any risk of either one of us losing our heads. We ought to be safe enough if we're always surrounded by other people. Neither of us is reckless enough to do something crazy in front of anyone else, right?"

"I used to think so," she said, then added candidly, "You confuse me, Caleb."

"I think I've been in a perpetual state of confusion since the day we met," he told her. "The pact would clarify things, make sure we don't do anything foolish."

Amanda gazed into his eyes for a very long time, then finally nodded.

But even as she agreed to do as he'd suggested, there was no mistaking the faint disappointment in her eyes. Caleb wished he hadn't noticed that. It pretty much shot to pieces his already wavering resolve to do the right thing.

Mary Louise looked up just before the end of her shift and saw Danny standing uncertainly on the opposite side of the counter.

"Is it okay that I'm here?" he asked, his gaze sliding down to her stomach, which wasn't even rounded yet, then coming back up to meet her eyes.

"Sure," she said a little too brightly. She

wished just seeing him hadn't made her heart lurch. She was reminded of way too many dreams she'd had to force aside to give him his freedom.

His gaze narrowed. "You don't mean that."

"Of course I do," she insisted.

"You never could fib to me," he told her. "Don't start trying now. If me being here is a problem, just tell me. I don't want to make this any harder on you than it is already."

Mary Louise drew in a deep breath. "Okay, it is hard, but I want to see you. I've missed you. You're not just the man I love, Danny. You're my best friend."

He looked relieved. "I've missed you, too."

"What are you doing home in the middle of the week?"

"Thanksgiving's Thursday, have you forgotten? And I don't have any classes tomorrow, so I came home tonight."

"Thanksgiving, of course. I guess I've been so busy I completely forgot."

"I don't suppose you'd like to have dinner with my folks and me," he asked, regarding her uncertainly. "They said it would be okay."

Mary Louise was torn between longing and anger. She went with the anger. It was safer. "Why would I want to do that?" she retorted. "Am I supposed to act like everything's normal when we both know it's not?"

He regarded her miserably. "Look, I know this is all my fault, but I do love you, Mary Louise. I can't just forget about that. And we are having a baby together. I wish I felt differently about us getting married, but I'm trying to think about the future for all of us, not just about what I want right now."

She relented. "I know. Me, too. But I still think Thanksgiving dinner with your folks would be awful. Could you bear having them stare at us through a whole meal, trying to think of something to say? Or worse, lecturing us on what we ought to be doing?"

He chuckled. "Yeah, they're not that enlightened. How about later, then? We could see a movie or something."

Before she could answer, Willie Ron walked in, took one look at Danny and grabbed his arm. "You and me outside," he said curtly.

"Willie Ron, no!" Mary Louise protested.

"I'm not going to beat the living daylights out of him, though I think that's exactly what he deserves," Willie Ron said.

"It's okay," Danny said, his expression resigned. "He's been a good friend to you. And to me, for that matter. Let him say his piece. It's not going to be anything I haven't thought about myself."

"Then Willie Ron can say it right here in front of me," Mary Louise declared. "I don't want the two of you out there getting into some kind of fistfight in the parking lot."

"I told you I wouldn't hit him," Willie Ron said indignantly.

"And I believe you mean it," Mary Louise said. "For now. But what if he ticks you off?"

Willie Ron rolled his eyes. "The boy has already ticked me off."

"You know what I mean," she said. "Come on, you two. There's no need for any of this. I love you to pieces for wanting to stand up for me, Willie Ron, but I've made my choice. Berating Danny for it is a waste of time."

"It's *my* time," Willie Ron said, heading for the door and dragging Danny behind him.

Mary Louise stared after them. Short of calling the police, what options did she have? Besides, Danny could stand up for himself. And she was *almost* certain that Willie Ron would keep his word and not hit him. A tiny, mean little voice in her head wished he would.

Still, her nerves were taut till the two of them came back inside. Willie Ron wore a satisfied expression and Danny looked chastened.

"Everything settled?" she asked.

"I think we understand each other," Willie Ron said, his gaze leveled on Danny.

"We do," Danny agreed.

"Then there was no bloodshed?"

"Do we look as if there'd been bloodshed?" Willie Ron scoffed. "We're civilized human beings here."

"Absolutely," Danny confirmed. He hesitated, his gaze shifting to Willie Ron, then back to her. "I'm thinking, though, that maybe going to the movies on Thursday night is a bad idea."

Mary Louise immediately scowled at Willie Ron. "What did you say to him?"

"Just some things he needed to hear," he assured her.

"I'll call you, Mary Louise," Danny promised hurriedly. "And I will see you before I go back to school."

She watched him leave, her emotions in turmoil. Then she whirled on Willie Ron. "You scared him off, didn't you? You threatened him."

"I most certainly did not," Willie Ron said, looking hurt. "I told him the truth."

"Whose truth?"

"There's only one," he said. "That he's hurt you enough and that a man faces up to his responsibilities."

"My choice!" she reminded him furiously.

"If I want to see him, if I want to let my heart get broken a million more times, it's my choice!"

"And it's my choice not to stand by and let it happen, if there's something I can do to stop it," he responded with quiet dignity. "That's what real friends do."

Mary Louise burst into tears. "Real friends do not keep people apart, not when they're in love."

"If Danny loved you —"

"He does!" she shouted, needing to believe that now more than ever. "He does love me."

"Okay, okay. Have it your way," Willie Ron soothed, looking shaken by her tears. "He does love you."

"Damn straight, he does," she said with a sniff.

Willie Ron looked deep into her eyes, his expression sad. "But in my view, if he doesn't love you enough to do what's right for you and *his* child, it doesn't much count."

She'd thought the same thing too many times herself to pretend otherwise. "You make it sound like it's easy," she whispered eventually. "It's not."

"It should be," Willie Ron said more gently. "With a baby on the way, it surely should be."

■ ■ ■ ■

Thanksgiving morning dawned with an orange sunrise that gave way to bright blue skies. Amanda took her first cup of coffee for the day into the backyard and sat down to reflect on how many things she had to be thankful for. The new house topped the list, followed very quickly by all the people who'd become friends in the past year. Caleb, despite the confusion he filled her with, was on the list, as well. In fact, he deserved credit for all the rest.

Then, of course, there were the kids, who were finally beginning to lose those pinched, frightened expressions they'd worn in the first weeks and months after Bobby died. They were back to being healthy, normal, carefree kids again. Even those moments when they turned into holy terrors seemed blessedly normal compared to the times when they'd been too silent.

She heard the screen door slam and saw Susie crossing the yard, barefoot and still in her nightgown. She crawled up into Amanda's lap and rested her head against Amanda's chest.

"Mommy, are we gonna have turkey today?"

"You bet."

"And pumpkin pie?"

"I imagine so."

"We didn't last year," Susie said.

Last year the whole Thanksgiving extravaganza had been beyond Amanda's means. Refusing to accept any of the invitations they'd been offered out of charity, they'd stayed at home in their cramped apartment. She'd baked a frozen pizza in their tiny kitchen and tried to make it seem as if they were the lucky ones, if only because the oven had actually worked for once. She hadn't been willing to risk the expense of a turkey, only to have the thing go to waste when it was still raw at the end of the day. The pizza had been a safer bet.

"This year we're going to have turkey and mashed potatoes and stuffing," she assured Susie. "Nadine's cooking, remember? She invited us to come over there with Caleb and Maggie and Josh and Mr. Winslow. It'll be the first time she's had people over since she moved into her new place."

"Oh, yeah." A worried frown settled on Susie's face. "But if we go to her house, we won't have any turkey for later like we used to have before Daddy went away."

"Nadine says she bought a very big turkey for that very reason, so we could take lots of turkey home for sandwiches."

Susie grinned. "That's good." Then her expression turned thoughtful. "Do you think Nadine's gonna marry Mr. Winslow?"

"I have no idea," Amanda said. It certainly seemed as if the two of them were getting closer, but Nadine hadn't expressed any interest in making the relationship permanent. She said she'd already made enough marital mistakes.

"What about you and Mr. Caleb?" Susie asked.

"We talked about this the other day," Amanda reminded her. "Caleb and I are friends."

"But not like he's friends with me and Larry and Jimmy," Susie said.

Amanda studied her daughter curiously. "Why do you say that?"

"'Cause he kisses you, like moms and dads kiss," Susie announced.

"How on earth do you know that?" Amanda asked, not trying to hide her shock.

"I got thirsty after I went to bed the other night and I came to get water, but Mr. Caleb was kissing you, so I went back to bed."

Amanda winced. "I see."

"So, are you gonna get married?"

"No, baby. We are not getting married."

"It would be okay if you did," Susie assured her. "Me and Jimmy and Larry love

Mr. Caleb, and if you got married that would make him our dad."

"I think you're going to have to settle for having him as your friend," Amanda repeated.

Susie frowned, clearly not happy at having her plan thwarted. "Maybe I should ask him."

"No," Amanda ordered, too harshly. "Absolutely not."

Susie looked startled. "How come?"

"Because I said so." Amanda gazed into her daughter's eyes, praying that her unyielding expression would get the point across. "Are we clear on that?"

Susie shrugged. "I guess so."

The response wasn't exactly reassuring, but it was probably the best Amanda could hope for. If she went overboard trying to extract a promise from Susie, it would probably guarantee that marriage would be the very first subject Susie brought up the next time she ran into Caleb.

Susie scrambled out of Amanda's lap and headed for the house. "I'm starving," she announced. "Can we have pancakes for breakfast?"

If it meant they wouldn't have to discuss Caleb and marriage, Amanda would make her a dozen pancakes and let her drown them in syrup. The whole conversation had stirred up a yearning she'd been working overtime to avoid. Apparently she was going to have to work a little harder.

Nadine's little rental house was crowded with guests for Thanksgiving dinner when George Winslow pulled Caleb aside.

"Could we talk for a minute?" he asked.

Caleb knew what was on George's mind, and the last thing he wanted to discuss with Amanda no more than a few yards away was Max. Too risky. George didn't know a single thing about discretion or keeping his voice down.

"Could we do this later?" he asked George. "Something tells me Nadine could use some help in the kitchen."

"Nadine can barely turn around in that kitchen when she's in there all by herself," George retorted. "She doesn't need you underfoot."

"Yes, but —" Caleb began, only to have George cut him off.

"Would you tell me why she insisted on renting a tiny little place like this when I told her I would help her find something nice?" George asked, gazing around the cramped space with irritation.

When Caleb remained silent, George gave

him a helpless look. "I'm really asking your opinion. Why would she insist on this place?"

"Maybe she needed to feel independent," Caleb suggested mildly, relieved to have George suddenly distracted by his frustration at his inability to get Nadine to fall in with his plans for her.

"She could have had a nicer place and her independence, too," George grumbled. "I wasn't going to attach any strings."

"George, you always attach strings, even when you do things with the best intentions in the world," Caleb said. "It comes from too many years of negotiating the best possible deals for your company. I doubt you could turn off that switch if you tried."

George frowned at him, then shrugged, looking sheepish. "You're probably right. Old habits and all that. Probably why Nadine fascinates me. I can't seem to get her to fit into a niche I understand. That woman needs me, but I'll be damned if I can get her to admit it."

"And that's probably a good thing for both of you," Caleb said. "By the way, have you had a chance to sit down with Cord and talk about the new housing project?"

George gave him a sour look. "Not since you told me I was going to be forking out a fortune for land, instead of buying some little plot for one small house the way I intended."

Caleb regarded him with amusement. "Something tells me you've been scouting out property, just the same. Found any bargains? I know how you love finding a good deal."

"I have my eye on one or two areas over in Mount Pleasant that could work and won't bankrupt me in the process," George admitted. "I'll get with Cord next week and take him to have a look."

"You're doing a good thing," Caleb told him.

"Speaking of good things, let's get back to the reason I wanted to talk to you in the first place. It's about Max."

"This isn't the time," Caleb said, casting a look in Amanda's direction.

"You telling me she doesn't know about his Alzheimer's?" George demanded, looking shocked. "Why the hell not?"

"Because Max swore me to secrecy," Caleb explained defensively, "so don't look at me like that. I imagine he did the same with you. For now, I think all we can do is honor his request. Let's table this discussion for another time."

George ignored his plea. "What do you

mean, for now?"

Caleb sighed. "To be honest, I'm with you. Amanda needs to know before it's too late. I've been working on getting her out there without mentioning Max's illness, but she's every bit as stubborn as he is. And, truthfully, I can't blame her. What he did was wrong."

"I can't argue with that," George said. "But it's time to let bygones be bygones for both of them. She'll hate herself if she doesn't have the chance to make peace with her daddy."

"I agree," Caleb said. "Now, please let's stop talking about this before Amanda catches wind of it and we ruin Nadine's party. Nadine would never forgive either one of us."

"You've got that right," George said. "Keep me posted. And keep going out there, Caleb. Max needs all the friends he can get now."

He walked away just as Amanda appeared beside Caleb. He could tell from her expression that, just as he'd feared, she'd overheard some of what George had said.

"What did he mean?" she asked him, her face tense.

"I'm not sure what you're talking about," Caleb said evasively.

"Don't you dare give me that, Caleb Webb. George said something about you visiting my father. Is he right? Have you been spending time with Big Max?"

Caleb couldn't bring himself to compound the problem by lying. "Yes," he admitted.

"How long?" she asked, barely concealing her fury.

"A while now."

"How long?" she demanded again. "And why?"

"A year or more," he admitted reluctantly. "We play cards from time to time."

"A year or more," she repeated incredulously. "And you didn't see any reason to tell me that?"

"What would you have done if I had?"

"Told you to get the hell out of my life," she said. "Which is exactly what I'm telling you now. Stay away from me, Caleb. Stay away from my kids."

"No," he said softly. "I understand why you're upset —"

"Upset?" she said in a barely controlled rage. "Upset doesn't begin to cover what I'm feeling right now. You betrayed me, Caleb. You've been friends with the one person on this earth who hurt me, and you saw no need to mention it. Obviously you get to be friends

201

with anyone you want to, but not to tell me when you know it's a man I despise . . ." Her voice trailed off and she shook her head. "All the times you've brought him up are starting to make sense now. You see yourself as some sort of great peacemaker, don't you?"

"That's not it." He was feeling his way along, trying to find a way to explain that she would accept. "Please, let's talk about this later. I'll explain everything, but let's not spoil Nadine's party."

"Why bother talking?" she retorted. "I don't see how I can ever believe another word out of your mouth. And I have to tell you, Caleb, that breaks my heart."

She whirled to walk away, but he caught her arm and forced her to face him. "I never lied to you, Amanda."

"No, of course not. You would never *lie*," she said derisively. "You just failed to tell me the truth — that you've been in cahoots with my father all along."

"Cahoots? What exactly do you think we've been plotting?"

She faltered slightly at the question. "I don't know exactly, but with my father involved it can't be good. Now let me go."

"Don't leave," he pleaded. "We haven't even sat down to dinner yet."

"I'm not leaving," she said impatiently. "I

wouldn't do that to the children or to Nadine, but I don't have to stand here and talk to you."

"We need to get past this misunderstanding," he persisted.

She gave him a pitying look. "It's not some little misunderstanding," she retorted. "Don't you get that? I won't forgive you for this, Caleb. Not ever."

"Then I'm to become one more person on your personal hate list?" he asked gently. "Careful, Amanda. Pretty soon there won't be anyone who hasn't offended or hurt you in some way. If you don't learn how to forgive, you'll wind up leading a very lonely life."

She yanked her arm free and headed for the kitchen. He noticed that just before she entered, she plastered a smile on her face. When dinner was served, she made sure they were at opposite ends of the table. Not once did she so much as glance his way.

Nadine's terrific meal tasted like sawdust to Caleb, and the conversation ebbed and flowed around him without any of it registering. He knew that it was going to be a thousand times harder to bring about a reconciliation between Amanda and Max now that he'd lost her trust, but he couldn't let that stop him from trying. Too much was riding on it . . . for all their sakes.

10

Amanda was still fuming when she went back to work on Monday morning. So when she looked up at lunchtime and saw Caleb coming in the door of the boutique, she immediately headed for the bathroom. She was not going to have another confrontation with him in public, not with her boss and several customers around. Obviously he'd counted on her sense of discretion and figured this would be the perfect place to have a quiet, reasonable talk with her. Fat chance! She was in no mood to be reasonable, not where he was concerned.

With the bathroom door securely locked, she turned the water in the sink on full force, then splashed some on her overheated face. When she heard the tap on the door, she ignored it.

"Amanda, Reverend Webb is here to see you," Joanna Mills called through the door.

"He says you have a lunch date."

"He must be mistaken," Amanda said tightly as she shut off the water. "Please tell him we're busy and that I can't leave now."

"Maybe you should tell him that yourself," Joanna said.

"Tell me what?" Caleb said from outside the door.

"You're on your own, you two," Joanna said. "Play nice."

Amanda could hear the tap of Joanna's high heels as she walked away and left them alone. She sighed and leaned against the door, wondering if she remained perfectly silent Caleb would eventually give up and go away. Probably not. One of the things she'd always admired most about him was his persistence. It just wasn't as admirable when it was being aimed at her.

"Amanda, we need to talk," he said now. "You can come out and go to lunch with me, or I can stand right here and say what's on my mind. Before you choose that option, though, you should know that there are a couple of fascinated customers lurking just outside. By one o'clock everyone in Charleston will know what we said. We might as well broadcast it on the midday news."

Amanda didn't doubt it for a second. It just reconfirmed her opinion that Caleb had counted on her reluctance to create a scene where she worked. He knew this job was important to her. How had she not noticed before that the man was so blasted sneaky?

Resigned to dealing with him, she flung open the door. "I'll get my purse," she said, clenching her teeth.

He beamed at her. "Good decision."

"I didn't make it to please you," she snapped.

He held up his hands and backed up a step. "Never thought you did."

He wisely said nothing more until they were safely outside. Then he asked, "Anything in particular you'd like for lunch?"

"Privacy," she said at once.

"Other than that."

"Anything's fine."

"Then we'll walk down the block and have some of Mirabella's homemade soup. Seems like it's a good day for it. The air finally has a bit of a nip in it. Did you notice? December's just around the corner."

She shot an impatient look at him. "Do you really want to discuss the weather?"

"It seemed neutral enough for a starter," he said.

"And you thought what, that it would help me to mellow out?" she asked scathingly.

"Not going to happen, Caleb. I'm furious with you."

He met her gaze evenly. "I know that. And I am sorry I didn't say something to you sooner about my friendship with your father."

"No, you're sorry I found out at all," she corrected.

"That's not true," he insisted. "I always meant to tell you, but with all the bad blood between you and your father, I wanted to pick the right time."

"You actually thought there would be a right time?"

He shrugged. "Yeah, I did."

"I know you're not stupid, so you must be naive."

"I prefer to think optimistic."

She studied him curiously. "How long did you say the two of you have been such buddies?"

He winced at her sarcasm. "As I told you at Nadine's, it's been about a year now. Maybe longer."

She nodded sagely. "Yes, that's what I recall you saying." She met his gaze. "And in all that time, you couldn't find a suitable moment to mention it to me? Please, Caleb. You were just being a coward. You knew how I'd react."

"Of course I did," he agreed. "I wanted you to trust me enough to maybe listen when I tried to patch things up between the two of you."

She pondered that for a minute. "Yes, that would explain what all those little mentions of Big Max lately have been about," she said. "You were testing the waters to see if I was ready to mend fences with my father."

"Yes," he admitted.

"I guess you know the answer to that," she said dryly.

"I know you're being stubborn."

She regarded him with shock. "You must be kidding! You think I'm the one being stubborn?"

"Oh, believe me, I've said very similar things to Max, as well."

"And how's that been going for you?"

He shrugged. "About the way you'd expect, since the two of you are exactly alike. Both of you have more pride than's good for you."

Amanda was not accustomed to anyone suggesting that she was a chip off the old block. "I'd like to think I'm more reasonable than my father," she said stiffly.

"Trust me, you're not," Caleb retorted. "Now, let's table this till we've ordered some lunch. Mirabella has Tuscan tomato-basil bisque on the menu today and I intend to enjoy it."

"Then perhaps you should have come alone," Amanda responded. "I'm going to do whatever I can to see that you wind up with indigestion."

Caleb's lips twitched at the threat, which only annoyed her more.

"Okay, actually I hope you choke on it," she said, flouncing past him and marching into the little café.

"I'd be hurt if I thought you meant that," he said as he slid out a chair for her.

Amanda deliberately yanked out a different chair and sat. Caleb shrugged and sat down on the one he'd pulled out.

Only after they'd placed their orders and been served their tea did Amanda finally meet Caleb's gaze and ask the question that had been bothering her ever since Thanksgiving.

"Why, Caleb?" she asked wearily. "Why of all the people in Charleston would you befriend Big Max?" She noted the startled look in his eyes, then pressed, "What made you think this would be okay, especially after you and I got to be friends?"

"Truthfully, I knew it wouldn't be okay," he admitted. "Not at first, anyway. But I trusted in your generous heart. I thought you'd forgive me and I thought in time you'd forgive your father."

"I can't," she whispered, not entirely sure if she meant him, her father, or both.

"He needs people to care about him," Caleb said. "He's lonely."

"And whose fault is that?" she demanded, still unyielding.

"His own, of course," Caleb agreed readily. "But that doesn't mean it ought to be that way. Somebody needs to take the first step. He should be surrounded by his family. He should have you and the kids in his life."

"We're not there because he doesn't want us there," she reminded him.

"I don't believe that," Caleb retorted. "Not for one single second. In fact, I think that's why he got in touch with me in the first place."

Amanda stared at him in shock. She'd assumed that the friendship had been at Caleb's instigation. "My father contacted you?"

Caleb nodded, but he looked oddly uneasy about the admission.

"Why?" she asked.

"To get to know me, I suppose."

She stared at him skeptically. "My father's not a religious man."

"No," Caleb agreed. "He's expressed his point of view on that subject more than once. We've had some invigorating debates."

That made sense. Her father did enjoy intellectual stimulation, as long as he was victorious. She doubted Caleb gave him an inch.

"So, what?" she asked. "You get together, debate religion and play cards?"

"Something like that," Caleb agreed.

"And my name has never come up?"

"I didn't say that."

She believed that, too. Her father had probably taken every opportunity to disparage her. "Has he been telling you that this rift between us is all my fault?"

"No. He's never said a bad word about you, at least not to me. Nor to anyone else I can think of. He's kept the feud between you to himself, probably because he knows in his heart he was wrong to start it and let it go on this long."

"You're assuming he has a heart," Amanda said, knowing she sounded every bit as heartless as her father. Maybe they were two of a kind, after all. "Do I need to remind you that he didn't bend even a little when Bobby died and everything in my life fell apart?"

"I think he regrets that," Caleb said.

"Do you really? What planet are you living on, Caleb? William Maxwell doesn't have regrets. He's always right about everything."

Caleb held her gaze. "Maybe once," he conceded. "You haven't spent any time with him for years now. You have no idea how he's changed."

"I think I've known my father a lot longer than you have," she said. "I've also been the victim of one of his personal vendettas. Big Max doesn't get mad. He gets even."

Caleb seemed startled by the depth of her bitterness. "How do you think he got even with you? You don't think he was somehow behind everything that happened to Bobby, do you?"

Amanda frowned under his direct gaze. "No, of course not. At least not the way you mean. I do think his disrespect and outright meanness drove Bobby to do some of the things he did."

"Maybe you're right, but ultimately we all make our own decisions, Amanda. Bobby could have made smarter choices, especially when it came to your finances."

She bristled at the criticism. "Don't you dare criticize Bobby," she said heatedly. "He spent our entire marriage trying to make up for everything he thought I'd sacrificed to be with him."

"Don't you blame him sometimes?" Caleb asked gently.

"No," she said. "I blame my father."

"Have you ever told him that? Have you ever just gone out to Willow Bend and tried to clear the air?"

"You know I saw him," she said defensively.

"Yes, but because you were hoping for his help, I imagine you were very careful not to say everything that you were really feeling," Caleb suggested. "Not even after he turned you down."

Amanda thought back to that humiliating confrontation. Caleb was right. She'd held her tongue because she'd felt she had to. She'd been too desperate to risk a shouting match. In the end, her discretion had been wasted. He'd still shown her the door.

"See him, Amanda. Get it all off your chest. Put this behind you once and for all, not just for his sake, but for yours," he urged. "Even if nothing changes, you'll feel a thousand times better for having made the effort."

"No," she said flatly.

"Not even a second's thought?" he chided. "Just no?"

"Just no," she repeated, avoiding his eyes. She knew what she'd see there. Disappointment.

"I thought you were a better person than that," he said.

"And I thought you would never betray me," she said just as quietly. "I guess we were both wrong."

Big Max stood in the middle of the kitchen trying to remember what he'd walked in there for. He'd probably done the same thing a hundred times before, but now an incident like this had the power to terrify him. Was his mind slipping faster than they'd warned him it would? Should he be making arrangements for the time when he wouldn't know anyone or how to do even the simplest tasks?

He sank onto a kitchen chair and stared out the back window. There had been a time when the view of his land with its ancient oak trees and trailing Spanish moss would have soothed him. Now he couldn't help wondering how soon it would all seem totally strange and unfamiliar.

"What are you doing sitting in here all by yourself?" his housekeeper asked when she found him at the table a half-hour later, still staring into space. "You come in here to get some lunch?"

He shrugged. "Is it lunchtime? I've lost track."

Jessie Heflin regarded him with dismay. She had been his housekeeper for nearly thirty-five years. She'd come when Margaret

214

had been pregnant with Amanda, then stayed after his wife was gone to help him with the new baby and just about everything else. He'd confided in her about the Alzheimer's, but he was beginning to regret that. She worried too blasted much. Her hovering was getting on his nerves.

"Should I call Doc Mullins?" she asked now.

"For what? So you can tell him I'm sitting at my own kitchen table thinking things over?"

"Maybe I should tell him that you're refusing to take that medicine he gave you," she countered. "How would that be?"

"I'm taking it," he muttered defensively. "Though I can't see that it's making a bit of difference."

"Maybe it's not the kind of difference you can recognize," she suggested reasonably. "Maybe things would be worse by now without it. You don't know." She patted his hand. "It's already one o'clock, Max. I'm going to fix you a nice chicken salad sandwich for lunch. You want sliced tomato on it?"

"Is the tomato any good? There's nothing worse than a mealy tomato."

"And when have you ever known me to give you one?" she retorted. "This one came from my garden. There are still quite a few

215

left on the vine. As long as we don't have a freeze soon, I think they'll ripen."

She made his sandwich and set it in front of him, then set another one on the table.

"You eating with me?" he inquired, surprised. Jessie had never taken what she described as liberties, no matter how many times he or Amanda had invited her to join them for a meal.

Before she could answer, the doorbell rang.

"That would be Reverend Webb," she said. "The sandwich is for him."

"Did I know he was coming by today?" Max asked worriedly.

"No, but I did. He called while you were outside taking your walk. I told him lunchtime would be a good time."

He frowned at her. "Who put you in charge of my social calendar?" he grumbled.

"No one," she said. "I just saw a need and stepped in, the same way I've been doing for more than thirty years. Now, hush up and I'll go let the man in."

"I'm surprised he doesn't just walk in," Max said. "Nobody seems to stand on ceremony anymore."

"They do with you," Jessie said. "Leastways, the ones who're scared of you do."

Max's spirits perked up. "You think Caleb's scared of me?"

216

"Don't you do your best to see that he is?"

"Indeed, I do." Max grinned, even though he suspected they both knew that Caleb didn't fear him in the slightest. "I can't have everyone thinking I've gone soft."

While he waited for Caleb, he sipped his tea and wondered what the devil had brought the man over here today. Probably another one of those lectures on telling Amanda the truth about his health. Caleb had had a one-track mind ever since the diagnosis. That was getting tiresome, as well.

Jessie ushered Caleb into the kitchen. "I put a sandwich on the table for you," she told him. "I'll be back in a while to give you both some pie. Made a blueberry one this morning."

"My favorite," Caleb exclaimed. "Thank you, Jessie."

She gave him a considering look. "I thought your favorite was my apple pie."

"Everything you bake is a masterpiece," he said quickly. "How could I possibly choose just one?"

"Nice save," Max complimented him as Jessie rolled her eyes and left them alone.

"It pays not to offend anyone who cooks like Jessie," Caleb said.

"So, did you come over here just for free

food? Thought the church was paying you a decent living."

"That depends on your definition of *decent,*" Caleb said. "By your standards, I'm probably at the poverty level. By mine, I do just fine. And I had some soup for lunch before I came, but since Jessie went to the trouble of making that sandwich, I'm not about to turn it down. I won't turn the pie down, either."

"Eating soup at your desk is a bad habit," Max scolded. "You need to get out."

"I'm out now," Caleb responded. "Besides, I didn't eat at my desk. Nor did I eat alone. I had lunch with Amanda before I came out here."

Max felt the old, familiar ache deep inside. "Oh? How did that happen?"

"I was trying to make peace. She's furious with me at the moment."

"Why's that?"

"She found out you and I have been spending time together."

Max's heart plummeted. "I imagine that means you won't be coming back here anymore," he said with real regret. His visits with Caleb were the one thing he had to look forward to lately. Even George's visits had tapered off now that he was chasing after that new woman, Nadine something-or-other.

"Why would I quit coming to see you?" Caleb demanded. "I just wanted you to know that she's aware of our friendship."

"You haven't told her about what's going on with me, have you?" Max dreaded the answer.

"I promised I wouldn't," Caleb reminded him. "You know you can trust my word."

"Always thought so," Max agreed. "But something tells me you'd break it in a minute if you thought it was for my own good."

"Could be," Caleb admitted. "We're not there yet." He regarded Max and said casually, "You could keep me from going back on it by telling her yourself."

"That'll never happen," Max said forcefully, then deliberately changed the subject. "Now then, how about a game of poker before you head back to town? Or do you have some souls you need to save this afternoon?"

"All the souls I'm worried about can wait for a couple of hours," Caleb said. "Besides, you don't think I'd leave before I have some of Jessie's blueberry pie, do you?"

Max shook his head. "I swear, I'm beginning to think that woman's food is the only thing that brings you out here."

"You're wrong," Caleb said. "I come for the chance to win more of your money."

"You won't live long enough to see me in

the poorhouse," Max retorted, then frowned. "If I'm lucky, neither will I."

"Max!"

"What? It's the truth. You think I want to be wandering around in some kind of daze, not recognizing anything or anyone?"

Caleb didn't look away from him, as Max suspected another man might. It was one of the things he respected about him. The reverend never shied away from the tough stuff.

"No," Caleb responded quietly. "I think that would be just about the last thing any man would want, but we will get through this, Max. We'll walk this road together."

"That's a bunch of hogwash and you know it," Max snapped. "I'll be the one on the road. You'll be standing on the sidelines with all your faculties about you."

Caleb's expression did waver then, but he didn't look away. Nor did he try to deny what Max had said. Instead, he said with what sounded like real pain, "And maybe that'll be the hardest place to be."

Max blinked away a sudden dampness in his eyes. "Damn, boy, don't say things like that. You'll have us both bawling."

Caleb didn't respond for an instant, but when he did there was a twinkle back in his eyes. "Maybe that's my plan. If your eyes are all watery, you won't be able to see the cards."

"If you're going to beat me today, you'll need a better scheme than that," Max said. "I'm feeling lucky."

And oddly enough, he was. He'd rather have one man as good as Caleb as a friend than the dozens who'd been in his life just because of his wealth and power. Too bad it had taken him so many years to value friendship over all the rest.

Amanda wished there were someone besides Caleb she could talk to about this feud with her father. Or someone with whom she could discuss Caleb, for that matter. Her emotions were all twisted into knots. Ironically, the first person she would have gone to with this sort of troubling confusion in the past would have been Caleb himself, but that clearly was impossible now, not with him at the core of her dilemma.

She was sitting in her backyard, sipping a glass of tea and enjoying the peace and quiet after getting the kids to bed, when she heard someone coming around the side of the house. Actually two people, she realized when she heard one person's muffled oath and the other's warning to watch where they were walking.

"There you are," Nadine called out cheerfully as she and Maggie rounded the corner. "We knocked on the front door, but I guess you couldn't hear us out here."

Amanda felt as if Nadine, at least, were the answer to her prayers. Josh's mother had befriended her during the building of the house, and for the first time in her life Amanda had felt as if she actually had someone in her corner, the way her mother might have been if she'd lived. Maggie was another story, but they'd resolved to be friends and her appearance here tonight with her mother-in-law suggested she'd meant it.

"What brings you two by?" she asked. "Can I get you something? There's iced tea made and I think I have some sodas in the refrigerator."

"Tea would be great," Maggie said.

"For me, too," Nadine agreed. "But sit there. I can get it. I know where everything is."

After being on her feet all day at the boutique, Amanda didn't argue. "If you don't find what you need, just poke around till you see it."

"Will do," Nadine said, walking into the house.

Maggie sat gingerly on the edge of the chair next to Amanda. "I hope you don't

222

mind us just dropping in like this."

"Of course not," Amanda said. "In fact, I was just longing for some company. I've missed the dinners we used to have together while this place was being built."

"Me, too, to be honest," Maggie said. "Especially now that Josh is over in Atlanta so much during the week. I had no idea I'd feel so lost without him."

Just then Dinah Beaufort turned the corner of the house. "I figured I'd find you all out here," she said. "Who knows how many more nights we'll have like this before cold weather starts in earnest?"

At Dinah's unexpected arrival, Amanda looked from one woman to the other, her suspicions suddenly on high alert. "It's not an accident that you three all picked tonight to drop by, is it?"

"I don't know what you mean," Dinah said, her expression innocent.

"Don't even try," Maggie chided her best friend. "She's obviously on to us."

"Caleb sent you," Amanda guessed.

"In a way," Maggie admitted. "Nadine and I saw what happened between the two of you on Thanksgiving. None of us overheard what you argued about, but we know you were angry."

"And then Nadine heard that you and

Caleb almost had another fight in the boutique today," Dinah added. "So, we're here to listen if there's anything you need to talk about. We all thought the two of you were getting close, so if he did something to upset you, we wanted you to know we're in your corner."

Amanda's eyes stung with tears. "Just like that, you're on my side?"

Nadine exited the house with a tray with three more glasses, a pitcher of iced tea and some sort of snacks she'd managed to put together from the meager contents of Amanda's refrigerator and cupboards.

"Well, of course we're on your side," Nadine said as she set the tray on a table. "Men are impossible, even my son." She grinned at Maggie, who nodded. "We women have to stick together."

"Of course, some of us thought Caleb would be better than most," Dinah added. "Him being a minister and all."

"He has testosterone, doesn't he?" Nadine said dryly. "Bad behavior comes with the territory. I doubt even seminary can train it out of them."

"Caleb *is* a good guy," Amanda felt compelled to say. "It's just that he's being pigheaded on this one particular subject."

"Which is?" Dinah prodded. "If you want

224

to tell us, that is."

Amanda did want to get it off her chest. She needed another perspective and three would be even better, especially when these women were all openly on her side. Even so, she knew they would try for a certain amount of objectivity. Dinah, as a journalist, certainly ought to be able to achieve that.

"You know about the rift between me and my father," she began.

All three of them nodded. It had been a hot topic during the building of this house.

"Well, I found out on Thanksgiving that Caleb and my father have become friends," she explained. "He's out there visiting all the time. That's his business, of course, but now he's pressuring me to make peace with Big Max, as if I've been the one in the wrong all these years." She looked from one woman to the next. "What do you think? Am I right to feel hurt and betrayed? Or is Caleb right that I'm acting like some sort of spoiled brat by not forgetting about everything my father did to me?"

"Oh, boy," Dinah murmured.

"What?" Amanda demanded.

"I can see both sides," Maggie admitted.

"Me, too," Nadine said. "Goodness knows, Josh and I had our issues when I got back to town. It would have been easier for both of us if he'd just given me some cash and sent me on my way, like I asked him to, but I'm thankful every day that he didn't. By keeping me right here, we were both forced to face the past and deal with it."

"I had plenty of issues with my mother, too," Maggie said.

"So did I," Dinah admitted. "I'm not saying they were the same as yours, Amanda, but I'm so glad now that we worked through them and didn't let them turn into such a big deal that we couldn't share the excitement of me getting married or being pregnant. You only have so many years with your parents."

"Right," Maggie agreed. "How would you feel if you never settled this and suddenly Big Max was gone? Wouldn't you always regret that?"

"I suppose," Amanda conceded reluctantly. She'd never let herself think about a time when the chance to make amends would be gone forever. Even when Caleb had tried to make her face that possibility, she'd resisted. "So, you're all saying Caleb is right?"

They each nodded.

"But not that you're entirely wrong, either," Maggie said at once.

Dinah nudged her in the ribs. "You're waffling," she accused.

"I'm being fair," Maggie argued.

"Okay, here's what you need to think about," Nadine said, leaning forward to clasp Amanda's hands in hers. "Just like Maggie said, how are you going to feel if this man you once loved — at least I assume you did — dies and you never once got to tell him again that you loved him?"

Amanda thought of all the years her father had been the only constant in her life, all the years he'd doted on her and she'd adored him. He could have turned her over to Jessie and let the housekeeper raise her, but he hadn't. Those years still meant something, despite everything that had happened since then.

"You've given me a lot to consider," she said, squeezing Nadine's hands. "Thank you so much for coming by tonight."

Maggie grinned. "Don't think you're getting rid of us now. We haven't even gotten to the good stuff."

"Good stuff?" Amanda asked.

"Sure," Dinah said. "You and Caleb. Have you slept with him yet?"

"Dinah!" Nadine protested. "That's too personal."

"Oh, so what?" Dinah scoffed. "I'm a journalist. I pry. It's second nature to me."

She turned back to Amanda. "So, have you?"

"I am not having this conversation with you guys," Amanda said, laughing despite herself. "Thanks for making me feel like a teenager at a sleepover, though. I never got to do that as a kid."

"Never?" Maggie asked, looking shocked.

"Not once," Amanda confirmed.

Maggie looked at Nadine and Dinah. "What do you think, ladies?"

"I say we stay," Nadine said at once.

"Okay with me," Dinah agreed. "Cord's in Atlanta with Josh."

Amanda stared at all three of them, stunned by the idea. "Really? Won't we be exhausted in the morning? I have to go to work."

"You'll manage," Maggie assured her. "It's not as if you drive heavy machinery. How alert do you have to be to sell clothes?"

"Good point," Amanda agreed, then glanced toward the house.

"Don't worry, we'll keep it down," Nadine said. "We won't wake the kids."

"Then let's make some popcorn and get this party started," Dinah said. She eyed Amanda. "Maybe we'll give you a make-over. Anybody have any makeup with them?"

"I have a makeup bag in the car," Nadine said.

Dinah's expression brightened. "Get it. Maggie, you make the popcorn. I'll see if I have anything in my purse. I usually have something for emergencies, in case I wind up on location on a news story."

"A makeover?" Amanda repeated worriedly. "Are you sure about this? It's not going to involve anything too drastic, right?"

"We won't cut off all your hair, if that's what you're asking," Dinah promised. "And everything we do will wash off if you hate it."

"Okay, then," Amanda said, brightening at the prospect. "This will be fun."

And it would get her mind off of her father and Caleb, she thought with relief. Those were subjects much better tackled in the bright light of day.

Or never.

11

It was the very first time Mary Louise had seen an ultrasound of her baby, the very first time she'd heard its little heartbeat. The baby had been real to her from the first moment she'd realized she was pregnant, but this was totally awesome. She couldn't seem to tear her gaze away from the monitor. To be honest, at not quite four months along, all she could really see was this tiny little pulsing motion, but it was amazing! She wished like anything that Danny could have been here, too, but she hadn't even told him about the appointment.

After Thanksgiving when things had been awkward between them, thanks, in part anyway, to Willie Ron's interference, she hadn't wanted to risk having Danny tell her he wasn't interested in coming with her. She knew she was probably clinging to a fantasy, but she wanted to believe that deep down he cared as much about this baby as she did. Every time he proved otherwise, it carved another chunk out of her already-broken heart.

Despite her fear that his reaction might disappoint her, the second she left the doctor's office, she pulled her cell phone out of her backpack and called him at Clemson. She knew his class schedule by heart and figured he'd be walking to his job off campus now. He picked up on the very first ring.

"Hey, Mary Louise," he said, sounding at least a little glad to hear from her.

"Hi, Danny. Is this a good time?"

"Sure. I'm on my way to work. I have about twenty minutes before I'm due there and it's only a five-minute walk. What's going on?"

"I just had a doctor's appointment," she began, trying to keep her enthusiasm in check in case he didn't show any interest.

He hesitated, then asked, "Are you okay? Is everything all right with the baby?"

Because he actually sounded genuinely concerned, she went on. "I heard the heartbeat," she told him excitedly. "And I could see him on the ultrasound."

"It's a boy?" he asked, his voice filled with wonder.

"No," she said hurriedly. "I mean, I don't

know that yet. It's too soon, but it was so incredibly cool. I could actually see the baby inside me. I mean, it didn't look too much like a baby yet, but it makes it even more real, you know. The doctor says I should be able to see even more next month."

He fell silent. For a minute, she almost thought they'd been disconnected.

"Danny?"

"I'm here," he said. "I was just thinking that I wish I'd been there, but that's crazy, huh? I don't have any right to be there."

It was exactly the response she'd hoped for, and it gave her the courage to go on. "It's your baby, too, no matter what," she told him emphatically. "I almost asked you to come with me, but, you know, after the way things went at Thanksgiving, I wasn't sure I should."

"I wish you had," he admitted, then sighed heavily. "This is such a mess, Mary Louise. I know I got exactly what I said I wanted, the chance to stay here and finish college without all that responsibility, but it doesn't seem right. I keep thinking about you going through this all alone, and it makes me crazy. I can't concentrate, anyway. Maybe I should just forget about college for now."

"No," she said sharply. "We decided —"

"*You* decided," he corrected. "I know you

did it for my sake, but it's not working out the way I thought it would. I can't just pretend everything's okay. Willie Ron was right. What kind of man lets his girl have his baby without marrying her? At the very least, the baby ought to have my name."

"Danny, it's okay. I understand. You need to finish college." She drew in a breath and added, "And I don't want to be married just for the baby's sake. If we ever do get married, it has to be because we're both ready and will try really hard to make it work."

"I think we should talk about this next time I'm home," he said. "Maybe we can find some sort of compromise."

"Like what?" she asked skeptically.

"I don't know, but there has to be something better than what we're doing. I'll call you when I'm coming home, okay? We'll get together and see what we can come up with."

Mary Louise didn't want to get her hopes up, only to have them dashed again. "Whatever," she said, faking indifference.

"I love you," he said quietly. " 'Bye."

"Oh, Danny," she whispered. Only after he'd hung up did she add, "I love you, too." Sometimes saying the words was just too painful.

Caleb knew he'd made a mess of things. Amanda was furious with him. The kids were totally confused. Big Max was slipping a bit more each day and was too blasted stubborn to reach out to the one person who meant something to him. It was enough of a disaster to make Caleb wonder if he hadn't gone into the wrong line of work. How was he supposed to help anyone with their spiritual needs when he couldn't keep his own life in order? He seemed to be failing everyone around him.

He'd prayed for guidance, but he knew in his heart that what happened next was going to depend on him doing some painful soul-searching of his own. He had to look back on his marriage and the reason it had fallen apart before he could begin to move on with Amanda the way he very much wanted to.

And by then it might be too late, he acknowledged candidly. There were too many secrets between them, and as a result she'd lost faith in him. He honestly couldn't say he blamed her, no matter how he'd tried to defend himself against her accusations of betrayal.

"You look as if you've had a tough day,"

Cord said when he found Caleb sitting in his office.

"Tough day, tough week," Caleb replied. "Everything's kind of blurring together."

"Want to talk about it?"

Caleb regarded him with amusement. "Not particularly. And something tells me you didn't come over here to listen to my problems."

"No," Cord agreed. "But I'm adaptable. Living with a woman like Dinah necessitates that."

Caleb grinned. "Yes, I imagine it does." He studied Cord thoughtfully. Maybe he could use some advice from this man who'd survived a few bumps in his *own* road to romance. "You two are really happy, aren't you?"

Cord's expression didn't register the kind of delight Caleb had anticipated. Instead, he seemed to be thinking over the question.

"Most of the time," Cord said eventually. "At the moment, we're at odds over how much work she ought to be doing with a baby on the way. I figure she'll end up in the hospital from overdoing it and I'll be right there beside her from stressing out."

Caleb laughed. "Then maybe you can use that time to sort out your differences."

Cord shook his head. "No, we'll just have

more time to argue over which one of us was right."

"With both of you being so stubborn, how *do* you work things out?" Caleb asked.

Cord studied him intently. "Is there some reason in particular you want to know?"

"Let's just say I'm mixed up with a couple of hardheads of my own."

"Amanda and Big Max, I assume."

Caleb regarded him with surprise. "You know about that?"

"Word gets around, especially when my wife, Maggie, Nadine and Amanda had an all-girls' night while Josh and I were out of town."

"Oh, brother," Caleb muttered. "How bad did Amanda make me look?"

"Let's just say you wouldn't win any popularity polls with that crowd right now," Cord teased. "Then again, they're all romantics, so in the end I think they're on your side."

Caleb shook his head, marveling at the way women's minds worked. "Good to know. Any advice?"

Cord leaned forward. "Here's the way I see it. You know Amanda's weak spot, right?"

"The children," Caleb said at once.

"Exactly. And those kids adore you. Use that."

"Isn't that sort of sneaky and underhanded?" Caleb asked.

"Do you want the woman or not?" Cord responded.

"Oh, I want her," Caleb admitted, ignoring all the very real questions about whether he could — or should — have her.

"Well, then . . ."

"I'll think about it," Caleb said, hating the idea that it might take sneaky and underhanded tactics to patch things up with a woman who deserved respect and admiration, to say nothing of a more straightforward approach. Of course, Amanda pretty much thought he was a sneak, anyway, so how much worse could things get?

Because he didn't want to think about using such questionable tactics, he changed the subject. "Why did you come over here in the first place, Cord? Don't tell me you were sent to scope out the enemy."

Cord chuckled. "No way. I try my best to decline that kind of mission. I'm here to talk about the new low-income housing project. George found some land. He's put in an offer and I'm fairly certain it will be accepted. Do you think we can get the volunteers to start working on donations of building supplies soon? We'll need to line up a crew, too. I don't want to get too far ahead of ourselves, but I don't want to waste time once the land deal goes through. If we have a mild winter, we might be able to get moving right after the holidays."

"I agree. I'll mention it in church on Sunday," Caleb promised. "Maybe we can get an organizational meeting set up for next Saturday. Can you be there?"

"Absolutely."

"And Josh?"

"I'll see that he's there, though I'm thinking that maybe I should bring Tommy Lee in on this. Josh is pretty tied up in Atlanta these days and I think Tommy Lee needs something to tackle on his own."

Caleb studied him thoughtfully. "You're talking about Dinah's brother, right?"

Cord nodded. "Tommy Lee Davis, right. He's turned into a real asset for Beaufort Construction. And of course, if Tommy Lee's in charge, it pretty much guarantees that Mrs. Davis will throw her heart into fund-raising for this."

"Speaking of sneaky," Caleb said, though this time the accusation was said with admiration.

"I do what I can," Cord acknowledged. "Now, let me get out of here. I haven't seen my wife all week. I need to see what sort of trouble she's managed to get herself into while I've been away. I'll be in touch to make sure we're on for next Saturday."

"Thanks, Cord."

After Cord had gone, Caleb went back to his musings about Amanda and Big Max. He'd literally run out of ideas for pushing the two of them back together short of telling her the truth, that her father had Alzheimer's. Maybe the time for that revelation was going to come sooner than he thought.

In the meantime, though, Cord's comment about getting to Amanda through the kids kept popping back into his head. Would it be so wrong, especially when he missed those kids every bit as much as he knew they missed him?

Okay, yes, it would be wrong. But he knew he was going to do it, anyway. He *had* made a promise to them that he wouldn't disappear from their lives. He didn't take that lightly. If that put him in proximity to Amanda, then that was just a very desirable bonus.

When Caleb turned up on Amanda's doorstep just before dinnertime on Friday, a part of her wanted to send him away. In fact, she wanted to scream and shout at him in a way that shocked her. She never let her temper get the better of her. And Caleb was the last man she'd ever expected to inspire such passionate fury.

But before she could utter any of the outraged words on the tip of her tongue, Susie caught sight of Caleb and screamed excitedly as she raced into the living room.

"Mr. Caleb, you came to see us!" she said, flinging herself into his arms and peppering his face with kisses.

Amanda heaved a resigned sigh and stepped aside to let him in. He gave her an apologetic look, but she didn't think there was much sincerity behind it. He probably counted on using the kids to get around her desire to keep him at arm's length.

Jimmy and Larry appeared just then, every bit as ecstatic as Susie to see Caleb.

"Can we play ball?" Jimmy asked. "I wanna learn to pitch."

"Then that's what we'll do," Caleb said, then quickly amended, "if it's okay with your mom."

"Of course," Amanda said, knowing she'd have a mutiny on her hands if she refused. "But only for a half hour. Dinner's almost ready."

"Can Mr. Caleb stay?" Susie asked. "Please!"

"Yeah, please, Mom," Larry said.

She exchanged a look with Caleb, hoping

he could interpret it. She was not happy about this end run of his. She added it to the list of reasons she had for wanting to scream.

"Fine," she said tightly. "He can stay."

She whirled around and headed for the kitchen before she exploded and said something in front of the kids she'd later regret.

Certain that Caleb would be wise enough to bypass the kitchen on his way outside, she was surprised when he appeared in the doorway.

"I'm sorry," he said.

"You seem to be sorry about a lot these days," she said, wishing that her heart didn't ache at the sight of him.

"I can't deny that," he agreed. "But I didn't mean to make you uncomfortable by showing up here. It's just that I made a promise to the kids. I didn't want to break my word."

"Which is the only reason I didn't toss you right back out of here on your backside," she retorted. "Next time, clear your visit with me ahead of time, okay?"

He nodded. "Are you ever going to forgive me, Amanda?"

She met his gaze. "I'm not entirely sure."

"What will it take to make up your mind?"

"Maybe a few less sneak attacks like tonight," she said.

He didn't look especially guilty. "Drastic times call for drastic measures."

"Which suggests you didn't mean a word of that apology a minute ago," she concluded.

"No, I meant it," he insisted. "I'm sorry it's come to this between us. You know I care about you, Amanda."

"You care about a lot of people. That's your job."

"It's not the same, and you know it," he said defensively.

"Oh? How is it so different?" she asked, then added with bitter sarcasm, "Oh, wait. I think I know. You would never betray them the way you did me."

He looked genuinely wounded by her accusation. "I didn't betray you," he repeated with barely disguised indignation. "I was trying to help two people I care about, two people who also care about each other, even if they *are* too stubborn to admit it. That's not a crime."

"Maybe not in a court of law," she agreed.

"But in your eyes it is," he surmised.

"Yes."

"Which brings me back to my question. What can I do to make things right?"

"Promise never to bring up my father's name again," she suggested, despite her resolution to give honest consideration to making peace with Big Max.

"I can't do that," he said.

"Why not?"

"Because I can't."

She shrugged, her heart thudding dully. "Then I guess there's nothing more to say, is there? Go on outside. I'm sure the kids are getting impatient."

"Amanda —"

"Just go, Caleb."

He hesitated, then sighed. "This isn't over, you know. Not between you and your father. And not between you and me."

She was very much afraid he was right on both counts.

Max was feeling restless and bored. He'd had way too much of his own company for the past couple of days. For the first time since he'd gone into retirement, he regretted not staying on some of the corporate boards he'd chaired over the years. He'd lost touch with too many old friends.

He was also missing Amanda more than he had any right to. Maybe that's what happened when a man saw his days dwindling down. He thought about the mistakes he'd made and the people he'd hurt and started wishing things could be different. Or maybe it was just Caleb picking at that particular scab every time he got the chance.

Every once in a while Max yearned just to catch a glimpse of his daughter and grandchildren. Caleb's secondhand reports weren't enough. The only reason he hadn't acted on his impulse was his fear of being caught. It would be damned humiliating if Amanda saw him riding by her house, checking things out like some sort of Peeping Tom.

Tonight, though, he couldn't seem to shake off the impulse. It was already dark, but not yet late enough that she and those kids of hers would be in bed. He might be able to spot them inside the house without her being any the wiser. The more he considered the idea, the better he liked it. Besides, the drive alone would do him good. He needed a change of scenery.

Glad that the Alzheimer's hadn't gotten so bad yet that he'd been forced to give up driving, he grabbed his keys and headed into town. Thanks to Caleb and to the copy of the deed he still held in his safe, he knew just where the house was located. Plus, he'd driven by it from time to time while it was being built, always when he knew Amanda wasn't anywhere around. He'd wanted to be sure they weren't taking any shortcuts on the construction. He probably knew the layout of the place as well as she did.

When he turned the corner onto her block, he spotted Caleb's car out front. He cruised to a stop and sat staring at it. He wasn't entirely sure how he felt about those two being close. Nothing in his conversations with Caleb had suggested there was anything inappropriate going on, but Max worried about Amanda being hurt again. Folks in Charleston loved to talk, and nothing would stir up a scandal like the notion of a minister having himself a fling with a member of his congregation. Maybe he needed to warn Caleb about that. Not that Amanda would appreciate him meddling in her life yet again. But no matter what a mess he'd made of things with her and Bobby, no matter how deep the hard feelings ran on both sides, he'd never stopped worrying about her. Not for a minute.

In the meantime, though, if he pulled up just a little ways down the block, he might be able to get a clear view of what was going on inside that house. He parked by the curb across the street and watched. Amanda came into view and his heart lurched. She looked more and more like her mama every day. Margaret had been a beauty with her cloud of dark hair and wide smile. Amanda had the same hair, the same sparkle in her eyes, the same lithe figure. Looking at her as she picked up toys, he was overcome by a wave of nostalgia that almost made him gasp. He couldn't even say for sure what he was missing most — his beloved wife or his daughter. He just knew it was painful to sit here so close with someone he loved beyond his reach.

Fumbling with the ignition, he finally restarted the car and pulled away from the curb. He needed to get home, back to the familiarity of his own life. Coming here had been a mistake.

He went to the end of the block and turned, drove a few more blocks and turned again, his mind on Amanda and on Margaret, confusing them a little as the images came and went.

He turned onto another road and looked around. Nothing looked familiar. He'd lived in Charleston all his life and he didn't recognize any of this. Shaking, he pulled to the side of the road and cut the engine. With all those turns, if he'd done them right, he should have been back out on Meeting Street. He could have gotten home from there. Instead, he seemed to be in a strange part of town.

"Come on, old man, think!" he muttered

aloud, but no matter how hard he tried, he couldn't figure out where he was or how to get home.

He reached into his pocket for his cell phone. He'd seen no need for it when he'd gotten the stupid thing, but Caleb had insisted. He'd even programmed his own cell phone number on speed dial. Scared and filled with uncertainty and impotent rage, Max pushed the button and waited.

"Hello?" Caleb said, his voice filled with worry.

"It's Max."

"I know," he said. "Where are you? Is something wrong?"

"I'm not sure."

"Not sure about what?"

"Where I am," Max said, hating the admission of weakness. "I took a drive and I can't seem to find my way back home."

"It's okay," Caleb soothed. "Where did you set out to go?"

"I drove by Amanda's and I saw your car. I remember that much. Then I took a couple of turns and nothing looked familiar."

"Are you parked now?"

"Yes."

"Stay put then. It's okay, Max. I'll find you."

"Don't tell Amanda, okay?"

Caleb hesitated a moment too long.

Max swore. "Don't tell her, Caleb. I mean it."

"We'll talk about it later. Right now, just sit tight and wait for me."

"Since I have no idea where to go, I imagine I'll be right here when you turn up," Max retorted.

He snapped the cell phone closed, then rested his head against the back of the seat. Once again the images of Margaret came to him. This time he knew for sure that's who it was, because he felt strangely comforted. In fact, it had been a long time since he'd felt so at peace.

12

"What was that about?" Amanda asked, studying Caleb curiously. The call had obviously upset him. He looked anxious and distracted.

"An emergency," he responded vaguely. "I have to go."

"Is there anything I can do?" she asked at once.

Caleb gave her a considering look, then finally shook his head. "No, I need to handle it, but thanks. I'm sorry I can't stay for dinner. Will you explain to the kids? Tell them I'll make it up to them soon."

"Of course."

She walked him to the door, thinking once more about what his life must be like, how many times it was disrupted by someone in need of comfort. Only a truly selfless person could spend so much time and energy on others and so little time on his own needs. It made her appreciate the time he spent with them all the more.

Of course, just because she admired Caleb's kindness and dedication, it didn't mean she wasn't just as furious with him now as she'd been earlier. One of those people he'd been comforting behind her back was her father.

"I won't forget that you and I need to have a talk," she said to him as he stepped outside.

He gave her a rueful smile. "Never doubted it for a minute. I wouldn't leave if this weren't really important. I hope you believe that."

"Of course I do. I never thought you were a coward, Caleb."

"Just a traitor," he murmured.

Amanda shrugged. "If the shoe fits . . ."

To her surprise he looked even more uncomfortable than she would have expected. Understanding suddenly dawned.

"Caleb, does this emergency have something to do with my father?" she asked.

He carefully avoided her gaze. "I can't get into it now," he said, brushing a distracted kiss across her cheek. "I'll be in touch."

"It does, doesn't it?" she called after him. "Damn it, Caleb, what are you keeping from me now?"

"Later," he said, and fled, leaving her to wonder if it would always be this way between them.

If there was a choice to be made, would Caleb always choose her father over her? Would he always regard her with disappointment for refusing to reconcile with the man who'd hurt her so deeply, while he . . . what? Gave her father a pass for his bad behavior? It hurt to think how much her father was capable of damaging her relationship with yet another man.

If Caleb were pressed to make a choice, at this point Amanda wasn't entirely sure where his loyalties would lie, and that hurt more than she could bear. Something told her, though, that the day was quickly coming when she would find out.

Amanda spent the whole night tossing and turning, wondering where Caleb had gone, whether it was, indeed, her father who'd had some sort of emergency. Surely if it was and it had been anything serious, Caleb would have told her. He wouldn't have deliberately kept her in the dark, even if he'd been sure that she would claim lack of interest.

She recalled the question Nadine had pressed her to answer. How would she feel if her father was ill? Or if he'd been in an accident? She tried to imagine the strong, vital man she'd known getting old, getting frail. She couldn't. Big Max was indomitable. He'd probably outlive them all out of pure cussedness.

But what if he didn't? How would she feel if she never had the chance to say goodbye? She didn't know. She honestly didn't know. But if that were true, why was there this ache in the region of her heart?

She was driving the kids to school in the morning, when she saw her father's car parked haphazardly a few blocks from the house. There was no mistaking it. Not only had he driven that same model of car for years in the exact same color, but the vanity BIG MAX license plate was a dead give-away.

Why on earth was it parked here, though? Her father had no reason to be in this part of town. Puzzled, she toyed with the possibilities as she dropped the kids off, until at last it came to her. Big Max had been this close to her house last night to spy on her. And Caleb had known it. Maybe the car had broken down and he'd called Caleb to rescue him. Or maybe he'd felt ill. Whatever the reason, Caleb had kept it from her. Just as she'd feared, when he'd had to make a choice, she had lost.

Filled with renewed fury, she whipped her car around and headed for the church, certain Caleb would be in his office by now. She'd hoped to run a few errands on her way to work, but this was more important. They needed to put an end to this whole secrecy thing around her father.

She'd worked up a full head of steam by the time she reached the church. Storming into Caleb's office, she flung open the door with such force it banged against the wall. Caleb's gaze shot up to meet hers. He sat back and regarded her evenly.

"Good morning to you, too," he said, amusement threading through his voice.

"Don't you dare act as if everything's just hunky-dory, when you know perfectly well you've been up to your eyeballs in keeping my father's secrets again."

"Have I really?"

He sounded so blasted calm, she wanted to hurl something at him. She didn't understand it. Caleb had always inspired serenity in her, at least until lately.

"What was my father doing in my neighborhood last night?" she demanded. "Was he there to spy on me?"

Caleb looked vaguely surprised and just a little alarmed by her question.

"What makes you think he was? Or that I

know anything about it?"

"Let me count the ways," she responded tartly. "You get a call from someone and the call obviously upsets you. You refuse to tell me a single thing about it. The pattern seems amazingly familiar, doesn't it?"

"That doesn't mean it had anything to do with your father."

"Oh, wait," she said as if it had just occurred to her. "Did I forget to mention that I found his car not five blocks from my house?"

Caleb winced at that. "You're sure?"

"Vanity plates," she said succinctly. "Now, give it up, Caleb. What the hell is going on?" Even as the profanity crossed her lips, she gazed heavenward and murmured, "Forgive me."

"I can't talk about it," he said.

"Can't or won't?"

"Same thing. I made a promise to your father."

"And what about the promises you've made to me? Or to the kids? What about all the apologies for betraying me once before? Yet here you are doing it again."

"Last night wasn't about you, Amanda," he said reasonably. "I had a call and I did what I had to do. It hardly matters whether it was your father or another parishioner."

"It does to me. Why won't you just tell me if that call was from my father and what it was about?"

He leveled a gaze directly into her eyes. "Would you want me telling him your business?"

She faltered at that.

He nodded. "I didn't think so."

She sank into the chair opposite him. "This can't keep happening," she said softly. She raised her gaze to meet his. "I thought something special was happening between us, Caleb."

"So did I," he said, then added with a touch of defiance, "It *is* happening."

She shook her head. "No, it will never happen, not with my father in the middle of it. He destroyed my relationship with one man I loved. I won't let him do it again."

"He can only mess up things between us if we let him," Caleb argued.

"You're right," she said, feeling defeated. "I guess I'm letting him, because I can't do this anymore. Please stay away, Caleb. You've done more for me than I ever had any right to expect and I'm grateful, but I can't have you in my life if you're going to be a constant reminder of my father. And if we're constantly fighting over this, it will only upset the kids. It's better to cut the ties now, make a clean break of it."

She got the words out because she had to, but sobs clogged her throat. She rose slowly and headed for the door, unable to look back, knowing she would cry if she did. She wasn't sure which hurt more, knowing how close she and Caleb had come to having something incredible or knowing that once again it was her father who'd ruined it for her.

Caleb watched Amanda walk out the door of his office and knew he had a choice to make. Like it or not, he was in the middle between these two, and he had to make a decision. He couldn't be fair to both of them.

Maybe in breaking his promise to Max and telling Amanda what she needed to hear, he would be doing Big Max a favor in the end. After last night's incident, Caleb had accepted that the secret couldn't be kept much longer, anyway. The timetable was moving up and the decision was going to be unilateral. Max would just have to deal with it.

"Amanda, wait," he called after her urgently. "Please, don't go."

She turned back slowly and he saw the tears spilling down her cheeks. "Oh, God, please don't cry," he whispered, going to her and pulling her into his arms. She held herself stiffly. "Come on now, don't cry," he soothed. "This will all sort itself out."

"I don't see how," she said, finally relaxing in his embrace.

Caleb made peace with his decision. He could only pray he was making it for the right reasons.

"Can you take the day off?" he asked.

She regarded him with surprise. "What?"

He grinned at her scandalized expression. "You know, play hooky with me. Can you do it?"

"Are you crazy?" she asked incredulously. "That would be totally irresponsible."

"I doubt the world will grind to a halt if you and I bow out and take some time for ourselves," he said wryly. "It's important, Amanda, or I wouldn't ask. Come on, let's be impulsive and do something crazy for once. We're both way too set in our ways."

She studied him as if he were spouting blasphemy, then slowly nodded. "You're right," she said at last. "I haven't done one single thing just for the fun of it for ages now." She eyed him with suddenly sparkling eyes. "What are we going to do?"

"We're going to pick up a picnic and take a drive," he said. "There's cold weather predicted for the weekend and this might be our last chance for a while."

"I could make sandwiches," she offered.

"No, you could not," he said. "We're having a holiday. That means no work for either one of us. You call your boss and I'll call Mirabella's and ask her if she can pack a picnic basket for us. Bread, cheese, wine and whatever decadent dessert she can come up with. How does that sound?"

"Romantic," Amanda admitted.

He grinned. "Good, then I got it right. Make that call to the boutique."

He ducked out of his office to place the call to the restaurant while Amanda used his phone. When he came back in, she was standing there with a bemused expression.

"What?" he inquired.

"Joanna told me it was about time I did something impetuous," she said with a note of wonder in her voice. "I thought she'd be annoyed."

He laughed. "See, even your boss thinks you're too stodgy. Come on, let's get out of here, before somebody catches up with us." He made a dramatic production of removing his cell phone and leaving it on his desk.

Once they were on the road, Caleb stopped by the restaurant and picked up the picnic, then headed out of town.

"Where are we going?" Amanda asked,

though she didn't seem to care enough to open her eyes and look around. She seemed content to rest her head against the seat while he drove wherever he wanted.

"Isle of Palms," he said. "I think we both need a real change."

She smiled. "I haven't been to the beach in ages. This'll be fun."

Caleb doubted she would feel that way if she knew what he was about to divulge to her, but he let her have this moment of anticipation. In fact, he did his best to keep things light while they walked barefoot along the cool sand, letting the waves chase them. When they tired of walking, they ate at a picnic table just beyond the dunes, the sound of the ocean their background music. The air was mild for early December and filled with a salty tang.

"This is heaven," Amanda said contentedly as she sipped the last of her wine, her eyes closed, her face turned up to the sun. "I haven't had a totally carefree day like this in a long time. Thanks for insisting we do this, Caleb. You always seem to know what I need, sometimes even before I recognize it myself."

"You weren't being so complimentary earlier," he reminded her lightly.

She winced. "Maybe I overreacted. I have

a tendency to do that when I'm feeling out of control of my life. And any mention of my father always pushes my buttons."

"To be honest, you didn't overreact," Caleb admitted. "I'm afraid you got it exactly right. There are more things I've been keeping from you. I was doing it because your father insisted on it, but I think you need to know. The time for lies, half truths and omissions is over."

She stiffened at that and the last faint hint of laughter in her eyes died. "Don't do this, Caleb," she pleaded. "Don't spoil the day by dragging my father back into it."

"I don't think I have a choice," he said. "Not even if both of you wind up furious with me for interfering."

He'd repeatedly tried nudging open the door to a reconciliation, but Amanda had just as emphatically slammed it shut each and every time. Now he knew he'd simply have to kick it down. Those two had to mend fences, not just because Max needed Amanda in his life, but because she would forever regret it if she and her father never had the chance to make things right between them. Continuing to keep Max's secret would cost Caleb Amanda's respect, just as surely as revealing it might cost him Max's trust.

"Yes, you do," she whispered. "You do have a choice."

"No, Amanda, not anymore. I need to talk to you about him," he said quietly.

She reached for the paper plates and started to rise from the table. "I need to put these in the trash before they blow all over the place," she said, her gaze averted.

He put his hand over hers and kept her from moving away. "Don't run from this, Amanda. Hear me out." She stilled, but didn't face him. "Amanda, please. You trust me, don't you?"

"More than anyone," she admitted, albeit reluctantly. "At least, I did."

"Then you know I wouldn't press you on this if it weren't important. Look at me, Amanda."

He waited until she finally faced him and met his eyes. "You need to see your father," he said flatly. "Now."

Her hands trembled visibly at that and she set the trash back down. A breeze caught the plates and napkins and scattered them just as she'd feared, but she didn't seem to notice. She regarded him with dismay.

"What do you mean I need to see him?" she asked, her voice shaky. "You make it sound so urgent, as if something's wrong."

"Something is," he told her.

She swallowed hard. "He's ill?" she asked, as if trying to grapple with the concept.

Caleb could sympathize. He, too, had known Max when he was strong and vital. It was hard to see him as he'd been last night, uncertain and shaky, and reconcile him with that once-confident man.

"Caleb, tell me. Is my father sick?"

He nodded.

"Cancer?" she asked, her voice barely a whisper. "Is he dying?"

"No, in some ways this is worse," Caleb said gently. "He has Alzheimer's."

Though her lips stayed in a firm, unforgiving line, her eyes welled with tears. "I see," she said tightly.

"Do you? Do you understand that you must see him now?"

"No," she said stubbornly. Only her visible trembling betrayed the fact that she was far less certain than she seemed. "I can't," she insisted. "I won't. Not even now. Besides, he probably doesn't want me anywhere around him. He made you promise not to tell me, right? There you go. He still doesn't want to see me any more than I want to see him."

Caleb refused to let her off that easily. He tried to hammer the point home, make her grasp what lay ahead. "Do you know there will come a time when he won't recognize you? When all the years of love you shared will be forgotten? Don't you think you should recapture those feelings, those memories, while you can?"

He watched as his words sank in, as she envisioned her father slipping from her forever, not with the quick finality of death, but bit by bit. He could see the agony in her eyes.

"Why is it up to me?" she asked plaintively. "He pushed me away, not once, but twice."

"I know it doesn't seem fair, but that's really not the issue now, is it? One of you has to make the first move, and given his pride, I think it will have to be you."

"Why?"

"Because Max is terrified you'll only turn to him out of pity or, worse, that you won't come back at all. He knows how badly he hurt you, Amanda. He knows he doesn't deserve your forgiveness, but he wants it desperately. You have to see that. He's been reduced to sneaking over to your house just to catch a glimpse of you. That's why his car was in your neighborhood this morning."

Her eyes were filled with uncertainty. "I don't know if I can do this, Caleb. He tore my heart out. He rejected my children. How can I forgive him for that?"

"You can, because you know in your heart that it's the right thing to do. Forgiveness is always the right choice."

"I think you're expecting too much from me."

"No, I'm not," he said confidently. "You're the strongest woman I know. Look at the heartache you've weathered."

"Lots of women are single moms," she said, dismissing the importance of one of her greatest achievements.

"But how many have fought their way back from despair?" he countered. "How many have been buried in debt and struggled to make restitution for every penny of it, even beyond what was required by the court? How many have protected their children from their father's folly and kept their love for him as innocent and pure as it ought to be?"

She gave him a wry look as he heaped on the praise. "Probably more than you or I know. I'm not that unique, Caleb. You seem to have a bias where I'm concerned."

"No question about it," he agreed. "But I also see quite clearly that you're strong enough to do what needs to be done for your father."

"And what is that exactly?"

"Love him, Amanda. Just love him the way

264

you once did, without conditions or reservations."

The tears that had clung to her lashes spilled down her cheeks. "I always have. It wasn't enough before. What makes you think it will be now?"

"Because it's time."

"And if he turns me away again?"

"Then you keep coming back," Caleb said. "He will say things to try to drive you away, Amanda. This is Max, after all. You simply have to tune him out. Hear what he's not saying, instead."

"Which is?"

"That he's scared and lonely and that he misses you and needs you." He reached for her hand and held it tightly. "Isn't that really what counts, what's in his heart?"

"Sometimes people need to *hear* the words, Caleb."

He gave her a smile edged with sorrow. "And sometimes you simply have to take them on faith."

"I don't have your kind of faith," she argued.

"Then lean on me," he told her. "I have enough for both of us."

13

Now that Caleb had persuaded Amanda to see her father — at least he hoped he had — he needed to prepare Max for the visit. He could have left it to chance, but he was convinced that wouldn't be fair to either one of them. No, he'd started this. It was only right that he do all he could to smooth the way. It would help if he happened to catch Max in a mellow state of mind.

Unfortunately, as it turned out, Max didn't seem to be in any mood to listen to anything Caleb had to say this morning. He'd had a restless night and when Caleb arrived, he was busy berating Jessie for everything from the pulp in his orange juice to the weather.

Jessie ushered Caleb into the kitchen to get his coffee, then made a face at Max's continuing tirade. "You're on your own with him. He's being even more impossible than usual."

266

"Any particular reason?"

She lowered her voice. "He's scared, but you never heard that from me." In a louder tone, she said, "I have cleaning to do. Help yourself to some of that pecan coffee cake while it's still warm. And there's more coffee when you're ready. You're going to need it."

"I heard that," Max hollered from the dining room.

"I meant for you, too," Jessie retorted.

Caleb warred with himself over the coffee cake, but it was a lost cause. He cut a large slice, poured himself a cup of coffee, then went to join Max. He gave the old man a chiding look. "Given the way you treat her, you're lucky that woman doesn't quit."

"What do you care?" Max growled. "Unless you're worried you'll lose access to all her baked goods." He pointedly eyed the coffee cake.

"That's part of it of course," Caleb acknowledged unrepentantly. "Then, again, I think she'd keep me supplied, anyway. At least I show her my appreciation."

"And I don't? I pay her a bloody fortune to keep up with this place."

"But not enough to make her take your abuse," Caleb chided. "She does that because she cares about you."

Max scowled at him, then sighed. "Okay,

you're right. Fortunately Jessie knows my bark is worse than my bite. She gives me a lot of latitude, especially these days."

"Feeling sorry for you?" Caleb inquired, knowing how much that must grate.

Max nodded. "Can't say I like it."

"Few people would."

"Then you might want to rearrange your face, as well. You've got that pitying expression back on it again," Max grumbled.

Caleb laughed. "Sorry. I'll see what I can do." He forced an exaggerated smile. "Is that any better?"

"You're not a bit funny," Max said, then gave him a hard look. "What brings you out here this morning, anyway? You still checking up on me after what happened the other night? I don't need you hovering. I get enough of that from Jessie. The woman hardly goes home to sleep these days. I think she's afraid I'll go off and leave something on the stove and burn the house down."

"Max, have you left anything on the stove?" Caleb asked, not even trying to disguise his concern. "Is Jessie right to be worried?"

"No, but there's a first time for everything. I've come to expect the unexpected when it comes to my memory these days." He frowned at Caleb. "It's not so bad, though, that I don't recall telling you to stop hovering."

"Sorry if my visits are getting on your nerves, but get used to it," Caleb replied. "I don't intend to stop coming around just because you're cranky and determined to run me off." He studied Max intently. "*Have* there been any more incidents like the one the other night?"

"Must have been a fluke," Max said with bravado. "I've been feeling fine ever since."

"That's great," Caleb said. "Did you mention it to Doc Mullins?"

"Didn't see any need to since I seem to have all my marbles about me now."

"Max, the doctor needs to know when these things happen," Caleb said. "There may be something he can do."

"He's already got me on every drug out there, including some experimental thing that'll probably destroy some vital organ if I don't die of something else first."

"You certainly are in a cheery mood this morning," Caleb commented. "Maybe my news will perk you up." He figured that was an optimistic assessment, at best.

"What news is that?" Max asked suspiciously.

"Amanda's thinking about coming out

here for a visit," Caleb said, his tone deliberately casual.

"Why the hell would she do that?" Max demanded, pinning his gaze on Caleb's face.

"Maybe because she wants to try one more time to make peace with the father she loves," Caleb said.

"Or maybe because some fool doesn't know enough to keep his mouth shut," Max suggested, his tone scathing. "That's it, isn't it? You blabbed something that wasn't yours to share. It's a sad day when a preacher's word doesn't count for a damn thing."

"So what if I did tell her?" Caleb replied, only a bit defensively. "Isn't the important thing that she's willing to make an overture to settle things between you?"

"Out of pity!" Max shouted, slapping his hand down on the table so hard the coffee cups bounced in their saucers. "I don't want Amanda here staring at me with that same sad look Jessie gets in her eyes. I thought you understood that."

"I do, Max. Believe me, I do. But you need your daughter now. And she needs to be here for you."

"Says who?"

"Says me," Caleb responded. "I think I know you both pretty well."

"If you knew me half as well as you think

you do, you'd have kept your nose out of this. I'm tempted to toss you out of here and ban you from ever coming back," Max said, though the threat sounded halfhearted.

Max's expression suddenly brightened. "You said she's thinking about coming," he said. "That means you don't know for sure."

"No, I can't swear to it," Caleb admitted. "But I wanted you to be prepared."

"I doubt she'll come," Max said, sounding as if he was afraid to get his hopes up. He seemed defenseless and vulnerable.

"I think she will," Caleb told him with more confidence, praying he was right. "Don't blow this chance, Max," he urged. "Don't push her away if she comes. Welcome her. Tell her you're sorry about everything that happened and put it behind you once and for all. Grab on to every second you can have with her. Get to know your grandkids. They're terrific. You'll love them. And they need you in their lives. They need a sense of family history and you can give them that. There are two little boys and a little girl who would benefit greatly from knowing their grandfather."

"Seems to me, Amanda's been pretty determined to make them O'Learys. She doesn't give two figs about their Maxwell genes," Max said bitterly.

"Maybe because your mule-headed attitude has made her less than proud of them," Caleb suggested.

"Then why now?"

"Because it's one of those pivotal moments we all come to from time to time. You faced one back when she wanted to marry Bobby O'Leary and look how that turned out. Now's another one. You can get Amanda back into your life and you can spend time with your grandchildren, if you don't let that pride of yours stand in the way."

"What do they need with me? They have you, don't they?" Max asked, his expression sly. "Seems to me you're around there a lot. That's where you were the other night when I called you."

"I'm not their grandfather," Caleb said, avoiding the trap Max was setting for him.

"What's your interest in all this?" Max persisted. "What do you get out of it?"

"Nothing more than the satisfaction of seeing the two of you back in each other's lives the way you should be. Family's important. It shouldn't be tossed aside."

"Sounds awfully damned noble to me," Max said. "You sure there's not some other payoff?"

"Such as?"

"I'm not sure, but I'll figure out what

you're up to, Caleb, make no mistake about that. And when I do, you'll pay for your meddling."

Max's gaze suddenly narrowed suspiciously, as if he'd just been struck by a less-than-pleasant thought. "You want that house of hers for somebody else now, is that it? You figure she'll move in here with those kids and free up the house? Remember, I bought that land. It's in Amanda's name, free and clear."

"Believe me, I remember that. That's when I knew you still had a heart. As for wanting to give it to somebody else, the thought never crossed my mind," Caleb said truthfully. "I want you two speaking again. I don't want you under the same roof — something tells me that wouldn't go well, at least not for very long. Besides, Amanda loves that house. She's happy there. Why would she want to move in here again, especially with you being as cantankerous as you're being this morning?"

Max regarded him with blatant skepticism. He gestured around them. His dining room with its formal antique table, ten matching chairs and expansive sideboard was almost as big as Amanda's whole house.

"You think that little cracker box of hers compares to this?" Max scoffed.

"Not in size certainly, but I think she views that *cracker box,* as you call it, as home," Caleb said. "And it's within her means. She doesn't have to rely on anyone else to pay for it. Independence means a lot to your daughter after everything she's been through. Stop fussing, Max. She's not interested in some grudging handout from you."

"Then I'll ask you again, why would she want to see me after all this time and after everything I did to make her life miserable?"

"You're her father," Caleb said simply. "That counts for a lot."

Max sighed heavily. "I've been a damned poor one for a lot of years now," he admitted with rare candor. There was even a hint of regret in his voice.

"Then you have a lot to make up for, don't you?" Caleb said mildly. "Do it while you can, Max. Don't let this chance slip away."

He stood up and gave the old man's shoulder a squeeze. "Just tell her you love her. In the end that's all that really matters."

He prayed that Max could utter the words and that Amanda would be ready to hear them. A lot was riding on that, for them and for him. If there was another blowup, another rejection, he suspected he would be the one they'd both hate for forcing the issue and putting them through it.

■ ■ ■ ■

Filled with mixed emotions, Amanda had driven along the road to her father's house three times since Caleb had told her about the Alzheimer's. And three times she'd turned around and driven back home without even reaching the winding, tree-lined driveway.

Ironically, what should have gotten easier with practice kept getting harder. She knew if she didn't turn into the driveway soon, she might never do it. She'd almost convinced herself that she'd be wasting her breath and her time. Only a nagging image of Caleb's disappointment had kept her going back after the first time.

After each aborted trip, she read a little more about Alzheimer's. The cold, hard facts of it terrified her. If she was scared, her father must be quaking, envisioning a time when he would be in his own private world and dependent on others for his care. For a man who'd always been so proud, so well respected and strong, it would be the height of humiliation to be reduced to that dependency.

She was sitting on the sofa at home, surrounded by books and pamphlets, chastising herself for her third cowardly retreat from his house, when Susie crawled into her lap.

"Are you crying, Mama?" Susie asked, patting Amanda's damp cheek.

Surprised, Amanda wiped away the tears. "Why, yes, I guess I am."

"How come?"

"I'm just a little sad," she admitted. "But it's nothing for you to worry about."

"Jimmy says it's because our granddaddy is sick," Susie told her, then regarded her with confusion. "I didn't even know we had a granddaddy."

Amanda was floored, not just because Jimmy knew so much, but because Susie sounded so wistful. She supposed it was natural enough for her children to be curious about their relatives and she'd never denied that they had a grandfather living nearby, but she certainly hadn't said much about him, either. Maybe that had been a mistake. Or maybe it had been a desperate act of self-protection.

"Tell me about him," Susie begged. "Missy Dandridge says her grandpa smells like pipe tobacco, but my friend Billy says his gives him candy whenever he comes to visit." She beamed at the thought. "I'd like that."

Amanda chuckled. "I'm sure you would, since your mean ole mom never gives you any candy."

"You give me some," Susie said fairly. "But I really, really *love* candy, 'specially chocolate."

"I thought Nadine had been sneaking chocolate to you," Amanda said.

Susie's eyes widened. "You know about that?"

"I know everything," Amanda said. "You and your brothers need to remember that."

Susie scrambled off the sofa, her interest in her grandfather forgotten for now. "I better tell Jimmy and Larry."

"I think your brothers learned that lesson a long time ago," Amanda said. "But it certainly won't hurt to remind them."

Relieved, she watched Susie leave, then picked up a photo of her father that she'd kept tucked away among a few other mementos of the life she'd left behind when she'd married Bobby O'Leary. This picture had been taken on his wedding day. He'd been a tall, handsome man, his hair as dark as hers and just as curly and unruly. It had given him a rakish, faintly dangerous look. She realized now that it was that same look that had drawn her to Bobby. How ironic! And how surprising that she hadn't realized it till just now.

She smiled at the image in the picture. It was little wonder her mother had fallen for him. A young William Maxwell had had the broad-shouldered strength that appealed to many women, a size that made them feel both fragile and protected.

To a scared little motherless girl that solidity had meant safety and security. The stubbornness and arrogance that went along with it had become clear only when she'd tried to break free.

"Oh, Daddy," she whispered, fighting the rise of tears. "Why couldn't you have trusted me? Bobby was a good man. If he hadn't been trying so hard to prove himself to you, maybe things would have turned out differently."

Of course, that was something they would never know. And continuing to blame her father for choices Bobby had made was pointless. Caleb was right. The past was over. The only thing left was now, and perhaps a different future, if she could gather the courage to face it.

Was it possible to recapture the sort of relationship she and her father had once had? Was it possible that he could be the kind of grandfather her kids deserved, one who tucked candy in his pockets, and spoiled them, and gave them well-meaning advice they'd most likely ignore? Could they have all that, at least for a time?

A part of Amanda wanted to believe it was possible. Caleb certainly believed it was, and he hadn't led her astray yet. She wanted to let go of the hate and anger and reach out, but she was terrified to let go of those powerful, familiar emotions and risk having her heart broken again.

The only way to know for sure would be to try. She knew if she didn't, Caleb would be disappointed in her. More important, she would be disappointed in herself. If Max weren't sick, perhaps she could drift along and see how things played out, but there was an urgency now she couldn't ignore. One day — perhaps even sooner than she knew — it would be too late.

She gathered up the pamphlets and books on Alzheimer's and stacked them on the table beside the sofa. Instead of tucking away the photo, though, she laid it on top, then gently touched a finger to the image.

"I'll try, Daddy," she promised. "Please, please don't make me regret it."

It was only a few days till Christmas and Max was sitting on the porch, shaded from the unrelenting afternoon sun, but not out of its surprising heat, when the small, well-used car rolled to a stop in front of the house. His heart beat unsteadily when he recognized it as the pitiful heap that Amanda had been driving ever since Bobby's death. The icy shield that had protected his heart for years now splintered and left him feeling vulnerable and uneasy.

So, he thought, she'd come, after all. He'd almost given up hoping that Caleb had gotten it right.

For the longest time they both sat where they were, him in the rocker that he'd favored for decades, her in a car that looked as if it were held together by rust and a prayer. Just when he was beginning to wonder if she'd changed her mind, she opened the door, climbed out and stood beside the car, the door a shield between them.

"Daddy," she said, her voice thick.

"Amanda." There was so much more he wanted to say, so much emotion he needed to convey, but he was taking his cues from her. He hadn't been this terrified years ago when he'd asked Margaret to marry him and spent what seemed like an eternity waiting for her to answer.

"It's hot out," she said at last. "Shouldn't you be inside?"

He fought a grin. So they were going to make small talk, after all. It was just the way he'd have done it, too, pretended it hadn't been a year or more since their last heated exchange and a decade since the one before that.

"Charleston's weather is unpredictable," he replied, matching her tone. "Nothing new in that. I'm used to it. I'd rather catch a breeze out here than be shut up in that blasted air-conditioning inside." He eyed her cautiously. "Jessie made some iced tea. You want some?"

"I could use a glass," she said. "It's a long drive out here and my car doesn't have air-conditioning."

"Well, come on up here, then," he said impatiently. "Don't expect me to bring it to you."

Her lips twitched. "No, I certainly wouldn't expect that," she said, closing the car door, then slowly climbing the front steps as if she still didn't quite trust her welcome.

Truth be told, Max wasn't sure of it, either. He didn't know what had brought her here, not really. Was it Caleb breaking his vow of silence about Max's illness? Did she pity him? Or was it simply time to call a truce? Maybe she'd figured she better make peace now while she could wrangle her way back into his will. He didn't want to believe that last one, but he couldn't be certain. The Amanda he'd raised hadn't been the least bit greedy, but maybe hard times had changed her.

Not knowing for sure why Amanda had come couldn't prevent Max from drinking in the sight of her. She looked good, especially given all she'd been through. The main difference he noticed was a trace of edginess, a brittleness that suggested she'd come through tough times and wasn't yet convinced they were behind her. Or maybe she was just anticipating the worst from him. He'd certainly given her reason to have those kind of doubts.

His hand shook as he handed her the tea, lemon and no sugar, the way he knew she liked it. Her fingers grazed his and for an instant her gaze flew to meet his.

Max sighed, suddenly feeling at peace. Perhaps it didn't matter why she'd come. Maybe the only thing that mattered was she had.

"I'm glad you stopped by," he said quietly, remembering Caleb's admonition to welcome her and not do anything that might send her fleeing. He braced himself, then said what was in his heart. "I've missed you, Amanda."

She met his gaze, clearly startled. Then, to his shock she blinked rapidly, fighting tears.

"I've missed you, too," she whispered, her voice choked.

Before he could rejoice in the wonder of

that, she stood up suddenly, the glass slipping from her fingers. It broke when it hit
the porch floor, sending glass and tea splat-
tering everywhere. Shocked, she stared at it,
then reached for a handful of napkins from
the tray beside him.

"I'm sorry," she said, mopping up the
mess with jerky movements.

"Stop it," Max ordered. "Leave it,
Amanda. It doesn't matter. Jessie will take
care of it. That's what she's here for. Just sit
back down."

She rose awkwardly, then regarded him
with a sad expression. "I can't do this," she
said, looking miserable. "I'm sorry, Daddy. I
just can't do this."

"Do what?" he asked, bewildered.

"I'm sorry, I have to go," she said, which
explained nothing.

Before he could ask what the devil had
gotten into her, before he could utter the
plea that was forming on his lips, she had
fled down the steps and into her car. The engine sputtered, and even from a distance
Max could tell Amanda was near tears, but
then the engine caught and she jerked the
gear shift and sent the car skidding on the
gravel driveway.

Feeling more lost and alone than he had in
years — which was saying something — Max

stared after the car as it raced down the driveway, kicking up dust.

The whole episode hadn't taken five minutes and not one thing had been resolved, but it had been a start, he told himself stoutly. For a man facing an uncertain future, any new start was welcome.

14

She'd tried so damn hard not to fall apart and bolt, but Amanda hadn't been able to stop the panic that had clawed its way up the back of her throat at her first glimpse of her father. So many awful memories had flooded over her, followed in quick succession by good ones that made her want to weep for time lost. The bad overshadowed the good by far, but it was the childhood memories that made her heart ache. She wasn't sure she could open herself up to him, let him back into her life, only to have him destroy her when she was least expecting it.

The two of them treading so damn carefully to make her visit seem normal took its toll, as well. What sort of father-daughter relationship was it when they had to try so hard just to hold a civil conversation?

He'd aged more than she'd expected, even since she'd last seen him only a year ago. His still-thick hair was now almost completely gray. His face, always tanned and weathered from his time outdoors, was pale and lined. Once an imposing man, he seemed to have shrunk, all the vitality sapped out of him. He was barely into his sixties, but he looked fifteen or twenty years older.

But the shock of his appearance and the difficulty having a conversation were nothing compared to the thoughts that assailed her about his future. No matter how angry she was with him, no matter how he'd hurt her, thinking about that was a thousand times worse than thinking about the past. Knowing that the man who'd fed her as a baby, who'd crooned her to sleep when she'd been restless would himself be helpless as a baby sometime in the not-too-distant future was unbearably sad. She'd hardly been able to look him in the eye without coming completely apart. And in the end, that's what she'd done. She'd panicked and fled. She was embarrassed and shamed by that. She should have been stronger.

Still shaken, she was barely in the front door at home when Caleb arrived.

"How did it go?" he asked, then took one look at her face. "Never mind. You can tell me later. Let me make you a cup of hot tea."

She lifted a brow. "Hot tea?"

"It's supposed to be soothing," he replied, ignoring her skepticism as he headed toward the kitchen.

"It'll take more than tea," she commented, following him, surprised that she didn't resent his taking over. In fact, it felt comfortable — comforting — to have him taking charge as if he had a right to. Given the rollercoaster state of her emotions toward him lately, that was a surprise.

She stood in the doorway, admiring the view from the back with guilty pleasure. Not only did the man have shoulders worth weeping over, but his backside was perfect. She felt an unexpected twinge of desire. It most certainly wasn't the first time, but it always caught her off guard and made her feel vaguely sinful. These twinges got all tangled up with her affection for him, her gratitude. It confused her that she wanted him in *that* way, but oh, how she did. Especially today.

"Caleb," she said, her voice edgy with nerves.

He turned and something of what was in her head must have been evident on her face. He regarded her with a startled expression. "What?"

"I need . . ." What did she need? Sex, so she could feel alive? Sex, so she could forget how hard that too-brief visit with her father had been? Or simply someone to hold her? Given that it was Caleb, she settled for the last. "I could really use a hug."

Without a moment's hesitation, he set down the half-filled teapot, turned off the water and opened his arms. Amanda stepped into them and rested her head against his chest. The steady sound of his heart soothed her, the strength of his arms reassured her. A sense of peace stole over her. It had been years since she'd felt so secure, so protected.

And there was this yearning. She lifted her face and met his gaze. The same yearning was in his eyes, the same heat. It had simmered between them before, but they'd both ignored it — or tried to dismiss it. This time it was plain that neither of them had the will to deny it.

When his mouth covered hers, she knew it had been inevitable. Not just the kiss — they'd kissed before — but everything that was to come. It was all inevitable, probably had been from the first time he'd treated her with so much kindness and compassion. She'd opened her heart to him and now he was a part of it.

But this wasn't about kindness or compassion now. Oh, maybe the hug was, but not the kiss. The kiss was about wanting and need and desire. It was about a man and a woman.

"We weren't going to do this anymore," Caleb reminded her, his breathing ragged as he pulled back just a little.

"I know," Amanda said, still holding on for dear life. "But I'm having trouble remembering why."

His lips curved slightly at that. "I could remind you."

"Don't," she pleaded. "Caleb, would it be so terribly wrong? I don't want you breaking a million vows or anything, but I want you. I need to . . . feel, I guess. You make me feel things I'd never expected to feel again."

"You do the same for me," he said, brushing a strand of hair from her cheek. "But I have to know, Amanda. Do you see this as the start of something? Or is it just about this moment? Is it about you feeling lost and alone and needing someone to hold on to?"

She knew those were fair questions, but she wasn't sure she had an honest answer to any of them. "I don't know," she admitted, then sighed. "That's not good enough, is it? Not with so much at stake, especially for you."

"For both of us," he corrected. He regarded her sadly. "I wish it were enough, Amanda, but we're the kind of people who need to know that something is right and lasting. Attraction can be fleeting. We need love and commitment. You have your children to consider. I have my congregation. Neither of us can live in the moment, no matter how much we might want to."

She could hardly argue the point. "Do you think we'll ever get it right?"

"Oh, I think we've gotten the kissing down perfectly," he teased.

"What about the rest?" she asked, unable to keep a wistful note out of her voice. There were times like this when she wanted it all more than she could say.

Something in his expression alarmed her. He seemed to be closing himself off from her, even as he still held her in a loose embrace. "Caleb? Am I pushing too hard? Is this so completely wrong?"

"No," he said fiercely. "Don't ever think this is wrong, Amanda. Or that your feelings aren't important or even that I don't share them, because I do."

"Then why are you so hesitant about us having some sort of future?"

He closed his eyes as if he couldn't bear to look at her, then deliberately opened them and met her gaze. "I simply don't know if it's possible, Amanda. There are so many things you don't know, so many things I can't explain."

"Tell me," she pleaded, sensing that it was

critical to get to the bottom of this before she lost him, lost the friendship that had become so important to her, lost the possibilities that had shone in his eyes only a moment ago.

He shook his head. "It's personal," he said, essentially shutting her out.

She frowned at the response. "More personal than the things you know about me?" she asked again.

"Yes, more personal than those. It goes to the core of who I am, what kind of man I am."

He looked so distraught that she couldn't bear to push him any further. "I wish you trusted me enough to tell me," she said softly.

He regarded her with sorrow. "I wish I trusted myself enough to live with the *consequences* of telling you."

Alarmed by that, she gave him a questioning look. "Caleb?"

He tucked a finger under her chin, then kissed her lightly. "Leave it be, Amanda. Today's been difficult enough for you already. Let's have tea and you can tell me about your visit with your father."

She gave him a rueful look. "It wasn't much of a visit," she admitted.

It suddenly seemed all of her contacts today with the men she cared about were destined to leave her with more questions than answers. She was also left with the vague sense that there was more she could have done to make both of those contacts go differently.

Standing on her feet all day was getting to Mary Louise. Her ankles were starting to swell, and according to the doctor, she could expect that to get worse as the pregnancy progressed. Every chance she got, she slipped outside to the bench on the sidewalk in front of the convenience store for some fresh air and to get off her feet.

When a car filled with a rowdy crowd of kids from the nearby high school pulled up, she stood up to go back inside.

"Well, if it isn't the little mama," Parnell Hutchins said, sliding out from behind the wheel with a sneer on his face. He was eighteen and already mean enough to be known to most of the cops in town. Mary Louise was one of his favorite targets. She had been ever since she'd turned him down flat when he asked her out. He'd accused her of thinking she was too good for him, told her she was out of her mind to think she was good enough for Danny Marshall.

Mary Louise walked inside, ignoring the gibe, and took her place behind the counter.

These boys scared her, but she wasn't about to let them see it. The only way to deal with bullies was to give as good as she got. She had her cell phone behind the counter programmed to call 911 if they ever got to be more than she could handle. Up till now that had never happened. They were usually happy enough to hassle her with words. Cruel words, but still just words.

"So, Mary Louise, who's the daddy?" Parnell asked, his gaze on her slightly rounded belly. "You gonna have one of them little coffee-colored babies, courtesy of Willie Ron? Is that why Danny ain't in no hurry to get hitched to you?"

The other boys snickered. Mary Louise stared them down. There was no use trying to tell them the truth.

Infuriated by her refusal to rise to his baiting, Parnell started to reach across the counter to grab her, but she backed up a step.

"You answer me, girl," he said heatedly. "I'm a customer in here and you don't want me tellin' your boss you're ignoring a payin' customer, do you?"

"You haven't bought anything yet," she said calmly. "When you do . . ."

"Grab a six-pack," Parnell ordered one of the other boys.

"Forget it," Mary Louise said. "Not a one of you is over twenty-one. I can't sell you beer."

"Then I suppose we'll just have to take it," Parnell retorted. "Make it a coupla six-packs, Jason. Rodney, you grab one, too."

"You will not get away with stealing from here," Mary Louise said. "I know exactly who to tell the police to chase down."

"You do, and you'll live to regret it," Parnell retorted, his expression filled with venom.

Just then he was grabbed from behind by Cord Beaufort, who'd come into the store without any of them noticing. Cord spun Parnell around and held him a couple of inches off the ground. "You watch who you threaten, punk."

Parnell's eyes were bulging. "Let me go," he croaked furiously, wriggling in a futile attempt to break free of Cord's grip.

"Not until you apologize to the lady," Cord said mildly. His searching gaze studied Mary Louise, as if to reassure himself that she was okay. She gave him a faint nod, trying to hide her relief at his arrival.

"I'm not hearing that apology, Parnell," Cord said.

"I'll apologize to the likes of her when hell freezes over," Parnell spit out.

"Then that's how long we'll stay here," Cord said, implying that it didn't matter a bit to him. "Mary Louise, you want to call the police and invite them to join us?"

She picked up her cell phone from under the counter, but before she could punch the button, Parnell said, "Wait."

Cord regarded him expectantly. "Well?"

"I apologize, Mary Louise. I didn't mean nothin' by what I said before."

The apology lacked sincerity, but she didn't care. She only wanted him gone. "Fine. Just get out of here," she said.

"And don't come back," Cord advised. "Mary Louise, you see any of these boys heading in this direction again, you call the police, you hear?"

She nodded.

Cord released Parnell and gave him an insincere smile. "I think we understand each other, don't we?"

"Yeah," Parnell said sullenly.

"That's 'yes, sir,'" Cord told him, an intimidating scowl on his face.

"Yes, sir," Parnell mocked, then turned and left, the other boys trailing along behind him.

Cord faced her. "Are you okay?"

"Just a little shaky," she said.

"Do they come in here often?"

"Often enough," she said with a shrug.

"Well, I meant what I told them. Next time don't wait for them to cross the threshold. Call the police. I know that boy's kind. Always looking for a fight, and I don't want you caught in the middle of it."

She gave him a shaky smile. "Thanks. Usually I can handle Parnell okay, but today he was meaner than usual. He was saying all sorts of stuff, trying to make me mad."

"What sort of stuff?"

She didn't want to repeat it. "It doesn't matter, really."

"You sure about that?"

She crossed her arms protectively over her stomach. "It was about the baby, that's all. He's trying to make something out of me being friends with Willie Ron. He was saying the baby is Willie Ron's, not Danny's. It's just a bunch of trash talk, that's all."

To her dismay, Cord looked more alarmed than ever. "Mary Louise, maybe you ought to think about quitting this job. I'm sure Dinah or I could help you find something else."

"Why? Just because Parnell's a bully? I won't let him run me off. I need this job."

"No, but he could get folks worked up about you being involved with Willie Ron. People around here are more enlightened these days, but that doesn't mean a certain crowd of folks as backward as Parnell might not want to make trouble for you and Willie Ron."

"But this baby is Danny's," she protested.

"It only takes one person spreading a lie to cause trouble," Cord said. "Just think about it, okay? Promise me. I'll send Dinah by to talk to you."

"I think you're worrying about nothing," she said, but she was beginning to feel shaky again.

"Maybe so," he said. "Where's your cell phone?"

She gave him a puzzled look. "Right here," she said, retrieving it from beneath the counter. "Why?"

"I'm programming my number in here, along with Dinah's. If these boys come back and you start getting any kind of bad vibes, you call the police first, then me and Dinah. Do not try to handle them on your own. And you'd better warn Willie Ron about them, too. You don't want him to be caught by surprise."

"You're scaring me," she said.

"I mean to," he replied. "I don't want you to take this lightly. I know these punks. They're not happy unless they're stirring up trouble."

"How come you showed up here in the first place?" she asked. "I don't think I've seen you in here before in all the time I've worked here."

"I was hoping you could put me in touch with Danny," he said.

She stared at him. "Danny? How come?"

"Caleb — Reverend Webb — told me he's interested in historic preservation. I've got a couple of jobs coming up I thought he might be interested in."

"Really?" she asked excitedly. "That's so cool." She grabbed a piece of paper and jotted down Danny's number, then glanced at the clock. "He's at work now and his boss doesn't like him getting personal calls, but he should be off in about an hour."

"Then I'll wait to call him," Cord promised. "You want me to hang around a while in case those kids come back?"

A part of her wanted to say yes, but she refused to give in to cowardice. "Nah, I'll be fine. They've more 'n likely had their fun for the night. And Willie Ron should be here any minute. He's been coming in early lately. He claims he likes to get a head start on things, but I know it's because he wants to get me off my feet."

Cord chuckled. "Sounds like he's a good friend. I wish Dinah would listen to me when I try to get her off her feet."

"She's having a baby, too?" Mary Louise asked. She didn't know the TV reporter that well, but she was fascinated by her. Dinah Davis Beaufort was famous. She'd been all over the world. She'd even covered war zones for a big cable network. Mary Louise didn't know how anyone could do that. She'd pee in her pants if she ever saw someone getting killed or a car bomb going off.

"Our baby's due around the same time as yours," Cord told her. "Maybe you and Dinah can compare notes."

She grinned. "Sure. I'd like that. My mom had me so long ago, she's practically forgotten everything."

"Oh, I imagine she remembers the important stuff," Cord said. "You take care, Mary Louise."

"You, too." She smiled shyly. "Thanks, you know, for what you did tonight."

"No problem. Just remember what I said. Give Willie Ron a heads-up and call the police if those boys come back around here."

"Sure."

"And think about looking for a different job."

She couldn't imagine another job she could get, especially with a baby on the way, but she nodded. "I will."

As soon as Cord was out the door, her knees seemed to give way. She sat down hard on the stool behind the counter and thought about just how close a call she'd had. It wasn't so much that Parnell might have stolen several six-packs of beer right in front of her eyes. It was the nastiness in his voice when he'd talked about Willie Ron and her. As much as she hated to admit it, Cord was right. There could be trouble and she'd inadvertently dragged Willie Ron right into the thick of it just by being his friend.

Caleb left Amanda's and headed to his office. There was no point in going home. He'd just toss restlessly, kicking himself for turning her down. What kind of idiot said no to the chance to sleep with a woman he was in love with?

The kind of idiot who knew that it would only complicate things, he reminded himself wearily. Much as he tried to tell himself he was taking the moral high ground, though, the more a little voice inside his head howled with laughter.

The truth wasn't half that noble. Ever since his divorce, he'd turned into an emotional recluse. All the bitterness and recriminations had taken a toll. No matter how many times he'd smoothed things over for couples going through a divorce, he'd been completely inept when it came to his own.

It didn't seem to matter that his wife's fury had been an extreme reaction under the circumstances. It wasn't as if he'd set out to deny her the child they both wanted. Hell, he hadn't even known till they'd been trying for three years that the fault was his. When the test results had come back, he'd been as shattered as she had been.

But Tess had acted as if he'd done it deliberately. Until then he'd only had an inkling of how spoiled and self-absorbed she was, but after the diagnosis, he'd borne the full brunt of her selfishness. She'd ranted for hours, demeaning him, oblivious to the pain he was suffering. She'd done everything she could to strip away his self-esteem on her way out the door.

And even though in the rational part of his mind he'd known her accusations were absurd, they'd found their way into his heart and left him feeling ashamed and inadequate.

And it was all over something that wasn't even his fault. The doctor had assured him that nothing he'd done — or hadn't done — had caused his infertility. Sometimes a low sperm count was just the hand a man was dealt. That diagnosis had given Caleb scant comfort when his marriage — and all of his dreams for a family — had been ripped apart because of it.

When his supposedly perfect marriage blew up, he'd struggled to endure the whispers of gossip, the pitying looks. Even those who didn't know what had happened — and few did — seemed to regard him differently. He'd withstood it as long as he could and then sought a transfer to a new parish. He'd hoped a fresh start would enable him to forget and move on with his life.

And slowly, since coming to Charleston, he'd healed. He'd felt more like the confident, optimistic man he'd once been. And in Amanda's family, he'd found the one thing that had been missing from his life.

Then he'd heard her offhand comment about wanting more children and he'd run headlong into reality. If he told her the truth — that he couldn't give her a child — would she regard him with the same disdain Tess had? He wasn't sure he could bear it if she did.

He was glumly pondering that when Big Max walked into his office. Caleb stared at him with surprise.

"What on earth are you doing here at this hour? It must be almost midnight."

"Time doesn't mean much these days,"

Max said. "I couldn't get to sleep, so I decided to test my luck and take a drive." He regarded Caleb with the pride of a kid who'd accomplished a brand-new feat. "Made it here without a hitch."

"Good for you," Caleb enthused, hiding his concern. Max desperately needed these triumphs to feel like a man. Caleb could relate to that. "What made you decide to come by the church? You normally wouldn't find me here at this hour."

"Just driving around, to tell you the truth, and saw the light. Figured you must be having trouble sleeping, too." Max studied him knowingly. "Want to tell me why that is?"

Tell Max about his quandary over loving Amanda? Not a chance, Caleb thought. He had a healthy instinct for self-preservation.

"I had a lot of paperwork piling up," he said instead.

Max gave him a chiding look. "I thought preachers didn't lie."

Caleb gestured toward the papers on his desk. "What lie?"

"Oh, I'm not saying you don't have paperwork, but I don't see much evidence you're doing it. Looked to me like you were staring into space when I got here."

Caleb deliberately changed the subject. "How did your visit with Amanda go?"

Max gave him a long, speculative look. "She tell you her version?"

"Briefly," Caleb acknowledged.

"That's pretty much how it was," Max grumbled. "Brief. One minute she was sitting there with a glass of tea, the next she was running away and bursting into tears."

"It had to be emotional for both of you," Caleb said. "How did it feel to you having her back?"

"She's too skinny," Max observed. "She could use some of Jessie's baking."

Caleb bit back a grin. "That's what you noticed about the daughter you've hardly seen for ten years, that she's too skinny?"

"Well, it's not like she gave me much time to get into anything important." He regarded Caleb warily. "You think she'll come back?"

Caleb nodded. "I think the ice has been broken now. She'll be back." He regarded Max intently. "Or you could visit her."

"And let her have the satisfaction of slamming the door in my face?" Max scoffed. "No, she'll have to come to me."

"Spoken like the unyielding man we've all come to know," Caleb commented.

"A man has his pride," Max countered.

"Some would say pride's the last thing you can afford these days," Caleb responded. It surely hadn't done much for him.

Max frowned. "I suppose. Okay, if she doesn't show her face around there in another week or so, I'll think about going by her place." He shook a finger at Caleb. "Remember now, I said I'd think about it. Don't go nagging me if I don't do it fast enough to suit you."

"It's not about me," Caleb said. "Or my timetable."

"Ha!" Max snorted. "If you're gonna set wheels in motion, boy, you'd better be prepared to accept responsibility when the train starts barreling down the track."

Caleb laughed. "Maybe I'll just jump out of the way." He stood up. "Come on, old man. I'll follow you home."

"I don't need you trailing along behind me like some baby-sitter," Max complained.

"Maybe I'm just hoping for a midnight snack," Caleb countered. "Jessie bake today?"

"Sweet-potato pie," Max said, his grim expression brightening at the memory. "Wouldn't mind having some of that myself. Come on, boy. Seems to me there might be some cold roast beef in the refrigerator, too. It'd make a mighty fine sandwich to go with that pie."

"Now you're talking," Caleb said, leading the way.

For all his blustering and his contrary ways, Max was the perfect antidote to the sour mood Caleb had been in earlier. Maybe he could even win a few hands of poker before the night was over. That would turn the day around.

15

When Amanda looked up after wrapping a package for one of the boutique's more demanding clients, Nadine was next in line. She had two incredibly sedate outfits in hand.

Amanda regarded the black linen pantsuit and lightweight pastel-blue wool dress with surprise. "Changing your style?" she asked.

"George insists on taking me to all these stuffy restaurants and country club parties," Nadine complained. "Even I'm bright enough to figure out that the clothes I like are unsuitable for that crowd."

Amanda bit back a grin. Nadine had the fashion sense of a Vegas showgirl. With her huge hoop earrings, display of cleavage and short skirts, she'd probably shocked the dickens out of some of Charleston's society matrons. In Amanda's opinion, it was probably good for them, something to keep their blue blood flowing.

"Has George complained?" Amanda asked, though she doubted he had. He seemed to have fallen for Nadine exactly as she was, probably because she was a refreshing change from the women who traveled in his usual social circle.

"No, he's never said a word, bless his heart, but I'm getting enough stares that it's embarrassing," Nadine admitted. "It might not matter a bit to me, but I don't ever want tongues wagging about his taste in women. He's been too good to me." She held up the clothes. "What do you think? Are these conservative enough?"

"They're conservative and boring," Amanda decreed. "Come on, Nadine. Let's see if we can't improve on those. You can be more conservative and still be yourself. I'm thinking something in red, especially with the holidays coming up soon."

Nadine's eyes lit up. "Red? You think so? There was a dress over on the rack that caught my eye."

She went right to it and pulled it out for Amanda's inspection. "What do you think?"

"I think those society women will need their smelling salts if you walk into a room in that dress," Amanda said honestly. "They'll gather up their men and run."

"It's the neckline, isn't it?" Nadine said, wistfully eyeing the low cut.

"And the hemline," Amanda told her. "It'd hit you at mid-thigh, which I understand is your preferred length, but I think something that skims the knee would be a better choice."

"Who gets to wear a thing like this?" Nadine inquired, reluctantly parting with it.

"Someone twenty-one and leggy going out with her sugar daddy," Amanda said.

Nadine grinned. "Too bad it's wasted on anyone that young. They can't possibly know how to flaunt it."

"Nadine, Southern girls grow up knowing how to flaunt their assets," Amanda said as she culled through the hangers till she found the red suit she'd remembered. "Now this will work for you. Try it on."

Nadine regarded it doubtfully. "It's just a plain old suit."

Amanda shook her head. "It's a plain old *red* suit with a classic cut. You'll be able to wear it forever. Come on. Be daring, Nadine. If I'm right, you can take me out and buy me lunch. If I'm wrong and you don't look like a million bucks, I'll buy lunch."

She waited outside the dressing room while Nadine changed into the suit. Nadine's usual line of chatter slowly died out.

"Oh, my," Nadine murmured a few minutes later.

She emerged from the room looking as if she'd stepped out of the pages of *Vogue.* With her hair up and a discreet amount of gold jewelry, she'd command any room she entered.

"I look . . ." Her voice trailed off.

"Amazing," Amanda supplied.

"And classy," Nadine said with wonder. "I actually look classy."

Amanda smiled. "Does that pleased look on your face mean I get a free lunch?"

"Honey, you can have lunch on me for a month," Nadine responded, her gaze still locked on her image in the mirror. "I don't want to take this off."

"Then don't, but you're going to be a little overdressed for the coffee shop on the corner."

"Right," Nadine agreed. "And I'd hate to spill ketchup on it, especially since buying it is going to bust my budget wide open. Give me two minutes, then we'll ring this up and go out to eat."

A few minutes later they strolled into the coffee shop and found a booth open by the window. Though the atmosphere was fifties diner, the menu had evolved. In addition to the grilled cheese sandwiches and burgers, there was an extensive listing of fancy salads and even Amanda's favorite chicken quesadilla with salsa and guacamole.

After they'd ordered and their iced tea had been served, Nadine sat back and studied Amanda.

"You want to tell me how things went when you saw your daddy?" she asked.

Amanda should have known it wouldn't take long for word to get around, especially with Nadine involved with one of Big Max's oldest friends. "George told you?"

Nadine nodded. "He stopped by to visit with your daddy yesterday. He said you could have knocked him over with a feather when Big Max told him you'd been by. Said you didn't stay long, though. Didn't things go the way you'd hoped?"

Amanda shrugged. "It was a little overwhelming. I mean, for years now I've hated my father for what he did to me, for how inadequate he made Bobby feel. All of a sudden I was sitting there drinking tea as if nothing had happened. A part of me wanted to throw that tea right in his face and scream at him for being so hateful to my husband, but I couldn't do it."

"Because he's sick," Nadine guessed.

Amanda regarded her with amazement. "You know about that, too?"

"Your father confided in George. The only reason George told me was because he thought you might need a friend to talk to, someone besides Caleb." Nadine's gaze was filled with sympathy. "Sweetie, it's okay that you're still angry with him, even if he *is* sick. That doesn't wipe the slate clean."

"But I feel like I'm the one being mean and hateful if I don't let it all go now," Amanda admitted. "We sat there making small talk, Nadine. It was ridiculous. I felt like such a hypocrite when there were so many things left unsaid."

"Then you need to clear the air," Nadine advised. "Say your piece, Amanda, and let him say his. That's the only way there won't be this big ole elephant in the room every time you see each other. From everything I've heard about your daddy, he can take it. Any man who can dish it out the way he has . . ."

"Did you and Josh ever sit down and have a conversation like that?" Amanda asked curiously, recalling how tense things had been between mother and son when Nadine showed up unexpectedly in Charleston the year before. "I know you two had a lot of old issues between you when you first came back to town."

Nadine chuckled. "We're talking Josh,

honey. Until he got involved with Maggie, 'stoic' was his middle name. He didn't discuss anything that went below skin-deep. If I'd started picking at the scabs on all those old wounds, he'd probably be living in Memphis by now or points even farther west. No, with Josh, things came to a head bit by bit."

"But you all get along great now," Amanda said, unable to keep a note of envy from her voice.

Nadine beamed. "Yes, we do. I think he actually likes having me for a mama almost as much as I admire the man he's become. I wish I could take credit for how terrific he is, but he did it all on his own and I couldn't be prouder of him for that."

"But if waiting it out was right for you and Josh, why do you think I need to get everything on the table with my father?"

"Time, sweetie," Nadine said quietly. "You might not have that much of it. Get the battle over with, so you can have as many peaceful days as possible. You want to start storing up some good memories. The holidays seem like the perfect time to start. I imagine your daddy would be real happy to spend Christmas surrounded by his grandkids."

Amanda couldn't imagine such a scene. "Couldn't I just pretend none of it ever happened?"

"I don't know. Could you?" Nadine asked, regarding Amanda with a penetrating look.

Amanda thought about how all that pent-up anger would eat away at her and destroy whatever time she had with her father. It had already taken a toll during that first visit.

"No," she admitted at last. "But I have to tell you, Nadine, given how I feel about confrontation, you just made the prospect of paying another visit to my father shoot straight to the bottom of my to-do list."

"Have a piece of double-fudge cake, then," Nadine said. "I find you can swallow almost anything as long as it's accompanied by chocolate."

Amanda had a hunch there wasn't enough chocolate in the world to make the inevitable confrontation with her father go down easily.

Caleb looked at the nervous young man seated across from him and had to fight a smile. Danny looked every bit as scared as he had the day he and Mary Louise had come to talk to Caleb about marrying them.

"What's on your mind, Danny?" Caleb asked, leaning back in his chair.

"I had a meeting with Cord Beaufort yesterday," Danny said.

"Really?" Caleb said, feigning ignorance. "What was it about?"

Danny's expression brightened. "He offered me a job for the summer. Can you believe it? It would be helping on his historic preservation project over in Atlanta."

"That's great," Caleb said. "It will give you a real taste of that kind of work. Maybe it'll help you decide if it's what you really want to do."

"That's what I thought," Danny agreed.

"Okay, then, what's the problem?"

"I was thinking I ought to be here," Danny explained, his excitement fading. "You know, because of Mary Louise. The baby will be here this spring and I probably should help out as much as I can over the summer. I don't want her to think I'm abandoning her."

"Have you talked it over with Mary Louise?"

Danny shook his head. "Not yet. I already know what she's gonna say."

"Really?" Caleb said, amused. "You can read her mind?"

"Pretty much," Danny said seriously. "She'll say I have to do it because it's exactly the kind of work I want to do someday and Beaufort Construction is one of the best."

"If she said that, she'd have a point."

"But come on, Reverend Webb, what about the baby?" Danny asked earnestly. "I

315

owe it to Mary Louise to stick around, at least when I'm out of school for the summer."

Caleb looked directly into his eyes and saw the confusion of a young man torn between doing what he perceived to be the right thing and doing what he'd dreamed of doing his whole life.

"Wouldn't you be helping Mary Louise most if you had a good job and could give her some money to help support the baby?" Caleb asked.

Hope flickered in Danny's eyes. "That's true." He shook his head. "But I don't want to let her down, not any more than I already have. I missed her first sonogram. I haven't even heard the baby's heartbeat yet."

"And you want to do that?"

Danny nodded slowly. "At first, I didn't think I did. But when she told me about it, I realized what I'm missing. It's gotta be amazing to see your own baby growing inside its mama, you know what I mean?"

Caleb wished he'd had that experience, but he could imagine it. "I'm sure it is. Why don't you talk to Mary Louise and make plans to go with her to her next doctor visit? Maybe she has one during the holidays."

Danny brightened. "Maybe she does. I'll check with her as soon as I leave here." His smile faded. "You don't think it would make it harder for her, having me around like that?"

"What do you think?"

"She's said it would be okay."

"Then I'd take her at her word," Caleb said. "And, Danny, remember this. In the long run, you'll let her down more if you're not true to yourself," Caleb said. "Talk over this summer-job offer with her. Mary Louise is a very mature young woman. I think you can count on her to give you good advice and to support whatever you decide."

"Yeah, she will," Danny agreed. "That's why I have to make the best choice for both of us. I can't have her letting me off the hook all the time."

Caleb frowned. He was beginning to sense that there was more going on here than a quandary over a summer job. "Danny, are you regretting the decision you made to wait to get married?"

"I guess," he said, still looking uncertain. "I know it would be really hard and all, but we do love each other. Maybe that's enough."

"I think you need to be more confident than that before you get married," Caleb said gently. "You'll know when the time is right. Don't rush into anything until you're absolutely certain you can make it work and are ready to make whatever sacrifices are necessary. You have your whole lifetime ahead of you."

"I guess," Danny said, his tone skeptical.

"You're a fine young man, Danny. I believe wholeheartedly that you and Mary Louise will be together when the time is right for both of you."

Danny stood up. "Thanks, Reverend Webb. I wish I could talk to my mom and dad the way I can talk to you. Before, I used to talk things over with Mary Louise. I really miss that."

"There's nothing to stop you from talking things over with her now. And try talking to your parents, too. Perhaps they'll surprise you."

A grin tugged at Danny's lips. "I'm pretty sure I'm the only one in the family who's full of surprises, and mine don't seem to be working out too well."

Caleb laughed as the boy left his office, his step a lot lighter than when he had entered.

Caleb sighed. He wondered how Danny would feel about his advice if he knew just what a mess Caleb seemed to be making of his own life.

Amanda was so terrified of facing down her father once and for all that she actually considered — if only for a fleeting second — taking the kids along to serve as a buffer. That would guarantee that she'd never raise her voice and might even stifle Max's desire to fight back. Obviously, though, it was a terrible idea. She didn't want her children anywhere near her father until he was ready to embrace them as family. She was far from certain that Max *was* ready.

This time when she drove out to see Max, she kept her foot pressed determinedly to the accelerator, whipped into the driveway and braked to a sudden stop right beside his car. She thought she saw him wince as she cut the engine, but his expression was neutral as she climbed the porch steps.

This time she actually took a minute to look around. The grounds were as well tended as ever with masses of azalea bushes bordering the porch, dormant now with winter just around the corner. In early spring, the colorful display was impressive. The porch's tongue-in-groove floorboards had been painted a glossy forest green to match the shutters on the house. The beadboard ceiling was a sparkling white, the ceiling fans a recent addition. In the old days they'd relied on breezes to cool the sultry temperatures.

"You look as if you've come barreling out

here ready for a fight," Max said. "What's on your mind?"

Amanda regarded him with astonishment. "What on earth do you think is on my mind?"

"You want to drag out every sin I've committed against you and make sure I pay, is that it?"

His blunt assessment pretty much took the wind out of her sails. "That's exactly it," she said, relieved to have the topic out in the open at last. "You hurt me, Daddy. And as much as I loved Bobby and he loved me, your behavior cost us something precious."

"I hope you're not going to blather on and on about how I ruined your wedding day," he retorted defensively. "I regret that, but at the time I thought I was doing the right thing. I took a gamble that my opinion meant something to you and might keep you from doing something crazy. Then when I lost, I didn't know how the hell to make it right."

"I don't imagine you gave the matter that much thought," she said.

"You're wrong about that," he said. "Oh, I was mad as spit that day, but when you walked out of this house with your head held so high and your shoulders all stiff and proud, it near to broke my heart. You ask Jessie. She'll tell you."

He gave her a rueful look. "You were a Maxwell through and through at that moment, sticking to your guns in a way that would have made me proud if you hadn't been defying me. Nothing I admire more than someone with the courage of their own convictions."

"I wish you'd told me that, maybe not then, but later," she said.

"And admit that the whole thing had been a desperate gamble and that you'd beaten me?"

She nodded. "Why not? Wasn't our relationship worth it? Until Bobby came along, you were my whole world. I never wanted to have to choose, but you made me."

"Only thing I knew to do," he said. "The boy was all wrong for you, all wrong for the future you could have had if you'd listened to me. I had to try to stop you from making a mistake you'd regret."

"I *never* regretted loving Bobby!" she snapped.

"Not even after he left you penniless?" Max taunted. "Wasn't that proof enough that I'd been right?"

Amanda's fury rebounded. "Don't you dare blame all of that on Bobby!"

"Who else should I blame?"

"You're the one he kept trying to prove himself to. Maybe if you hadn't made Bobby feel so inadequate, he wouldn't have taken so many financial risks."

Her father stared at her incredulously. "You can't blame me for your husband's folly."

"But I do, dammit. You cost me time with the man I loved."

Max regarded her with shock. "You blaming me for that boy's death, too?"

Amanda knew better than that. "No, I'm talking about the hours in the day he should have been spending with me and the kids. Instead, he was driven to succeed, driven to prove you wrong."

"If he felt inadequate, that was his problem," Max said. "He wasn't good enough for you, and that's the truth."

"That's *your* truth!" she said furiously. "Bobby O'Leary was a kind, decent husband who was willing to do whatever it took to make up for the things he thought I sacrificed to be with him. Everyone should be loved that much."

"Love," Max scoffed. "You can't pay the bills with love. Found that out, didn't you?"

"Don't you dare throw that in my face. Don't you dare!" She was shaking so hard, she could barely speak. "Whatever made me think you might have changed, that you might have mellowed? You're the same cold-hearted bastard you were on my wedding day."

She whirled around and started down the steps. Only when she was halfway to the car did she hear him call her name. At first she wasn't sure it hadn't been her imagination. She turned slowly and saw her father struggling to his feet. To her astonishment, there were tears on his cheeks.

"Don't go," he said softly. "Please, Amanda. I deserve everything you said to me, even being called a bastard back then, though I'll thank you not to use that word around here again."

She almost smiled at that. He'd always hated it when she swore. He'd drilled it into her head that it was unladylike. Maybe that was one reason it had been so satisfying to call him a name that would make his hackles rise.

Still, it had gone against the grain of her own beliefs, so she apologized. "I'm sorry if I offended you," she said. "But you make me so furious. If only you'd gotten to know Bobby, if only you'd given him half a chance, things might have turned out differently for all of us." She approached the steps and met her father's gaze. "Do you know something ironic? I think I fell in love with Bobby because he reminded me of you."

"That boy was nothing in the world like me," her father declared.

"He was stubborn and determined and proud," she countered. "Yet he would do anything in the world for those he loved. Remember when he came to you after our first son was born? He did that for me. You've no idea what it cost him."

Max winced. "I remember that day," he admitted. "And I remember how I treated him."

"You said unforgivable things," Amanda said, the old hurt bubbling up. "You talked about my baby as if he didn't matter, as if he were trash — when it's Maxwell blood flowing through his veins, the same as it is through yours and mine!"

Max sank back into his rocker. "That was the most shameful moment of my life," he said sorrowfully. "I wanted to take back the words as soon as they were out of my mouth, but I couldn't. I wanted to ask that boy for his forgiveness, but I couldn't do that, either."

Amanda heard real regret in his voice and it bewildered her. "Why couldn't you?"

"Because I was embarrassed that a man I'd treated so abominably had come here to make amends, when it should have been the other way around. On that day, I knew that Bobby O'Leary was a better man than I'd ever acknowledged — a better man than I was — and it shamed me."

"So you let those awful words stand, you deepened the rift between us, all because you were *embarrassed?*" she asked in disbelief.

"That stubborn Maxwell pride," he said, as if it explained everything. "It's a trait you share, darlin' girl, so you should understand it. Once I'd headed down that road, I didn't know how to turn around."

Amanda couldn't entirely deny that she was guilty of the same sin, but she saw now what a waste it was to let pride determine the outcome of some things. Caleb had seen that, though. He'd encouraged her to put pride aside to come here one more time. It remained to be seen if it had been worth it.

She met her father's gaze. "Maybe it's time to bury that particular trait. Seems to me it's already cost us too much. Maybe there's still time to make sure it doesn't condemn the next generation to repeating our mistakes."

"I wish now that I'd learned that lesson at your age," Max said. "What's it say in the Bible? Pride goeth before a fall?"

Amanda regarded him with astonishment. "You're quoting the Bible these days? When was the last time you set foot in a church?"

"The day I said goodbye to your mama," he said without any hint of an apology. "These days the Bible quotes come to me."

"Caleb," she guessed at once.

Max grinned. "The man does have one for every occasion. It gets tiresome."

"And yet you two have become fast friends," Amanda noted.

Max looked vaguely uncomfortable. "He plays a decent hand of poker, that's all."

"Meaning he lets you win," she said, amused.

"Actually, he doesn't, which is the point," her father said. "For too many years folks seemed to think they had to let me win at everything — business, poker, it didn't matter. Caleb doesn't bat an eye when it comes to taking my money."

"You're actually playing for money?" she asked, more shocked by that than anything else that had been said.

"Have you ever known me to gamble for toothpicks?" Max scoffed.

Amanda chuckled. "No, but I thought Caleb might find it objectionable."

"He's got money for the food bank and a new stained-glass window for the church on the line. He'd have all of it by now, if he'd play for more."

"He's that good?"

"That man could bluff his way past the tightest security network in the world," Max said with admiration. "Hard to imagine a preacher would have that much skill lying through his teeth, but he doesn't even hesitate."

Amanda grinned at her father. "Maybe I'll join you next time you play," she said impulsively.

A slow smile spread across Max's face. "You serious?"

Amanda considered her impetuous offer and decided it felt right. "Sure. Why not? It sounds like fun."

"The man won't know what hit him," Max observed. "You sure you want to do that to him?"

"Oh, I think he's about due for a surprise," Amanda said, thinking of all the things Caleb had kept from her.

"You think you can remember everything I taught you?"

She decided not to tell him about the strip poker games she'd played with Bobby. "I remember," she said confidently.

"Then how about I call him and get him out here right now?" Max asked.

He sounded so eager Amanda couldn't bring herself to say no. "Let me see if I can make arrangements for someone to stay with the kids for a couple of hours," she said.

"They could come out here with Caleb," Max suggested. His tone was carefully neutral, but there was a wistful expression on his face.

Amanda shook her head, then noted the disappointment in her father's eyes. "I'll bring them next time," she told him. "Before Christmas, I promise."

He nodded, his relief plain. "Caleb says they're pistols."

"They're wonderful," Amanda confirmed. "Now, let me call Nadine. If she can watch them, then you get in touch with Caleb and lure him out here. Think you can?"

"Jessie baked a pie today. That'll get him out here if nothing else does." He gave Amanda a knowing look. "Something tells me he'll get here even faster if I mention you'll be sticking around."

Amanda wasn't about to have that particular conversation with her father. It was enough that they'd dredged up all the past and made a start on putting it to rest. She wasn't anywhere near ready to have him meddling in the present. She'd resisted his attempts to control her life once, but if he got it into his head that there ought to be something between her and Caleb, she wasn't sure she'd have the strength to fight him this time.

16

Caleb wasn't entirely sure what was going on. He'd arrived at Max's to find Amanda seated comfortably on the porch looking very much like a cat that had just gotten into a particularly delectable bowl of cream. Her presence rattled him. Max hadn't said a word about Amanda being here.

"Everything okay?" he asked, studying both Max and Amanda for signs of tension. To his relief and amazement, they seemed relaxed enough.

"Perfect," Amanda said cheerfully. "Can I pour you a glass of iced tea, Caleb?"

"Sure." He glanced at Max. "Are we still playing poker?"

"That's what I invited you out here for," Max said. "You think I had some ulterior motive?"

"I almost never try to second-guess you," Caleb said. "I was just thinking you might want to reconsider, since Amanda's visiting."

"She wants to play, too," Max said. "It was her idea we give you a call."

"Is that so?" His gaze shot to Amanda. "You want to play cards with us?"

"If you don't mind," she said sweetly. "I've been hearing so much about these friendly games the two of you have, I thought I'd sit in."

Caleb got a very funny feeling in the pit of his stomach. She was acting too darn nonchalant, to say nothing of being awfully cozy with a man she'd claimed to despise not that long ago. If she and Max had miraculously cleared the air today, they'd done a darn fine job of it. He should be pleased. Instead, he was suspicious.

"Are you two trying to hustle me?" he asked.

Max gave him a scathing look. "We play for peanuts. What does it matter?"

"Oh, I suspect it matters quite a lot," Caleb said. He studied Amanda's expression. "How good are you?"

"Good enough," she said modestly, then added, "You might need to refresh my memory on a few of the finer points."

"Now I know you're up to something," Caleb said.

"Why?" she inquired indignantly. "Because I admitted I might need some pointers? I was merely being honest."

"Yeah, sure," Caleb said.

"You want to back out?" Max inquired.

Caleb grinned. He might not know what was going on with these two, but the atmosphere was promising. He wasn't about to do anything to rock the boat. "Absolutely not."

Max nodded approvingly. "Thought I had you pegged right. I like a man who doesn't back down from a challenge. Amanda here wasn't so sure."

Caleb regarded her with amusement. "Is that right? You thought you'd scare me off?"

"Well, I do know how badly you want that new stained-glass window," she said. "And the food bank can always use an infusion of cash, especially with Christmas right around the corner."

"Your father told you about that?"

She nodded pleasantly. "Exactly how much do you have in that fund at the moment? Daddy says you usually have the figure right at your fingertips."

Caleb retrieved the paper from his pocket and handed it to her, then took another sip of his tea as he watched her.

"Nearly eight thousand dollars," she said admiringly. "That's a lot of poker. Want to play the first hand double or nothing?"

He laughed. "Not a chance, sugar. I'll need to figure out your strategy and your skill before I take a risk like that." He studied her over the rim of his glass. "You sure you ought to be gambling at all, Amanda? Your finances are . . ." He deliberately let his voice trail off in an unspoken warning.

"Oh, don't worry. Daddy's staking me. I wouldn't dream of putting any of my paycheck at risk, especially since I'm thinking of quitting my second job after Christmas if Joanna comes through with the raise she's promised me." She smiled, her expression smug. "Truthfully, though, there's not that much risk involved."

"And only moments ago you were claiming you might require pointers to keep up," Caleb reminded her. "If you're going to bluff, Amanda, it's better to be consistent."

She studied him, her eyes wide with innocence. "Really? I'll have to keep that in mind. If sounds as if you might know quite a bit about bluffing." She stood up. "Shall we go inside, gentlemen?"

Caleb regarded her with growing amusement. "I'll want to inspect the cards we're using."

Amanda turned to her father. "Did you hear that, Daddy? Caleb all but accused you of trying to cheat by using a marked deck. I'd be insulted if I were you."

Max chuckled. "Suits me fine. He'll have no excuse when he loses."

Caleb frowned at the pair of them. "I'm not going to lose," he said. "In fact, since you're staking Amanda, I'm especially looking forward to doubling my take for the evening."

He laid his accounting of their past games on the card table in Max's den and smoothed it out. "In fact, I'm so confident, I'll even let you have the first deal, Amanda. It'll give me a chance to see just how clever you are."

"Okay with me," she said cheerfully, then handed him the deck. "See, no markings. This is a perfectly ordinary deck. Brand-new, in fact." She waved the box and now-unsealed wrapping under his nose. "Opened right before your eyes."

Caleb made a great show of examining it closely, then handed it back. "It'll do."

Amanda shuffled the deck with a skill that seemed to shock even Max.

"Where'd you learn to do that?" Max demanded.

Amanda grinned. "Nadine worked as a dealer in Vegas for a while. She's taught me a few things. Have you met Nadine, Daddy?

She's been dating George Winslow for several months now."

"Driving him crazy, the way I hear it," Max said. "She refuses to marry him." His eyes sparkled. "Have to admire a woman who has the gumption to turn down George."

"Next time we play cards, I'll ask her to come along," Amanda promised. "I think you'll find her surprising."

"That's what George says," Max replied as he looked over his cards, then tossed down two.

Caleb studied him intently, then discarded three of his.

Amanda dealt them their new cards, then said, "Dealer takes one."

Caleb exchanged a look with Max, trying to get a read on just how likely Amanda was to try to bluff her way through the very first hand to set the tone for the game. He couldn't read a single thing into Max's bland expression.

He looked at the pair of jacks in his own hand and decided to play the hand out. "I'm in," he said, tossing an additional penny into the pot.

"Me, too," Max said. "And I'll raise you one."

"I'm in for five cents," Amanda said, her

gaze locked with Caleb's, daring him to challenge her.

He couldn't help it. He admired a good bluff as much as the next man. He tossed in the additional four cents to stay in the hand. "I'll call."

"I'm out," Max said, throwing down his cards, then watching the two of them expectantly.

Amanda slowly pulled out a pair of tens and laid them on the table. Just as Caleb was about to claim victory with his jacks, she pulled out two more cards.

"Sorry, I almost forgot these," she said as she set a pair of aces beside the tens.

"Beginner's luck," Caleb scoffed, enjoying the quick rise of indignant color in her cheeks. "Now it's time to get serious."

Amanda lifted her gaze to his. "When it comes to poker, there's something you should know, Caleb."

"Oh?"

"I am always very, very serious."

In that instant, he realized for the first time just how alike she and Max were. Suddenly she was no longer Amanda O'Leary, damsel in distress, but Amanda Maxwell, a woman capable of bringing a man to his knees. It was a daunting discovery. Fascinating, too.

■ ■ ■

Amanda happily pocketed her $10.85 winnings at the end of the evening. She'd been the big winner, but Caleb had held his own. Max had seemed content enough to hand over his pennies to the two of them. She'd never known her father to be so complacent about losing before.

"I'll get it back next time," he said confidently as he walked them to the door.

"Not if I have anything to say about it," Amanda retorted. "This is just a little pocket change, Daddy. Next time I'm going to talk Caleb into upping the ante."

Caleb looked at her. "How did I miss the fact that you have the heart of a gambler?"

"Should have been plain as day," she told him honestly. "Daddy thinks he's the one who took a gamble on my wedding day and lost. I gambled more. In fact, I gambled everything I had. Some would say I'm the one who lost," she added with a pointed look at her father. "But I'd say I was the big winner. I had ten years with a man I loved and came away with three incredible kids. That more than outweighs whatever losses and problems I've had since."

"Nobody can say you didn't inherit the Maxwell spunk," her father said with real ad-

337

miration. "I should have realized I never stood a chance against that." He winked at Caleb. "Something you might want to remember, too."

Caleb looked flustered. "Me?"

"Yes, you," Max grumbled. "You want my girl, you're going to have to fight for her."

"I never said —" Caleb began, even as Amanda's cheeks flushed with embarrassment.

Max scowled at him. "Either you do or you don't, son. I'd advise you to make up your mind before it's too late."

"Yes, sir," Caleb said, sounding surprisingly meek.

Outside, Amanda regarded him with dismay. "I'm sorry about that. I don't know what got into him. We've barely reconciled and he already thinks he has a right to meddle in my life. Wouldn't you think he learned his lesson last time?"

Caleb laughed. "Men like Max don't learn lessons. They teach them. The rest of us just have to keep up."

"Still, don't let him bully you into doing something you don't want to do," she said.

Caleb seemed taken aback by the idea that he might be bullied into anything. "You think I don't want you? I could prove otherwise."

"Oh, I know you *want* me, but trust me, that is not what my father has in mind."

"I know exactly what your father has in mind. Now that he's been given a chance, he wants to see you settled before it's too late."

"Too late for me?" she scoffed. "I'm not that old."

"Too late for him," Caleb corrected. "I think he'd like another chance to walk you down the aisle."

Amanda blushed furiously. "I think that idea's a bit premature, don't you?" she said stiffly.

"I believe you know my position on that," Caleb responded. "But you certainly don't think a little thing like timing would stop your father, do you? Have you forgotten that much about him?"

Amanda considered the question. There was no doubt her father would push and shove to get his way, even if he knew he was treading on very thin ice with her. He wasn't the type to proceed gingerly just because he'd barely made his way back into her good graces.

"Still, he can't make us do anything," she said staunchly.

"Of course not," Caleb said, his gaze steady. "But there could come a time when it's not worth fighting him."

"You'd give in just because he's sick?" she asked incredulously. "After all those conversations we've had when you've declared any future between us to be impossible?"

Caleb gave her an odd look she couldn't quite interpret.

"I think you know me better than that," he said mildly.

"Then what?" she demanded.

He trapped her against the side of her car and kissed her thoroughly. With his hands braced on either side of her, she couldn't get away. Not that she was inclined to run. Caleb's mouth was very clever as he plundered hers. His unmistakable arousal sent desire rampaging through her bloodstream.

They really had to stop doing this, she thought weakly, hanging on to him. It was becoming addictive. One of these days neither of them was going to think of a single reason to stop.

Or a single reason not to do as her father wanted and get married.

"Oh, my," she murmured as understanding dawned.

Caleb grinned, his mouth hovering just over hers. "I thought the idea would sink in eventually."

She gave him an ineffective shove. "We can't let him win," she said fiercely.

340

"Because you don't want me or because you need to spite him?" Caleb inquired mildly.

Amanda stared at him, her heart thumping unsteadily and her blood sizzling. "I don't know," she admitted. "It's starting to get a little mixed up."

Caleb rested a hand against her cheek. "That's okay. I suspect things will become clear one of these days."

She frowned at him. "Do you know what you want?"

"As you well know, my feelings are every bit as muddy as yours. What I want and what I think is right are two entirely different things."

"Then we really do have to stop with the kissing," Amanda said. "Especially in plain view of my father's house. A cozy little scene like this will be all he needs to remain motivated and focused."

"Or to get out his shotgun," Caleb said, not entirely in jest. "I suspect Mary Louise's daddy was mild-mannered compared to Max when it comes to an outraged defense of his daughter's honor, and I had all I could do to calm him down. Your daddy might be more than I can handle."

The image of her father trying to push Caleb down the aisle at the barrel of a shotgun struck Amanda as hysterically funny. Not that she could have said why. Big Max was perfectly capable of doing exactly that. Maybe it was the image of Caleb trying to reason him out of it.

"You shouldn't be laughing about a thing like that," Caleb said.

"I know," she said, sobering. "Don't worry. I'll protect you. There was a time when I was a pretty decent shot myself."

Caleb moaned, evidently unamused. "That doesn't reassure me, Amanda."

"It should. Maybe a gunfight at Willow Bend is exactly what Max and I have been moving toward all these years."

"Not funny," Caleb reiterated.

"I'm thinking high noon," she continued. "Aren't gunfights always at high noon?"

"I have no idea, not being a big fan of gunfights as a way to resolve problems." He shook his head. "I think I'm beginning to see what happened between you and your father all those years ago."

"You already knew that. He betrayed me and disinherited me on my wedding day."

"No, it was two immovable objects slamming into each other. The only wonder is that both of you lived to feud about it for the next ten years."

"Maxwell stubbornness," Amanda said

succinctly. For the first time she was beginning to understand the value of it. Without that inherited gene from her father, she might have withered and died in the face of so much adversity.

She'd have to remember to thank her father the next time she ventured out here.

Mary Louise turned Willie Ron down the first dozen times he tried to convince her to go with him to get something to eat. Parnell's ugliness and Cord's warnings had scared her, but she hadn't had the heart to tell Willie Ron about what had happened. Now she could see that her unexplained refusals were hurting the man who'd been nothing but kind to her these past few weeks.

"You need to get some food into you," Willie Ron said earnestly. "I'm not asking you on a date, for goodness' sake. Skinny little white girls who are four months pregnant ain't my type."

Mary Louise sighed. "I know that. Look, there's something I should probably tell you."

His gaze narrowed at her somber tone. "What's that?"

"Parnell Hutchins was in here a while back," she began.

Willie Ron shook his head. "That boy's

nothing but trouble. Did he shoplift something? He's always trying to sneak beer out the door."

"Oh, he tried that this time, too, but Cord Beaufort came in and stopped him. That wasn't the problem."

"Then what was?"

"He was saying some stuff, you know, trash talk about you and me," Mary Louise said.

Willie Ron's face went perfectly still. "What kind of trash talk?"

She felt sleazy just mentioning it. "You know, that the baby might be yours, that kind of thing. I didn't pay a bit of attention to him," she said. "No one with any sense would, but Cord said I should watch out for him, and you should, too. That's why it might not be a good idea for you and me to go anywhere together." She looked into his eyes. "It's not me, Willie Ron. I swear it. You're my friend and I don't care who knows it."

A pulse in Willie Ron's forehead jumped. "I know that," he said.

"Let's just go," Mary Louise said, regretting that she'd even mentioned the incident. "I mean it's Parnell, right? He's a coward. He won't do anything except talk."

Willie Ron shook his head. "I don't think

we can count on that, especially when he finds somebody to sell him some beer. He's mean enough when he's sober. He gets some booze in him and, well, he might do anything. And there are plenty of fools around who'd go right along with him. I'm not going to put you in danger."

Mary Louise regarded him worriedly. "You're not going to go after him, are you? Just leave him be, okay? Promise me. This will blow over eventually and he'll find someone else to bother."

"I'm not an idiot," Willie Ron said, dismissing her fears. "I never go looking for trouble, especially with a two-bit punk like Parnell. But I will keep my guard up."

As he spoke, Danny walked in and overheard him. "Why would you need to do that, Willie Ron? What's going on?"

Willie Ron looked at Mary Louise. "Up to you," he said with a shrug. "I've got work to do in the back."

Danny's gaze followed Willie Ron as he left them alone, then he faced Mary Louise. "Tell me."

"It's no big deal, really," she said. "How are you? You look great."

"Stop stalling and tell me."

She sighed. "I just had a run-in with Parnell Hutchins the other night. I was telling

345

Willie Ron about it."

Danny's gaze narrowed. "Why would you and Parnell have a run-in?"

"Because he likes to stir up trouble. You know that, Danny," she said earnestly. "You know exactly how he is. Remember when he told everybody that Mitzi Lewis had some sexually transmitted disease, just because she wouldn't sleep with him? He's mean, that's all."

If anything, Danny looked even more tense. "What was the run-in about, Mary Louise? And why didn't you tell me about it before this?"

"I didn't see any point in you worrying about it," she said reasonably. "You had exams going on. When did you get home, by the way?"

"Yesterday," he said. "And stop trying to change the subject. What was Parnell going on about?"

Mary Louise gave up trying to keep it from him. "Willie Ron, if you must know." She explained what the bully had said and how Cord had come in just in time to kick him out the door.

Alarm creased Danny's face. "You have to quit this job," he said urgently. "It's too dangerous for you to work here anymore. You just said it yourself, Mary Louise. You know

346

how Parnell is, especially after Cord humiliated him in front of his friends. He'll be back. He'll want you or Willie Ron to pay."

"I'm not quitting this job," she said fiercely. "I need it. And I'm not abandoning Willie Ron. He didn't do anything wrong. If anything, this is my fault."

"You're willing to put our baby at risk just to prove something to that scumbag Parnell?" he asked indignantly. "Use some sense, Mary Louise. It's not worth it."

Mary Louise flinched at his tone, but she held her ground. "I need the job," she repeated.

"Dammit, Mary Louise, I'll quit college and go to work for Cord Beaufort full-time before I'll have you or our baby endangered," Danny said. "Give your notice before you leave here tonight. I mean it. If you don't, I'll call your boss myself."

She frowned at his commanding tone. "Excuse me. When did you get the right to make any decisions for me?"

"When you stopped making smart ones for yourself," he retorted.

She was so angry, her stomach started doing backflips. "Danny Marshall, you don't have the right to tell me to do anything. You lost that right the day you admitted you weren't interested in marrying me."

347

"But I love you!" he shouted.

"And I love you!" she shouted right back. "But I'm on my own here and I'm doing the best I can, so you'll just have to trust me to take care of our baby the only way I know how."

Danny looked as if he might explode. Mary Louise dared to reach out and touch his cheek.

"It's going to be okay," she said quietly. "I can handle Parnell. And you are not going to quit college over this, Danny. That's ridiculous."

He frowned at her, but his temper seemed to cool. "When did you get to be so stubborn?" he asked.

She shrugged. "When I figured out that this baby and I are on our own."

"You don't have to be," Danny said, looking wounded. "I want to help."

"Then support my decisions."

"Even when they're crazy?"

"Even then," she said. "You don't have the right to tell me what to do."

He studied her curiously. "Would I have that right if I'd married you?"

Mary Louise managed a wobbly grin. "Nope."

Danny sighed. "I didn't think so."

For the first time since she'd given Danny

his freedom, Mary Louise felt a real sense of triumph. Not because she'd bested him in an argument, but because she was finally figuring out who she was. It turned out she was a lot stronger than she'd ever imagined. She loved Danny Marshall with all her heart, but she didn't need him to survive. How about that? she thought with amazement. She couldn't seem to stop grinning.

"What?" Danny demanded.

"Nothing," she said, smart enough not to tell him what she'd just discovered. Even *she* understood the male ego was a fragile thing. "I guess I was just thinking about how much things have changed the last couple of months."

Danny studied her skeptically. "In a good way?"

She gave the question some thought, then nodded. "Yeah, I think so. I really do." She stood on tiptoe and kissed his cheek. "Merry Christmas, Danny! I'm glad you're home."

He looked for a second as if he might argue some more, but then he sighed and wrapped his arms around her and rested his chin on top of her head. "Merry Christmas."

17

When Caleb turned up on Amanda's doorstep on a Friday night in mid-January just as
she arrived home from work, she scowled.
She was bone tired and in no mood for company, not even Caleb's. "Did I forget you
were coming by?" she asked irritably.

"Nope. I never told you. It's a surprise,"
he said, evidently not the least bit daunted
by her inhospitable attitude. "And I'm not
staying."

"Is that part of the surprise?"

"I was hoping it would be a disappointment," he said dryly. "I'm just here to get the
boys."

She regarded him with confusion. "The
boys, as in Larry and Jimmy, my sons?"

He grinned. "Those would be the ones."

"And why would I let them go somewhere
with you when you didn't ask in advance or
tell me where you're taking them?" she in-

quired testily. Ever since their poker game at Willow Bend before Christmas, the man had started to take way too much for granted. He was a lot like her father that way. She should probably point out that emulating Max in *any* way would not endear him to her.

"Because you're a wonderful mother and you wouldn't want to disappoint them just because you're annoyed with me," he said. "And because you won't want them underfoot during girls' night."

Amanda regarded him blankly. "Girls' night? I don't know anything at all about girls' night. Between the holiday rush and the post-holiday sales at work, then taking down Christmas decorations here, I'm too exhausted to even consider a girls' night."

The words were barely out of her mouth when Nadine strolled up the walkway, quickly followed by Dinah, Maggie and Mary Louise, who looked as if she couldn't quite believe she was being included.

"I hope you don't mind that Dinah asked me to tag along," the girl said, her expression hopeful.

"Of course not," Amanda said automatically, then scowled at Dinah. "It might have been nice, though, if someone had mentioned any of this to me."

"If we'd given you any advance warning,

you would have come up with an excuse to say no," Maggie said confidently. "You did last week when I wanted to have it at my house and the week before that when Dinah was willing to host it. We decided sneakier tactics were called for. It was Caleb's idea to take the boys with him, Josh and Cord. And Nadine's idea to bring the party to you."

Amanda's head was reeling. She wasn't sure how she felt about so many decisions being taken out of her hands. Truthfully, she could use another one of those laugh-filled evenings she'd had with these women before, but she'd felt guilty about taking the time away from her kids. She'd had so little of it with all the overtime work Joanna had given her during the holidays. She'd barely had any celebration at all. It had been just the excuse she needed to avoid spending the holidays with her father. She wasn't ready for that yet.

However, since Larry and Jimmy were going to be over the moon about being included with the men tonight, she hardly had any reason to fight this unexpected plan. Still, she couldn't give in too quickly or they'd be sneaking around her every chance they got. She had to put on a small show of defiance. They expected it. Heck, they *deserved* it.

"And what about Susie?" she asked, dredging up another problem they apparently hadn't considered. "Is she to be banished to her room? Or is someone coming to swoop her off, too?"

"Susie's staying with us," Nadine said. "I'm going to teach her to use nail polish."

"Over my dead body," Amanda snapped.

"She'll love it," Nadine said, not impressed with her vehement objection.

"I'm sure she will," Amanda said. "She's five. She loves chocolate and ice cream, too, but she doesn't get to have those just because she wants them."

Dinah draped an arm over Amanda's shoulder. "We'll do your nails, too," she cajoled. "You're just jealous because Max never let you go to sleepovers and do silly things when you were five."

"I am very sorry I told you all that." Amanda scowled at her, then relented. "Okay, you have a point."

Caleb had listened to the exchange with undisguised amusement, but now he focused his attention on Amanda. "Does this mean the boys are going with me?"

"Of course," she said with a sigh. "That was a foregone conclusion from the minute you showed up here."

He dropped a kiss on her cheek. "I'll find

353

them and tell them. There's too much estrogen floating around here for me. I need to go before I find myself getting too in touch with my feminine side."

As soon as he'd left the room, Maggie dramatically waved a napkin in front of Amanda's face. "Is that man half as sexy as he seems to me?"

Mary Louise regarded Maggie with widened eyes. "Can you say stuff like that about a preacher?"

"When he's as gorgeous as Caleb, it's an obligation," Dinah confirmed. "A preacher would insist on us being honest."

Amanda rolled her eyes. "Ladies, please watch the lessons you're imparting to this sweet young girl. She's innocent."

"I'm almost five months pregnant," Mary Louise replied tartly. "I'm not *that* innocent."

Amanda chuckled, delighted that Mary Louise hadn't lost her sense of humor despite all the difficulties she was about to face as a single mom. "Okay, but still, we need to preserve at least the illusion of respect for the clergy around here."

"I'll bet you've respected him all the way to your bedroom by now," Maggie taunted.

"Magnolia!" Dinah said, looking downright scandalized, then turning to Amanda with evident fascination. "Is Maggie right? Have you and the reverend done the deed?"

"I am not talking about this," Amanda said. "Since Mary Louise's presence wasn't enough to tame you, I'm going to get my five-year-old daughter. Maybe then you all will curb your tongues."

Maggie grinned unrepentantly. "You are without a doubt the most optimistic woman I've ever known. No wonder Caleb's so smitten."

"Not hearing this," Amanda declared as she went in search of Susie.

These women delighted her, shocked her and gave her the first taste she'd ever had of real friendship, but she had a hunch if she didn't set some limits right now, they'd spend the rest of the evening dissecting her relationship — or lack thereof — with Caleb. She wasn't sure she was anywhere near ready to hear their opinions on that, not until she'd figured out a few more things for herself.

Mary Louise couldn't get over the fact that all these women had included her in their girls' night. She hadn't said two whole sentences all evening because she was so busy taking in every word they said. And the conversation had gotten a whole lot more interesting since Susie had been sent off to bed, her tiny fingernails now a bright red.

Mary Louise knew she could never be a TV reporter like Dinah, but she'd love to own a little shop someday the way Maggie did. Or even work in one like Amanda. Anything would be better than spending the rest of her life working for minimum wage in a convenience store and putting up with jerks like Parnell.

She must have sighed or something, because all of a sudden they were all staring at her as if they'd just realized she was there. "What?" she asked, bewildered by the sudden attention.

"What's the scoop with you and Danny?" Amanda asked. "Has anything changed?"

Mary Louise flushed. "I guess I should have let you know what we decided, after you talked to me and everything. I'm sorry."

"You didn't owe me an explanation," Amanda responded. "I'm just asking because you've been so quiet all night. I figured you should have a turn to grumble about your man, too."

"Danny's not my man," Mary Louise said regretfully. "Not the way Cord is Dinah's or Josh is Maggie's, anyway."

Amanda regarded her with sympathy. "Then you decided against getting married?"

Mary Louise nodded and suddenly she couldn't seem to stop the tears that welled up in her eyes. She brushed at them impatiently and then Nadine handed her a tissue.

"I'm trying so hard to be sensible and do what's best, but it hurts, you know," she said, swiping at the tears. "I never thought I'd be having my first baby all by myself."

"You are not by yourself," Dinah said fiercely. "You have all of us and your folks."

"I don't think my folks are gonna be much help," Mary Louise said candidly. "They've been great about not getting on my case and everything, but I can tell they're real disappointed in me. They kind of pretend this isn't happening. My dad barely looks me in the eye anymore, much less at anything else. It's like if he doesn't see my stomach getting bigger, it won't be real or something."

"Oh, honey, once they see their first grandbaby, I guarantee you they'll forget all about how the baby came to be and just love it to pieces," Nadine said, giving her hand a squeeze. "And if you need a surrogate grandma around, you let me know. I wasn't the most doting mama in the world when Josh was a baby, so I can't wait to make up for that." She gave Maggie a pointed look as she spoke.

"I know. I get it," Maggie responded. "I'll

hurry up, or I would if Josh were in town for more than fifteen minutes at a time." She frowned at Dinah. "Tell your husband I need my husband back here more often. It's virtually impossible to get pregnant long distance. Or is that the way you're making sure I won't catch up with you?"

"I think we've already established that this is one race you cannot win," Dinah retorted. "As for Josh being gone, the man has a perfectly good motel room in Atlanta. You ever thought about driving over there? I'm pretty sure I conceived on one of my surprise visits to Cord."

Maggie's expression instantly brightened. "Is that so? I'll have to remember that for next week. Something tells me by the time he and the guys wind up their boys' night tonight, he'll crash and it'll be more than even I can do to wake him up." She grinned. "Even though I do have a very sexy red camisole I've been wanting to show off."

"If that won't keep him awake, you're doing something wrong," Dinah told her.

Mary Louise giggled. "You all are so funny. I wish I had friends like you."

"But you do!" Dinah declared. "You have us."

Mary Louise regarded her with wonder. "You really mean it? You guys will be my friends? I'm just a kid and you all are kinda . . ."

Dinah frowned. "Surely you were not going to say *old?*"

Mary Louise giggled. "How about more mature?"

"Shall we kill her now?" Maggie asked.

"Stop teasing, you guys," Nadine ordered, then turned to wrap Mary Louise in a hug. "Sweetie, we are your friends. We all think you're brave and mature and wonderful. If you need one single thing, you just ask one of us."

"And if you want Josh to have a few words with Danny, you let me know," Maggie said.

Mary Louise immediately shook her head. "No. I made the decision to have this baby on my own," she said, feeling more confident than she had in weeks. "I can do it. And it's not like Danny won't be around some of the time. He even went to one of my doctor appointments with me the other day. I thought he was gonna pass out when he saw the baby for the first time."

"That's great," Dinah said. "But if he can't be here, then I expect you to take birthing classes with me and Cord."

"And I'll be your coach," Amanda offered.

"I could do that," Maggie said.

Amanda frowned at Maggie. "How many

babies have you had?"

"Yes, Magnolia," Dinah taunted. "Maybe you ought to concentrate on the getting-pregnant part."

Maggie held up her hands. "Okay, okay, I defer to the mother of three."

"Thank you," Amanda said, grinning at Mary Louise. "Is this okay with you?"

"Sure," Mary Louise said eagerly. "I was wondering what I'd do. I don't think Danny's going to want any part of the delivery. Willie Ron would probably do it as a favor to me, but that's probably a really bad idea, especially with the way Parnell Hutchins has been spreading talk about us."

Maggie held up her hand. "Whoa! What kind of talk? I know Parnell. He's a low-class troublemaker. And Willie Ron's a doll. He's been a real blessing to his mama. There should be more men in the world who take on that kind of responsibility without giving it a second thought."

"Amen to that," Dinah said. "Now, tell the rest of them about Parnell. Cord's already filled me in."

Mary Louise realized she'd just opened up a real can of worms. "It was nothing," she said halfheartedly.

Dinah regarded her with sympathy. "It wasn't nothing," she said quietly, then told the others what Parnell had said. "Cord's afraid he'll stir up some of those low-life characters he hangs out with and something will happen to Willie Ron or to Mary Louise. Cord tried to convince her to quit, but she refuses."

"Danny's tried, too, but I can't quit," Mary Louise protested. "I have to work to save money for the baby."

"I can understand that," Amanda said. "But what if there was another job out there? There's an opening for a sales clerk at the boutique."

Mary Louise could hardly believe her luck. "Really? Do you think they'd hire me?"

"We can certainly check into it," Amanda said.

"Or you could work for me," Maggie chimed in. "One of my clerks just had an amazing show at the gallery and wants to start concentrating on her art full-time."

Mary Louise stared from one woman to the other and burst into tears.

Nadine was right there, this time with a whole box of tissues. "What on earth?" she asked. "Why are you crying, sweetie?"

"Because everyone's being so nice," Mary Louise said, blotting at the tears she couldn't seem to stop. "And I would absolutely love working at either of those places, but I don't think I should leave my job. It would be like letting Parnell win."

"No, it would be protecting yourself, your baby and Willie Ron," Dinah contradicted. "Be smart about this, Mary Louise. This is one fight it would be best to avoid."

The others nodded.

"You really think so?" she asked, her gaze on Nadine, who gave her an encouraging nod.

"That's settled, then," Dinah concluded. "Which place would you rather work? The boutique or the gallery?"

"The gallery's a sure bet," Maggie reminded her. "I'm the boss and the job's yours if you want it."

Mary Louise couldn't believe it was that easy. "Would you maybe teach me how to run a business? I mean, I know I'd have a lot to learn about all the things you sell in your shop, but after that?"

Maggie grinned at her. "I think we have a budding entrepreneur here," she said with approval. "Sweetie, I will teach you everything I know."

"Careful, Maggie," Dinah teased. "She could wind up being your strongest competitor one day."

"Oh, no," Mary Louise assured her. "If I ever had my own business, it wouldn't be a gallery. It would be a yarn shop, you know, where women would come and take knitting classes and sit around and talk the way we're doing now."

Amanda regarded her with surprise. "You knit?"

Mary Louise nodded. "My grandma taught me before she died. I'm making some things for the baby right now." She glanced around and realized they were all looking at her with real interest. "Would you like to see the blanket I'm knitting?" she asked shyly. "It's in Dinah's car. I work on it when things are slow at the Stop and Shop."

"Absolutely," Amanda said.

"You stay put," Dinah told her. "I'll get it. Is it in that tote bag you had with you when I picked you up from work?"

Mary Louise nodded.

"I'll be right back," Dinah said.

While she was gone, Mary Louise turned to Amanda. "Do you think I could have some more soda?"

"Water," Amanda said. "You need to cut back on the soda."

"Sure. Water's good," Mary Louise said, amazed that she felt protected when these women pressed her to do something. If her mother pressed, she felt smothered.

"And while we're waiting for Dinah, I'll

get the dessert," Maggie said. "Nadine baked brownies and I brought ice cream." She grinned. "I assume everyone here wants both."

Mary Louise listened to the chorus of enthusiastic responses and shook her head. "How do you all eat like this and stay so thin?"

"Trust me, we do not eat like this all the time," Nadine assured her.

"We reserve it for girls' night," Amanda said. "Which is probably why we've only had two girls' nights so far. Otherwise we'd all be big as blimps."

"Oh, that's why you came up with all those excuses," Maggie taunted. "To protect your waistline for Caleb."

Amanda ignored her. She handed a tall glass of ice water to Mary Louise, then started scooping ice cream onto the brownies Maggie had been setting into bowls. The desserts were ready when Dinah returned. She had this weird expression on her face as she handed the tote bag to Mary Louise.

"You okay?" Maggie asked.

Dinah nodded, then gave Mary Louise an apologetic look. "I peeked."

"That's okay," Mary Louise said at once, though she felt vaguely embarrassed. "It's not like I'm an expert or anything. I'd need to take some classes if I ever opened a shop."

"Stop it," Dinah said. "The blanket is beautiful, Mary Louise. Show them. And then promise you'll knit one for me. I want one exactly like it for my baby."

Mary Louise regarded her with uncertainty. "You mean it? You really like it?"

"Come on. Show us," Amanda pleaded.

Mary Louise pulled the nearly completed blanket from the bag. She'd chosen a pale green yarn and added white trim. It was the softest yarn she'd been able to find and it felt kind of like she imagined a cloud would feel, just barely there and gentle against a baby's skin. The pattern wasn't all that complicated, but she'd added a little row of fluffy yellow ducks around the border that she thought made it different.

"Oh, my," Amanda whispered, her eyes wide as she held it almost reverently against her cheek. "It's lovely, Mary Louise. It's absolutely charming."

"The ducks are just precious," Nadine said.

"When you're finished, would you let me show it to my boss?" Amanda asked. "She's been talking about adding a baby boutique to the store. I'll bet she would take as many of these as you could make." She grinned. "And charge an arm and a leg for them, too."

Mary Louise was overwhelmed. "You really think it's special?"

"I think you have a gift for design," Maggie confirmed. "And remember one thing if you sell any of these to Amanda's boss. She only gets an exclusive for, say, the next year. After that, we're going to see what we can do about opening your own shop."

"Absolutely," Dinah said. "I'll invest."

"You'll have to get in line behind me," Maggie countered.

Mary Louise clutched the baby blanket to her chest and blinked back more tears. For the second time since her dream of marrying Danny had gone up in smoke, she felt a sense of her own self-worth coming back. She realized she might be able to make a real future for herself and her baby all on her own. It was amazing how good that made her feel.

Caleb knew the instant he spotted Max making his way into the restaurant that he'd made the biggest mistake of his life by insisting that Amanda let Jimmy and Larry come along with him this evening. She was going to blow a gasket when she found out that the boys had met their grandfather when she wasn't there to supervise. She'd already postponed two meetings between them, making excuses about work pressures during the holidays. Caleb thought she was just terrified that once Max had met her children, there would be no turning back.

Cord spotted Max at the same time Caleb did. "Oh, boy," he muttered. "Is this going to be as bad as I think it is?"

Josh, who'd never met Max, looked bewildered. "What's the problem?"

"Could you take Jimmy and Larry for a walk?" Caleb asked Josh urgently. "Now!"

Josh didn't hesitate. "Hey, kids, let's go outside, okay?"

Jimmy stared at him curiously. "How come?"

Cord ruffled his hair. "Because if we get some exercise, we'll have more room for dessert. I'm thinking hot fudge sundaes. How does that sound?"

"Totally awesome," Jimmy said.

Larry, however, said nothing. His gaze seemed to be riveted on Max, who was making a beeline in their direction. "Who's he?" he asked Caleb.

Caleb forced a smile. "I'll tell you when you get back, okay? Just go with Josh."

Jimmy bounded out of his seat, but Larry was slower. He seemed to sense that the excitement was going to be right here.

"Larry, go with Josh," Caleb said firmly,

then turned to face Max, who was standing by silently, his avid gaze locked on the boys.

Cord stood up and nudged Larry along, then cast a sympathetic look at Caleb.

"They're Amanda's sons," Max said with certainty after the boys were gone. He regarded Caleb with a hurt expression. "Why did you send them away?"

"Because it's not up to me to introduce you to them," Caleb said. "Amanda would be furious if I took that decision out of her hands."

"It's not as if you arranged it," Max scoffed. "What do you think I'm going to do — scare the two of them?"

"No, of course not," Caleb said. "It's just awkward."

"And you don't think it was awkward shooing them out of here as if I were the devil incarnate?" Max asked. "I imagine they're pestering Cord and that other fellow with questions right now."

Caleb sighed. "Yes, I suspect they are."

"Think they'll rat you out?" Max asked.

"No, I think they'll be very discreet," Caleb said. "Unlike you, they seem to know what's at stake."

Max's gaze narrowed. "Which is?"

"Your relationship with your daughter," Caleb responded at once. "And mine."

Max sat down suddenly as if his legs would no longer hold him. "You think she wouldn't forgive you?"

"Or you," Caleb said. "Max, we have to tread lightly with Amanda. This truce between you is still a fragile thing. If you upset her, it could go up in smoke."

Max looked genuinely bewildered. "But I thought we'd made progress. She stayed there a couple of weeks back and played poker with the two of us."

"She's mellowed, no question about it," Caleb agreed. "But these are her babies, Max. You said some awful things about them once. She's going to have to decide when you get to see them. She's just trying to protect them."

"I never said a thing to their faces," Max blustered indignantly, but it was evident from the regret in his eyes that his tone was mostly for show. He knew how badly he'd behaved.

"I would never deliberately set out to hurt a child, especially not my own grandchild," he added for good measure.

"But you did hurt them, at least indirectly," Caleb admonished him. "When you cut their mother out of your life, then turned their father away, you made sure that they wouldn't have a grandfather in their lives.

You robbed them of that. I think that's more important than ever, now that they've lost their dad."

"Is that what you're worried about, or are you upset because I didn't hand Amanda the money to dig herself out of the hole that O'Leary scoundrel put her in?"

"It's not about the money, Max. That's the least of it," Caleb said. "All I care about are people."

Max rubbed a hand across his eyes. "Okay, I get it. I've made a lot of mistakes. I know that. I'm trying to fix things."

"By coming here tonight?"

"I told you it was an accident," Max said, but without real vehemence.

"Then George didn't happen to mention anything about this boys' night out when he stopped by to see you?" Caleb asked mildly.

Max looked startled. "You know about George being at the house?"

Caleb smiled. "He said that's why he couldn't join us, because he was coming to see you. I imagine he told you exactly where we'd be and that we'd have those boys with us."

"You're too damn smart for your own good," Max grumbled.

"And you're not half as clever as you think you are," Caleb retorted. "Why don't you go home before you stir up a ruckus in here, Max? Amanda will bring the boys to see you soon."

"You sure about that?"

"Didn't she promise she would?"

Max nodded grudgingly. "She said it would be before Christmas, though, and that didn't happen."

"Well, I know the one sure way to guarantee that she won't keep her word would be for you to force the issue right now," Caleb said confidently.

Max frowned, but he stood up. "Okay, you win," he said, his expression sad. "Least I got a glimpse of them. They're Maxwells through and through, aren't they?"

Caleb couldn't deny him that. "They have your stubbornness, too," he said. "And trust me when I tell you that is not a compliment."

"Watch your tongue, boy." He gave Caleb's shoulder a squeeze. "I suppose you think I ought to thank you for keeping me from stirring up trouble."

"I'd appreciate it, but I don't expect it," Caleb retorted.

"In that case, I thank you," Max said, a twinkle in his eye. "See, even an old man like me is capable of a few surprises."

Filled with relief, Caleb watched him go.

Now all he had to do was keep Larry and Jimmy from asking a thousand unanswerable questions, then reporting back to their mother.

18

Amanda took her exhausted sons upstairs and tucked them in without the usual nighttime rituals, then went back down to find Caleb standing at the kitchen window, his expression pensive as he stared out into the darkness.

"Is everything okay?" she asked. "I hope the boys weren't too much trouble."

"Your sons couldn't possibly be too much trouble," he said. "There's nothing I'd rather do than spend time with them."

"Are we talking about the same boys? Eight and nine, about so tall?" She held up her hand, palm down. "I seem to recall an adventure with a nail gun while we were building this house and another surprise excursion up to the roof."

Caleb's lips curved slightly. "Typical boys, that's all."

Shaking her head at his nonchalance,

Amanda said, "You might not find it so charming if they were yours. My heart still starts pounding when I think about it. Took ten years off my life."

"I imagine they'll do worse before they're grown," he said.

She regarded him with alarm. "Please don't say things like that."

This time he gave her a full-fledged smile, the kind of smile that made her tingle with the suggestion that they were somehow in this together.

"Prepare yourself, Amanda. Just wait till they hit their teens. Get all the sleep you can now, because during those years it'll be in short supply. Wait till they're out on their first dates, or out beyond curfew with the car."

"Now, aren't you the cheery soul?" she said, then studied him. "How do you know so much about teenaged boys?"

"For starters, I was one. For another, I spend a lot of time with the youth group at church. It's about time we got you started with that, too. I'm thinking sometime in the next few weeks. I didn't press before the holidays, but things shouldn't be so rushed now. Once you've spent some time with these kids — and let me add that these are all *good* kids — you'll see what I mean. It might prepare you."

"Prepare me?"

"For a few years from now when Larry and Jimmy hit their teens," he said. "Isn't that what we were talking about?"

Surprised by the edge in his voice, she studied him intently. "What put you into this odd mood, Caleb?"

He avoided her gaze, then sighed. "I'm trying to decide whether or not to tell you something."

Amanda was surprised by the cautious note in his voice, to say nothing of the fact that he hadn't yet learned that keeping secrets from her was a sure way to provoke her. "Evasions, Caleb? I thought you'd learned that lesson."

"I'm afraid I'm still tempted to try it when it comes to anything related to your father," he replied. "That topic usually gets you pretty stirred up."

Her heart flipped over in her chest. "Is he worse?"

He immediately looked apologetic. "Oh, no, nothing like that. I'm sorry. I didn't mean to scare you."

She was startled by the depth of her relief. Apparently she'd made more progress in forgiving Max than she'd realized, or maybe the concern was simply instinctive, ingrained by all those years when she had cared. "What about him, then?"

"We ran into him tonight," he said, studying her closely.

Amanda went perfectly still. "You ran into Max? While the boys were there?"

He nodded.

"Did you plan it?" she asked, ice in her voice. "Did you decide I wasn't moving fast enough to suit you?"

Caleb shook his head. "No, I didn't plan it, Amanda," he said, looking hurt by the accusation. "It just happened. And I did the best damage control I could. Josh and Cord got the boys out of the restaurant and I talked to your father and asked him to leave."

"And did he leave?"

Caleb nodded. "Reluctantly, yes. They barely crossed paths." Then he added with some urgency, "He's dying to meet them, Amanda. Surely you can understand that. You even promised him you'd take them out there over the holidays."

"I was busy, dammit!"

"I know that," he soothed, "but you know that Max isn't a patient man."

"Maybe I should rethink that promise," she retorted coolly. She wasn't sure if her forgiveness extended to Max's rejection of her children.

"Please, don't."

She watched Caleb suspiciously, certain that he hadn't told her the whole story. "I know you're trying hard to make it sound like it, but this wasn't an accidental encounter, was it? If you didn't set it up, he did."

"Yes," Caleb admitted. "George saw him earlier tonight and mentioned where we'd be and that Larry and Jimmy would be with us. I suppose your father couldn't resist. I can't say that I blame him, but I swear I did everything I could to keep them apart. They never even exchanged a word with him, and none of us explained who Max is. Still, I imagine the boys will have a lot of questions in the morning. They certainly had them tonight."

Her heart started to pound. "What did you tell them?"

"The truth, up to a point. I said he was someone you know and I was sure you'd take them to meet him one day soon, but it was up to you to do that."

"And of course that only made them more curious," Amanda concluded wearily, recalling that Larry had already picked up on Max's existence and had even found out somehow that he was ill. He'd even shared some of what he'd figured out with Susie, more than likely with Jimmy, as well. She wasn't ready for all the explanations this was going to require. Taking the boys and Susie to see her father would mean the end to the war of wills between them. It would amount to saying that she'd forgiven him completely and trusted him not to hurt them. Once she'd allowed him into their lives, she couldn't change her mind.

But even if her own feelings were mellowing, did she trust Max? He'd been her rock for nearly twenty years and he'd almost destroyed her. How could she entrust her children's fragile young hearts to a man capable of that?

"I hate being in this position," she said angrily. "I'm not ready for this."

"Nonetheless, you have to deal with it," Caleb said, refusing to cut her even an inch of slack. "I'm sorry this happened tonight, but that's where we are. If you ignore it, I wouldn't put it past Larry to go looking for his grandfather. I think he suspects that's who Max is. Jimmy was more oblivious to the undercurrents, but Larry wasn't. He didn't want to leave the table when Max arrived."

She regarded Caleb with dismay, fully aware of her son's determination and daring. "You don't think he'd try to find his way out there on his own?" she asked, then shook her head. "Of course he would. Larry's the one with absolutely no fear."

"Then you can't take a chance, Amanda. Take them to see your father, and do it soon," Caleb pleaded. "That way you control the situation."

"As if anyone ever controls anything when it comes to Max," she scoffed, then sighed. "Okay. I'll take them, but you're coming with me."

"Fine." He met her gaze. "What is it you think my presence will accomplish?"

"You'll be handy when this meeting blows up in my face. I won't have to go hunting for you to kill you."

She wasn't entirely joking, and based on the expression of alarm in Caleb's eyes, he knew it.

Max hadn't suffered many humiliations in his life, but being forced to leave a restaurant without saying so much as a word to his own grandsons was just about at the top of the very short list. He was still stewing about it on Sunday afternoon. Worse, Caleb hadn't called to say how things had gone when Amanda had found out. Nor had Amanda shown her face.

He should have forced the issue right then and there, he thought, feeling totally out of sorts and out of control. Leaving had been a mistake. Amanda would probably turn this into some sort of big whoop-de-do and use it as an excuse to keep him from those kids forever.

The only reason he hadn't stayed was out of respect for Caleb. The man had been a good friend, and he'd worked to help Max make peace with Amanda. How could Max have turned his back on that and left Caleb stuck out on some limb all by himself? Max had experienced the full brunt of Amanda's fury. He couldn't very well subject his friend to that on his behalf, especially not if what he suspected about their feelings for each other was true.

He supposed the next couple of hours would tell the story. Caleb usually came by in midafternoon. Once he showed up, he'd fill Max in on just how ticked off Amanda was about the other night. There wasn't a doubt in his mind that she knew every detail. Caleb didn't have enough sneakiness in him to keep that kind of secret, not after he'd vowed to her that the secrets were over.

Jessie appeared on the porch, that dadgum pitying look back in her eyes.

"What do you want?" he growled.

"I was just wondering if you're getting hungry or if you want to wait to eat when Caleb gets here?" she responded, unfazed by his grumpiness.

"Why would I wait on him? Do you think he does me the courtesy of letting me know if he's coming?"

She grinned at that. "He comes every Sunday, Max. Don't pretend you're sitting around on pins and needles waiting for his phone call. The two of you don't stand on ceremony."

"Well, maybe we should," he grumbled. "Maybe he should wait to be invited."

Jessie merely rolled her eyes. "Am I putting some lunch on the table for you or not?"

"I'll wait to eat with Caleb when he shows his face," he said. "But bring me a sandwich out here so I don't starve to death in the meantime."

"Any particular kind of sandwich?"

"You have any of that meat loaf left?" he asked hopefully.

Jessie hesitated. "Uh, no, you finished it."

Max frowned at her. "Something wrong with me asking about the meat loaf?"

"No, of course not," she said a little too hurriedly. "Nothing at all."

Max sighed at her pitiful attempt at evasion. "We haven't had meat loaf in a while, have we?"

She shook her head. "It's not surprising you'd think about it. It was always one of your favorites."

"Next to your fried chicken," he said. "That's Caleb's favorite. I imagine that's what we're having for supper, since you have a soft spot for him."

Her tight expression eased. "Of course, but it's got nothing to do with Caleb. You know perfectly well that Sunday fried chicken is as much a tradition around here as my sweet potato casserole on Thanksgiving or my black-eyed peas on New Year's Day."

Max regarded Jessie with genuine fondness. There'd been a time when they might have been more to each other, but his heart had always belonged to Margaret, even after all the years she'd been gone. "You know how important you are to this family, don't you? I know I don't say it half enough, but Amanda and I wouldn't have made it without you. And I'm not sure I could have carried on when she left, if you hadn't been around to nag me."

"Oh, hush that nonsense," Jessie said, her cheeks turning pink and tears welling up in her eyes. "You're gonna make me cry, old man."

"Maybe you ought to sit down here next to me and we could both have ourselves a good cry," Max suggested. "Seems to me we're due. Lord knows we shed enough tears the day Amanda left here."

"Which would never have happened if you hadn't been your stubborn, contrary self," she admonished him. "I hope you don't do anything to ruin this reconciliation."

"I'm not going to ruin anything," Max huffed indignantly. At least he hoped not. Of course, based on Friday's incident, there was a good possibility he already had.

Asleep in his rocker on the porch, Max was awakened by the sound of a car winding its way up the driveway. He pulled himself out of a troublesome dream and watched anxiously to see who was coming. He told himself he wasn't disappointed that it was just Caleb's familiar sedan.

Only after it had pulled to a stop did he see that there were other occupants in the car. Amanda was sitting stiffly in the front passenger seat and her three children were in the back. Max felt his heart clutch at the wondrous sight. Only Jessie knew how much he'd longed for this day over the years.

All three kids were spilling out of the back seat before Caleb could get out from behind the wheel. Amanda was much slower to exit. In fact, she waited until Caleb circled the car and opened her door. Max didn't think it had a blessed thing to do with manners. He was pretty sure she'd have stayed put without Caleb standing there waiting for her to move.

He saw her shoot a scowl up at Caleb, reserving another one for Max as she slowly crossed the lawn, the kids running ahead. They hung back when they reached the bottom of the steps till she joined them.

Max clutched the arms of the rocker, willing himself to let Amanda handle this in her own way. If it had been up to him, he'd have scooped every one of those kids into a bear hug by now. All the vicious thoughts he'd ever had about their daddy faded as he studied those precious faces.

"Hello, Daddy," she said at last, her voice even shakier than it had been on her first visit.

Max realized she was nervous or angry or both. He nodded at her and waited, but his gaze kept straying to the boys standing on either side of her and to the girl clutching Caleb's hand. That darling child was the spitting image of Amanda when she'd been that age.

Amanda turned her back on him and hunkered down in front of the children. "This is your grandfather," she told them, that hitch back in her voice. "He's been wanting to meet you." She glanced over her shoulder with a look that warned him not to make a liar out of her.

Max stood up then. "I surely have," he said, taking a step toward them.

Jimmy's face lit up in recognition. "I know you. You were the man at the restaurant Friday night. How come Caleb made us leave without talking to you?"

"He was just trying to do the right thing," Max said. "He knew your mama wanted to be the one to introduce us."

Susie took a cautious step forward, her sweet little face filled with curiosity. "How come we never knew you before? Did you live far away?"

Max shook his head. "No, I've always lived right here." He faltered after that, unsure of what to say.

"Your granddaddy and I had a big disagreement a long time ago," Amanda said quietly. "I was very mad at him and we haven't seen each other since then."

Larry inched closer to her, his attitude admirably protective. "Are you still mad at him?" he asked her, regarding Max with suspicion.

Amanda rested a hand on his shoulder. "We're working on making things better," she said.

"I'll bet it's 'cause he's sick," Susie guessed. "Mommy's always extra nice to us when we're sick."

Max felt that odd sensation in his heart again, an old pain that had never really gone away. "Whatever the reason, I'm real glad of it, Susie. I've missed your mama."

Susie crept closer, then held out her arms to be picked up. Max scooped her up and held her tight against his chest. To his astonishment, she gave his cheek a pat, just as Amanda used to do.

"It's okay, Granddaddy. You can cry if you want. I cried my first day of school 'cause I missed her."

Max felt the tears cascading down his cheeks and wasn't the least bit ashamed of them. "Caleb, why don't you go inside and tell Jessie we have company. I think she baked cookies today. I imagine a few won't spoil Sunday dinner."

"Cookies?" Susie asked, squirming to get down. "I'll go with Mr. Caleb. He probably needs help."

Max released her with regret, then smiled as she scampered inside ahead of Caleb, practically bouncing with excitement. His gaze sought Amanda's. "I could always win you over with cookies, too."

Her lips curved slightly, but the smile

didn't take. "I'm not as easily won over now," she told him.

Max nodded. "I understand that." He smiled at his grandsons. "What about you? You want to help with the cookies while your mom and I have a talk?"

"Sure," Jimmy said at once, and raced inside, letting the screen door slam behind him.

"Larry?" he asked.

"I'm staying with my mom," he said fiercely.

Max nodded. "That's fine with me."

Amanda, however, ruffled the boy's hair. "It's okay. You go on with the others. I'll be fine."

Larry's gaze narrowed. "But *are* you still mad at him?" he asked again.

"I'm working on it," she said.

"How come?" Larry asked.

"Because, no matter what, he is my father, just like I'm your mom. I hope if we ever have a fight, you'll forgive me."

Larry looked bewildered. "We have fights all the time."

Amanda grinned. "Those are little disagreements," she told him. "The one your granddaddy and I had was a humdinger."

"Oh," Larry said, still looking puzzled.

"You don't need to understand," she told

him. "It's between your granddaddy and me, and we'll work it out. I want you to get to know him, okay?"

"I guess," Larry agreed reluctantly.

"Go have some cookies and think about it," Amanda encouraged. "And make sure Caleb doesn't let Susie have too many, especially if Jessie made fried chicken for dinner."

Larry grinned and looked at Max with the first less-than-hostile look since they'd arrived. "Susie gets sick and throws up," he said happily. "You'd better watch out."

Max laughed at the warning. "Good advice. I'll be sure to stay out of her path if she has too many cookies, and between Jessie and Caleb, I imagine she will."

Larry finally went inside, leaving Max alone with his daughter.

"Thank you," he said, his voice thick with emotion.

"For what?"

"Bringing them out here. I know I probably don't deserve it," he said.

"Especially after that sneaky trick you played on Caleb Friday night," she said.

Max shook his head. "He told you? I wondered if he would."

"Caleb's an honest man."

"He is," Max agreed, then grinned. "Something tells me he struggles with it from time to time."

"Only when you swear him to secrecy," Amanda retorted.

Max flushed guiltily. "Still, I don't suppose the story was the first thing out of his mouth when he brought them home."

"No, as a matter of fact, it wasn't," she admitted.

"Then there's hope for him yet," Max said approvingly.

Amanda frowned. "Let's pray he doesn't adopt your attitude toward honesty, that it's something to be reserved only for those occasions it's convenient."

"You always been so concerned about honesty?"

"Of course."

"Then how the devil did you let Bobby O'Leary get away with lying to you for so many years?"

Max knew as soon as the words were out of his mouth that he'd said exactly the wrong thing. He closed his eyes against the anger on Amanda's face and tried to block out the heat in her voice.

"Saying things like that about my husband is no way to keep me here," she said coldly. "Keep it up and your first visit with your grandchildren could be your last. I won't have you criticizing their father, especially not when they might overhear you. They have no idea it was Bobby's fault that things have been so difficult for us. I won't have their memories of him tarnished by you out of spite."

"You're absolutely right," Max said, hanging his head. "I should never have said such a thing when they could hear it. Children should never hear a harsh word spoken about their parents. I held to that when *you* were a child."

Even before Max realized what he'd let slip, Amanda regarded him with a stunned expression. "Meaning what?"

"Forget I said that," he muttered.

"No, how can I? I want to know what you meant."

"Nothing," he insisted. "I was just rambling on."

"About what?" she demanded again. "You weren't rambling, Daddy. You said exactly what you meant to say. What kind of harsh words did you keep to yourself when I was a child? Are you talking about my mother? Was there something about her you never told me? You always put her up on a pedestal, so I assumed she belonged there."

Max cursed his stupidity. He'd kept the secret for more than thirty years, only to come close to blurting it out now when it could do even more damage.

"That's exactly what a child should believe about her mother," he said.

"But it was a lie?" she asked.

Max kept silent.

"Daddy, tell me," Amanda demanded. "If there's something I should know about my mother, then I want to hear it. I have a *right* to hear it."

All the fight seemed to drain out of Max under Amanda's condemning gaze. Maybe the damn secret wasn't worth keeping anymore, but right this second he wished like hell it had died with him . . . or with his faltering memory, at any rate.

"I swear, Daddy, if you don't speak up, I'll . . ." Her voice faltered.

"You'll what? Beat the truth out of me?" he asked, amused by her ferocity despite the disaster he'd set in motion. "Take the kids and leave? How will you learn anything if you're not underfoot to nag me?"

"Oh, for pity's sake, you're impossible!" she snapped. "You probably made the whole thing up just to see if you could get me all stirred up."

For a fleeting instant, he considered letting her believe that. It would be easier on both of them.

Then her expression changed. "But you didn't do that, did you?"

God help him, he couldn't see a way around the truth. "No," he admitted. "I never should have gotten into this, not after all this time. It won't do a bit of good."

Amanda's gaze remained steady as she waited, her hands clenched nervously in her lap as if she knew whatever was coming would shake her world forever. And it would. There was no question about that. That's why Max had never had the nerve to tell her when she was younger. He'd worked hard to give her an image of her mother that she could treasure.

"Okay, yes, it is about your mother," he said quietly.

She nodded. "I figured that much," she said impatiently.

"I loved her more than you can possibly imagine," he said, his heart aching at the memory. "She was my life, at least till the day you were born."

"The day she died," Amanda whispered.

Max took a deep breath, then slowly shook his head. "No, Amanda. It didn't happen like that."

For a moment, she merely looked confused. When the implication registered, shock spread across her face. "What are you saying?" she asked weakly. "Did you . . . ?"

He stared at her in confusion, then realized the leap she'd taken. "Did I what? Kill her? Is that what you're thinking? Good God, Amanda, is that what you think of me?" He sighed, hurt to the quick. "I suppose you have reason enough to think I'm capable of anything, but no, nothing like that."

"What, then?"

He had to brace himself to voice the truth. "Your mother's not dead, Amanda," he said slowly. "A few days after you were born, she left me."

Amanda looked as if she might faint from the shock of his announcement. Max regarded her worriedly. "Are you okay?"

She stared at him incredulously. "My mother's alive? Still?"

"Last I heard, yes," Max said.

"And when was that?" she asked, disbelief and fury warring on her face.

Max winced. "A week or two ago," he admitted, racked now with guilt over all the years of deception. "I've gotten a report once a month since the day she left."

Amanda sat back, suddenly looking more

bewildered than angry. "Why?"

"Why did she go or why did I keep it from you?"

"Both."

"It's a complicated story, but I suppose it can be boiled down to one thing. She wanted more excitement than I could give her."

"She just walked away from me? From us?" Amanda sounded breathless. "Without a fight?"

"It was the deal we made. I insisted on a clean break, even though it tore me apart to do it. I couldn't have her changing her mind every few weeks or months, turning our lives upside down. She wasn't ready to be a mother, to give up all the dreams she'd had to stay here at Willow Bend." He gave her a sad look. "She was a lot like Bobby, you see. She was a dreamer. She always wanted something that was just out of reach. I gave her everything she ever asked for — I would have given her the moon if I could have — but it was never enough. So I let her go off with someone she thought could make her happier."

"She left with another man?"

He nodded, trying to hide his bitterness. Losing Margaret had been hard enough. Losing her to a no-account charmer who was destined to break her heart within a year had been a thousand times worse.

"Are you sure you didn't send her away?" Amanda asked heatedly. "That sounds more like you."

He shook his head, thinking of the day he'd watched his beautiful Margaret go and how it had ripped out his heart. It was exactly like the day he'd lost Amanda. Worse in many ways, because it had set all these years of deception in motion.

"How dare you keep this from me?" Amanda demanded furiously now. "How dare you let me spend my whole life thinking my mother was dead?"

"I thought it was best," he said simply.

"Best? How could it possibly have been best?"

"Wasn't it better than knowing that you weren't enough to keep her here?" he asked gently. "Knowing that I wasn't enough was hard on me and I was a grown man. How could I put that kind of burden on a little girl?"

He watched as his words sank in and Amanda seemed to shrink right before his eyes. No question her heart was broken by a woman she'd never even known and a father who'd blurted out a truth best left unsaid for all eternity. He'd curse himself for that till the day he died.

"I'm sorry, darlin' girl. I never should have told you," he said.

Amanda looked at him with a mixture of hurt and contempt. "Yes, you should have," she said quietly. "You just should have done it thirty years ago."

19

Amanda felt as if her head were going to explode. Her mother was alive! All these years she had mourned someone she'd never even known. She'd pitied herself for not having a mother to bake cookies for her, to listen to her talk about school, to explain about her first period, to hold her when her first boyfriend broke her heart.

Instead, it had been Jessie who'd baked the cookies and listened and explained about becoming a woman. Max had been the one to hold her and let her tears soak his shirt. She'd had both of them, and it should have been more than enough.

But it hadn't been. She'd longed for a mother. She'd even tried a time or two to pick out one for herself, but Max had been stubbornly resistant to her matchmaking schemes, even when it came to Jessie, already an integral part of their lives. Or maybe *especially* when it came to Jessie.

To discover now not only that her mother was alive but far from the idealized version her father had described made her feel sick inside. She looked at her father, fighting the all-consuming anger and renewed sense of betrayal that was bitter on her tongue. She wanted desperately to lash out, but always in the back of her mind was the reminder that he was ill.

"Did you love her all this time?" she asked. "Is that why you never looked at anyone else?"

Max nodded. "Pitiful, isn't it? That's what I didn't want for you, Amanda, an all-consuming love like the one you felt for Bobby, a man who was as unworthy as your mother."

"But how?" she asked. "How could you go on loving her after what she'd done?"

He smiled at that. "You should know. A part of you still loves Bobby, doesn't it? Love doesn't die easily, even when you see the other person's flaws. People are more than their failings, Amanda."

His expression turned nostalgic. "Your mother was ten years younger than I. She was vital and amazing and beautiful. She captivated everyone who met her. Everything I ever told you about her was true. I just didn't paint a complete picture. She was also selfish and immature. She wanted what she wanted when she wanted it, with little regard for the consequences. Under the right circumstances, that could be charming and impetuous. Under others, it was far less attractive. I recognized some of those same traits in Bobby and knew firsthand the damage they could cause. I know it wasn't fair to judge him based on what had happened to me, but I couldn't help it. I wanted to protect you from the same kind of mistake I'd made, one that nearly destroyed me."

Amanda could hardly argue with his motives, now that she had a more complete picture, but none of that made it right. And she couldn't imagine anything that would make his lie about her mother okay.

"I should have known," she said wearily. "It might have made all the difference."

"Perhaps," he conceded. "But you were my world and I didn't want you to hurt the way I did when your mother left. I didn't want you to make a rash decision and suffer as I had."

"And yet I did suffer," she told him. "Out of your desire to protect me, I never had a chance to know my mother and then I lost you and, in the end, I lost Bobby. How did that make anything better?"

"If I'd been able to see into the future, I'd have done things differently," her father said.

She regarded him with skepticism. "Really?"

He gave her a wry smile, then shrugged. "No, probably not. I was convinced I knew what was best."

Amanda fell silent, her thoughts whirling. Finally she met her father's gaze. "Has my mother ever asked about me?"

He shook his head. "As I said before, that was our agreement. There was to be absolutely no contact, not with me directly, not with you, not with anyone in Charleston who might give away the secret. It was the price she agreed to pay for her freedom to go chasing after her lover. We had to come up with this whole elaborate plan to let her slip away from here so no one would know the truth. Everyone believed the story that she'd died after giving birth to you and that I'd taken her ashes back to Georgia for burial. If anyone questioned that, they never dared to mention it to me. In return, I paid her enough to live on comfortably for the rest of her life."

"But why not just admit the truth, that she'd left you?" she asked, then shook her head. "Never mind. It was that Maxwell pride of yours, wasn't it? You couldn't just lose her. She had to be dead to everyone."

"Something like that," he admitted.

"And the man? What happened to him?"

Her father shrugged. "The allure wore off eventually, I suppose. They weren't together more than a few months."

"And you know that because you kept tabs on her," Amanda said, "even though she wasn't allowed to contact me."

"I needed to know she was okay," he said simply.

"And if she hadn't been?" she asked curiously. "What would you have done? Would you have gone to her? Brought her home? Unraveled all the lies?"

His expression wilted at that. "I don't know," he said softly. "I have no idea. I suppose it's just as well I never needed to find out. As near as I can tell, she's had the life she wanted. She's been content."

"How could she be?" Amanda asked, bewildered, trying to imagine her own life if she'd simply abandoned her children and left them to someone else to raise. "What sort of woman leaves her daughter behind and never looks back? She must have had regrets."

He sighed. "Perhaps she did, but she wasn't like you, Amanda. Mothering wasn't instinctive to her. She wanted to travel, meet new people, have new adventures. I had rashly promised her all of those things when I married her, but when I took too long giving them to her, she grew restless. My mistake was thinking she'd come to love this place as I do, that she'd settle down."

Amanda felt completely overwhelmed. "I have so many questions, but I can't think now. I need to go. If I take Caleb's car, do you think you could make sure he and the kids get home?"

"Of course," Max said without hesitation.

In fact, Amanda thought he seemed almost eager for her to go. Perhaps he needed time to himself, as well. His revelations seemed to have taken as much out of him as they had out of her.

"Should you be driving?" she asked belatedly. "If not . . ."

A few years ago, perhaps even a few months ago, Max would have railed at her doubts, but he seemed to accept them, which somehow made Amanda terribly sad.

"It's okay," he said without rancor. "Jessie will drive them."

She studied him sorrowfully. "You know, I always thought Jessie was the one you really loved."

"I know," he said. "And in my own way, I suppose I do. She just had the misfortune to come along after my heart was already taken." He shrugged, his expression resigned. "Things are better this way."

"You all alone and Jessie just as miserable?" Amanda asked. "And my mother, who knows where? How is any of that better?"

"If I make Jessie's life miserable now, just imagine what I could do if I were ever to marry her," he said, his tone wry. "Besides, it wasn't possible."

"Why not?"

He gave her an impatient look. "Your mother's still very much alive."

It finally dawned on Amanda what he meant. "You never divorced?"

"How could we? Everyone thought she was dead. See what a complicated web we weave . . . ?"

What Amanda saw was a man who'd made impossible choices and found a way to live with them. She just wasn't sure quite yet whether she admired him or hated him because of it.

When Caleb and the children exited the house, he realized Amanda was gone and so was his car. Larry apparently noticed it at the same time. He whirled on his grandfather.

"What did you do to my mom? Why did

she leave?" he asked Max, his fists balled up as if he wanted to strike out at this man who had the power to hurt his mother.

Caleb rested a hand on the boy's shoulder, but he, too, regarded Max curiously. "Did something happen?"

"We talked, that's all," Max said defensively.

Caleb kept his gaze steady on the older man. There was more. He could tell it not only by Max's tone, but it almost seemed as if new lines had been etched into his face.

"Kids, why don't you all explore a little?" Caleb suggested. "Just stay within sight of the house."

Jimmy could hardly wait to take off and Susie was right on his heels, but once again Larry hung back. Caleb hunkered down and looked into his eyes. "I'm sure your mom is just fine. You don't need to worry about her."

"But if he did something . . ." the boy began, casting an angry look at his grandfather.

"Then it will be up to him to fix it," Caleb said. "Go keep an eye on your brother and sister, okay?"

He waited until Larry was out of earshot, before he turned to Max. "What happened?"

"You don't need to worry about getting home," Max said, avoiding the question. "I'll have Jessie take you all."

"A ride is the last thing I'm concerned about," Caleb snapped. "What did you say to upset Amanda? You did upset her, didn't you?"

Max suddenly looked defeated. "She'll have to be the one to tell you," he said. "If that's what she wants to do."

"Dammit, Max, the two of you were just starting to get close again," he said, not even trying to hide his frustration. "You know how fragile this truce is."

"Don't you think I understand that, boy? I didn't intend to open up this can of worms, but it happened and there's not a blessed thing I can do about it now." He regarded Caleb sadly. "Maybe you all should get on out of here. Go check on Amanda. She said she wanted to be alone, but something tells me she could use a friend about now."

"I could be a better friend if I knew what was going on," Caleb said.

"Then you'll have to ask her," Max repeated, struggling to his feet. "I'm tired. I'm going in to take a nap."

Caleb tamped down his irritation and studied him worriedly. "Are you okay?"

Max gave him a resigned look. "I think we both know the answer to that, don't we?"

Caleb watched him go inside. Just as the

screen door was about to close, Max caught it and looked back at Caleb. "Tell her I'm sorry, okay? About everything."

Caleb nodded. "Sure."

But first he had to learn what *everything* was. Something told him Amanda was going to be no more eager to talk about it than Max had been.

She wasn't going to get rid of Caleb. Amanda could tell that from the set of his jaw and the way he'd ignored every one of her hints about being tired and tomorrow being a workday. More telling was the fact that he hadn't said a single word about her abrupt disappearance from Max's. No, he was saving that for after the kids were in bed. So far, she'd let them stay up a half hour past their bedtime just to avoid being alone with Caleb and all his questions.

Finally, she had no choice. She had to get the kids upstairs so they'd get a decent night's sleep before school. She tried staring Caleb down. "Isn't it time you were going?" she asked bluntly.

His mouth curved into a slight smile. "You're not shaking me that easily, Amanda. We're going to talk."

"Does it have to be tonight?" she asked. She was emotionally wrung out. She wasn't sure she had anything left for a conversation about Max's devastating revelation.

Caleb studied her for an eternity before finally nodding. "Yes," he said quietly. "I think it does. Otherwise, neither one of us will get any sleep."

"Okay, fine," she said irritably. "Give me a few minutes."

"Why don't I help you out?" he offered. "I'll read the boys their bedtime story and you get Susie tucked in."

Amanda was too tired to argue, so she nodded and let him lead the way down the hall. Susie had already given herself what passed for a bath. She was still covered in bubbles when she climbed out of the tub and her hair was curling damply against her cheeks. Amanda got her tucked in, then leaned down to brush a kiss across her forehead.

" 'Night, baby."

" 'Night, Mama," Susie said sleepily, then opened her eyes. "I like my grandpa."

Despite her own heartache, Amanda smiled. "I'm glad."

"Do you think if I told him I'd like it, he'd keep candy in his pockets?"

Tears stung Amanda's eyes. "I imagine he would do anything in the world you asked of him," she said. That's what he'd done for her, anything she'd ever wanted. She needed to keep reminding herself of that, letting it balance out all the rest.

Only now she understood that it had been about more than his love for her. It had been about guilt. Out of his own stupid pride, he'd managed to deprive her of a mother. Of course, he would say that her mother hadn't fought to keep her.

As she went back into the living room, she heard the low murmur of Caleb's voice as he read the boys to sleep. He was so good with them. And he'd filled a huge gap in their lives, in *all* their lives. When she was at her lowest, she wished with all her heart that she could snuggle into his arms and let him take care of her, of them.

But she would never again rely on a man for her family's security. The two she'd loved the most — her father and Bobby — had let her down. From now on, she had only herself to count on. As much as she trusted Caleb, as much as she already relied on him, she wasn't sure she could ever take that final leap of faith that he would always be there. And that hurt, because she did love him, more and more each day.

Admitting that surprised her. She'd tried so hard to pretend it wasn't happening, but it had. It had snuck up on her despite all her defenses, thanks to his steadfast presence.

Caleb would never lie to her. He would never keep secrets from her, she assured herself, only to remember, of course, he already had. Worse, he, like Max, had done it in the name of love, in the name of protecting her. It wasn't enough to keep her from loving him, apparently, but it was more than enough to make her wary.

When he joined her downstairs, she had just enough resolve left in her to look him in the eye. "Please go," she begged him softly.

"We need to talk," he repeated.

Amanda shook her head. "Not tonight. I can't do it, Caleb. I don't have the stomach for it."

Alarm flared in his eyes. "It's that bad?"

"Let's just say it was a shock and leave it at that."

"Is there something I can do?" he asked at once. "Do you want me to speak to Max for you?"

Instinctively, she rested her hand against his cheek, drawing his warmth around her like a cloak. "No. You have to let me handle this on my own, Caleb. It's between me and my father, and right now I have no idea what, if anything, I want to do about it."

"You're not going to cut him out of your life again, are you?" he asked. "Surely you wouldn't do that now, no matter what he's done."

"No," she said, resigned. "I can't do that."

But the visits promised to get a whole lot more complicated before they got better, which meant she didn't want the kids out there as witnesses to any of it.

Caleb studied her with a narrowed gaze. "What are you thinking?"

"Just that I can't take the kids back out there right now," she said. "Not till the rest of this is resolved." The look she gave Caleb pleaded with him to understand.

He nodded, but his disapproval was evident. "Then don't take too long working this out, Amanda. He needs those children, and something tells me they need him."

She thought of Susie's plan to ask him to keep candy in his pockets just for her. It was silly, really, but her own childhood wasn't so long ago that she couldn't remember how delightful such treats were.

"I'll do the best I can, Caleb."

He stepped closer and cupped her face in his hands. "I wish you'd talk to me."

"I know, and I will. I promise."

He touched his lips to hers. He didn't linger long, just long enough to scramble her pulse. And in that instant, she regretted more than anything that she couldn't plead with him to hold her, to love her.

He released her reluctantly, then brushed a curl away from her cheek. "Good night."

"Good night, Caleb." She opened the door before she could foolishly ask him to stay. There was no room in her life for being impetuous, not when it came to a man, even one as decent as Caleb.

Whatever questions were still on the tip of his tongue, he swallowed them and gave her a smile. "If you need me, you know where to find me."

Amanda nodded. But she had a feeling they both understood that she wouldn't go looking for him, no matter how desperately she needed him.

Two endless weeks passed before Amanda could bring herself to visit Max again. It was just as awkward as their last encounter. She went armed with a list of questions about her mother, some of which he answered, most of which he evaded. He wouldn't tell her where her mother was or even if she was still living under her real name.

"You know I'm going to find her," she finally said. "Why won't you help?"

"I'm thinking of you," he insisted, then sighed at her expression of disbelief. "Okay, I'm thinking of her."

"Or yourself," Amanda accused.

"No, it's about your mother," he said more emphatically. "Can you imagine what a shock it would be to have you appear after all these years?"

"No more of a shock than it was to me to learn she's still alive," Amanda retorted. "She's as much at fault in all this as you are, so pardon me if I'm not feeling terribly sympathetic to her."

"Well, you should."

"How can you possibly defend her?"

"Because she's your mother, dammit!"

"If you start quoting the Commandments to me, I swear I will walk out that door and never come back," Amanda said heatedly. "I get enough of that from Caleb about you."

Max actually smiled at that, but was quick to turn away. When he met her gaze again, his expression was neutral. "Maybe you need to remember this, then. Your mother gave birth to you and she did the right thing, leaving you here with me. She could have dragged you along with her, then ignored you while she went searching for whatever it was she was looking for. She had enough love for you to know you'd be better off with me."

Amanda blanched. She tried to imagine her childhood anywhere but here, with anyone other than Max. It was impossible, but that was only because she'd never had even a hint that any alternative existed. "I imagine I would have adapted," she said optimistically, mostly because she knew it would irritate her father. She'd seen the effect having an impetuous mother had had on Josh. He'd adapted, and not always well. It had taken a woman like Maggie to bring peace and stability into his life after the nomadic existence Nadine had provided for him.

"Would you really?" Max said skeptically.

"I adapted to not having a mother and I did it again when you cut me out of your life," she said, needing to believe that she wouldn't have been harmed as Josh had been. The irony, of course, was that she'd been emotionally scarred, anyway.

Her father's gaze caught hers and held, his steady and filled with regret. "I deserved that," he said wearily.

"And more," she shot back, unable to stop.

Max closed his eyes. It seemed for a minute as if some of the color had washed out of his face, and she thought perhaps she'd finally gone too far.

"I'm sorry," she forced herself to say.

He shook his head. "No, I deserve whatever you need to say, if it's going to make you feel better. Keeping your feelings bottled up doesn't do anyone any good. Resentments infect everything. The only way to cure them is to scrape the wound clean."

Amanda leaned forward and clasped his hand, shocked at its fragility. He'd always been so strong, his hands those of a man who knew the meaning of hard work, even though he'd spent his professional life in boardrooms. Now his grip was loose and cool, an odd reminder that time was slipping away. If she was to have all the answers she wanted, she needed to press for them now, before they disappeared into the dark recesses of his faltering memory.

Before she could open her mouth to frame the words, her father looked at her curiously.

"You have children now, don't you?" he asked.

She nodded, unable to speak around the sudden lump in her throat. In an instant, everything else was unimportant.

"Where are they? Why aren't they here with you?" he asked, sounding agitated.

"Because there were things I wanted to discuss with you in private," she said, struggling to keep her voice calm.

"Do you have any pictures with you? I'd like to see their pictures."

"Sure," she said, retrieving her purse and pulling out the kids' most recent school pictures, along with a snapshot of all three of them together in front of the new house.

She handed them to her father and watched as he studied each image intently. She couldn't tell if he was trying to remember them . . . or trying to memorize their faces so he'd recognize them on their next visit.

"You should have brought them," he said, sounding angry. "Why are you trying to keep them from me?"

"I'm not," she said. "But they're in school right now and I wanted to talk to you alone."

"About the will, I imagine," he said, scowling at her.

Amanda stared at him in shock. "What?"

"Oh, I know what's going on. My mind might be slipping, but it's not gone yet."

"Daddy, I don't have any idea what you're talking about," she said. His unexpected flash of irritability had caught her off guard. Out of the blue, he seemed to be harboring some sort of resentment or anger, which didn't make any sense at all, given the way the earlier part of the visit had gone.

When he continued to snap at her over the most innocuous things, Amanda picked up the nearly empty iced tea pitcher and headed indoors.

"I'll get some more tea," she said, needing

to put distance between them before she said something that would destroy their hard-won peace. Maybe Jessie could give her some insight into the best way to handle him or at least tell her whether these abrupt mood swings and severe memory lapses were becoming more commonplace.

In the kitchen she set the pitcher on the table and braced herself against the counter, slowly counting to ten.

"He's having a bad day," Jessie said quietly behind her.

"No kidding."

Jessie clasped Amanda's hands in hers. "Don't hold this against him, Amanda. He needs you so badly."

"I seem to be upsetting him today."

"An hour from now, he'll be his old self," Jessie assured her. "These mood swings come and go. I think he gets frustrated when his memory slips, and he takes it out on whoever's handy. You know how he's always hated any sign of weakness. Remember how he used to get when he had the slightest bit of a cold?"

Amanda's lips twitched at the memory. He'd been an absolute bear. "I know you're probably right," she said, giving Jessie a rueful smile. "But his words still have the ability to cut right through me. I feel like I'm six again and got my best dress dirty right before we were going somewhere important."

Jessie smiled. "Then you should be used to it. You did that a lot, as I recall."

Amanda chuckled, despite her frustration. "Yes, I did, didn't I? It's a wonder he was as patient with me as he was."

"Patience was definitely never your father's best trait," Jessie said. "And this illness of his is bound to test it."

"I guess I was hoping he'd try harder now since we're trying to find our way back to each other," Amanda said.

"It doesn't have anything to do with you, Amanda. And it doesn't matter if he tries or not, these slips of his will happen. He's going to have times when he's angry and frustrated because of the disease. It makes him feel out of control. You can imagine how that feels to a man like your father."

"Of course I can," she said at once. Then, "Did something happen before I got here?"

Jessie sighed. "I suppose it's my fault. Your father and I got in to it because he wanted breakfast . . . for the second time. I couldn't convince him he'd already eaten. I should have followed the advice I just gave to you and cut him some slack. I should have fixed it for him and kept my mouth shut."

"Oh, no, I'm so sorry," Amanda said,

knowing how hard that must have been on Jessie.

The woman shrugged. "You know how it goes with us. We argue all the time. But when I realized he really didn't remember, I pretty much came unglued, and that upset him more."

Amanda couldn't seem to get past what had started it all. "He really didn't remember having breakfast?" she asked, her heart aching. "What time was this?"

"Around nine, I think. He'd only been away from the table for a half hour or so. I'd fixed him pancakes and bacon, his favorite."

Amanda pulled out a kitchen chair and sank onto it, her knees weak. "It's happening, isn't it? It's really happening. He's going to slip away by degrees."

Jessie pulled out a chair and sat beside her, then clasped her hands. "You remember how strong he was for you when you were a little girl?"

Amanda nodded, her eyes stinging with tears.

"That's how strong you're going to have to be for him now. Think you can do it?"

"I suppose I have to," she murmured with very little conviction. How could she watch this deterioration of the man who'd once meant everything to her? It would have been easier if she'd never come back, if she could have remembered him as he'd been. She met Jessie's gaze. "I wish Caleb had never told me. I wish I'd never come back."

Jessie smiled, though her expression was sad. "No, you don't. You know you have to be here for him now. These last glimpses of him as you remember him will mean the world to you one day."

"I don't have to be here," Amanda said fiercely, then sighed. "No, of course, you're right. As painful as it is, this is where I belong." She couldn't explain to Jessie about her mother and how that had left her emotions more conflicted than ever.

"You need to go back out there," Jessie said, a teasing glint in her eyes. "You know your father. He'll think we're in here plotting against him."

"I can fix that," Amanda said, forcing a smile. She plunked some of Jessie's freshly baked cookies on a plate. "I'll tell him I was baking cookies. Maybe he won't remember that you're the one who baked them."

Jessie rolled her eyes at Amanda's pitiful attempt to make a joke out of what was truly tragic. "You'll never get away with it," she warned. "But I've half a mind to come along and watch you try."

"Then do it," Amanda said. "I could use the backup."

Jessie draped a comforting arm around Amanda's shoulders and gave her a squeeze. "You be there for your daddy," she said quietly. "And I'll be there for you. Caleb will be, too. That man loves you both, you know."

Amanda nodded, unwilling to get into that discussion.

Outside, they found Max as irritable as he'd been when Amanda had left him. Not even the fresh pitcher of tea and plate of cookies seemed to appease him. He scowled at Amanda.

"What are you doing here?" he demanded as if she'd somehow slipped in while he wasn't paying attention.

"I've been here awhile, Daddy."

"I know that," he said impatiently. "But why did you come?"

Amanda was at a loss. She looked to Jessie, but she merely shrugged.

"I wanted us to be a family again," she said at last.

Her father regarded her with the sort of disdain he'd expressed years ago when he'd banished her from his life. Amanda felt every humiliating exchange they'd ever had wash over her.

"You know, don't you?" he demanded.

Amanda regarded him blankly. "Know what?"

"You know I'm sick," he accused.

Amanda nodded.

"How long?"

She remained silent, befuddled by his confusion and his anger. She knew she had to find some way to accept it and not overreact, but she wasn't there yet.

"Dammit, I asked how long you've known? Is that what brought you running back here?" he demanded, his accusing gaze shifting to Jessie. "I suppose you told her."

"Jessie didn't tell me anything," Amanda said. She seized on the one thing that might calm him. "I want you to spend more time with your grandchildren. Susie's very anxious to come back. She's hoping you'll tuck some candies in your pocket just for her. How about Sunday? Would that be a good time to bring them back?"

Max clearly wasn't appeased. "What am I? Some sort of damned sideshow for you all?"

"Max!" Jessie protested.

"Well, that's it, isn't it? The old man's losing it, so let's hang around and maybe he'll forget there was a reason he cut us out of the will. Maybe he'll put us back in again." He glared at her. "That would fix things for you, wouldn't it? Getting all my money?"

Amanda's gut twisted at the vicious words. "Is that what you think? That I came back for your money?" she snapped before she could stop herself.

"It's a lot of money," her father said defensively, though there was the faintest hint of regret in his eyes.

Amanda stood in front of him, shaking, but her spine was straight and her shoulders were squared. "Don't you dare accuse me of coming here for money! I don't want your stupid money. I might be poor, but I never lost my dignity and self-respect, two things you taught me. Those are more important than whatever you've got stashed away in the bank."

Max's expression instantly changed. As quickly as the blink of an eye, the anger was gone, replaced by uncertainty. "I'm sorry."

"You ought to be," she said, not quite ready to forgive the outburst or the unwarranted accusation. "I think I'll go now before either of us says something more we'll regret."

She was halfway to the car when he called out to her. "You coming back tomorrow?"

She bit back a sigh and the urge to tell him no just for spite. He deserved to pay for thinking the worst of her, and for so much more, she thought angrily.

But the truth was, she couldn't seem to sustain her anger anymore, not seeing him slip slowly away day after day. Today had slammed her headfirst into reality. There were going to be more moments like this, more unpredictable outbursts. She had to find some way to handle them. And she wanted her children to spend time with him before the outbursts became so frequent they were frightened of him.

"I'll be back," she said eventually.

"Bring the kids, then. I'll have Jessie bake cookies," he promised, oblivious to the plateful of just-baked cookies right beside him. "Chocolate chip still your favorite?"

"Of course," she said, fighting to choke back an unexpected sob. Oatmeal and raisin. That had been her favorite. It was a silly mistake, hardly a cause for tears, but once she'd reached the end of the driveway, she put the car in neutral and sat there, letting the tears flow freely.

20

Caleb couldn't seem to get a lick of work done. He'd gone for a walk to try to clear his head. He'd piled up the most mundane paperwork on his desk, figuring that would be the easiest to cope with in his distracted state, but it was still all right there, untouched. He was worried sick about Amanda, but it was plain she wanted to handle whatever problem she was facing on her own.

That hurt. He'd hoped by now that she trusted him enough to know she could count on him. He'd hoped she respected him enough to seek out his advice. But in nearly a month she hadn't come to him for help. He'd caught only glimpses of her when he'd dropped by to spend time with the children. He was still in the dark about what had sent her into this dark place.

"Somebody steal your favorite prayer

book, son?" Max inquired from the doorway to Caleb's office.

Caleb blinked and stared at the older man in confusion. "What?"

"You're scowling, so I figured somebody had messed with the nice, tidy order of your life," Max explained, walking in without waiting for an invitation.

"Your daughter, if you must know," Caleb admitted.

Amusement flared in Max's eyes. "Then we can commiserate. Amanda's been on my mind for a while now, too."

Caleb thought he heard a note of uncertainty in Max's voice. "Oh? What happened? Did you two have another disagreement?"

"You want the whole ugly story or the condensed version?" Max asked.

"I think the highlights will do," Caleb said. He suspected the longer version could take quite a while. "Though I'm surprised you want to tell me any of it. You refused on Sunday. And the three weeks before that, too."

"Things change," Max said with a shrug.

"Meaning you're scared you've really blown it," Caleb concluded.

Max nodded.

"Then talk to me, Max. I'll do what I can to help."

He listened as Max told him about Amanda's mother being alive, then about the fight that had sent Amanda fleeing from Willow Bend.

"I'll be surprised if the girl ever sets foot on my property again. Can't say I'd blame her. I should never have kept a secret like that all these years," Max said, unable to disguise the real worry in his eyes. "In my own defense, I meant to tell her when she was older and able to handle it." He shrugged. "But you know what happened. I couldn't tell her much of anything when the two of us weren't even speaking."

Caleb nodded. "It *is* something she had a right to know."

"Don't you think I know that?" Max snapped. "But I should never have blurted it out the way I did. I should have prepared her, put a better spin on it."

Caleb regarded him incredulously. "Do you honestly think there's any spin that would have made it okay?"

Max sighed. "No, I suppose not."

Caleb sensed that he still didn't have the whole story. "There's more, isn't there? What else did the two of you argue about?"

Max flushed. "It was a week or so ago when she came back looking for more answers. Apparently I accused her of being after my money."

"Are you crazy?" Caleb said before he could stop himself. "Max, surely you know better than that."

"Well, of course I do. Believe me, Jessie tore a strip out of my hide over that one, too." His expression turned sad. "Truth is, I didn't even remember doing it."

At the reminder of how fragile Max's memory was these days, Caleb's attitude toward him softened. He suspected Amanda's would, as well, once she'd had time to think things through. "Amanda won't hold it against you," Caleb assured him.

"She probably should. I don't seem to be able to control what comes out of my mouth these days."

"She said she'd come back, didn't she?"

"Yes, but what if she thinks it over and changes her mind? It's been more than a week now, and I haven't seen hide nor hair of her."

"Then you'll go to see her," Caleb said simply, though even he knew there was nothing simple about it when it came to these two and their stubborn pride.

"Do you think that God of yours will forgive me for all the pain I've caused that girl?" Max asked.

Caleb smiled. "He's in the forgiveness business," he told Max. "We're the ones who seem to struggle with forgiving ourselves." He gave Max a sly look, deciding to take advantage of his troubled mood. "Maybe you should think about getting in touch with Amanda's mother for her. If you could bring about a reunion, it would go a long way toward fixing things."

Max shook his head. "I don't know if that's such a good idea. Springing this on Margaret might be the worst thing for both of them."

"You know if you don't make it happen, Amanda will," Caleb warned him. "She's as stubborn and determined as you are, Max. She won't let it drop. She'll find her mother on her own."

"I suppose you're right. She said as much herself." Max still didn't look entirely convinced.

Caleb studied him closely. "What are you really worried about, Max? That Margaret won't come to see her daughter?"

Max shook his head and suddenly the truth hit Caleb right between the eyes. "It's not about Amanda at all, is it? You're afraid if Margaret finds out about your health, she'll pity you, and you don't want to see that look in her eyes. After all these years, you still love her."

Max shrugged, not admitting it, but not

denying it, either.

"Well, you don't have the right to worry about that," Caleb said heatedly. "For once, it's not all about you, Max. It's about doing what's right for your daughter. You owe this to Amanda. Now, will you do it or not?"

Max seemed startled by his vehemence. It was the most blatant clash of wills between them yet. For a moment, it looked as if Max was going to refuse, but then his shoulders sagged. "I'll call her," he said.

"Now," Caleb said, shoving his phone in Max's direction. "And don't even try to pretend you don't know how to reach her."

"You know I have problems with my memory," Max said.

Caleb merely stared him down. Eventually Max took out his wallet and retrieved a dog-eared slip of paper. He scowled at Caleb, but then picked up the phone and dialed.

When someone eventually answered, Max paled a bit, but his voice shook only a little when he announced, "Margaret, this is Max. I need to ask a favor of you."

A rueful smile touched his lips. "Yes, I know I have a lot of nerve turning up after more than thirty years and asking for a favor, but it's about Amanda. I figure you owe her one, even if you don't owe me anything."

Satisfied, Caleb stood and left the room.

Max needed privacy for this conversation. And Caleb needed time to absorb all the implications of Max's lies and what they must have done to shake Amanda's world yet again.

Mary Louise was taking a break at the Stop and Shop when Danny suddenly appeared. She knew he'd been coming back to Charleston more frequently lately because of the work Cord was training him to do full-time this summer, but she hadn't seen all that much of him. He looked different, stronger and more confident, maybe. Her stupid heart did a little dance at the sight of him.

"Mind if I join you?" he asked, regarding her with uncertainty.

"Have a seat," she said, and scooted over on the bench. "You working for Cord this weekend?"

He nodded, then studied her worriedly. "I didn't think I'd find you here."

"How come? It's where I work."

"Cord said something about you going to work at that gallery in town. Images or something."

"Next week," Mary Louise said, excitement creeping into her voice. Every time she thought about it, she could hardly believe her luck. "Maggie says she'll teach me how to run a business, and then, after the baby comes in a couple of months, if I'm any good at it, she and Dinah Beaufort are going to help me open my own shop."

Danny regarded her with surprise. "You're kidding! I never knew you wanted to own your own shop. What kind?"

"A knitting shop. I'll sell yarns and teach classes and stuff." She was about to launch into the whole business plan she'd been drawing up whenever she had time, but she figured Danny wouldn't want to hear it.

"You really think you can do this?" he asked.

She frowned at his skepticism. "I can do anything I set my mind to," she said irritably. "Same as you."

"That's not what I meant," he said hurriedly. "I know you're smart. It just costs a lot to start a business."

"Which is why I'll have investors," Mary Louise said. "And I got a book from the library that shows how to create a business plan. I've been working on mine so they'll take me seriously and not worry that I'll be squandering their money." She regarded him with disappointment. "I thought you'd be happy for me."

"I am," he insisted, but he didn't *look* happy.

"Danny, is there some reason you came by here today?"

"It's only a couple more months till the baby's due," he said.

She bit back a smile. "I know."

"Well, I was hoping we could talk about getting married," he admitted, knocking the breath right out of her. Then he added, "But with all these big plans of yours, it sort of sounds like you don't need me anymore."

Mary Louise looked at him as if he'd gone nuts. "I never needed you to give me money, Danny. I'm a hard worker and I'm not proud. I'll always be able to provide for the baby and me."

"Then you really don't care about getting married?" he asked incredulously.

Sometimes men were so damn dense, she thought. "I care about marrying you because I love you, you idiot. And that's the same reason I let you go. Money and child support never entered into it."

He seemed to mull that over. "I've really made a mess of things, haven't I?"

She regarded him blankly. "How? By getting me pregnant? I was there, too, so you don't need to shoulder all the blame for that. For not wanting to get married right now? I agreed with you. The timing's all messed up. It still is, so let yourself off the hook."

He scowled at her. "Maybe I don't want to be off the hook, after all. Maybe I don't want to lose you. Maybe I want to be a full-time father to our baby."

She heard something unfamiliar in his voice. He sounded sad and hurt. And scared. He was still scared. "Maybe?" she repeated, picking on the word he'd used in every sentence. Because she didn't want to sound mean, she leaned over and pressed a kiss to his cheek. Funny, she didn't love him one bit less, but she felt older and wiser than Danny at this moment. "Come see me when there's not a doubt in your mind, Danny. Until then, let's just leave things the way they are."

He looked at her with dismay, then sighed. "You're probably right."

She grinned then. "I *know* I'm right. That's the difference between us, Danny. You may be a big college guy with everything in the world going for you and all sorts of knowledge getting crammed into your head, but I'm the one who knows my own mind. I think I'm the one who's way ahead here."

"I do know I love you," he said with more certainty. "There's not a day that goes by that I don't miss you, miss talking things over with you."

She hugged him then, because she couldn't resist. "If you ask me, that's a pretty good start. I imagine everything else will come in time."

He regarded her curiously. "You really mean that, don't you? You're not in any hurry to get married anymore?"

"Nope," she said confidently. "Because when we finally do get married, I know it's going to last."

"And if it never happens?"

Her heart thumped unsteadily at the thought, but she looked him in the eye and said bravely, "Then it wasn't meant to be."

But it *was* meant to be, she thought staunchly. She just needed to sit tight and wait till Danny saw it, too. One of these days he'd have — what did they call it in her English class? — an epiphany. If those unexpected awakenings happened to some of literature's greatest characters, some of whom were dumber than dirt, in her opinion, then surely one could happen right here in Charleston to a guy as smart as Danny!

Amanda had been making stupid mistakes all day long. Fortunately she'd caught most of them before the customers at the boutique had noticed, but not before her boss had observed a few of them. Finally during a lull after lunch, Joanna pulled her aside.

"Is something going on with you? You

seem distracted today." Her voice was filled with concern, not anger.

"I'm sorry," Amanda apologized. "It's been an upsetting few weeks, but I really don't want to get into it."

"Maybe you should, if not with me, then with someone. Why don't you call Caleb and go meet him for coffee or something?"

"I can't call Caleb every single time I'm upset about something," Amanda protested.

Joanna grinned. "He doesn't seem to mind."

"But that's the point, isn't it?" Amanda replied. "I'm taking advantage of his good nature."

"No, you're counting on a friend to be there for you," Joanna corrected. "And Caleb's more than a friend, isn't he? I've seen the way you two look at each other."

Amanda held up her hands. "Not talking about this," she said, embarrassed.

Joanna looked beyond her and her eyes suddenly lit up. "Well, speak of the devil," she said, then chuckled. "Whoops! Bad choice of words."

Amanda turned and saw Caleb, then frowned at her boss. "Did you call him?"

"I most certainly did not," Joanna said. "His appearance here, while not entirely unexpected, is pure coincidence."

Amanda wasn't sure she believed that, but a part of her was very grateful he'd turned up, no matter what had brought him by. Then she took a good look at his somber expression and had second thoughts.

"What's wrong?" she asked.

"Nothing at all," he said at once. "But we need to get out of here, if Joanna doesn't mind."

"Go," Joanna said, snatching Amanda's purse. "Her mind's not here, anyway."

"Oh?" Caleb said.

Amanda frowned. "Never mind, but I'll ask again. What's wrong? Are the kids okay?"

"The kids are perfectly fine."

"Well, I can't play hooky from work every time you get some crazy idea to take a day off, Caleb. And I have to be home when the kids get home from school."

"I'm giving you permission to go," Joanna said. "So you're not playing hooky."

"And Nadine will wait for the kids at your place after school. She'll stay with them till we get back. Now, come on." He took her purse from Joanna, then guided her toward the door.

Amanda balked. "Back? From where?"

Caleb regarded her impatiently. "Just for once, could you trust me and not ask so many questions?"

436

"Something tells me that when you're being so mysterious, it is exactly the time I ought to be asking every question that pops into my head," she said, but she followed him to the car.

"Well, please refrain, or it's going to be a long trip."

Amanda stared at him. He wasn't making a lick of sense. "Trip?" she demanded. "What on earth are you talking about, Caleb? I can't go on a trip."

"Get in the car, Amanda," he coaxed, then closed the door behind her. "The trip is just overnight. We'll be back in time for work in the morning. I have a change of clothes for you in the trunk."

"Well, you and Nadine just thought of everything, didn't you?" she said nastily. "In case you haven't caught on yet, I don't appreciate other people trying to run my life."

"Really? I would never have guessed that about you," he said, amusement lurking in his eyes.

"Oh, go to hell," she said, then immediately apologized.

He laughed. "I've been told worse things in my life."

"Yes, I imagine you have, being the know-it-all control freak that you are."

He was about to turn the key in the ignition, but he paused and faced her. "Do I need to kiss you to shut you up?" he inquired.

Amanda decided that would be a very bad idea. Given the level of agitation she was feeling at the moment, a kiss would either go very badly . . . or way too well. Which raised an interesting point, she realized suddenly.

"Are you taking me away to . . ." Her voice faltered.

"To what?" he asked, then chuckled at her expression. "No, I am not taking you away to seduce you, Amanda, though if you were to show the slightest inclination in that direction, I could be persuaded."

She frowned at him. "Sometimes I wish you weren't such a blasted saint."

He chuckled. "Me, too, darlin'. Me, too. Maybe we should get back to that topic another time, though."

"When?" The word popped out of her mouth before she could stop it. She blushed furiously. "Pretend you didn't hear that."

"Sorry. Impossible," he said. "I'll add that to the list of topics for later discussion."

Amanda sighed. "Yes, I imagine you will."

That was the trouble with Caleb. He never forgot anything, least of all the things she most wanted him to forget.

Since Caleb obviously didn't intend to be

any more forthcoming about their destination, Amanda tried to force herself to sit back and relax. When she realized they were heading into Savannah, she turned and regarded him with renewed curiosity.

"Why didn't you just tell me we were going to Savannah?" she asked. "It's one of my favorite cities. Daddy used to bring me here all the time when I was a little girl."

Caleb nodded. "I think he mentioned something about that." He glanced at a slip of paper, then turned into the historic part of the city.

The squares around which the older houses had been built were well tended and shaded by huge old trees. She recognized the famed Mrs. Wilkes's boardinghouse, where she and Max had once stood in line to eat a traditional Southern lunch family-style with strangers from all over the country.

Then Caleb turned onto a quiet block where there were no tourists strolling along. He pulled to the curb in front of a town house with wide brick steps and wrought-iron trim. The shutters and front door had been painted a shiny black, and a brass knocker was in the shape of a lion's head. Amanda couldn't seem to pull her eyes away from that knocker. It was just like the one on the front door at Willow Bend.

She turned slowly to face Caleb. "Why are we here? Who lives here?"

"You'll know soon enough," he said, cutting the engine, then getting out of the car before she could ask more questions.

When he opened her door, she stayed right where she was, her heart thumping unsteadily. She lifted her gaze to meet his. "Caleb, tell me, please."

Just then the front door of the town house opened and a tall, thin woman with auburn hair stood at the top of the steps. The sun caught her hair and turned the color to fire. She was dressed impeccably in a knit suit, designer shoes and discreet but unmistakably expensive jewelry. Amanda's gaze was drawn to her perfectly manicured hands . . . and to the simple platinum-and-diamond band on her ring finger. She'd seen one picture of her mother in all these years, her wedding picture. A band just like that had been plainly visible.

Amanda tore her gaze away from the ring to study the classically elegant woman waiting in the doorway. For all of her care with her appearance, there was fear and uncertainty in the woman's eyes. Something told Amanda that anxiety wasn't part of her normal nature.

"Who is she?" she asked Caleb, hardly

daring to believe what her head was telling her. She needed his confirmation.

His lips curved ever so slightly. "Unless I've turned up at the wrong place, that is Margaret Maxwell, your mother," he said quietly, then searched her face. "Would you like to go and meet her?"

Amanda sat frozen right where she was. "I'm not sure I can stand up," she whispered. "I wasn't expecting this. How did you talk my father into telling you where she was?"

"He loves you," Caleb said simply. He gave her an encouraging smile. "Do you really want to keep her waiting?"

A flash of anger streaked through Amanda. "Why shouldn't I?" she asked bitterly. "She kept me waiting for more than thirty years. She and my father."

Caleb regarded her with sympathy. "Then why waste another minute?"

Amanda noted that her mother's expression had wilted a bit when Amanda didn't immediately emerge from the car. She realized then that her mother really was as terrified about this meeting as Amanda was. Somehow that made it better. Not okay, but better. Perhaps her mother had a conscience, after all.

Amanda took Caleb's hand and got out of

the car, then slowly crossed the sidewalk and climbed the steps. At the top, she looked into eyes as blue as her own. Right now they were just as tear-filled as hers, too.

"Amanda?" her mother said softly, her voice filled with a mix of wonder and uneasiness.

Amanda couldn't speak, so she merely nodded.

For an instant, she thought her mother was going to embrace her, but apparently she thought better of it, because she stepped back, transforming herself into the gracious Southern hostess she no doubt was. "Come in, please." Her gaze sought out Caleb, who'd retreated to the sidewalk by the car. "Reverend Webb, aren't you going to join us?"

Amanda turned and looked at him in dismay. "Caleb?"

He shook his head. "I'll be back in a couple of hours. I think you two need time alone to catch up."

He said it as if they'd been apart weeks or months, rather than a lifetime. Amanda wanted to bolt down the steps after him. Instead, the Maxwell pride kicked in and she stood her ground. She faced her mother with her chin held high.

"Caleb's right," she said. "We do have a lot

to talk about. You can start with why you abandoned me and allowed me to grow up believing you were dead."

She brushed past her mother and went inside, instinctively finding her way into the formal living room, where she sank onto a chair before her knees gave way.

Her mother was slow to follow, which was just as well. Amanda wanted every second she could grab to restore her composure. And to frame the thousand and one questions she'd spent a lifetime wishing she could ask of the woman who'd given birth to her.

21

Caleb stood on the sidewalk in front of Margaret Maxwell's house for several minutes after the two women had gone inside. He couldn't seem to tear himself away. A part of him worried about Amanda and wanted to stay close in case she needed him. Another part wanted to be privy to what was going on inside.

Since the latter smacked of a kind of nosiness he disliked in others, he forced himself to get behind the wheel of the car and drive away. He intended to go to the hotel where Max had made reservations for him and Amanda, check in, kill a couple of hours and then go back.

Just as he was about to drive away, his cell phone rang. He knew even without checking the caller ID that it would be Max.

"What's going on down there?" Max demanded without preamble. "Have they met yet?"

"They're inside Margaret's house right now talking," Caleb told him.

"Where are you?"

"On my way to the hotel."

"What? Why aren't you with them?" Max demanded. "Those two shouldn't be left alone."

"They're not going to tear each other's hair out, Max. You just want me to be able to give you a play-by-play of what they say," Caleb accused.

"Well, of course I do. Dammit, I knew I should have taken Amanda down there myself."

"I thought you told me Margaret refused to see you," Caleb reminded him.

"I didn't have to listen to her," Max grumbled.

Caleb grinned. "To be perfectly honest, I'm surprised you did."

Max fell silent, then admitted, "I figured me being there would just stir things up. Better to let them have this time alone to work things out, if they can."

"She's still a beautiful woman, your Margaret," Caleb said, knowing Max wanted to ask. "And she seems very gracious."

Max sighed. "She's aged better than I

have. I've seen pictures from time to time. Don't know why she had to go and turn her hair red, though. Brown was the color God gave her, just like Amanda's. She should have kept it."

Caleb laughed. "Women like a dramatic change from time to time. Hair color seems to be the thing they choose."

"I suppose. I imagine red suits her better, anyway. She was a real spitfire once upon a time."

That image didn't quite fit with the elegant woman Caleb had just met. "Tell me more about her, Max."

"Margaret was unpredictable and full of life back then," he said, sounding nostalgic. "She was always ready to try something new." He chuckled. "Even in my thirties, I couldn't keep up with her. I suppose I should have seen right off we were a bad match, but I saw potential in her. Not sure she ever saw it in herself, though."

Caleb thought of her classy appearance now and tried to reconcile that with the independent spirit who'd walked out on a husband and baby. "I'd say she figured it out, Max. Based on appearances alone, she seems to have changed, become the woman you imagined she would."

"You don't suppose she's mellowed

enough to consider coming back here for a visit?" Max asked wistfully. "I'd like to see her one more time."

"You're the one who spoke to her," Caleb said. "What do you think?"

"That she'd still like to serve up my head on a platter," Max replied. "Don't know why that is, though. I gave that woman everything she ever asked for and then some. It was her idea to leave here with someone else. I didn't kick her out."

"Maybe she regrets what she did in leaving you and her child, but has too much pride to admit it," Caleb suggested. "You ought to be able to understand that."

"I do," Max said. "I surely do. You call me later, okay? I want to hear how things went."

"I'll call when I can," Caleb promised.

"And make sure you and Amanda use *both* those rooms I reserved for you. I don't want any monkey business on my dime," Max said.

"You don't get to control everything, Max," Caleb chided. "And you gave up any right to tell Amanda what to do years ago."

"Which is why I'm telling you," Max said. "Besides, misbehaving shouldn't even be on your mind, Reverend."

Caleb laughed. "No, but where your daughter's concerned, I don't always use

447

good sense. Now, let me go. I'm turning into the hotel. I'll speak to you later, Max. And stop worrying."

"I'm not worried. I know you'll do the right thing."

"I wasn't talking about me. I meant you don't need to worry about how things are going with Amanda and her mother. It may take some time, but they'll work this out. At least they'll find some common ground."

Max sighed heavily. "I hope you're right about that. Amanda's got my stubbornness and Margaret's got her own share. They could be butting heads, even as we speak."

"No question about it," Caleb agreed. "But like I said, they'll work it out in time, the same way you and Amanda have."

Though he did his best to sound confident for Max's sake, Caleb hoped he was right about that. Amanda and her mother didn't have the history she shared with Max. Despite the bad times, there were at least some good for those two to build on. Not so with her mother.

He hoped Amanda would thank him for bringing her here, rather than taking his head off for interfering. Right now, he'd have to say it was probably a toss-up.

"Would you care for some tea?" Amanda's

mother asked politely.

Amanda wanted to shout that she wasn't there for tea or to exchange pleasantries. She was there for explanations and apologies. But years of training in social graces — lessons from Jessie that this woman should have been the one to teach — kept her silent. She nodded, then forced herself to say, "Yes, thank you."

"I'll be right back, then."

Once her mother had left the room, Amanda looked around. To her astonishment there was a picture of her father on an antique table beside the chintz-covered sofa. And next to it in a tiny frame was a baby picture, one of those they took in the hospital with the baby's face still all scrunched up and red. Amanda recognized this one because Max had one exactly like it in his wallet, or at least he had while she was growing up. He'd always told her it reminded him of the best day of his life. Even as she'd grown and he'd added her latest school pictures, that baby picture had stayed in his wallet.

Seeing the same tiny photo here brought salty tears to her eyes. She swiped at them angrily, not wanting her heart to soften even a little bit toward the woman who'd callously walked away from her. If she'd mattered so little to her mother, why had she kept that picture?

When her mother returned, she set a silver tray on the table, then poured them each a cup of tea. She handed a cup to Amanda. "If it were a few hours later, we could have a drink. Something tells me we both could use one."

Amanda fought a smile as she accepted the tea. A sense of humor wasn't something she'd expected, either. Truthfully, she didn't know what she'd expected. An ogre, perhaps. Someone so flighty and disreputable that Amanda would be glad to have been left behind. The woman seated across from her was neither of those. She was studying Amanda with intelligent eyes, regarding her with undisguised curiosity.

"You're as lovely as I imagined," she told Amanda, a catch in her voice.

"It's nice to know you gave me at least a moment's thought in all these years," Amanda retorted.

Her mother blinked at the heat in her voice, then nodded. "There it is," she said, amusement lurking in her voice. "Your father's wit and temper. I suspected you'd have that, too."

"I wish I'd had half a chance to consider what you were like or what traits I might have inherited from you," Amanda said. "I thought you were dead. All I had were the stories he told me about you."

"Your father thought it best," Margaret said. "How could I argue when I was the one walking away? He had to handle it in a way he could live with."

"Obviously it didn't matter to you as long as you got your freedom," Amanda said.

Her mother winced, but she didn't shy away from the barb. "Something like that."

"Why?" Amanda asked. "Why did you have to leave at all? Daddy obviously adored you. He's never even looked at another woman."

"At twenty-five, all that devotion was smothering me," her mother said candidly. "I didn't know what to do with it. I didn't have any idea how to break free of it except to run. And then someone daring and adventurous came along who wanted to take me with him."

"What about taking a vacation, instead?" Amanda snapped. "That's what most people do when they need a break. They don't leave forever with the first interesting man who wanders by."

"I thought 'forever' was my only option, especially with you to consider. I couldn't keep walking in and out of your life."

Amanda still couldn't grasp it. "Didn't you love my father at all, at least in the beginning?"

"Of course I did. William Maxwell was larger than life. He was only ten years older than I and already a powerful force in Charleston. If I asked for something, if I even mentioned something, he bought it for me. He was generous and attentive, the ideal husband in so many ways."

"And yet you left."

"I shouldn't have married so young. I wanted to experience more of the world. It was my own fault, but you know how persuasive your father can be. He convinced me I would have all the excitement I wanted, that we'd go everywhere and do everything. But the reality was something less than that. Business always took precedence. He wanted me at his beck and call, so I couldn't find an interest of my own that might have fulfilled me."

Something in her words resonated with Amanda more than she wanted to admit. Her adoring father had smothered her, too. He'd wanted only the best for her, and sometimes that had meant not allowing her to stretch her wings and make her own mistakes. He'd covered his obsession with business by making Amanda part of it.

452

She wondered if he'd ever realized the mistakes *he* was making, first with her mother and then with her. Perhaps if he'd been a different kind of man, her mother would have stayed. Perhaps if Amanda had been permitted smaller mistakes, she wouldn't have seized on Bobby with such fervor. Not that Bobby was a mistake, except in her father's eyes, she thought staunchly.

"Have you been in Savannah all this time?" Amanda asked her.

"No. When I left, I knew I had to go far away, or it would be too easy to go back again the minute I got scared or the relationship I was in burned itself out. I'm not sure how your father would have explained it, but I knew he'd take me back despite whatever humiliation my departure caused him. I couldn't do that to him, so I traveled for many years. I lived in London for a time, and in Paris. I spent several years in New York and eventually two years in Atlanta. That's when I realized how much I missed the South. Going back to Charleston was out of the question, so I came here."

She gave Amanda a weary smile. "It was a risk and I knew it. If anyone from Charleston had come here and recognized me, it would have been the end of the charade. I think after all that time maybe a part of me wanted to be exposed. It would have allowed me to come back to Charleston at last. I would have been disgraced, of course, but I think I could have lived with that if it hadn't meant hurting your father again. I'd put him through enough."

"Very noble," Amanda said sarcastically. "Of course, you gave no consideration to what any of these choices might do to me."

"You're wrong," her mother said. "Max was the better parent to raise you. I recognized that. Even if he hadn't insisted on it, I would have left you in his care. You needed a stability that I wasn't capable of giving you back then."

"And later?"

Her mother's eyes filled with tears. "Later, it was too late. There was no turning back. I knew your father wouldn't permit me to be anywhere near you. That was our agreement and I knew he'd never change it. I'm sure you've seen his stubbornness and pride first-hand."

"You could have fought him," Amanda said. "Wasn't I worth fighting for?"

Her mother's smile turned sad. "You were worth everything. That's why you deserved the life only he could give you."

"Why didn't you just divorce him? Why this huge charade about dying? How much freedom could you ever have, really, as long as you were tied to him?"

"I suppose a part of me didn't want to cut the tie. Maybe I saw it as a safety net, that if everything fell apart, I could go back. Perhaps if I'd met someone else, someone to take seriously, I would have pursued a divorce on some island, but there was never a need for that. It wasn't about men, Amanda, though I'm sure that's what your father thought since I left with someone. It was about finding me, figuring out what I was capable of, learning to stand on my own two feet."

"With his money to back you," Amanda said with scorn.

"At first, yes," Margaret admitted. "But I found my own way in time. I've worked, had a few accomplishments of my own. I'll tell you about them sometime, when you're ready."

The offer hung in the air as the doorbell rang, startling them both. Her mother looked as if she wanted to ignore it, but she rose and went to answer. When she returned, Caleb was with her.

"Would you like me to leave and come back later?" he asked, his gaze on Amanda.

She shook her head. As brief as the visit had been, she wasn't sure she could bear another minute of it. "No, I'm ready to go."

Her mother nodded, her expression resigned. "Will you come again?"

"I'm not sure," Amanda said. "I am glad you're alive, but I don't know yet if I'm ready to have you be a part of my life."

"I know I'll need to earn that right," her mother said.

"Will you bother trying?" Amanda asked, aware that her mother had never acknowledged any desire to fight for a relationship in the past.

"Of course I'll try. I want to get to know the woman you've become, but it will have to be here," she said. "My coming to Charleston is not an option, for all those reasons I was giving you when Reverend Webb returned."

Amanda studied her intently. "Do you know Daddy's sick?"

Immediate alarm flared in her mother's eyes. Amanda thought it was genuine.

"Sick? What's wrong with him? Max was always one of the strongest men I knew. And he sounded fine when we spoke on the phone the other day."

"He has Alzheimer's," Amanda told her. "I'm not sure if he'd want you to know that, but I think you should."

Her mother gave her an odd look. "Why?"

"So you can decide how important it is to you to have his forgiveness before it's too late," she told her quietly. She turned to Caleb. "I'm ready. Shall we go?"

She was silent on the ride to their hotel, and Caleb, bless him, didn't pester her with a lot of questions. When he showed her to her room, she lifted her gaze to his.

"Don't leave," she said quietly. "Please, Caleb."

He searched her face. "Amanda, you're hurt and vulnerable. I don't want to take advantage of that."

"I may be vulnerable, but I know my own mind. I need you, Caleb. I won't regret this. Not ever." She studied him. "Will you?"

"Never. I could never regret loving you."

"Then stay."

She wasn't sure he would until he stepped across the threshold and closed the door behind him. Then he opened his arms and Amanda stepped into his embrace.

Caleb awoke filled with contradictory emotions. Holding Amanda, loving her, had been everything he'd spent months imagining and more. He wanted a future with her more than ever, but one thing hadn't changed. He couldn't give her the children he knew she wanted, and until she knew that — and if

God was generous, accepted it — they had no future.

At the same time, he felt a deep awareness that what they had done in this bed had been a kind of commitment. Amanda was bound to have certain expectations, whether she voiced them or not. And a man in his position understood all too well the ramifications of any involvement that wasn't leading to marriage. He would be condemned for it, not just by Max, but by his entire congregation, who expected him to set a good example.

Even as he cursed himself for the weakness that had allowed his yearning for Amanda to overrule his head, she awoke and curved her body into his. Just like that, with the barest brush of her skin against his, he wanted her again.

Because he wanted her so badly, he pulled away and sat on the side of the bed, all too aware of her puzzlement.

"We need to talk," he told her, forcing himself to meet her gaze.

"Not about last night," she said firmly, her own gaze unflinching. "We agreed, Caleb."

"I know, but —"

"No buts," she said. "Last night was amazing. Being with you was exactly the way I imagined it would be. You're a passionate, generous lover, Caleb. You made me feel things I'd never expected to feel again. I'm glad we made love and I won't apologize for it." Her expression challenged him. "Are you the one with regrets?"

"Not regrets," he said, brushing a stray curl from her cheek. "But you have to see that this complicates things."

"What things?" Unexpected amusement danced in her eyes. "Do you think folks back in Charleston are going to take one look at us and know what went on in this room last night?"

"I can think of one person who might," he said gloomily.

"Who?" Then her grin spread, as understanding dawned. "You're scared of my father finding out, aren't you?"

"I'm not scared of your father," he said defensively. "But I do respect him and I know he expected me to look out for you, not seduce you the first chance I got."

"Then we'll just tell him I seduced you," Amanda said lightly. "He'll probably be relieved to know my taste in men has improved, at least by his standards."

Caleb frowned. "That's not even remotely funny, Amanda."

"It is, if you stop and think about it. We're both in our thirties, Caleb. We're not young, impressionable kids. We both knew what we were doing."

"I'm not sure you did," he said.

Heat darkened her eyes. "Are you suggesting I didn't know my own mind?"

"It had been a stressful day."

"No question about that," she agreed. "But you gave me about a hundred chances to change my mind, Caleb. You have nothing to feel guilty about. I'm exactly where I want to be this morning, though you're beginning to annoy me."

"I'm just trying to be sensible," he muttered defensively.

"Well, stop it and come back to bed," she said. "Or I'll think I did something wrong last night."

"Wrong?" he repeated, perplexed.

"Missed an erogenous zone or something," she said, suddenly grinning.

Caleb shook his head. "You didn't miss anything," he assured her.

"I'm not convinced," she said, her expression enticing. "Show me."

Caleb warred with himself for two whole minutes while Amanda lay sprawled provocatively beside him. Maybe she had been a little lost and vulnerable last night, but this was a whole new side of her, one he'd never seen before. She was confident and absolutely certain of what she wanted. It seemed to be him. Only a saint could argue with that.

"When we get back to Charleston, we are going to have to sit down and have a serious conversation about where we're headed," Caleb said in one last attempt at rational thought.

"Of course we will." Amanda ran her hand along his thigh.

"I'm serious," he insisted.

She laughed. "I'm sure you are, but so am I."

"Oh, really?" he said skeptically as her touch became even more inventive and daring.

"Just not about conversation," she said, reaching up to pull him down until his lips met hers. "Shut up, Caleb."

As their mouths merged, he realized that silence was right up there at the top of the list of virtues. Under certain circumstances, there were much better forms of communication.

22

Max took one look at Amanda's face and knew that things had changed between her and Caleb. He sent a scowl in the minister's direction. "You and I need to have a talk," he said meaningfully.

To his credit, Caleb didn't look away. He merely nodded. Max approved of the way this young man never ducked a conversation that might prove difficult. Amanda could do worse. In fact, in Max's opinion, she had, but to this day she didn't see it. He had a grudging admiration for that kind of loyalty. He only wished Bobby O'Leary had been deserving of it. Of course, if they knew the truth, some might say the same about his unwavering love for Margaret.

Eventually Max turned his attention back to his daughter. "How did things go with your mother?"

"We made a start," Amanda said.

A million and one questions came to mind, but Max couldn't seem to find the words to form any of them. An image of Margaret as she'd been on their wedding day settled into his mind and he focused on that, drifting into the past, which these days was sometimes clearer to him than the present. It was a comfort to spend time in a world he still recognized.

"Daddy?" Amanda asked, her voice filled with alarm.

Max blinked, groped his way back to the present, and stared at her. "What?"

"You looked as if you were a million miles away all of a sudden," she told him.

"Sorry. My mind wanders a lot these days," he told her. "Funny how I can remember your mother's wedding dress clear as a bell, but I can't recall what I had for breakfast this morning."

Amanda's smile seemed forced. "Knowing Jessie, it was probably bran flakes and a banana," she said lightly. "She's still fighting the cholesterol battle for you."

"Seems like a waste to me," he said, then looked at Caleb, trying to recall what it was he'd been wanting to talk to him about. He knew it had seemed urgent only moments ago.

"You seem tired this morning," Caleb

said. "Maybe Amanda and I should let you get some rest."

"There'll be time enough for resting when I'm in the ground," Max said heatedly. "I wanted to talk to you about something."

"It can wait for another time, Max," Caleb said, that damnable pitying note back in his voice.

"No, it can't wait!" Max thundered, pounding the arm of his chair. "I know it's important."

Amanda laid her hand over his. "Then it will come back to you," she said. "Don't try to force it, Daddy. It only upsets you."

"Well, of course I'm upset. You try spending your day searching for things around the house or searching for words and ideas that were plain as day just an hour ago."

Caleb regarded him with sympathy. "You always feel better after you've had some sleep. Take a nap and I'll come back this afternoon. We'll talk then."

Max looked at Amanda. "You, too?"

"Not this afternoon, Daddy. Since I was gone yesterday, I need to spend some time with the kids when they get home from school."

Max struggled to remember where she'd gone. He knew it was important, but the memory was just out of reach. Filled with frustration, he merely nodded. Maybe it was best if they left. He didn't want either of them to see what a struggle every day was becoming.

"Go," he said impatiently. "Just go on and get out."

He was aware of the quick flash of hurt in Amanda's eyes, but still she leaned down and kissed him.

"I love you, Daddy. Don't forget that."

Max clung to the words tenaciously after she'd gone. Even after all he'd done, his daughter still loved him. If he remembered nothing else, he couldn't forget that. Surely, he would never forget that.

Mary Louise had been accumulating yarn catalogs for weeks now, ever since Maggie and Dinah had told her they'd help her start her own business. There were more colors and types of yarn than she'd ever imagined. A part of her was overwhelmed by the magnitude of the decisions she would have to make to choose what would sell and what wouldn't. Another part of her could barely contain her excitement. She wanted to run these colorful strands through her fingers, work them into glorious sweaters and jackets that people would clamor to have; knit soft-as-a-cloud blankets for babies. She could visualize the displays already, each one tempting and inviting the stroke of a finger or a quick gasp of delight.

She'd dragged the entire collection with her to show Willie Ron when she stopped by to visit him at the end of her first month working for Maggie. She knew he probably didn't give two hoots about yarn, but he shared her enthusiasm for this chance that would change her life.

"I sure do miss seein' your beautiful face round here," he told her as they sat outside the Stop and Shop an hour before his shift was scheduled to begin. "But this is the right thing for you to do. I can tell you're already learning a lot just from being around Miz Parker and Miz Beaufort."

She studied his sad expression. "You sound like we're never gonna see each other again," she said.

"It's different now," he told her.

"Different how? I may not be here, but I'm still counting on you to be around to change diapers for me from time to time."

He shook his head. "You know that's not going to happen, Mary Louise. You and me don't travel in the same circles."

"But you're my friend, Willie Ron," she protested.

"I'm your *work* friend," he corrected.

His insistence that there was some sort of social distinction between them was crazy. It was an idea Parnell had probably put in his head.

"No, Willie Ron," she said fiercely. "You're my best friend. I don't want to hear you say otherwise."

Suddenly car lights flashed in their eyes as Parnell and his buddies turned into the parking lot. Of all the times for that piece of no-account trash to show his face, she thought bitterly.

"Well, well, well, if that ain't a picture, the two of you sitting there all cozy like," Parnell said as he slid out from behind the wheel and sauntered in their direction.

Beside her, Willie Ron stiffened. When Mary Louise rested her hand on his forearm, he jerked away.

"Isn't that something?" Parnell gloated. "Even a man like Willie Ron don't want a little slut like you touching him."

Willie Ron was on his feet in a heartbeat. "Don't be saying things like that about her," he commanded, a quiet dignity to his voice that Mary Louise had never heard before. "Mary Louise, go inside."

Terrified that things would escalate if she left him with Parnell and his cowardly thugs, she shook her head. "I'm staying right here."

Willie Ron cast a pointed look at her swollen belly and repeated, "Go inside."

Knowing he wanted her and the baby safe, she backed reluctantly toward the door of the convenience store. Inside she could call for help. She could call the police and Cord, and they would put an end to this before anything bad happened.

She got the door open an instant before Parnell threw the first punch. It split Willie Ron's lip and blood spurted everywhere.

"No!" she screamed. "Leave him alone, Parnell! You just leave him alone."

When Parnell whirled in her direction, she caught the first glimpse of the gun in his hand. "Oh, God," she whispered, terror-stricken by the sight. She crossed her arms protectively over her baby, torn between helping her friend and saving herself and her child.

"Man has to be able to defend himself, now, doesn't he?" Parnell asked when he recognized her fear. "It's our right under the Constitution of the United States of America."

"I doubt you've ever even read the Constitution," Mary Louise snapped back before she could stop herself.

Parnell's gaze narrowed. "You don't want to be making me mad, do you, Mary Louise?"

She dared a look at Willie Ron and drew strength and determination from his quiet, calm demeanor. Once more, he mouthed the words *Go inside.*

Without responding to Parnell's taunt, she turned and ran, flipping the lock as she closed the door and dove behind the counter. It was then, just as she was frantically dialing 911 that she heard the gunshot.

Forcing herself to stay where she was, she spilled out the story to the dispatcher, then pressed the button to get Cord and repeated it.

"I'm on my way," he said quietly. "Stay right where you are, Mary Louise. Whatever you do, don't get up, don't look outside, okay?"

Sobbing now, she nodded, then realized he couldn't see her. "Okay," she murmured, then dropped the phone and huddled behind the counter, rocking herself and holding her stomach. "Please God, let Willie Ron be okay. Please, he never did anything to hurt anyone. He was just trying to protect me."

At the sound of sirens in the distance, she heard car doors slam and the squeal of tires as Parnell and his cowardly friends fled. Despite Cord's advice, she eased to the end of the counter and peeked outside.

There was blood smeared on the door as if someone had used it to begin some hateful message. Sick to her stomach, she crawled closer to the door.

Willie Ron was sprawled on the ground, blood seeping from a wound in his chest. On her feet now, Mary Louise grabbed a handful of paper towels, unbolted the door and ran to him.

"Don't you dare die on me," she sobbed as she pressed a wad of towels against his chest. "I will never forgive you if you die, Willie Ron, do you hear me?"

His pain-filled eyes cracked open. "Deaf man could hear you, girl. Stop all that caterwauling. It's not good for the baby."

A hysterical laugh bubbled up. "You can't be telling me what to do," she said. "Save your strength. I won't have you dying because you were trying to boss me around."

An ambulance turned into the parking lot, along with two police cars and Cord. Dinah was out of Cord's car before he'd cut the engine. She wrapped Mary Louise in her arms and rocked her. "Come on, sweetie, let's give the paramedics room to do their job, okay?"

"I'm not leaving him," Mary Louise said fiercely.

"Of course not," Dinah soothed. "We'll just stand right over here. And when they take Willie Ron to the hospital, we'll follow right behind."

Mary Louise kept her gaze locked on the paramedics, who were working to stem the bleeding and hook Willie Ron up to an IV. Now that he was in good hands, she began to shake from the inside out.

"Let's go sit down," Dinah said, urging her toward the bench where all her precious yarn catalogs were strewn and spotted with blood.

Just then Mary Louise's belly tightened in a spasm that had her gasping for breath. "The baby," she whispered, panicked. "Oh, God, I think I'm in labor and it's too soon."

"Cord!" Dinah yelled, holding her hand tightly and rubbing her belly soothingly.

Cord materialized instantly in front of them. "What?"

"We need to get her to the hospital now. There's not time to wait for another ambulance to get here."

Mary Louise thought Cord looked a little faint. "You'd better not pass out," she said. "If you're this messed up when *I* go into labor, you won't be a bit of help at all when it happens to Dinah."

He grinned at her. "You have a point. How about I get a paramedic to take a look at you before we go?"

"No," Mary Louise said firmly. "They shouldn't leave Willie Ron. I'll be okay if you just get me to the hospital."

Cord spoke to one of the policemen, then hurried to his car, where Dinah had already settled Mary Louise into the back seat.

She didn't remember much of the ride. Dinah sat next to her, punching in numbers on her cell phone as if working some late-breaking news story for her TV station. Mary Louise tuned out the conversations and concentrated on trying to stay calm, despite the pains twisting her belly.

Cord slammed to a stop at the emergency entrance, then charged around the car to pick her up as if she weighed no more than a feather. He carried her inside as if she were the most precious thing he'd ever handled.

She summoned a smile when he put her down on a gurney provided by a couple of nurses. "Maybe you'll do okay when your baby comes, after all."

He smiled back. "Thanks for the endorsement. Be sure to tell Dinah."

Then another pain had her writhing and clutching her stomach. Murmuring every prayer she'd ever been taught, she willed her baby to slow down and stay inside where it belonged. Then the doctor gave her some sort of shot and the last thing she remembered was looking up into Danny's panic-stricken eyes. Dinah must have called him.

"Marry me," he pleaded just before she slipped away.

Later she wondered if she'd said yes, or only dreamed it.

Caleb was exhausted from spending the night at the hospital with Mary Louise and her friend Willie Ron, waiting until the doctors said both of them were stable before he went home. He should have collapsed into a sound sleep when he finally crawled into his bed, but instead his head was whirling with his dilemma over Amanda. Watching the doctors work to stop Mary Louise's premature labor and save her baby had reminded him of what a miracle a baby was. It had also reminded him of the secret he was keeping from Amanda.

He wanted to ask her to marry him, wanted to ask Max's blessing before it was too late, but he couldn't bring himself to do it, not with that one huge secret — okay, two, if he counted Max's owning the land her house was sitting on — left between them. Unfortunately, though, for a man who found the words he needed to help others, Caleb couldn't find the right ones to help himself. He had no idea how to tell Amanda the truth.

It was midday before he finally fell into a restless sleep. He awoke before sunset and made his way to meet Amanda and the kids at Willow Bend as they'd planned several days ago.

"Max had a difficult day," Jessie told them when they arrived. "He's in his room resting now. I don't want to disturb him."

"Of course not," Amanda agreed, then looked at Caleb, her gaze intense. "Could we stay awhile, anyway? The kids need some time to run off some of that energy they've stored up in school. And I'd like to sit on the porch and rock for a bit. It's soothing."

"Sure," he agreed.

"I'll bring you some iced tea," Jessie said. "Then I'll go and sit with Max awhile. He seems to like it when he wakes up and finds me there."

"Don't bother with the tea," Amanda told her. "I'll get it."

When the women were gone, Caleb sat in a rocker, wondering if the motion would soothe him, too. To be sure, the back-and-forth motion did have a calming effect, but he still hadn't found the answers he needed.

Then, when Amanda returned, the issue was taken out of his hands. She sat down in the rocker beside him. The kids were playing hide-and-seek in the last dusky light of the summer day.

"There's something I've been thinking a lot about lately," Amanda said, breaking the comfortable silence. "Ever since Savannah, in fact."

"Oh?" He became suddenly wary.

"I know a woman is supposed to wait for a man to make up his mind, but I don't think I have time for that."

Caleb regarded her with alarm. "What on earth are you talking about?"

She looked directly into his eyes and blurted, "I think we should get married."

He stared at her blankly. He'd known Savannah would push things to a new level for them, but he hadn't expected this.

"You're asking me to marry you?" he asked, just to be sure.

She grinned at him. "Sounded like that to me. Didn't I make myself clear enough? I love you, Caleb. You have to know I would never have gone to bed with you in Savannah if I didn't. I know I told you it didn't have to lead to anything, but I've changed my mind since I've seen how fast Daddy seems to be slipping. I don't want to wait. I want us to be a family. I want us to have a baby, maybe even two. And I think it would make Daddy happy to see me settled with someone he respects, too. I want to give him that."

He seized on the one part he was ready to deal with. "So, this is just about making Max happy?"

"No," she insisted. "It's about making us a family."

Joy burst inside him, then withered and died. "I can't."

Her expression faltered. "You can't? Why?"

"You don't . . ." Caleb swallowed hard. "You don't know everything about me."

"I know everything that matters. You're kind and decent and strong. I trust you with my life and with my kids. What could be more important?"

Caleb knew it was now or never. It wasn't fair to let her think he didn't want her, didn't love her. She had to understand that he was only trying to protect her, save her from heartbreak.

She frowned at his silence. "Caleb, answer me. What could be so important that it would keep us apart?"

"You just said it yourself. You want more children, Amanda. You deserve them." He drew in a deep breath and finally blurted the words that had been eating away at him for years. "And I can't give them to you."

■ ■ ■ ■

Amanda saw the shame and embarrassment in Caleb's eyes and felt her heart twist. She knew she needed to handle this exactly right or he would walk away from her out of some misguided notion that he couldn't give her what she needed. She'd already had one man in her life who'd felt inadequate. She wouldn't tolerate another one misjudging what mattered most to her.

"You think that having another child is more important to me than you?" she demanded.

"I've heard you say more than once that you want more children, Amanda. There's no use denying it now to make me feel better. I can't give them to you and that's that."

She continued to regard him with disbelief. "And that's the only reason you won't marry me? Because you can't have children?"

"I'd say that's a good enough reason," Caleb said stiffly.

"Not to me," she said heatedly. "Why would you ever imagine that the quality of your sperm is more important to me than the man you are? Am I that shallow? Is my love so unreliable?"

"No, of course not. It's just that . . ."

"Just that what?"

"It was important enough for my wife to leave me," he said, barely managing to choke out the words.

"*That's* why you got divorced?" she asked incredulously. "Whatever happened to 'for better or for worse'?"

"How could I blame her for breaking those vows? She wanted children."

"Hadn't she ever heard about adoption?"

"She wanted her own," Caleb said, still determined to defend his ex-wife.

"Because of the whole childbirth experience?" Amanda asked. "Trust me, it's not that much fun."

Caleb's lips twitched. "I think she was more focused on the miracle aspect of it. I felt it myself last night when I was at the hospital praying for Mary Louise's baby to have a chance."

"Every child is a miracle. It doesn't matter who gives birth to him or her. Of all people, *you* should certainly understand that."

"I do," he said, but without much conviction.

She cupped his face and looked into his eyes. "Tell me something, Caleb. Do you love my kids?"

"Of course."

"Do you see the way they look up to you,

the way they care about you?"

"I suppose."

"That's the love and respect they'd show a father. It doesn't matter that it's not your blood flowing through their veins."

His eyes brightened at last. "You really don't care about this?" he asked, an incredulous note in his voice.

Amanda chose her next words very carefully. "I care, because I can see how much it matters to you. I would love to carry your baby inside me. But would I let something like that rip us apart? Not a chance."

Though his expression was lighter, he still hesitated. "I think you should take some time. Think this through."

"I don't have to," she said emphatically.

"Then do it because I want you to. I want you to be very sure, because if we get married, Amanda, I'll never let you go."

Her heart leapt at his promise, but for now she merely nodded and said, "I'll think about it."

She knew she wouldn't think long.

"You gonna marry my girl?" Max asked Caleb a few days later. "I figure a man in your position sleeps with a woman, then he must be serious about her. Am I wrong?"

Caleb fought back the desire to chuckle.

Apparently no one in this family was willing to wait around for him to do the asking.

"Amanda asked me pretty much the same thing the other night."

Max looked horrified. "You waited so long that she had to ask you? What's wrong with you, man?"

"Just trying to do the right thing," Caleb said.

"Who left it up you to decide what's right? I made that mistake once and look at all the years it cost me. Do you love her?"

"Yes."

"Then get the show on the road while I'm still able to walk her down the aisle."

"I'm afraid it's out of my hands. I tossed the ball back into her court."

Max glowered at him. "Why did you do a damn fool thing like that?"

Caleb winced at Max's displeasure. "It seemed like a smart thing to do at the time."

"Oh, for goodness' sake, do I have to take care of this for you?"

Caleb saw the grim determination in Max's eyes and felt momentary panic. "Absolutely not. I'm not entirely sure having you on my side will work in my favor."

Max stared hard at him, then sat back and hooted. "You could be right about that, son. There are a lot of days lately when I think that girl's forgiven me, but sometimes I see a look in her eyes that tells me she hasn't forgotten what I did to her."

"Isn't that what real forgiveness is all about?" Caleb asked. "We remember the hurt, but we forgive, anyway, and we move on."

"Maybe that's the one good thing about this disease I've got. Sooner or later, I'll forget the bad times I've had in my life, the sins I've committed."

"That may be a blessing," Caleb agreed. "But losing the good memories, too, that's the unfairness of it."

Max sighed heavily. "You and Amanda and those kids of hers will just have to do the remembering for me."

23

Mary Louise walked gingerly down the hospital hallway to Willie Ron's room. To her surprise, when she went inside, she found Danny sitting beside his bed. They were deep in conversation about the police arresting Parnell and his no-account friends when Willie Ron spotted her.

"Looks like we've got company," he said to Danny. "It's these quiet ones you have to keep an eye on. They sneak up on you."

Looking scared, Danny bolted out of his chair and took her arm. "Are you okay? Should you be out of bed? You almost lost the baby once. Are you trying to do it again?"

Mary Louise regarded him with a mixture of impatience and amusement. "The doctor told me to walk. The crisis is over for now and he wants me to get some exercise before he lets me out of here tomorrow."

"Seems too soon to me," Danny said. "I want to talk to him myself. I know you, Mary Louise. You're likely to twist his words to suit your own purposes."

She scowled at the accusation. "I most certainly will not twist his words, not if it could put my baby at risk."

"Uh-oh," Willie Ron murmured from his bed. "If you two are about to have yourselves a brawl, take it somewhere else."

Mary Louise grinned at him. "No brawl. I'm just going to remind Danny that he has no right whatsoever to go talking to my doctor about anything."

Danny stared at her. "Is that so? That baby inside you is mine, too, and I have a right to protect it. Besides that, I asked you to marry me not two days ago, and I'm still waiting for an answer. It's downright rude to ignore a question that important."

Willie Ron chuckled and Mary Louise frowned at him before she whirled on Danny. "If you're going to ask something that important, don't you think you ought to make sure a person is conscious before you do it?"

Danny regarded her with confusion. "Did you hear me or didn't you?"

"I *thought* I heard you, but for all I knew, I could have been dreaming. I've been waiting for you to get around to repeating it. I figured if it wasn't just some momentary panic sort of thing or wishful thinking on my part, you'd ask me again."

Danny cast a helpless look toward Willie Ron, who merely shrugged. "I were you, I'd be down on one knee about now," he told Danny.

"Maybe we could go someplace a little more private," Danny said.

Mary Louise hid a grin at his sudden discomfort and shook her head. "If you ask me to marry you and really mean it, I want a witness so you can't back out later."

"Oh, for pity's sake," Danny muttered, but he dropped to one knee and reached for her hand.

Mary Louise stared at him in astonishment. Until this instant, she hadn't really believed he intended to do it. She'd convinced herself that he'd only said the words when he was worried she might die on him.

"The other night when I thought I could lose you and our baby, I've never been more scared in my life," he began.

Huh, she thought. Proves my point. "But you didn't lose either of us," she said.

"Would you hush and let me say this?" he pleaded.

"Yes, please, before my sedative kicks in,"

Willie Ron chimed in.

Mary Louise shut up.

"I realized then just how much I love you," Danny continued. "And how much I want to be a real father to our baby, no half measures. So, I'm asking you again in front of God and one witness who will probably beat me to a pulp if I mess this up again, will you please do me the honor of being my wife? And would you do it quick, before this baby comes? He or she seems impatient."

Mary Louise saw the sincerity and love shining from his eyes. Tears welled up in her own and spilled down her cheeks. "Oh, Danny," she whispered, her heart overflowing.

"Is that a yes?" Willie Ron asked impatiently. "All this dillydallying is getting on my nerves."

Mary Louise laughed and launched herself into Danny's arms. "Yes," she said jubilantly. "Yes, I'll marry you and make a family with you."

"Seems to me like you've got a head start on that," Willie Ron noted. "Now, go away, so I can get my beauty sleep."

"As if you could be any handsomer than you already are," Mary Louise said, pressing a kiss to his cheek. "In fact, you're so good-looking, I think I'll have you stand up for me at our wedding."

"Now, won't that be a pretty sight," Willie Ron murmured. There was a smile on his lips as he drifted off.

She turned to Danny. "You wouldn't mind, would you?"

"He protected you and our baby," Danny said. "I'd say he's in our life to stay. I'll owe him for that till the day I die."

She gave his hand a grateful squeeze. He winked at her.

"Want to go back to your room and make wedding plans?" he asked.

"Sweetie, we won't need to do much planning," she told him. "I've had my wedding all worked out since I was four. We'll just have to tweak it a little to make sure we can pull it together before I'm too huge to waddle down the aisle."

"You'd still be the prettiest bride ever," Danny said. His expression sobered. "I'm going to make you happy, Mary Louise. That's a promise."

"Oh, Danny," she whispered, her voice choked with tears. "Don't you know, you already have?"

Caleb's mind wasn't on their card game, Max concluded when he won three straight hands. "What the devil's gotten into you?" he demanded. "There's not much point in playing if you're not going to concentrate."

"I thought you'd be happy to win some of your money back," Caleb retorted.

"Well, I would be, if I thought I was winning it fair and square and not because your head's a million miles away. Haven't you talked Amanda into marrying you yet?"

Caleb scowled at him. "I told you, I left the decision up to her."

"And I told you you were a damn fool," Max said in disgust. "What kind of man leaves his destiny up to somebody else?"

"One who's trying to do the right thing," Caleb said.

Max studied him. "Is there something I don't know about you? You got a bunch of skeletons kicking around in the closet?"

"None that concern you," Caleb assured him.

"But they might matter to my daughter?"

"They might," Caleb acknowledged.

"Care to explain that?"

"No."

Max glowered at him, but Caleb didn't wilt — or change his mind. He just dealt another hand and feigned concentration on his cards.

"Okay, be that way," Max muttered just as

the doorbell rang. "Now, who on earth would that be at this hour?"

"Want me to go answer it?" Caleb asked.

Max heaved himself up. "The day I can't answer my own door is the day I take to my bed and give up."

He walked to the front door, flung it open impatiently and then stared in shock at the woman standing there. "Margaret!"

Her confident expression wavered ever so slightly. "Max, it's good to see you."

Max felt as if someone had yanked the rug right out from under him. "Wh-what are you doing here?" he asked, thoroughly flustered.

"If you'll ask me in, I'll explain," she said, her lips curving into a small smile.

He backed up a step. "Of course," he said, his heart thundering in his chest every bit as hard as it had on the day he'd waited at the altar for her to say "I do."

She walked past him and headed straight for the living room, barely sparing a glance for anything along the way. Only when she spotted Caleb did she hesitate.

"Reverend Webb, I wasn't expecting to find you here. I thought Max would be alone. That's why I called so late in the evening."

"Please, call me Caleb. We were just playing a few hands of poker. Since Max is winning for a change, you've given me the perfect excuse to call it a night."

Max wasn't at all sure he wanted him to go. He'd been feeling okay most of the evening and his mind hadn't betrayed him, but he wanted backup in case that changed. "Stay," he ordered, drawing surprised looks from both of them.

Caleb seemed to catch on quick enough. He nodded and sat back down. Margaret shot a questioning look in his direction, but then sat on the edge of the sofa, her hands folded in her lap. Max sat in his favorite chair and took the time to look at her.

She was more self-possessed than she'd been as a young wife. Her face had matured, though there was hardly a line in it. She'd dyed her glorious hair a dark shade of red. Despite his earlier misgivings, he was forced to admit it suited her. It seemed to emphasize the sparkle in her blue eyes.

"I suppose you're wondering why I came after all this time," she said eventually.

He nodded. "Seems like a logical question."

"Amanda told me you're sick," she began.

Max felt something inside him shrivel and die. "So you came to make sure I've taken care of you in my will," he accused. "Amanda should have kept her mouth shut."

Margaret looked vaguely taken aback by the venom in his voice. "Actually, I came because of something else Amanda said. I wanted to ask your forgiveness." She paused, then, "I treated you badly, Max. Over the years I've regretted it more than I can say, but I couldn't bring myself to call or write it in a note. I figured you wouldn't believe me, anyway. Or that it wouldn't matter in the end, even if you did think I was sincere."

Max recalled the day Margaret had walked out of their lives as if it had happened yesterday. She'd taken his heart with her. He'd alternated between hating her for that and missing her desperately, especially when he was at a loss with Amanda. He'd always believed Margaret would have known how to keep their girl safe and happy. Instead, he'd been left to muddle along doing the best he could. Thank God he'd had Jessie.

"You can't change the past," he told her now. "And regrets are a waste of time. I've had more than my share and they haven't changed a blessed thing. All you can do is accept where you are and move on."

She regarded him with curiosity. "You've changed," she said. "You're more mellow now."

Max gave a shout of laughter. "I imagine

there are plenty of folks who'd dispute that."

"You know what I find sad?" she asked.

"What's that?"

"You say that moving on is what's important, but you haven't done that, not really. Neither have I."

"Of course we have," he insisted. "Years have passed, Margaret, and we've lived them. We haven't holed up somewhere in isolation."

"True, but is that all there is to moving on?" she asked. "You never asked for a divorce, Max."

He got her point and it rankled in a way he couldn't entirely explain. "Neither did you," he retorted defensively.

"As I said, neither of us took that final step to move on with our lives. We kept the tie. Why do you suppose that is?"

He shrugged. "Never saw the need to get a piece of paper. Besides, we'd told people you were dead. I couldn't very well ask for a divorce from a woman who was supposed to be in her grave. You could have gotten one, though. You could have gone off to some island, gotten a quickie divorce with no one here being the wiser. Why didn't you?"

Her gaze locked with his. "I think because some part of me always knew I'd come back here someday."

Max felt his heart leap, then his temper. "Hold on just a cotton-pickin' minute, woman. Are you telling me you want to come home at this late date and turn the last thirty years into a lie? You'd humiliate me like that, after all I did to give you the freedom you insisted you had to have?"

"Max," Caleb said softly. "No need to work yourself up."

"There damn well is a need! I won't have it," he said, slamming his fist on the arm of his chair. "I won't be made a fool of." He scowled at this woman he'd loved for so many years despite what she'd done to him. "What made you think for a minute I'd agree to this?"

"I thought . . ." Her voice faltered. "I thought you might need me."

"Well, I don't," he blustered. "I've gotten along just fine without you and that's the way it'll stay."

Her expression turned sad. "I see. I suppose you're right. I suppose it's far too complicated, which is why you insisted on doing things this way in the first place. You wanted to be sure that coming back wouldn't be an option, didn't you?"

"Well, of course I did. I did it for Amanda's sake." He scowled. "Did you give one second's thought to her? Do you think she wants you here after you abandoned her?"

"I was hoping for a chance to make peace with her, too," she said. "But I can see that coming here was a mistake." She stood up. "I'm sorry I've upset you, Max. I really am."

"Hold on a minute," he commanded when she started to walk away. "That's it? I say no to this crazy plan of yours and you just walk away?"

She regarded him curiously. "What did you expect?"

"I expected you to fight to stay the same way you fought to go," he told her fiercely. "I expected you to make me believe that staying really matters to you."

"You want me to fight you on this?" she asked.

"The Margaret I knew could hold her own with anybody, even me," he said. "Not many people could do that. I suppose that's why I never forgot you. Don't destroy my memories now. I haven't got that many good ones left."

She cast a helpless look at Caleb, then chuckled. "You always were the most perverse man on the face of the earth, Max. I'm glad to see that hasn't changed."

He frowned at her. "Well, then?" he prodded.

"I'm still going," she said, then touched

his cheek with a brief caress. "But I'll be back from time to time, so you start figuring out what you want to tell people about my miraculous recovery."

Damn, but she was a pistol. Always had been. He grinned at her. "Maybe I'll just keep you hidden away here and let them think I've lost what little's left of my mind. The whole town will be talking about me spending my final days talking to a ghost."

"That's one approach," she agreed wryly. "But it might be hard on Amanda and our grandchildren." Her expression sobered. "Max, you were right about one thing. Before I start spending too much time around here, talk it over with Amanda and see how she feels about it. I know I haven't earned the right to come back in her eyes, or in yours, for that matter. An occasional visit in the dark of night will do for now."

Max saw the sense in what she was saying. If he had years left, an occasional visit would be a sensible start. But he wanted to store up a few last memories while he could.

"We'll work it out," he told her. He would convince Amanda, if not to forgive her mother, at least to give her a chance, same as she had him.

Margaret gave his hand a squeeze. "Good night, Max. I'll let myself out." She nodded at Caleb. "Good night."

After she'd gone, Caleb turned to Max. "Are you okay?"

"Have to say my head's spinning a bit," he admitted. "How do you think Amanda will take all this?"

"If it's what you want, she'll go along with it for your sake," Caleb said. "But I'm a little surprised you'd agree to it so quickly."

Max gave him a wry look. "Aren't you the one who's always preaching forgiveness?"

"I am, but you usually ignore me."

"Then consider this one of those times when you managed to get through my thick skull," Max told him. "Besides, even I recognize that I don't have time to waste holding a grudge when that woman's the only person in this world who ever meant a thing to me besides Amanda and those kids of hers. A few weeks ago, I'd have sent Margaret packing out of stupid pride. Now I don't much see the point."

"You've just proved one of those invaluable life lessons I like to preach about," Caleb said. "Sometimes, if we're lucky, with age comes a little wisdom."

Max regarded him with uncertainty. "Then you don't think I'm being a sentimental old fool?"

"No. I think you've recognized what's important and you're grabbing for it and holding on for dear life."

"What about you? You going to grab Amanda and hold on for dear life?"

Caleb chuckled. "You never give up, do you?"

"Only once before — when I let that woman get away from me — and it was a mistake. Now, tell me. Are you going to fight for my girl?"

"If Amanda considers everything I've told her and still wants me in her life, then believe me, Max, I will never let her go. She's the best thing that ever happened to me."

Max regarded him with disgust. "Sometimes you're too damned noble for your own good, Reverend."

"Sometimes it's the only choice a man has."

"Well, it's a big risk, leaving a thing like this up to a woman's whim. I did that once and look what it got me. Years of being alone."

"Marriage is more than some whim," Caleb corrected. "I'm comfortable with letting Amanda think things through and make this decision."

"Then why do you look like a groom who's been left standing at the altar an hour too long?"

"Maybe because you won't let the subject drop," Caleb said. "You're getting on my nerves, old man."

"If I were you, I'd stop wasting time talking to me and go over to Amanda's and see if she's come to a decision."

"I don't want to pressure her."

Max rolled his eyes. "Whatever happened to sweeping a woman off her feet? I'd have filled her house up with roses and champagne by now."

"Your daughter doesn't care about roses and champagne."

"All women *say* they don't care about roses and champagne till the flowers and expensive bottles of Dom Pérignon start turning up on the doorstep," Max said. "I could make a couple of calls for you, get this thing started."

"Stay out of it," Caleb warned.

Max sighed and shrugged. "Up to you. I just know what *I'd* do."

"As if your love life has much to recommend it," Caleb retorted.

Max grinned. "Thirty years later my woman came back to me. I must have given her something good to think about all these years."

"Roses and champagne?" Caleb asked skeptically.

"I had one or two other tricks up my sleeve back then, but I'm not sharing all my trade secrets. Let's see how you do with the simple things first. Now, get out of here. You're wasting time."

He watched Caleb leave, then sat back down and thought about the unexpected events of the evening. As gloomy as his outlook had been for weeks now, it was a revelation to discover that life still had a few surprises left in store for him.

Amanda took an entire week to consider Caleb's announcement about his infertility, not because she needed to, but because he expected it. She used the time to make arrangements for the wedding she wanted to have in a month's time.

When she invited him over for dinner, she was stunned when he showed up with two dozen white roses and a bottle of fine champagne.

"They're beautiful," she whispered, burying her face in the roses and breathing in the sweet scent. "What made you think of them?"

"I shouldn't admit it, but Max seemed to think I was messing up the whole courting thing. I decided to give his way a try. Is it too much?"

"I wouldn't want these every week, but it's the perfect way to start this evening," she told him. "Let me put the flowers in water and we'll have dinner. We have a lot to talk about."

He studied her intently. "We do? Where are the kids?"

"They're spending the night at Willow Bend," she said. "Jessie's helping my father look after them."

"I see."

"Do you really?" she asked, amused by the confusion in his eyes. It was good to know she could throw him off balance once in a while.

"What is it you want to talk about, Amanda?" he asked at last.

"These for a start," she said. She handed him a draft of her proposed wedding invitation, a list of potential caterers and a confirmation from his church that the date was available.

He looked everything over, then met her gaze. His eyes were filled with such relief that she knew she'd done exactly the right thing to prove to him that she wanted this marriage as much as he did.

"You didn't leave much to chance, did you?" he asked, his lips curving into a slow smile.

Amanda shrugged. "I thought if I started spending money after a couple of years of being so frugal, you'd take me seriously."

The smile spread across his face. "Then I guess we're getting married."

She studied his face. "You okay with that?"

"If you're sure, then you've made me the happiest man alive. Your father will probably be the second happiest."

"I know. He called me and told me he thought it was time for me to stop waffling around and give you an answer. He's still trying to control my life, but somehow it doesn't seem to matter so much."

"Because this time you're on the same page?" Caleb asked.

"Because I can finally accept that he's doing it out of love."

Caleb looked satisfied, but then his expression changed.

"What?" she asked.

"I have one more thing to tell you, one last thing I've kept to myself."

Her stomach sank. "Oh?"

"It's about your father."

Amanda simply waited while he tried to find the words. She used the time to pray that whatever this revelation was, it wouldn't change anything.

"He bought this land, Amanda." He met her gaze, his expression earnest. "It was the only way he could bring himself to reach out to you."

She stared at Caleb, stunned. "When?"

"Before he came to me about building the house. He was behind all of this. He wanted you and the kids to have a new home and a fresh start. He was afraid if you knew that, you'd turn it down."

Amanda sat back, trying to take in the news. "If he was willing to do this, why couldn't he just let me back into his life?"

Caleb smiled. "Because this is Max. He's only now beginning to grasp that pride is a sorry replacement for love." He touched her cheek. "I'm sorry I kept it from you."

"I'm glad you did. He was right. I probably would have refused."

"Then it won't stand between us?"

"No, Caleb. I still want to marry you. I think we've both learned our lessons about pride and secrets."

He nodded, then regarded her curiously. "Did Max tell you the latest?"

"About my mother coming back to spend some time with him?"

Caleb nodded. "How do you feel about that?"

"Honestly, I'm not sure. I thought I'd have

501

him to myself for whatever good days he has left, but if this is what he wants, I'm hardly in a position to deny it to him."

"Will you be able to deal with her and give her a chance?"

Amanda didn't answer at once. It was a question she'd been struggling with ever since she'd found out her mother was alive. "I'll try to keep an open mind," she said at last.

"No one could expect more than that."

She looked into Caleb's eyes and saw everything she'd ever need in life. "Love's a funny thing, isn't it?"

"How so?"

"It's unexpected and unpredictable, but once the real thing comes along, it really is strong enough and powerful enough to last forever."

"Ours will," he said. "I believe that with all my heart. And oddly enough, I think maybe your parents' love has, too."

Amanda felt at peace, even knowing how many struggles lay ahead. With Caleb by her side, she would get through them all.

"I love you," she told him. "You have no idea how much."

"Given how much you're overlooking to marry me, I think I do," he said. "All I can tell you is that I'm grateful and I will spend every day of my life making sure you don't regret it."

"No regrets," she assured him. "Not ever."

After all, he was the man who'd made her believe in herself again and made her believe in love.

EPILOGUE

The baptism of Daniel Marshall Jr. and Mariah Dorothy Beaufort was a bittersweet moment for Caleb. Mary Louise had insisted on waiting to hold the service for her son until after Dinah's baby was born.

"Besides, it's bad enough that everyone in the congregation knows that Danny and I barely got married before the baby was born without having them back for the baptism a couple of months later. I don't think our son's soul will be in jeopardy if we wait till Dinah has her baby," she'd told Caleb with that stubborn jut of her chin that he'd come to respect.

Mary Louise might be barely nineteen, but she was a woman to be reckoned with. Danny was going to have his hands full, but judging from the contented expression on his face as he held his son, he was ready for whatever came their way.

Caleb turned his attention to Cord, who looked as if he were terrified that the tiny girl in his arms might break. Dinah was regarding her husband with amusement. She glanced at Caleb and winked.

"You'd think a big strong man like my husband wouldn't be scared to death of a tiny little baby," she said.

Cord scowled at her. "You can take over anytime."

Dinah laughed at that. "Since when? Ever since we brought Mariah home from the hospital, the only time she's in my arms is when I'm breast-feeding."

"Are you sure we ought to be discussing this in church?" Cord asked.

"Nothing more natural," Caleb assured him. "But maybe we ought to leave the topic till after the service."

He glanced over the congregation to see that everyone was settled, then paused when his gaze met Amanda's. He saw the wistful expression on her face and regretted for an instant that there would be no baby for them. Then he looked at the troubled ten-year-old foster child they'd taken in the week before and knew that their lives would be fulfilled in other ways. The world was full of children who needed protecting and loving, even for a short time. He and Amanda had decided their home would be a safe haven, a stop-over for these kids.

"Everybody ready?" he asked as the designated godparents stepped forward. Maggie and Josh were there for Mariah. And Dinah and Willie Ron would be promising to keep young Daniel on the right path in life. Willie Ron nervously ran a finger around the collar of his shirt, but his awed gaze never left the little boy Danny carefully handed to him.

"Let's get started before these two forget about being on good behavior and decide it's time for lunch," Caleb said, and began the service.

As he made the sign of the cross on their foreheads, Daniel smiled as if he knew just what it meant to be so blessed. Mariah, in the fine tradition of her rebellious mama, screamed her head off until she was safely back in the arms of her doting daddy.

"No question she's her daddy's little girl," Dinah commented.

Cord laughed. "And I was just thinking she's an awful lot like her mama, carrying on till she gets her way."

Dinah tucked an arm through his. "Either way, you're the center of both our universes."

Caleb's gaze went back to Amanda, who was the center of his. He knew it might not be entirely appropriate, but he winked at her just the same. And, as always, a blush stained her cheeks.

Beside her, their temporary foster daughter smiled, something she'd done far too rarely since coming into their lives. Caleb winked at her, too.

He knew he would remember that wide smile long after she'd moved on to a permanent home and the next child had come into their lives. Sometimes the best parts of life were made up of small moments, of precious memories like the baptism of these two new lives today.

If he had any regret at all, it was that as he was accumulating a lifetime of these moments, Max was losing touch with the memories that he'd once held precious. The man was slowly slipping away from them, still strong in body, but losing ground daily in mind. And it was breaking Amanda's heart.

"Who's this?" Max asked Amanda later that afternoon, pointing to a picture with a shaky finger.

"The caterer, Daddy. You didn't know her."

Relief flickered in her father's eyes. "Didn't think so," he said, a triumphant note in his voice.

It had been only a few months since Amanda's wedding to Caleb, and each day of it brought a new torment in the progress of Max's disease. He seldom left the house anymore. At Max's insistence, she and Caleb had moved in with the kids, forcing an awkward truce with her mother, who was there on a regular basis. The time she spent with her father was precious to her, because she knew it was finite.

Her father plucked another picture from the pile, and a smile spread across his face. "I know this one," he said, beaming. "No one's ever been prettier than your mama."

"No one," Amanda agreed, battling tears as she stared into her own face in the photograph.

She gave her father a fierce hug, then gathered up the remaining pictures and put them back in the box. Looking through the pictures had become her father's favorite pastime lately.

When he nodded off, still clutching the last snapshot in his hand, she took it from him and put it in the box on top, then touched a finger to the image as her tears fell unchecked. It saddened her now that she hadn't forgiven her mother and asked her to attend her wedding. She recognized that it had been petty revenge for a lifetime of neglect. And she knew she needed to put the resentment behind her if she was ever to find peace.

"I wish you had been there that day, Mama," she whispered with one last glance at the picture. "I really did look as beautiful as you."

ABOUT THE AUTHOR

Originally from Arlington, Virgina, **Sherryl Woods** graduated from Ohio State University with a degree in journalism. In 1986 she began writing full-time, and now, over a hundred books later, Sherryl enjoys the phenomenal success of her books.

A member of Novelists Inc., Sisters in Crime and the Mystery Writers of America, Sherryl also served as president of the Guild for the Miami City Ballet. She currently divides her time between her oceanfront home in Key Biscayne, Florida, and her childhood summer home in Colonial Beach, Virginia, where she owns and operates her own bookstore.

If you can't visit Sherryl at her store then be sure to drop her a note at P.O. Box 490326, Key Biscayne, FL 33149, or visit her Web site, www.sherrylwoods.com.